TIMESTORM

ALSO BY JULIE CROSS

Tempest

Vortex

TIMESTORM

A TEMPEST NOVEL

JULIE CROSS

THOMAS DUNNE BOOKS
ST. MARTIN'S GRIFFIN
NEW YORK

THOMAS DUNNE BOOKS.
An imprint of St. Martin's Press.

TIMESTORM. Copyright © 2014 by Julie Cross. All rights reserved. Printed in the United States of America. For information, address St. Martin's Press, 175 Fifth Avenue, New York, N.Y. 10010.

www.thomasdunnebooks.com
www.stmartins.com

The Library of Congress Cataloging-in-Publication Data is available upon request.

ISBN 978-0-312-56891-7 (hardcover)
ISBN 978-1-250-02073-4 (e-book)

First Edition: February 2014

10 9 8 7 6 5 4 3 2 1

TO MY KIDS: CHARLES, ELLA,
AND MADDIE

TIMESTORM

CHAPTER ONE

DAY 1

I stood in front of the cell staring at . . . well . . . staring at *me*. The caged, unshaven, animal version of me. The way he looked, not at me but through me, brought on the sudden self-awareness that I probably hadn't survived the bleeding brain or whatever the hell happened to me when I jumped into the future. My eyes dropped to my arms as I lifted a hand toward my face. Transparent. I was transparent.

A magnetic force seemed to pulse in the space between the two versions of myself, pulling us together. Footsteps echoed from behind me and I jumped out of the way as Senator Healy stalked right up to the cell, opening the door and somehow cutting off whatever force had been dragging me forward. The other me stood up slowly, shakily, bruises marring his face and legs.

"Senator Healy!" I tried to croak, not hearing a sound outside my own mind.

"Come on, son. Let's get you out of here," Healy said, his voice gentle, barely above a whisper. It reminded me of the way he had spoken to me while I had hung my head over a sink after watching Mason get blown to pieces. Even just thinking about what happened still made me feel nauseous.

The other me shuffled closer, leaning heavily on Healy for support as if his legs weren't used to walking. The urge to somehow unzip him and crawl inside so I could be seen and heard intensified. I had to find a way! Somehow I just knew that I was dying. And then the old warehouse dissolved and pain shot through every inch of my body.

"He can't breathe! We've got to do something!"

A truck.

A truck sat on my chest and every ounce of energy I had was

devoted to shoving it away. Air. I needed air. Nothing would enter. Nothing would exit.

"His lungs are full of fluid! Open him up!" someone shouted.

And I felt the stab to my chest, skin splitting open and my ribs cracking. I had to get out of here. People aren't supposed to feel these things.

"Pulse is fading and then coming again . . . I can't get it steady," a woman's voice spoke right next to my ear.

"He's jumping," someone said.

Silence followed for a full five seconds, then I heard Dad's voice in my other ear, sounding more terrified than I've ever heard him in my life. "Jackson, just stay here . . . please."

But I couldn't. There was no way to control it.

"Are you all right, son?" Healy said to the other me, hand clutching his shoulder.

The other me had sunk to his knees with a loud crack as his kneecaps made contact with the hard floor. He clutched his chest, a look of panic in his eyes, and then raised his shirt. A faint line appeared slowly down the center of his chest, blood trickling from the wound.

Which one of us is dying? I thought it was me. He's not in the future. How can he feel what is happening to me?

A gunshot rang from right behind me, breaking my concentration. Healy fell to the ground, blood oozing from his head. Eyes wide open.

"What the . . ." the other me said, staring at Healy's body. Then he looked up, right at me. Or through me.

"Who . . . who are you?" he stuttered, still on his knees, attempting to stand.

Was he talking to me? No, he was talking to whoever had just shot Healy. But for some reason I couldn't make my body turn around to see who it was. I needed to breathe air. To feel my heart beat again.

"I'm the only one with enough guts to do this," the deep voice boomed from behind me.

Chief Marshall. I didn't have to look.

"Do what?" the other me said, his eyes wide.

Using all my willpower, I forced my body to start to move. The gun fired again. Not just once, but three times. I heard myself scream inside my head . . . heard the other me's scream cut off as he slumped to the ground.

Thump . . . thump . . . thump.

My heart gave three quick beats as I finally turned, just in time to see Chief Marshall vanish.

CHAPTER TWO

DAY 5

"He's waking up."

"Jackson? Can you hear me?"

I found my hands and brought them to my face, rubbing the sleep from my eyes. The room came into focus—white walls, a few gray cabinets, a table beside the bed. The bed had metal rails and white sheets that covered my legs. It looked a lot like a hospital room in 2009. Maybe this wasn't the future after all?

Dad and Courtney stood at the foot of the bed, watching like they'd been staring at me for weeks and I had finally moved.

"Chief Marshall," I managed to say, looking at Dad. "He killed me." I took a breath, slowly letting the scene fall into place in my head so I could articulate it. "The other me. He killed the other me. And Healy. He killed Healy."

My heart raced, causing a searing pain to rip through my chest like it was being split open all over again. "Healy told me before . . . he said that he had someone doing his time-travel changes for him, someone doing the alterations like putting Holly and Adam in the CIA! He did that, Dad. But he said it's not Thomas. It's Marshall! I *know* it is. He vanished right in front of me. He can time-travel!"

Dad's eyes widened, but not because of what I'd just revealed but because of the loud beeping on the monitor beside me. "Jackson, I need you to calm down. Breathe . . . focus on the present for the moment and then we'll figure out what you saw or *think* you saw."

"I know I saw it . . ." The pain in my chest increased, shutting me up. I relaxed back into the pillow, closing my eyes briefly, breathing as slowly and deeply as possible without aggravating my pain. After a couple minutes, the monitor stopped beeping and Dad let out a sigh of relief.

"Good, very good."

I opened my eyes again. "Where are we? Did we make it back?"

Dad shook his head and patted my foot over the covers. "It's still the same place. Same year."

My heart sped up as I touched the back of my head, feeling a large bandage behind my ear. Then I remembered my dream, or was it a half-jump? My fingers fumbled around, moving toward my chest. I drew in a deep breath and felt the tightness of stitched skin pulling apart. There was another bandage horizontally placed between my sternum and left armpit.

"I'm not dead?" I looked up at Dad and Courtney, who were both standing still as statues. "Obviously, I'm not dead . . . I just . . . I thought I was."

Before they could respond, a man with light brown hair and a striking resemblance to Thomas walked into the room, followed by a red-haired woman. I remembered her welcoming us here with Dad, just before my almost death.

The man held up his hands as if in surrender. "I know, we look alike, but don't worry, my name isn't Thomas and I'm not a clone either."

Courtney laughed and my eyes bounced to her and then back to Dad, who seemed at ease, not worried at all about these strangers.

I sighed with relief.

"I'm Grayson and this is Lonnie." He nodded toward the red-headed woman "You met her five days ago."

"Five days." I could hardly wrap my head around the idea that I'd lost that much time. More details about how we'd ended up here hit me all at once. I tried to sit up too quickly and was instantly knocked back down as pain shot through my head and chest. "Holly . . . Emily . . . Mason . . . are they—"

"They're all fine," Dad said.

"Except for the being-stuck-here part," Courtney added.

After holding a stethoscope to my chest briefly, Grayson held up a giant syringe with a long needle. "Pain medication. I wanted you to wake up first and see how your heart and lungs were functioning."

He plunged the needle into my IV. "You're going to experience some drowsiness in about five minutes. Luckily, you guys got trapped on an island with a doctor who's practiced medicine in two different centuries. I used a combination of new technology and old-school methods to relieve the pressure in your skull and stop the bleeding as well as saving your collapsed lung."

"Wow . . . so I was pretty messed up?"

No one said a word for several long seconds but I could see it all over their faces. I really *had* almost died.

Dad gripped the rail at the foot of the bed with both hands and looked me in the eye. "Grayson says you'll be good as new in a few days."

The pain in my head and chest reached an almost unbearable level and I tuned out until Grayson, Dad, and Lonnie left the room to get supplies and talk about me behind my back.

Courtney walked closer and sat beside me on the bed. "I really, really hate you for scaring me like that. And Dad, he's been in hell for the past five days."

I moved my hand closer to Courtney's and squeezed her fingers tight. "I'm sorry."

Tears spilled from her eyes but she started laughing at the same time, wiping her cheeks quickly. "God, this is so weird. I still can't get over how old you are and how old I'm not. And this thing with Holly. She's not saying much but we all heard you. Loud and clear."

The fogginess of the drugs started to set in, but not enough that I didn't feel a sudden sense of alarm. What had I said to Holly?

Oh right.

I love you.

I looked down at my hand, now covering my sister's. "I thought . . . I thought it was you," I lied.

Courtney's eyes widened. "Seriously? You were saying good-bye?"

A knot formed in the pit of my stomach. "Yeah, something like that."

I wasn't quite swept under by the pain meds yet, but I closed my eyes anyway, pretending until it really happened so we could end this conversation.

When I woke from my drug-induced sleep, Courtney was gone and Holly sat in a chair beside my bed, knees pulled up to her chest, arms wrapped tight around her legs. Her eyes were focused on the monitor to my right, but she blinked rapidly and yawned.

I didn't speak at first because my mind was so groggy I had to remind myself which Holly this was. What had we done together? How did she feel about me?

It came back in an instant. Agent Holly. The one who saw her best friend Adam lying dead on the floor in a puddle of blood. The one who thought I'd killed him. The Holly who wrote that terrible letter about herself, about the hopelessness of her life now and how survival—self-preservation—was the only reason she had to get up in the morning.

The ache of these revelations hit me like a punch in the stomach.

"Hey," she said, noticing I had woken up.

"Hey." I suddenly felt very insecure about the state of my personal hygiene and the fact that I had tubes and wires coming out of *way* too many body parts. "Where is everybody else?"

"It's the middle of the night." Holly yawned. "We've been taking turns watching the heart monitors, switching the bags of fluids. Stuff like that."

My eyes carefully avoided hers. "Well, that answers my question about whether or not you've decided to continue working for Eyewall."

"Nobody's enemies here. What's the point?" Holly sighed and gave me a tight smile. "This is awkward, isn't it?"

I finally looked at her and knew in an instant that I was going to lie, just like I had with Courtney. Not because I smelled bad and looked like hell but because I couldn't imagine being in Holly's position: having someone tell you that another version of you was *in love* with this person you sort of hate. A person who held you at gunpoint and dragged you into the future.

Everything that had happened since I left August of 2009 trying to save the other version of Holly had created a hell on Earth for this version of Holly. She had had no choice about any aspect of her life from the point that Adam had first asked her to help with a CIA mission. This time around, I was determined to make damn sure she got to choose who she fell in love with, if anyone at all. From now on, Holly would be in full control over the course of her life.

Eyewall had her boxed in with no way out and I wasn't about to do the same thing to her. Not after getting her trapped here. I still couldn't believe, after all my efforts to keep Holly safe, she'd ended up working for 2009 Eyewall, a division of the CIA that seemed determined to take down my own division, Tempest. And Eyewall hadn't exactly been a pleasant work environment for Holly. I hated to think about being the reason she was stuck here, but at the same time, I couldn't forget what had happened when I "held her hostage" before the jump to the future. Her own people, her own division, had been poised to write her off without a second thought.

"I know what you think," I said to Holly, making a quick decision.

Her eyebrows lifted as if to ask if I also had mind-reading abilities in addition to time-travel powers. "What I think is . . . that you know me a little better than I know you. And I'm not sure how I feel about that. How would you feel?"

"I don't know." I rubbed my face with my hands. "About what I said, Courtney filled me in and honestly, I thought it was her. You have to realize, I hadn't seen my sister in years, and then she's here and I'm dying."

"So you were trying to tell Courtney you loved her before you died?" Holly clarified.

My eyes froze on hers, unwavering as I forced my pupils to stay normal-sized. "Yes."

"But you did know me, things I don't have any memory of because of time travel, right?" She looked so focused, so incredibly on-task that it occurred to me for the first time that Holly probably made a fantastic CIA agent. A lot better than I would have if I didn't have superpowers.

Now for the cover story.

"Adam," I said, forcing calm. "Adam was my best friend. We were working together on time-travel stuff. He was also your friend, so obviously I knew you then, too."

"But you didn't know I was an agent, did you?" she asked, drilling me as if I were a hundred percent healthy and not at all in danger of heart failure or whatever.

"That kinda shocked me," I admitted, because it lined up perfectly with my cover story. "Which I'm sure you noticed."

I could tell she was deep in thought, reviewing those memories, but after a few seconds she nodded. "Yeah, I noticed."

The back of my throat felt like sandpaper and I coughed a few times before asking Holly if there was water or anything to drink. She jumped from her chair and opened a cabinet, pulling out this flat, round water bottle. When she unscrewed the cap, a rubber straw popped out.

"Weird." I looked it over carefully before taking several big gulps. It hurt like hell, but I was too thirsty to care. "What's it like out there, anyway?"

Holly took the bottle from my hands and set it on the table before sitting down next to me again. "It's so odd, seriously. There are a few cabins and some tents, and a building with all this weird-ass technology and supplies. It's like they want us to stay alive but also not be all that comfortable. Mason thinks they're watching us constantly. Most of the area isn't all that futurelike considering the year."

"If we're being watched, why don't they just kill us?" I asked, regretting my choice of words immediately. "Sorry, that wasn't the positive thinking I had been trying to display."

Holly laughed. "Believe me, that was the first thought to go through my head. But I think Mason could be right. We're in some kind of guinea-pig maze. Like a social experiment or something."

"How many people are here?"

"Mason, Courtney, Emily, your dad, me," Holly rattled off. "Grayson, Lonnie, Sasha, and Blake."

"Making friends?"

Holly rolled her eyes. "Yeah, it's just like summer camp."

"I've met Lonnie and Grayson. I have no idea who Sasha is," I said. "Blake? Why does that name sound familiar?"

"The guy with the ponytail," she said, reminding me that I'd already met him. "He's our age. They've been here awhile, you know?"

"How long?"

"Almost two years," Holly said.

Our eyes met again and we sat in silence, letting the gravity of two years sink in slowly. If there was a way out of here, they would have found it by now.

But did it even really matter to me how long we were stuck here? I had Courtney, Dad, and Holly with me. Three people I loved more than anything else.

Could I secretly be happy in this place?

I had a feeling if I brought this up with anyone else, I'd be in need of more medical attention. Or maybe they'd excuse it and label the behavior as one of the weird things that happens to people after they almost die.

CHAPTER THREE

DAY 10. LATE AFTERNOON

"Doing okay so far?" Courtney asked, holding a hand out as if preparing for me to topple over any second.

"I'm not hooked up to needles and tubes, I can go to the bathroom on my own, I've showered, and I'm wearing normal clothes, preparing to see actual daylight for the first time in nearly two weeks." I smiled at her. "So yeah, I'm doing better than okay."

Sunlight hit me right between the eyes as we stepped outside. The muggy air hung with dust but I took a deep breath anyway, filling my lungs.

Emily's face lit up when she saw me and Courtney. She kicked up dirt and grass running over to us. Her cheeks looked rounder and more colorful than they had the night Kendrick and I found her wandering around Central Park, starving and lost. *Lily Kendrick. My Tempset partner. I wonder if she's okay?*

Emily was still scrawny as hell but no longer to the point of being sickly.

I took a minute to look around while Emily grasped my hand, tugging it gently toward a fire pit a hundred feet away. A small brick building sat behind the pit and several wooden cabins and tents were scattered around the grassy area. In the distance the grass was much taller, or maybe it was weeds, and there was also a small lake with bluish green water.

That must be the source of the fish they've been feeding me for the past four days. Blake—the guy with the ponytail, someone I hadn't seen since collapsing and nearly dying ten days ago—stood on the far side of the big fire pit, swinging an ax, splitting wood in half.

No wonder they called this place Misfit Island. It was like a weird, forced-camping experience.

Just as I was contemplating walking over to say hi, Blake suddenly dropped his ax and looked up, his face filled with alarm. "Get away from each other!"

Both Courtney and Emily stayed at my side, frozen and confused. Blake ran toward us, grabbing Courtney's arm and pulling her away.

"What the hell—" I started to say and then I smelled it. The sense of smell is supposed to leave the longest-lasting impressions. And I remembered this. Too well. The metallic scent filled my nostrils and I did exactly what Blake had said. I hauled ass away from Emily and Courtney, and the abrupt movement caused pain to shoot through nearly every inch of my body. I might have been better, but I wasn't completely healed yet.

Suddenly, Adam Silverman lay at my feet. I stopped, completely frozen. "Adam, what are you doing here?"

His face and leg were covered in blood and he wasn't moving. His eyes stared up at me, questions . . . too many questions in them. Questions I couldn't answer. I dropped to the ground, panic setting in, causing me to lose sight of reality, which wasn't *this* at all. I pressed my fingers to his leg, applying pressure to the wound that I'd seen once before. "Adam, you're okay! There's a doctor here. It's okay."

I shook him hard, trying to get him to wake up. *I've seen this before . . . I've been here before. What is this?*

Memory gas.

I blinked my eyes several times and focused on the object in front of me. It wasn't Adam. Somewhere in my mind I knew it wasn't Adam. I pulled my shirt over my nose and held my breath, squeezing my eyes shut.

When I opened them again, a giant log sat in front of me. My hands were scraped and bloody, splinters covering both my palms. My heart began to slow down and I breathed normally, testing the air. The metallic smell was gone. I hadn't almost murdered someone this time thinking he was Thomas, like I did during training, when Chief Marshall tested the gas out on several of us unsuspecting trainees.

Chief Marshall.

I ground my teeth together at the thought of his shooting Healy and the other version of me. When I had told Dad and Grayson about it in more detail a couple days ago, they both concluded that I had probably done a half-jump, despite the invisible force field over us preventing time travel. Of course, being able to do a half-jump did absolutely no good considering my body was still here and we were no closer to escaping from the year 3200. But the half-jump did provide an important piece of information: Chief Marshall was a bad guy.

Very bad.

A high-pitched scream brought me back to reality. I stood up and saw Courtney covering her face, screaming at the top of her lungs. Dad came barreling out the door of a nearby cabin, racing toward her.

Emily was closest to me, and I reached her before anyone else. She was huddled in the grass, knees pulled to her chest, crying quietly. I picked her up, feeling a pull in my chest where the long scar was still working hard to hold my skin together, and let her bury her face in my shoulder while I carried her toward Courtney.

Dad shook Courtney's shoulders a little, then tried to pry her hands from her face. "It's not real, honey. It's just an illusion. You're okay."

Her hands visibly shook but she dropped them to her sides. Her face had gone completely pale. In fact, she looked a little green, like she might spew any minute. She sank to the ground and Dad sat beside her. "Put your head between your knees, it helps." He looked up at me and Emily. "You okay?"

"Yeah, fine," I said, glancing around.

Mason pulled himself off the grass, his face colorless.

Emily sniffled a few more times, then lifted her head. "I'm okay."

I set her down on the ground and counted heads. Blake and

Grayson stood near each other, appearing less shaken than the rest of us. I could see Lonnie and Sasha, the dark-skinned girl with the almond-shaped eyes, down by the lake.

"Where's Holly?" I asked no one in particular.

"I think she was sleeping in one of the cabins," Courtney said between shaky breaths.

I headed for the closest cabin and had to check three more before spotting blond hair and white tennis shoes huddled in the far corner.

"Holly? You okay?" I walked slowly toward her still figure. Too still. I squatted on the floor beside her and barely rested a hand on her back.

"Don't touch me!"

Startled, I fell back onto my hands and scurried away, putting a few feet between us. "Holly, it's okay. It wasn't real, it's this stuff—"

"Don't touch me!" she repeated, shouting into her knees. Then she lifted her head and I was surprised that her cheeks were dry, no sign of tears. Her eyes were hard and cold when they zoomed in on me.

Was she seeing me or an illusion of someone else? And if so, who?

"Okay . . . I'm not going to touch you." I moved back a couple more feet and held up my hands. "It's me . . . Jackson."

"I know who you are, asshole," she snapped. "I know it's not real. Just leave me alone. Go help someone who actually needs it."

Stung by her words, I scrambled to my feet, slightly dizzy from all this movement after ten days of being in bed, and left her alone. When I went outside again, everyone was sitting around the fire pit. Blake tossed some logs into the hole and followed them with a flaming match.

I couldn't fathom why we needed a fire in this heat and humidity. And it was more than strange to see them gathered together like it was story-and-song time.

Mason caught my eye and gave me a smile that was more like a grimace. "Just like old times, huh, Agent Meyer?"

I let out a breath. "At least this time I only injured my hands and not another person."

That's when I remembered Blake, yelling at us to get away from each other. I turned my eyes to him. "Has this happened before? Where's it coming from?"

"We're not sure how it's released into the air." He laughed darkly. "And yes, it's happened many times. First time since you guys arrived, though."

Grayson stood up from his spot next to Blake. "Blake, Lonnie, Sasha, and I have a tradition after each memory-gas episode. We sit out here and tell each other what hallucination manifested from our minds. We've done this twelve times, and it seems to reduce the intensity of the next episode."

"I have a theory," Blake said. "I think when you talk about the hallucinations out loud, it moves the memory it is based on from the subconscious to a different part of the brain. Somewhere the gas can't reach."

A door swung open and Holly emerged from the cabin she'd been holed up in. She breezed past me and took a seat next to Mason. Her face was calm and collected. As if she hadn't just screamed at me and called me an asshole.

"I'll go first," Sasha said. "On one of my trips to Eyewall headquarters, I got attacked by the faceless men. One of them had a razor blade to my throat, my legs pinned to the ground."

Courtney pressed her hands over Emily's ears and I moved closer to the fire, sitting down beside them.

"I didn't know if they were going to kill me," Sasha croaked, choking on her words a bit. "Somehow I managed to get away, but it was the closest I've been to death."

Grayson spoke next. "My first delivery in 1985, I hadn't studied childbirth enough in that year, it was stupid for me to think I could handle it. Probably the biggest regret of my life." He cleared his throat, regaining composure. "Anyway, the shoulder got caught on the pelvic bone and the cord was wrapped around the baby's neck. I should have caught it earlier. We got her into the OR but the baby had been without oxygen for too long to not suffer a great deal of brain damage."

Everyone was silent for ten long seconds and then Blake spoke up. "I watched someone kill a good friend's mother, father, and younger brother. I just watched and I couldn't stop it."

Lonnie told a story about her mother dying, and Mason's memory was of getting caught and interrogated by several Iraqi soldiers when we were doing training in the Middle East. I remembered the area he was talking about, but it must have been a mission with his Tempest specialty group. Something I didn't have the privilege to know. Dad didn't look too surprised so I assumed he probably wasn't hearing about this for the first time.

When it was Courtney's turn, she laughed and her face flushed. "I can't tell you mine. It's going to sound so frivolous after all these horrible stories."

Mason rolled his eyes. "No it won't. Just tell us."

"All right." Courtney smiled a little, then glanced sideways at me. "I watched my brother fall out of a tree and break his arm when we were six."

I started laughing, too, realizing that Courtney, at this point in her life, had had it pretty easy. Dad was grinning too and he lifted his hand to indicate his turn. "That was actually mine, too. Same memory."

Grayson's eyebrows lifted and I looked at Dad and then back at Grayson, who had probably done this with him already in the four weeks that Dad was stuck here with him before we arrived. I seriously doubted that my broken arm was at the top of Dad's horrible-events list. His list was probably worse than anyone else's here. There was Courtney's death, Eileen's, probably several close calls with me that I didn't even know about.

I spoke quickly, interrupting everyone's train of thought before they had a chance to figure out that Dad was lying. "I saw my dad smoking a cigarette in 1953."

Everyone laughed and Mason threw a twig in Dad's direction. "Don't you know smoking can kill you, Agent Meyer?"

"A slow death spread over the course of fifty years," Dad said. "Sounds nice, actually."

"My turn," Emily said. "My chicken died."

Courtney squeezed her around the shoulders. "I lost a hamster when I was your age. Dad tried to switch him for another one but I could tell the difference."

I scratched the back of my head, diverting my eyes from Courtney's. Dad coughed loudly as if telling me to come clean. "Actually, he didn't die. Not right away . . ."

I felt Courtney's eyes burning a hole in the side of my face. "Jackson!"

"He seemed really unhappy locked up in that cage. I thought he might want to go outside. He was on the balcony, totally fine. I didn't know he would walk right off the ledge. I think he had brain damage even before he fell. Not the smartest hamster in the litter."

Mason snorted back a laugh, but Courtney's glare stayed on me. "I can't believe you did that!"

"It was an accident," Dad said, holding back his own laughter, although when we were eight, I had gotten seriously chewed out by Dad for that event.

"Yeah right," Courtney said, snapping her head in Dad's direction. "He accidentally opened the cage, removed Jell-O, walked him to the balcony, put him down, then watched him waddle to his death? Explain how that works, Dad?"

"Your hamster's name was Jell-O?" Mason asked. "Why?"

Grayson clapped his hands together, interrupting the family feud. "Holly, you're up next."

Everyone looked at her and her light blue eyes widened as she sat up straighter. The fear only lasted for a split second before her face became totally unreadable. "It's too hot to sit by this fire any longer." She brushed off her jeans and then stood up. "And I don't agree with Blake's theory. It doesn't help to talk about it, and my guess is at least half of you are lying, anyway."

Mason let out a low whistle as Holly took off toward the lake. "*Somebody* is obviously trying to damage our happy circle of feelings."

I rolled my eyes at him. "Lay off her. She's just freaked out." I turned to Grayson. "Who's doing this? Setting off the memory gas and keeping us here?"

Grayson let out a breath, glancing first at Lonnie then Blake and Sasha, getting nods from each of them. "The four of us are a lot like you, Jackson. And I guess like Courtney and Emily, too. Except your existence is a direct result of our existence, and I know that the logic seems mixed up since we're from . . ."

"The future?" I prompted. "My future, anyway."

"That's right."

"Time travel was always going to happen," Lonnie added. "The four of us evolved naturally. In our present times, no one knew who would possess the ability to time-jump."

"As opposed to the cloned people who were made for it?" Mason asked.

"Exactly," Grayson said.

"So, like, a whole ton of people can time-travel in the future?" I asked. That seemed like one nasty mess if it was true.

All four of them shook their heads. It was Blake who explained, "We only know of seven true, naturally evolved time jumpers. I was the second to last to be discovered. Sasha wasn't even born yet, wouldn't be for a long time."

"Eyewall headquarters is in this year," Sasha said. "It's quite a ways from here. About a two-day walk."

"But if you guys are from my future," I asked, "maybe you can tell me what time period Thomas showed me in a time jump?"

I took a minute to explain to them about the perfect future I saw with Thomas. The green landscape everywhere, right in the

middle of New York City. The eerie quiet, the perfect temperature, the children with their superhuman powers, climbing and
jumping.

All four of the future time travelers were quiet for a while, exchanging weary glances. Grayson took a deep breath before speaking. "You've studied history, right? World War II?"

"Yeah," Courtney, Mason, and I all said together.

"A utopian society that evolves by creating a master race,"
Grayson said. "That's what you saw. Not the aftermath of World
War II but of a similar war, a war that caused the destruction here,
and in the outcome Thomas showed you, the new Hitler won."

I knew there was something weird about that place. I didn't feel
the warmth of the world when I was there, nothing good, but it was
so hard to judge because it had *looked* amazing. It seemed perfect.

"And they keep us here," Grayson said. "Because we're rare and
Dr. Ludwig can't bear the thought of getting rid of us. He doesn't
even want us to suffer too much. That might make it more difficult
to use us for whatever experiment he's working on. Notice we're
given plenty of supplies—food, sources of water, medical equipment."

"It's not because they care so much," Lonnie said, bitterness
spilling from each word. She glanced behind her at the bright sun,
moving lower in the horizon. "We should get our gear. The sun's
about to set."

Courtney touched my arm. "It gets really cold at night for some
reason. The temperature drops a lot—like going from summer to
winter."

Grayson stood up, prepared to follow Lonnie, but then turned
to face me, Dad, Courtney, Mason, and Emily. "I think the best
thing you can do right now, all of you, is accept this place as home.
Don't let the negative thoughts creep in and do something stupid.
There's no fight to be won, nothing to make this life seem temporary. Make the choice to accept it and to be happy with what you
do have."

Hadn't I decided that already? But what about Dad and Courtney . . . *and Holly*? What did they want?

"Jackson," Grayson added, "if you have more questions, Blake can tell you his story. He's seen a bit more of Eyewall than I have."

Everyone began shuffling around, heading for supplies in different cabins. I moved over and sat beside Blake, who hadn't made a move to leave. I glanced up at the sky, pink and purple from the setting sun. "So, they're up there, watching us in this bubble, like gods."

"They're not gods," Blake said firmly. "They're human. Unfortunately, it seems they've forgotten that fact."

"Right," I said, not sure exactly what he meant by that.

Blake's gaze darted around, and then he lowered his voice. "Can I show you something?"

I followed him into the small building and then into a tiny room with several computer screens lining one of the walls. All of the screens were blue and blank. Blake sat on the tile floor and removed an army knife from his pocket. He yanked off his right tennis shoe and his white sock. "I've been waiting almost two years to do this."

And before I could stop him, he sliced a hole in the bottom of his foot.

CHAPTER FOUR

Blood oozed from his foot onto the floor. "Dude! What are you doing?"

"Just wait," he said, leaning forward, pressing his fingers inside the cut. Finally, he held up something silver and bloody between his fingers. "In the year I'm from, we all have memory files. Usually behind the ear." He tilted his head and I had a good view of the one-centimeter scar behind his ear.

"Here." I spotted a sink in the corner of the room and ran over to it, grabbing handfuls of paper towels. "Use these. That's gonna bleed for a while."

"When everything started going bad," Blake said, pressing paper towels to his foot with one hand and wiping the floor clean with the other, "Grayson took out my original memory file, put a fake one behind my ear, and then we hid the real one. I needed to remember what happened. To have those thoughts with me at all times just in case. With the others, I've told them my story. But I want to show you these instead so that our world and where we came from makes more sense to you."

"I doubt anything's going to make much sense to me."

"Well, it's possible I have other motivations outside of Grayson's goals for showing these to you," Blake said, wiping the tiny metal chip clean. "But we'll get to that part later."

He stood up and walked carefully on the ball of his right foot. I waited quietly while he fiddled with a computer and slid the chip into a tiny slot.

"Just so you know, in case you need it for anything, this room is virtually soundproof." One of the blue screens turned black. "Some of these files I recorded onto the chip myself as a journal entry and some were plucked from various regions of my brain. I couldn't save everything. I just kept the important ones."

A robot voice filled the tiny space, "December 8, 2873. Audio recording by host."

Then Blake's voice came through, though it sounded a little different, younger maybe. And the words moved across the black screen accompanying the audio.

I never imagined my parents would be so eager to hand over their fifteen-year-old son to the U.S. government. But boy were they ever. It happened on my way to school two days ago. My outer gear is fourth-hand, passed down from my three older brothers, and has lost its wind-resistant ability. The air was bitterly cold, my eyes half-closed, and I could hardly put one foot in front of the other, when suddenly, sunlight hot enough to be July beat down on me. It took me several seconds to realize what had happened. What I'd just done. Unlike my parents, elation wasn't my first reaction. It was utter panic. I didn't know how I'd done it and how to get back.

My legs had never moved as fast as they did in that first time jump. I tore my outerwear open as I ran home, bursting through the front door, yelling for them to tell me what day it was. My mother took one look at my clothing and dropped the glass dish she had been holding. My father came running into the kitchen after hearing the glass shatter.

Turns out I had jumped almost exactly three months into the past. I couldn't even spit out the words to reflect my fear of getting stuck there or just of the unknown because Mom had already picked up her telecom, making the one call every parent dreams of making. And even in my panic, I did feel a small surge of pride as she said the words to the dispatcher on the other line, "My son has just come from the future." The way she said *my son* meant something entirely different now. Before it just meant one of four nearly identical boys, almost exactly three years spacing each of us apart. Now these words seemed to separate me from the three shadows I had chased my entire life.

My moment of pride only lasted a few minutes, until my father returned with a slightly tanner, sweaty, and confused version of me. This was how they proved it. The only way to know for sure. Not that time travelers are discovered all the time. I'm only the seventh in the history of mankind. No wonder my parents are so proud.

As I stood looking at this barely younger version of myself, I couldn't grasp much else. The government workers showed up almost instantly. Their navy uniforms crisp and stiff in an inhuman way. They recorded the details I gave them—when did you leave? Approximately what time? What was your location?

Then they gave my family and the other me memory injections so we would spend the next three months knowing nothing of what would happen on December 6, 2873. Once the shock had worn off and reality set in, I knew how to get back.

The cold wind returned, freezing the air into my lungs, but still, as I turned to walk back home, I slowed my pace, knowing they were there. Waiting to take me away. Waiting to make me the envy of every boy and girl in my class. Possibly the envy of everyone in the country. Everyone except the five others like me.

I only had ten minutes to pack my bags and say good-bye before being teleported to an apartment in the nation's capital, New York City. The apartment is twice the size of my family's home, and instead of sharing space with five others, I'm only sharing with one. His name is Thomas and he looks about ten years older than me. I only met him briefly this morning. He came in with a navy-suit worker and told me to try not to feel overwhelmed and that we'd talk later. That was hours ago and now I really just want to call home, but I can't find a telecom anywhere.

I guess receiving this honor, having this rare talent, requires a great deal of patience. A virtue I have yet to acquire.

Blake hit a button on the control panel and the words froze on the screen.

"So Thomas is one of the originals! That explains why he's able to do the complete jumps so easily. He can go back and forth in the same timeline like regular time travel. Is that the only kind of jump you guys do?" I drilled Blake. "Or can you bounce off World B, too? I know I'm the one who opened that portal, and I also know that cloned time travelers have jumped over there."

"Until your dad arrived and told us about you, I hadn't really heard of any other way of time travel besides the complete jump, as you call it. And yes, Thomas is one of the original time travelers and we are the strongest. Last I heard, the clones hadn't been able to come even close to matching us."

"Except Emily."

He nodded solemnly. "She's a special project. Thomas's own brainchild."

I knew this already, but thinking about Thomas's bringing a child into the world under those pretenses left me completely disgusted. I had to change the subject. "So . . . you were only fifteen and you had to leave home. That sucks. And living with Thomas, what was that like?"

Blake's eyebrows lifted. "You ready to hear more?"

I nodded. There was never any way to stop my curiosity when it had latched on to something. I had no idea what Blake wanted me to get from this info, but I wanted to know about this world where time travelers naturally occurred and were worshipped and adored by all. That would have made my life a hell of a lot easier. Except the living-with-Thomas part.

The audio robot began again and I watched the words on the screen, reading them quickly.

DECEMBER 14, 2873.
AUDIO RECORDING BY HOST.

Everyone has been so nice to me this past week, even the navy-suit workers. Well, they aren't exactly nice, but they're not mean either like when they first came to my house after my mom's call. The scientists in the lab, the ones taking all my data and doing test after test, have bent over backwards to get me everything I need *and* a whole bunch of stuff I don't. Thomas keeps asking how I'm doing, telling me how special I am, that he was seventeen years old before he did his first time jump, and before me, he was the youngest reported time traveler in history. So, not only am I one of a handful in the world who can travel through time, I'm now the youngest, at fifteen, ever to time-travel.

Thomas thinks in another thirty or forty years, we'll have small children who can time-travel. I know he's twenty-five and much older than me, but still, I don't ever spend time guessing what might happen in thirty or forty years. Thomas is like that, though. He sits in on conferences with all the other scientists working for the government, studying the Tempus gene, and it's like he's one of them. I'm so behind. And so immature. Thomas is very well respected among the entire crew of government workers. He has this aura that shines the minute he walks in a room. I need to work harder, to study more, so that Thomas and the others will have just as much respect for me.

A couple of days ago, I met two of the other travelers: Nora and Jean. They live in our building downtown. Nora is twenty-six and Jean is eighteen. Jean has the brightest red hair and green eyes I've ever seen. Thomas says it's a sign that these physical traits could be a future indicator for identifying time travelers before their first jump. I just think she's really pretty which means, like with all the pretty girls at my former school, I'm going to have a lot of trouble talking to her. Nora is super nice and almost motherly to Jean, and now to me, too. So, even though she's also very attractive, I don't have any trouble talking to her because she reminds me of my own mother and fits a little better into that category than any other.

So far, I've been showered with gifts, expensive clothing (brand-new, not handed down from my brothers), the most amazing entertainment devices that my family could never afford, not to mention the food . . . better and larger in quantity than anything I've ever had before. But I still miss my family, my friends, my hometown, my school and all its quirks. Thomas says it's best to sever contact, at least in the beginning, but I really wish there was a way to have both worlds.

I wonder if they miss me, too?

"Every time I've seen Thomas," I said once Blake had frozen the words again, "he's been much older than twenty-five. Probably thirty or thirty-five. Maybe even a little older. When did he change? He seemed all right at twenty-five."

Blake stared over my shoulder, deep in thought. "It wasn't like you'd think, a sudden shift due to one influence. I think he was always working toward a different goal than everyone else, but his ideas, his theories and views of the world were so close to being right and yet so wrong at the same time that I couldn't see it, not for a while. And as he got smarter and more powerful, more respected, it made changing our system easier."

"Lots of gray areas," I concluded. "That's why you can't pinpoint one moment that made everything go wrong. Sometimes I wonder if time travel is wrong, and by wrong I mean unethical. I know your ability evolved naturally, but just because we all have the capability to murder someone doesn't mean we should do it."

"I agree a hundred percent," Blake said.

"Where are Jean and Nora? Why aren't they trapped here?"

"Jean's infatuation with Thomas led her to follow him. But I know deep down she doesn't share his beliefs," he said. "And Nora . . . I don't know exactly where she is but Grayson does and I'm pretty sure she's safe."

The words moved again as the computer voice said the date.

FEBRUARY 1, 2874.
MEMORY EXTRACTED FROM HOST.

Thomas grasped my arm and I could almost feel the weight of his effort—the brainpower it took to make this kind of jump and take me along in the process. I felt the warm air before I even opened my eyes. Then I heard it. Both Thomas and Dr. Ludwig, who's sort of like our brainpower coach, prepared me for the noise, but I had no idea it would be this loud.

Cars. I'd read about them in the education files on

my computer, but seeing them move so recklessly, people running in front of them, I wasn't at all prepared.

"It's chaotic, isn't it?" Thomas said, releasing my arm and then resting a hand on my shoulder.

"I don't even know what to look at first."

He pointed to a building right in front of us. The sign on the outside said NYU MEDICAL CENTER. "This is the 1987 version of a medical-treatment facility."

"Okay, but what are we doing here?"

Several people darted around us as we stood in the center of a sidewalk, throwing us dirty looks as if we had ruined their day by slowing them down.

"Don't worry about them," Thomas said. "You'll never see any of these people again. And to answer your question, this is why we're here." He pulled several small vials of a cloudy white substance from his pants pocket and held them out for me to see before stowing them away again. "You understand how the Tempus gene works, right?"

"Yeah . . . I mean, mostly," I stammered, still distracted by the honking and screeching going on around me. I fought off the urge to cover my ears. "It's not here in this year, right? Not a fully formed Tempus gene, anyway. It's first discovered in the year . . ."

"2234," Thomas finished for me, not carrying one bit of the condescending tone some of the navy-suit workers had whenever I didn't know the answer to a question they asked. "But it took all the way until early 2800 for time travel to show up and that woman was thirty-four when she discovered her ability. You and I are proof that the gene is evolving over time. Eventually, the entire human race may possess the ability to time-travel and possibly at an age even younger than fifteen."

"Wait." I'd known there were still two remaining time travelers I had yet to meet, but I hadn't really thought about the age difference being so huge. "One of us is that old? Is she still alive?"

Thomas grinned. "Stick with me, kid, and you'll get the real answers. And no, she's not alive anymore. She passed away a couple years ago. And the Tempus gene shows up in our history maps in earlier years because of missions like this one. But don't worry, you and I are still part of the original group. Nothing can change that. We'll always remember that information because we hold all the versions of our lives within our minds even if we alter history. Even if we alter the future."

"But what are the vials for?"

"The Tempus gene," Thomas said as he took a step across the sidewalk and pulled open the door to the medical center. "We're introducing it earlier, hoping the future looks different."

I couldn't move for several seconds even though so many people would have loved for me to vacate the middle of the sidewalk. This wasn't a small little adventure for the fun of discovery and creating accurate records of our country's history. This was big. Very big. And I couldn't believe Thomas would allow me to take part in it.

Finally, Thomas reached out a hand and pulled me through the door. "I had a feeling you'd be impressed with this mission. But don't forget the number one rule of time travel . . . always blend in with your surroundings."

Thomas breezed past security guards and official-looking people like he owned the place. I saw several men and women squeezing themselves into what I knew from studying history in school was called an elevator. Thomas shook his head and opened another door, leading to a flight of stairs.

"Never trust technology in this year," he said in a low whisper. "Those things are held by cables and a pulley system. Can you believe how they pack themselves inside, like there's no risk?"

We went down three flights before reaching a door with a security code that Thomas had obviously been given. He used another code to enter a lab where a guy, probably a few years older than Thomas, stood wearing a white coat and safety goggles.

"Always taking the stairs, huh?" the guy said, not even looking up at us.

"I think President Healy would be a bit perturbed with me if I killed myself riding in an elevator when a perfectly good set of stairs was available," Thomas said.

The guy turned his back completely on us and stuck his face in what looked like a microscope—a device I'd learned about in history class.

"Of course, President Healy. Wouldn't want to do anything to disappoint him," the guy said.

Even I could hear the edge in his voice. Thomas cleared his throat as if to alert him that they weren't alone. "Grayson, this is our newest recruit, Blake."

Grayson looked up at me suddenly, and his smile was warm and didn't carry any of the edge he'd had just seconds ago. He stuck out a gloved hand to shake mine. "Nice to meet you, Blake. Thomas mentioned a newbie a while back, but I didn't realize how young you were. You can't be more than—"

"Fifteen," Thomas finished. "Broke my record by two years."

I stood up straighter, trying to grow instantly. "I'll be sixteen in a month."

Grayson smiled and it went all the way to his eyes like my mother's smiles. I hadn't seen an expression that honest since I left home. Impassiveness is something the government instills in all workers.

"How are you getting along so far?" Grayson asked me.

"Good . . . I mean . . . this is my first mission, but it's been pretty exciting these last couple of months." I got a good look at Grayson's face now that he had turned toward me. His hair color was light brown like Thomas's and his eyes were also blue like both Thomas's and mine. The similarities were too great to ignore. It was like seeing what I might look like in ten years with Thomas and in twenty years with Grayson.

"But it must have been hard for you," Grayson said. "Leaving home. I was nineteen and already on my own. Thomas was raised in the White House, he didn't need any adjusting. But you're just a boy."

Thomas rested a hand on my shoulder again. "That's why Dr. Ludwig is taking it slow with him. It'll be a while before he's doing his own missions."

Grayson stared at me for a long moment, then his face formed the emotionless smile I had become used to in the last couple of months. "Well, let me show you what we're doing here today." He turned to Thomas, who dropped his hand from my shoulder and removed the vials from his pocket. "Thank you.

Now, Blake, we have sixteen women who will undergo a procedure called in vitro fertilization in this hospital today. Basically, traditional methods of conception, in this year, anyway, haven't been successful for them and they've sought the assistance of a fertility doctor."

Grayson pointed to his chest, indicating that he was the fertility doctor these women sought out. He walked over to the center lab table and pointed to a small dish with clear liquid in it. "All of the women today have husbands who have donated specimens—sperm—to be joined with their wives' eggs. You understand how this process works, correct?"

I gave a quick nod and felt my face heating up at the mention of conception, though this was a very technical scientific version that didn't seem to involve contact between the two parents at all. But still, my mind couldn't help but wander to thoughts of more traditional methods, and I hoped with all my power that these thoughts wouldn't show up in the mission report.

"What we're going to do today," Grayson said, "is supplement the fathers' specimens with that of a man carrying the Tempus gene in your present."

"Do they know this?" I asked. "The parents? Won't they know that there's no genetic link between the real father and the child, at least after it's born?"

Grayson nodded his approval. "Very good. You're a smart one. All my patients sign a clause as part of our research program. The procedure cost is more affordable for a larger percentage of families, and in return, we get their permission to use a substitute specimen as needed to increase the probability of successful conception."

"In other words," Thomas added, "we tell the families that the father's semen has a low sperm count, whether it does or not, and they consent to a donor because having a child is that important to them. Something I can't even fathom, but it's a very useful motivation for the purpose of our experiment."

I was so blown away by the complexity of this project and the importance of our missions that I barely spoke for the rest of the trip. I watched Grayson carefully as he went through the steps to prepare each specimen for the procedure.

Later, when Thomas and I returned to our apartment, after being debriefed in the White House by Dr. Ludwig and his team, I finally asked him the question that had been on my mind since first being introduced to Grayson.

"So, is Grayson's mission a long one? Like a few months? He seemed very comfortable in 1987."

"He's been on the same mission in the past for two years and hasn't done a time jump since," Thomas said. "Before that, he had a bad habit of using his time travel for personal reasons. He jumped too often and sustained an injury. His last jump for this current mission nearly killed him. The risk of bringing him back was too much. Dr. Ludwig decided that he needed to stay and be the field man for the Tempus gene experiment. He still has a chance to heal; it's very possible he will in a year or two."

"Wow . . . I don't even—"

Thomas waved my response off as if to say there was no need to feel sorry for him. Maybe because he did it to himself? Or maybe because he was happy in 1987? How could he enjoy living in that chaotic and dangerous world?

"Now we need to verify our impact," Thomas said,

opening my handheld computer and holding it out for me. "What was that year I mentioned earlier? The first detection of the Tempus gene?"

"2234," I said right away.

"Correct." He pointed to the tiny screen in front of me. "Look it up, again."

I typed in the question and nearly dropped the computer onto the hard floor. "2208 . . . how . . . I mean . . . we did this? Changed the date by twenty-six years?"

Thomas's face split into a wide grin. "Yes, we did this. This is why you're here, Blake. Do you understand how important you are now? How much of an impact you can have on creating a future that is bigger and better than every man and woman in 1987 could ever imagine?"

All I could do was nod and try to hide my shock. Could I really be that special? That important? Me, the fourth son of Jessica and Stephen? A hero to my entire country?

And I knew right then I'd do anything to make sure I didn't let them down. This was too important.

"So, that's what Grayson meant when he said he'd been a doctor in two different centuries," I said. "I was born there, you know, at NYU Medical Center. Me and Courtney both, obviously. Wouldn't it be so weird if Grayson was running around the hospital at the same time as Dr. Melvin?"

"Dr. Melvin?" Blake said, suddenly looking over at me, now seated in the only chair in the room. "Andrew Melvin?"

"Yeah, that's him," I said. "Why? You know him, right? The creator of experiment Axelle?"

I swallowed back the bile drifting up to my throat as the image of Dr. Melvin dead on the floor of his office replayed in my mind.

"Yeah, we've met once," Blake said with a sigh. "Your friend Mason is a product of the Tempus Gene Project. He was conceived in Grayson's lab and delivered by him. That's why your side wanted Mason."

"They put him in the CIA really young," I said. "And he's a genius, I thought that was why."

Blake shook his head. "They knew he'd be a genius in your present long before he joined the CIA. Most likely his identity was revealed and they took him to protect him from being studied."

"Wow, so everyone in your present is smarter? That's so crazy," I said. "Do you know any more spawn of the Tempus Gene Project?"

Blake's face clouded with some emotion I couldn't nail down. Grief or longing or just sadness. Whichever it was, it instantly made him look five years older.

"Just one," he said.

My thoughts shifted suddenly and I eyed Blake with suspicion. "Wait a second . . . Grayson's a doctor."

"Uh-huh . . . ?"

"If he wanted you to show me this memory file, he would have cut it out of your foot himself and stitched it up properly," I said. "And wouldn't he have wanted you to show it to my dad weeks ago?"

Blake's mouth fell open. He was caught. Obviously, his being taken from home at fifteen to work for the government didn't include any form of CIA-type training because he had made too many mistakes to count since we walked into this room.

A knock on the door startled both of us. As if to answer my question, Blake ejected the memory chip, hid it in the bottom of his sock, and stuffed his foot in there before putting the shoe back on. "Yeah . . . ?"

He flung the door open and Lonnie stood there, taking in both of us. "I thought you preferred female lovers, Blake."

He rolled his eyes and laughed at Lonnie, then turned to me. "We have a joke about this room. It's the only truly private sound-proof area on Misfit Island."

"We've affectionately named it the reproduction room," Lonnie said. "Because it's ironic, or at least it was before all of you got here. See, Grayson prefers men, or one man, at least, who unfortunately died before Grayson was trapped here. Sasha is a ladies' lady, which leaves only me and Blake to make special time-travel babies, but how old did we decide I am?"

"Fifty-one," Blake said, giving her a very nonromantic smile.

"Fifty-one," Lonnie repeated with a sigh. "Way too old to conceive with little man Blake here. And pretty soon, way too old to conceive with anyone."

This conversation had gone in a wild direction but neither of them seemed at all uncomfortable with the subject matter.

Blake leaned on one elbow and looked Lonnie over. "I think you look great for fifty-one. I would guess thirty-five if I didn't know better."

She rubbed the top of Blake's hair. "You are wonderful. Keep it up, kid. Also, Grayson needs your help skinning some fish."

Blake and I headed out of the room and back outside. The cool air bit us right away and I couldn't believe the shift in temperature.

"Sorry about that," Blake said, as we walked toward the lake. "Grayson and Lonnie are so blunt and open about everything, I've become desensitized to all their jokes, though there is a root to them—the time-travel-baby concept. It's not the first time Dr. Ludwig would instigate something like this, but if that was his original plan, he messed up big-time. He couldn't have picked a worse combination of four people to achieve that goal. Other than the fact that Grayson can deliver a baby."

Blake glanced around again, looking for any listening ears. "We'll finish this soon, okay? I didn't mean to trick you and I do have a point to all this."

I decided that I wanted to wait around to find out what that purpose was. "Good."

"Nobody's going to care that I'm telling you these things but

Grayson might suspect that I'm not coping with the reality of being stuck here. It's not that exactly." He looked around, as if checking for any sign of the others. "If anyone asks, I was impressing you with technology from your future in the control room, okay?"

"Got it," I said with a nod.

As I walked toward the building where I'd been sleeping for the past ten days, I noticed Courtney and Mason sitting close together on the porch of a nearby cabin. Their heads were ducked and they were engaged in some kind of whispered conversation.

I eyed them suspiciously and then went inside to search the supply cabinets for tweezers since my hands were still covered in splinters from gripping the wood during the memory-gas episode. Exhaustion from my first day venturing out hit me hard and the second I found the supplies I needed, I collapsed onto my back on the bed, holding my hand in the air to pluck the bits of wood from it.

"There you are," Dad said.

I looked up to see him standing in the doorway. He slid inside the room and shut the door. "Hey, Dad . . . I'm just removing the leftovers of the memory-gas drama."

He sat in the chair across from the bed. "Yeah, that was pretty rough. Only my third experience with that."

"And the first time you had to lie about what you saw?" I prompted.

He sighed, sinking back into his chair. "Yes."

I set the tweezers down and sat up. "You saw Courtney, right?"

His face paled. "Yes."

"I figured." I let out a breath, knowing exactly why he had to lie. That wasn't the moment to tell Courtney what had happened to her. What most likely would happen all over again. My heart ached at the thought and I forced it away for now. "I saw Adam dying."

"I see," Dad said. "You thought it might be hard on Holly, bringing up Adam?"

"Yeah." I flopped onto my back again, staring up at the ceiling. "She was so weird when I found her in the cabin, totally aware. She wasn't in the hallucination anymore and she didn't want me coming near me. I don't think her delusion included Adam's dying, it just doesn't fit with her reaction, but I'm not sure why."

"She worked for the other side, Jackson," Dad said. "She was trained by the other side. We can't even begin to know what Eyewall put her through."

I rolled on my side, staring at Dad. "You're right."

Maybe someone like Holly, trained as our enemy, would like to see the proof that Blake presented me with today? Maybe she needed to be in on our next secret session.

CHAPTER FIVE

DAY 11. MORNING

The world seemed brighter this morning, sharper, more focused. I noticed small movements and the difference in size in every object in the room in a way I couldn't remember experiencing. It must have been the whole near-death episode that made me see, smell, and measure even more acutely.

I set out to find Blake to continue where we had left off yesterday. It wasn't like I had anything more interesting to do.

He was outside by the lake with Holly. They were standing beside the water. Blake had Holly's pistol pointed at a thick tree stump with a white T-shirt pinned to the front of it. She angled herself partially behind him and partially beside him. Her hands covered his, her arms around his back.

I couldn't help thinking the first thought that popped into my head . . . *the reproduction room* . . . and then I wondered what had gone on during the ten days I was injured and stuck in bed. I froze in the grass, still quite a ways from them. Intense fury pumped through me. I squeezed my fists open and closed several times, trying to compose myself. Jealousy was not an option without doing what I swore to myself I wouldn't do—tell Holly about us. Instead, I took in slow, deep breaths, calming myself down.

I was nearly under control until she reached down and touched his right leg, moving it back several inches.

"Bend your knees a little," I heard her say as she returned to holding Blake's hands. "Choke up on the gun more."

"Choke up?"

"Slide your right hand higher," she said. "When you fire it, the gun's gonna twist sideways and then try to point up. You want to keep that from happening. This will give you a better grip."

They stood still for several seconds and then finally Blake sighed and shook his head. "I can't do it . . . I'm afraid of missing and the ricochet off the tree . . ."

So I was right about Blake's not having any kind of agent training while working for the government in his present. Although with memory gas around, maybe they didn't need guns in the future.

Holly took the gun from his hands and stepped sideways. "It's okay. It's hard for everyone the first time. I'll show you one more time, okay?"

He watched her carefully as she took her stance, held the weapon out, and fired three times in a row, knocking three perfect holes through the center of the white T-shirt.

Blake ran his fingers through his hair. "It makes perfect sense. I've got the angles and distance all memorized, it's just getting myself to actually pull the trigger."

So his brain worked like mine. That was how it was for me the first time I picked up a weapon. I could measure the distance, see the angles, and project where it would land. It was like this door had swung open revealing a whole new layer to the world.

She smiled at him, causing me to scowl. "You'll get it. I know you will."

I'd had enough of this cozy moment and felt a strong need to break it up. "Nice shooting, Agent Flynn."

They both jumped and then spun around to face me.

"Jackson . . . hey," Blake said. "How are you feeling today? Still good?"

"You know . . ." I eyed the tree stump, staring at the bullet holes. "I'm not too bad of a shot myself if you're looking for some help. They wouldn't let me handle much else besides a gun in Tempest."

"Is that right, Rambo?" Holly said.

My eyebrows lifted up, sensing a challenge. "Yeah, that's right."

"Talk is cheap, Agent Meyer." She slapped the gun into my palm and stepped out of the way.

"How are we doing on bullets? Are we going to run out?"

"We've got plenty of bullets. I'm not sure how, but your dad has a very generous supply, though it doesn't appear that we'll be putting them to any real use anytime soon, other than this pissing contest that I will most definitely win," Holly taunted.

I laughed under my breath, knowing I was actually pretty damn good at this. But when I took my stance and held the gun out, there was an unmistakable tremble in my left hand.

Holly reached out and set her hand on top of the gun. "Don't. It's too risky. If you miss—"

"Yeah. I'm not stupid." I let out an angry breath and handed the gun back to her. "Guess I know who's getting picked last for the next mission."

Holly rolled her eyes. "Come on, your brain practically exploded. Give it some time. I'm sure that screwed with your nervous system or something."

Blake frowned. "Maybe it's the medication?"

"It's weird," I said, looking at Blake and then Holly. "Because I feel better than ever, more observant. Like my aim should be better, but my hands aren't on the same page as my head."

"We should ask Grayson," Blake said right away, frowning.

I shrugged. "I'll ask him later. Actually, I wanted to talk to you about yesterday's stuff."

Blake's eyebrows lifted. "Right. We should continue that."

I glanced at Holly, then back at Blake. "And I think we should let Holly join us."

"Why?" Blake said.

"She's one of them. I'm guessing you're going to show me how your roommate went to the dark side and she needs to see who she's working for."

"I'm one of who?" Holly asked. "Care to fill me in?"

"Eyewall," Blake said with a defeated sigh.

I hadn't really given him much of an option, but I knew this was the right choice. Holly put on a positive face most of the time, but I'm sure she was extremely conflicted given what Dad said last night about us not knowing what kind of hell Eyewall had put her through.

"Come on," Blake conceded. "No one's in the reproduction room right now."

Holly and I followed Blake and she hissed in my ear, "Did he just say 'reproduction room'?"

I shrugged and kept my eyes on Blake's back. "I don't know, maybe it means something else in this year?"

Let someone else explain that one to Holly.

AUGUST 3, 2874.
MEMORY EXTRACTED FROM HOST.

1987 looked just the same as I remembered from my first and only trip here with Thomas. Now I was here again on my first solo mission. This time I landed a week after my last visit. I ignored the pounding in my heart and the fear rushing through me as I weaved my way across the street, into the hospital, and down the stairs to the lab where Grayson worked alone.

"Blake! Good to see you again," he said with a genuine smile. "How long has it been for you?"

"About six months," I said as my heart slowed down, relieved to be in a near-empty and silent room.

"I thought you looked taller. Sixteen now, right?"

"Yes, that's right." My eyes swept over the lab, looking for brewing experiments or anything remotely interesting to make this first solo mission a little more exciting.

"What brings you to 1987 this time?" Grayson asked.

I jolted back to reality, remembering I was here for a reason. I reached into my coat pocket and removed the vacuum-packed bag of vitamins, holding them out for Grayson.

"Ah, B-29 supplements, of course." He waved his gloved hand toward a cabinet against the back wall. "Would you mind stowing them away for me? I've just scrubbed up and don't want to contaminate the specimen."

I walked over to the cabinet and opened the metal door, eyeing rows and rows of medical supplies and pills. An entire shelf was filled with unopened bags of B-29 supplements identical to the one in my hand. "Do you not have access to B-29 here?"

Grayson glanced at me through his safety goggles. "Actually, B-29 hasn't been discovered yet. Not until 2048. And won't be widely used for another fifteen years after that."

I had learned about the necessity of B-29 in health education in school but hadn't known it was a more recent discovery. In my present, it was received as a vaccine once a year on the first day of school. I knew B-29 was an emotion regulator, but I had never thought about what would happen if people went without it, since it works to keep the mind focused on calm, rational thoughts and actions. Not that anger, fear, and sadness no longer exist. I've definitely experienced my share of fear and anger growing up with three older brothers. But was the lack of B-29 in 1987 the reason for the noise and chaos in the world? Did quiet places exist outside New York City?

"So, do you give them to people here?"

Grayson shook his head. "No, we don't tamper with the past unnecessarily."

"Right." I swung my arms back and forth, not sure how to maintain a conversation with this much older time traveler and not sound like an immature child. I'd rather he think I was mature and responsible, following orders the United States military had given me. "Um, Dr. Ludwig said not to come back right away. Since I'm alone this time. My mind needs rest."

Grayson's eyebrows knitted together. "Yes, it's very risky, indeed, that long a jump." He pulled out a stool and pointed at it, indicating I should sit, which I did right away. "Let's give you a quick check, all right?"

I nodded and allowed him to shine a light in my eyes, listen to my heart, and measure my pulse. Grayson seemed very different than the others I'd come to know. He seemed more expressive and full of secrets that he couldn't hide completely. Somehow this made me feel calm and secure, probably because a lot of times I felt the same way. Like I couldn't keep my feelings from showing on my face. That's probably what delayed Dr. Ludwig from letting me jump on my own. He could tell I was scared to try even if I didn't say it out loud.

"I think about two or three hours' recovery time will be just fine," Grayson finally said after his thorough exam. "Probably best if you hang out here, stay out of trouble."

"Sure."

He pulled up another stool and sat across from me. "Tell me about your family. How are they handling things so far?"

"I haven't really talked to them much," I admitted. "My mother called on my birthday. Thomas said I wouldn't be able to go back home, too much of a security risk, I guess, and it would be easier if I just let them go."

"Easier for whom?" Grayson asked, then shook his head. "He's partially correct. Since your identity and ability have been revealed worldwide, there are all kinds of possible terrorist threats, and targeting your family, who aren't as well protected as you are, is a definite concern."

I looked down at my hands, trying to hide any fear. "That's what President Healy said, too."

"Do you have brothers or sisters?"

"Three older brothers. I'm the baby of the family."

He smiled. "What are they like? Do you get along?"

I spent three hours talking to Grayson about everything from my oldest brother's new wife and daughter to the girls at my old school and my mother's inability to remember which kid was named what whenever she got angry with us. He said that parents had very similar experiences in 1987 and that increased brainpower and technology over time wouldn't change family dynamics. Some things were just human nature.

It made me miss them all over again, and after returning to the present, I decided to contact my oldest brother, Henry. Seeing my little niece toddling around on the screen after all these months had passed caused me to feel sadder than I have since I first left home last December.

"So what's the deal with this B-29 stuff?" Holly asked before I had a chance to.

We had also listened to and read the text of the memory files Blake showed me yesterday for Holly's benefit.

"It's not what you think," Blake said. "Honestly, I think it's probably a very useful and important supplement. What you guys have to realize is that the world I lived in, before everything started changing, before Project Eyewall, was a really great place. I've spent a lot of time in your present and I can make an accurate comparison. The future was a better place to be than the past. The forward motion was mostly positive, as it had been in the history you two probably studied in school."

I leaned against the wall, watching Holly twist back and forth in the only chair in the room. "But what changed for you? And what kind of forward progress happens between my present and yours? I know the Tempus gene evolves and people become smarter, a few time travelers appear, but what else?" Holly asked.

Blake folded his arms across his chest, his forehead wrinkling like he was deep in thought. "Well, there's a broader acceptance of differences—race, religion, politics, sexuality." Blake's eyebrows shot up and he returned his hands to the control panel. I noticed pink creeping up his neck toward his face and wondered what kind of filed-away memory would cause him to turn red like that. "There's also the Plague of 2600. It was a dark time but the government did what they had to for humanity to survive. Basically, there was a very deadly disease spread by skin-to-skin human contact. For nearly thirty years we fought it, and the population of the United States decreased by half."

"By half?" Holly and I said together.

"Yes. It was devastating. Many people covered their hands and faces at all times. Reproduction happened in a lab for most families. And while the government worked to come up with a vaccine, they offered drugs that blocked certain responses in the brain such as . . . libido," he finally said, and I had to assume that was the reason for the red face. "Nothing was mandatory, it's just people were panicking and there was no vaccine. They had to do something. Of course, there were the rebels who were against people taking the inhibitors. They called it mind control, but no one wanted to control people, it was the disease that needed controlling. Anyway, they finally managed to produce a working vaccine, lifted all the warnings, and no longer coordinated couples genetically based on their immunities to the disease."

"Wait," Holly interrupted. "They coordinated people? That seems really weird and very communist or something."

"Like I said, it was a desperate time," Blake answered with a shrug. "And the government went into huge debt over developing the coordination system and funding all the fertility labs. They couldn't wait to get rid of it. They even had to borrow money from China."

This was like the most interesting history (or future, I guess) lesson I'd ever heard. What would people in 1900 have thought of everything that happened between then and my present? I bet it would seem just as crazy.

"So it didn't spread worldwide?" I asked.

Blake shook his head. "Nope. As soon as they discovered the transmission, there was no foreign travel allowed. No crossing borders. Nothing. And even though the government went to great lengths to encourage people to live and take risks once the vaccination program had been implemented nationwide, people were still conservative, kept all the same precautions for a long time. Once you see a loved one's skin rot and fall off in a three-day period, it's hard to shake those habits. So, even in my time, some of that still lingered just a little, and that's the reason certain items legal for consumption in your present had been outlawed for decades in my present. Which you'll see in this next entry."

AUGUST 15, 2874.
MEMORY EXTRACTED FROM HOST.

"I have big news for you," Thomas said, entering our apartment, Jean and Nora trailing behind him.

He went on to talk about the big committee meeting that afternoon with Dr. Ludwig and several other scientists and government officials and they all determined that I was now allowed one personal time jump per week. There are virtually no limitations on when and where I can explore, just no major alterations without clearing them first. I can use the time to study the past—science and history, anthropology—anything to gain cultural experience and knowledge that will help me blend in with different time periods when I'm on a mission.

It's a big deal. A huge privilege. I know that, but it's hard for me to be excited about gaining permission to go back in time and observe strangers in a period that isn't my own, when I still have this constant ache to go home. To visit people I know and love. I've been down ever since I called Henry. Dr. Ludwig must have been able to tell because he increased my B-29 injections to four a year rather than the standard one every twelve months. Maybe Thomas was right. It would have been easier if I had just left it alone.

And I can't help wondering if this additional freedom I gained today was based more on my lackluster performance and effort lately than on real merit.

"This is so exciting!" Jean said.

For once, I actually managed to meet her eyes, though only for a few seconds, without feeling my face flush.

"You deserve a little fun and freedom," Nora said.

Somehow, after talking for a few minutes, Nora and Thomas ended up leaving me alone in my apartment with Jean, who produced a bottle of what she called wine from a bag I hadn't even noticed she'd been holding.

"To celebrate," she said with a grin. "I got it from 2014. Think it has a long shelf life?"

It was a poor attempt at a time-travel joke, but I laughed anyway because it was, well, *Jean.* Beautiful Jean.

She used some strange mechanical device to remove the stopper in the bottle and then poured two full glasses.

I took a long sip. It tasted like fruit and water and another flavor that was completely new to me. After several more swallows, it became more than a taste—a dozen emotions, a song I couldn't recall, something strong and soft all at the same time.

"Good, huh?" Jean said.

"Yeah." I glanced down at the dark purple liquid sloshing around the sides of the glass. "Why would they stop making this? It's amazing."

She shrugged. "I have no idea, but I do know what my next research project will be. During my allotted free time."

"Let me know what you find out."

In no time at all, Jean and I had finished the entire bottle and were now seated on the couch, searching my handheld for any information we could find on the history of wine.

For some reason, after sharing the beverage with Jean, I didn't feel nervous sitting so close to her, laughing and talking almost as easily as I had that day with Grayson. And it wasn't just emotionally altering. Physically, my limbs almost felt detached from my body or like my bones had thinned and suddenly become more agile, increasing their range of motion. My eyes had trouble focusing on the screen held between me and Jean, but I didn't really mind the blurriness at all. I didn't really mind anything. And I didn't feel sad.

Jean glanced up at me for a split second, those green eyes shining with all kinds of hidden secrets. "I think I might understand now why wine is unavailable in 2874."

"Uh, me, too." Then both of us started laughing so hard that my handheld dropped to the floor and my fingers were suddenly free to touch Jean's bright red hair. Something I'd thought entirely too much about in the past eight months. "It's so . . . orangey," I mumbled.

"And yet they still call it red," Jean said, laughing some more. "And orangey isn't a word."

"It is now. I've just named your hair. It's orangey."

She reached up and gently weaved her fingers in my hair, sending a jolt through my entire body. "Then we'll call yours sandy. Have you seen the beach before?"

"I lived near the beach," I said, feeling the tiniest pang of longing—for home, for summers on the beach. My hands were moving on their own, traveling across her cheek, tracing the outline of her jaw and chin. "I saw someone do this once, in a jump with Thomas a couple months ago, this guy and girl sitting on a bench, right near the street, with all the chaos surrounding them. I think I get it now. Touching is human nature."

Jean clapped a hand over my mouth, her eyes suddenly turning dark. "Don't let them hear you talk like that. *Ever.*"

I dropped my hand to my lap. "Like what? It's not going to kill either of us. This isn't 2600. We've been vaccinated."

"I know but it sounds like Grayson," she said. "He got so caught up in, well, I don't know what exactly, but I've read his old reports. His philosophies on human nature and the lack of influence from technology are so different from everything Dr. Ludwig preaches. Dr. Ludwig's goal is to control the future by altering the past based on what we learn over time. It's smart when you think about it, really. Why shouldn't we learn from our past mistakes? Why shouldn't we strive for a better world for the next generation if our abilities make this possible? It's not like man manufactured time travelers. We're made this way for a reason."

I agreed with Jean, I truly did. But at the moment, I didn't want to talk about the bigger picture or the world beyond our time. I just wanted her to understand what I had felt only seconds ago. There was no fact to dispute it. It just was. I took her hands and placed them on my face, moving them slowly down toward my neck. She stopped talking and drew in a sudden breath, unable to exhale.

"See?" I said.

Until this very moment, I'd never touched anyone unless it was necessary—a planned gesture to display emotion or kindness. That was how everyone was, except for that guy and girl I'd seen in the past. And except for my parents, who I'd seen on a rare occasion unconsciously seeking out contact with the other. This, tonight, it didn't feel like a plan. It felt more like a desperate need, or a want. I couldn't tell the difference and somewhere in the back of mind, I knew that there was probably a big difference between the two emotions—need and want.

And yet I didn't care in the least.

I leaned into Jean and felt the heat of her surrounding me. And then my mouth was on hers . . . *kissing* . . . the most effective way to spread communicable diseases. Logic was losing big-time.

All four of our hands suddenly sought out more skin to touch—bare necks, under our shirts. Eventually it became apparent how much easier it would be to just throw them on the floor.

"Open your mouth," she whispered after the shirts hit the floor and I kissed her for the hundredth time. "I saw this once . . ."

Blake hit the button to stop the recording and his face was bright red again. He kept his eyes on the control panel, and mumbled, "Sorry, I didn't realize how much detail was inserted into my memory file."

I glanced at Holly, who looked wide-eyed, but not a trace of the blushing that had infested Blake was on her face. My Holly would have been at least a little bit pink out of sympathy for Blake. Agent Holly seemed to have every emotion under control.

"Okay, so you were drunk," she summarized. "And people in your present don't get drunk or kiss, apparently."

"They do kiss and everything else," Blake said, finally looking at us. "It's not usually so impulsive, more careful and planned. You get checked for immunities and cleared by a physician first. That's how I was raised, anyway, and it's all I knew. It could be different for some people in my present. I'm not really sure. Obviously, it was the same for Jean, too."

"If you know all about the Plague of 2600," I asked, "then why didn't any of you go back to 2600 and give the government the secret formula for the vaccine or whatever?"

Blake sighed. "The division of government that supervised us wouldn't allow any jumps to the plague period. It was off-limits. I think they were convinced that it would change too much about the future, that the world would have been overpopulated and too fearless."

"But they could go around altering people's genetics?" Holly said. "I think we need to hear the rest of this one. Hit that button or I will."

Blake eyed Holly's gun tucked in the side of her jeans and then sighed before starting up both the audio and visual replay.

I did open my mouth, but more to reply than because I wanted to figure out what she was going to do. Her tongue carefully slipped into my mouth and I froze, not sure what came next. She closed her mouth again and started kissing things that weren't my lips— cheeks, neck, collarbone. Then she grabbed my hand and placed it on her breast. I became so lost in feeling this whole new type of skin, I didn't even notice the door open.

"Jean!" Nora said. "Blake! What are you . . . ?"

We both jumped apart, reaching for our wrinkled shirts on the floor and banging our heads together in the process. Once my shirt was safely returned to its original spot, I glanced at Thomas, standing behind Nora. His expression was completely unreadable. But at least he didn't look shocked or angry.

"That wasn't exactly what I had in mind," he said to Jean.

Jean's cheeks were flushed to a beautiful rosy color that clashed with her hair. My eyes bounced between the two of them, trying to understand Thomas's words.

He just shrugged and picked up the empty bottle on the counter, holding it for Nora to see. "Dr. Ludwig wouldn't exactly be disappointed if two of his beloved time travelers were caught reproducing."

"Reproducing?" Jean and I said together.

Then I moved to the opposite end of the couch.

Creating offspring wasn't exactly on my evening to-do list. Although I knew how it worked. Why couldn't I have seen that was where we were headed a few minutes ago? I just didn't think about it. I was too absorbed in the moment.

"He's sixteen," Nora said to Thomas under her breath. "He can't do *that* yet."

"Apparently he can," Thomas said, shrugging again.

Jean scrambled to her feet and headed toward the nearest exit. "I'm not feeling well."

I sighed with relief the second she was out the door. Now I really wouldn't be able to make eye contact with her ever again. Not without turning the color of a tomato.

"Did you tell her to do that?" Nora asked Thomas.

"Not *that*. No," he confirmed. "I told her to entertain the kid, make him feel more at home here."

My stomach sank and flipped all at the same time. And then I felt the wine bubbling up inside me, working its way toward my throat.

I barely made it to the kitchen sink before regurgitating the dark purple liquid. "Impurities, right?" I gasped as my head hung over the drain. "In the water . . . the water used to make wine."

Nora raced over, standing behind me, and placed a hand on the back of my neck like my mother did when I was sick as a child. She pressed a button above my head, turning the stream of water on, allowing me to rinse my mouth.

"Impurities for sure but also alcohol," Thomas said. "It's toxin that was banned decades ago for its negative effects on health and unpredictable behavioral side effects, not to mention its addictive nature."

Thomas and Nora helped me walk to my bed after deciding my balance was less than a hundred percent. Nora placed a cool rag on my forehead and then left to check on Jean. Thomas stayed in my room, sitting in a chair next to the bed.

"I'm sorry. I didn't realize Jean was experimenting tonight. I've seen how you admire her," he said quietly, so as not to disturb my upset stomach and pounding head. "I just thought it might help cheer you up a little, spending time alone with Jean. She agreed without question."

I couldn't be upset with Thomas for trying to help me, but finding out he had instigated this whole evening made everything seem like just another mission or experiment. Nothing personal. It wasn't like Jean would have said no to Thomas. Everyone respected him. Everyone knew he'd never ask for something that he didn't think was important.

His intentions might have been out of kindness to me, but Jean's were out of kindness and admiration for Thomas, not for me. Only the wine made her look at me differently and enjoy the time alone together.

"I wasn't completely honest with you, Blake," he said. "When I told you that Grayson had been injured."

"He's not injured?" I tried to sit up and decided it wasn't worth the effort.

"He spent a lot of time in and around the year 1991 for the Tempus Gene Project and then eventually for his own personal time. The same freedom you've just been given to explore the past." Thomas repositioned his chair so he was facing me and looked me right in the eyes. "He fell in love with a man in 1986. An agent working for the Central Intelligence Agency."

Shock must have filled my expression though I

tried my best to conceal it. "He could come back? Anytime? He chooses to live there?"

"I haven't relayed this information accurately to Dr. Ludwig or anyone else. Grayson was my mentor. He helped me through my early missions and I had hoped if I allowed him some time, he'd realize his weakness and overcome it. A physical injury would keep his record clean," Thomas said. "But a mistake, a judgment error, would mean his ability could be taken from him."

"Taken?" I asked, finally able to sit up and lean against the headboard. "How do they take it?"

"I don't know all the details," Thomas said. "But trust me, there are ways. I don't want you to fall into the same trap, feeling too much emotion for your family. That kind of behavior can really make this job difficult. I thought maybe having fun with Jean would help you overcome this. Perhaps I was wrong, and I'm truly sorry if her intentions hurt you at all."

"It was just the wine," I said. "I don't know if it would have been a pleasant experience, spending time alone with her, if it weren't for the . . . alcohol. Of course I look at her, think about her that way, but she's the only female even remotely close to my age that I've seen since leaving home."

"I understand," Thomas said, standing up. "I won't interfere in that way again. You have my word. And you also have my word that I'll do everything in my power to keep my head clear and not abandon my position as your mentor for as long as you need me."

"Did you mean it?" I asked him before he could leave the room. "When you said Dr. Ludwig wouldn't be upset about two time travelers reproducing?"

He turned his back to me, flipping off the light before saying, "It's a concept the government is currently exploring."

"What about the Tempus Gene Project?"

"It's certainly changing history, showing itself much earlier, but has yet to create the larger number of time travelers intended. President Healy wants to abandon the experiment in the next twelve months if it continues to be unproductive." He shut the door halfway, leaving me in the dark. "Get some sleep. You'll feel better tomorrow."

And because Thomas told me to, I pushed my worries aside for now and fell right to sleep.

"Huh," I said. "Are you sure this is the same Thomas that I knew?"

"Yes," Blake said firmly. "And Grayson didn't only stay in the past because of his partner. He also began to disagree with Thomas and Dr. Ludwig."

"Sorry about the girl's setting you up like that. Totally sucks," I said to try and make the air in the small space slightly more comfortable for him.

"Yeah, totally," Holly chimed in. She lifted her feet onto the long desk and leaned back in her chair. "I've been there, too. One time I was at this party and this guy I didn't even know hit on me at the bar and then when I asked him to dance, he was really into it. Turns out he was just another agent trying to get information out of me about my best friend—"

"Wait," Blake interrupted looking confused. "What—?"

"He's dead," she said, jumping back in. "Not the guy at the bar. My best friend. And the guy I danced with . . . apparently he's hung out with various versions of me and doesn't feel like it's important to give me any details about those encounters."

I stayed leaning against the wall, staring at Holly while attempting to look like I wasn't completely in love with her. "That's a great story, Hol, but—"

"So this guy was a time traveler?" Blake asked. "Who did he work for? Tempest?"

"Supposedly Tempest," Holly said. "Good guys, bad guys, I'm not sure and it really doesn't matter. Just another asshole trying to hook up with me for a mission."

"*He* was trying to hook up with *you*?" I rolled my eyes and let out an angry breath. "If I remember right, you were the one that asked to come home with me. And I said no!"

Blake's eyes bounced nervously between the two of us. "Um, okay, I'm lost."

Holly dropped her feet to the floor with a loud thud and leaned forward in her chair, angling it away from me and facing Blake. "Let's try this a different way. Let's say another time traveler, one you don't know very well, maybe not at all, seems to know a hell of a lot about you. And then you find out he *or she* has been jumping into the past and hanging out with you or doing God knows what with you. Then he *or she* erases everything and won't tell you a fucking thing about what happened, would that piss you off?"

"You know what, *Agent Flynn*?" I snapped. "I never took you as the passive-aggressive type."

She spun her chair around to face me. "Oh, I think I'm being very direct."

Panic crept up inside me, mixing with anger. Why couldn't she see that I was trying to make things better for her? "What? Am I supposed to relay every single second to you? Seriously? I already told you everything days ago, or don't you remember?"

She stood up and walked closer to me, arms folded across her chest. "I've been thinking about that a lot lately and too many things don't add up. If you only knew me through Adam, why did seeing me with Brian at the bookstore piss you off so much? Don't deny it either, I could tell you were furious. And why did you almost kiss me during that fifty-thousand-dollar dance?"

I held my breath, feeling my heart thud too loud. I swallowed back the words I wanted to say and kept my mouth shut. She was too perceptive to miss the waver that would inevitably be present in my voice.

"You were about to kiss me, I know you were. It was like you forgot that you weren't with a version of me who wouldn't think that was weird. Like another version of me would expect to be kissed by you."

My eyes were locked on hers, nowhere to run. All I could do was say, "Just let it go, Hol, please. It doesn't matter."

With that lame reply, I turned around and left the room. I couldn't keep looking at her and not give everything away. What would she do if I told her?

Don't. You've made the right choice.

CHAPTER SIX

DAY 11. LATE MORNING

I found Courtney and Emily in one of the cabins. They both sat on the bottom bunk of one of three sets of bunk beds, sifting through a giant pile of clothes.

"What's wrong?" Courtney said as soon as she looked up at me.

Twin perception. It got me every time.

"Nothing," I muttered.

Courtney looked at Emily and shook her head. "Jackson is a big fat liar. And a hamster murderer, too, apparently."

Emily giggled and tossed items from the top of the pile to the floor by my shoes.

I laughed, too. "Okay, seriously, you need to forgive me for that. We were eight."

"Fine," she said. "Help us find pants for Mason. Something close to a thirty-inch waist and thirty-two-inch length."

My guard flew up instantly as I stared Courtney down. "Let Mason find his own damn pants."

"That's nice, Jackson," she said, rolling her eyes at me. "Who do you think dug through an entire supply closet to find jeans in your size?"

"I was incapacitated," I said. "Last I checked, Mason was in perfect health."

"Don't be such a jerk," Courtney snapped.

I reached into the clothes pile, throwing a few T-shirts to the ground before retrieving some dark blue jeans that looked close to Mason's size. "There. Happy now?"

She snatched the pants from me. "Thanks."

Emily and I watched as she stomped out of the cabin, probably to go find Mason. "That's the second girl I've ticked off today."

Emily sat up straighter, her tiny body barely covering any space on the bed. I took Courtney's spot on the bottom bunk and leaned against the post and closed my eyes.

"What happened before this?" Emily asked.

"Holly's a little upset with me."

"I'm sorry. I know how you feel about her."

My eyes flew open again, zooming in on this little kid who might be the one person who could ruin my plan with the Holly issue. "You do know how I feel about her, don't you?"

Emily nodded.

"My journal, right?" *That damn journal and damn fingerprint clone.* Right after I began Tempest training, Dr. Melvin had given me a lockbox that required my fingerprints for access, and of course Emily being my clone and all meant she was a match. Reading my journal, reading all the things I'd wanted to use time travel to fix, had been the reason we'd ended up here in 3200. She also read a copy of the original 009 Holly's diary that someone had left in Stewart's hands before our jump to the future. I hadn't been able to bring myself to read much of it, but I'm sure Emily absorbed every page. And probably in seconds with her brainpower.

My annoyance must have been clearly written on my face because before I could cover it, she was crying and trying to hide the tears from me.

"I'm sorry. I shouldn't have read it," Emily said.

My entire gut twisted with guilt. Make that three girls I'd upset in one day. That had to be a personal record for me. I shoved the clothes to the floor and scooted next to Emily, putting an arm around her shoulder. "Hey, it's not your fault. They would have found a way to trick me. And honestly, everybody I love the most is here and maybe that's okay."

She sniffled a bit more, nodding and wiping her nose at the same time. "But Adam . . . he's not here. I almost got him, too, I just didn't have time."

I wrapped my head around the idea of Adam's being here, alive. Then I really would be okay. "Emily, do you think . . . I mean hypothetically . . . if we ever did get out of here and we could go back to the present, a complete jump back, could we land on a date before Adam died and keep it from happening?"

"You've done complete jumps before," she said, then looked up at me with a sheepish grin. "I read about those in your journal when you saw your two-year-old self and Eileen Covington."

"Right, yeah, that was a complete jump."

"Well, did you think about what mark you were going to hit on your way back?" she asked.

I shook my head. "Not really. Just like the half-jumps, I have to go back to home base, back to the exact moment I left."

"I think you could go somewhere besides home base in a complete jump," she explained, as if thirty years older than me. "The problem is, you're going to have to deal with a duplicate version of yourself. It's not like when you switch timelines from World A to World B. The other Jackson doesn't vanish."

"What if someone killed him," I muttered under my breath, but she heard me.

"I heard Grayson talking about that," Emily shook her head. "It's confusing, I know, but everyone would have another version of themselves in 2009 if you go back and it's not the moment you left. But aligning with the moment you left won't be difficult. Your body is naturally going to seek out the former home base where there aren't two Jacksons. Anything other than that would be very difficult."

Grief swept over me. It was a hopeless situation. "It doesn't matter anyway. We're all stuck here with no prospect of escape anytime soon." I glanced down at her weary face. "It's not your fault, Emily. They would have come up with dozens of ways to get us here, or at least me. Imagine how crazy I'd be if I were stuck here alone."

She nodded and wiped away a few more tears. "You don't want me to tell anyone about you and Holly, right?"

"I'm not trying to lie to her intentionally, I promise. It's just . . . she should have a choice about who she loves. A choice that isn't influenced by what happened in the past. Or in another time-line. She deserves it. I've put her through hell and I won't do that again."

"If she asks me anything, I won't tell her, I swear," Emily said.

I glanced down at her and smiled. "Are you sure you're only eight? Maybe clones age slower? You must be at least twenty-seven."

Emily giggled and jumped off the bed, pulling a pair of red high heels from the clothes pile now on the cabin floor. "You're right. I'm twenty-seven. That means I can wear these, right?"

"Go for it, kid." I stood up and watched as she kicked off the little tennis shoes she had on and slid her feet into the pointy red heels. They were the most impractical shoes for Eyewall people to store in a supply closet for the prisoners of Misfit Island. I had to assume that either Sasha or Lonnie showed up here wearing those the day they got trapped.

Emily scooted at a snail's pace across the slippery, dust-covered floors. "Look! I'm five point three eight centimeters taller!"

"Really? I would have guessed at least five point three nine."

"Nope." She laughed again and headed for the cabin door. "I have to show Holly."

Her hand froze on the door and she turned slowly to face me. "It's too bad she doesn't know what you did for her. I think she's really scared but in a different way than the others. There's nothing worse than thinking that no one cares about you."

I walked closer and squatted in front of her. "I care about *you*, you know that, right? From the first time I met you, I knew we'd need each other someday. I knew you were important to me. And it is possible for good things to come from bad ideas." Not that Emily herself was a bad idea, but cloning time travelers and forcing children were.

"Do you really believe that?" she asked.

"I do. I really do."

She gave me a sad smile and then turned to leave again. "I won't tell her anything, I promise."

When I went back outside, the first thing I noticed was Courtney standing in front of the cabin next door. Her arm was wrapped around the tall wooden post in front, and Mason stood across from her, a little too close, and leaning closer every second. I stormed up behind him and grabbed the hood of his sweatshirt, tugging it hard and pulling him farther from my sister.

"Excuse us," I said to Courtney. "Mason and I have some Tempest business to discuss."

"Okay . . . ?" she said.

I gave Mason a shove in the direction of the lake. "Walk with me."

"Uh, doesn't look like I have a choice," he said, attempting sarcasm, but I could hear the tiniest indication of fear in his voice, which made my blood literally boil.

Guilt. His intentions must not be very innocent.

The lake looked more green than blue now, and I waited until we had nearly reached it before stopping and yanking Mason to a halt by grabbing his hood again.

"What do you think you're doing?" I demanded.

He shrugged, looking anywhere but at me. "Nothing."

I snorted a laugh. "Yeah right. Don't think I don't know what's going on in your head. Just put a stop to it now. Whatever you did to send her digging through clothes and memorizing your waist measurements needs to end."

"I didn't do anything," he said, his voice going up an octave. "It's not my fault we have things in common."

"Like what? What do you possibly have in common with my sister?"

Mason folded his arms across his chest, staring hard at me.

Oh right, the being-dead thing. I swallowed and took a step back from Mason. "If you touch her, I'll seriously kick your ass, and if that doesn't scare you enough, I'm sure Agent Meyer Senior will."

He held up his hands in surrender. "Okay, fine!"

After Mason stomped off, I moved closer to the lake, picked up a few rocks from the grass, and started tossing them in, trying to skip them across the water and blow off steam at the same time. Mason knew what was going to happen to Courtney. He knew everything about my family, so what was he thinking? And he's seventeen, she's fourteen. I could see it in his eyes, just then, he liked her. In that way that I remembered all too well from being Mason's age. It led to kissing and removing bras and—

I shuddered, forcing the mental picture from my brain.

I wasn't alone for long before I heard Holly's and Emily's voices coming from the grass behind me. They were all the way over by the tree stump with the T-shirt still pinned to it and didn't appear to be coming closer anytime soon. At least I had smoothed things over with Emily. Holly and Courtney still hated me, but one out of three was better than zero out of three.

It had just occurred to me that in my idiotic grief, I had left Holly and Blake alone in the reproduction room. Good thing Blake didn't have access to wine.

Being jealous of the two of them left me completely demoralized by my moral decision to let Holly choose her own path. What if that path was Blake? What if we were stuck here forever until we got really old and died of natural causes? Did I want to keep this secret from Holly for that long—to never attempt to make her love me again? I didn't know if it would even be possible, but I did have a record of two out of three with getting the different versions of Holly to do exactly that. This one would be the most difficult, though.

I put a lot more force behind the next rock I threw into the lake as disgust filled me completely. How could I look at being in love that way? Even in my head, using information from 009 Holly and 007 Holly to lure Agent Holly in felt like a total sleazeball thing to do. Plotting to make a move on her, to trick her into loving me—it diminished everything I thought our relationship stood for. It played out in my mind like just another mission. A task full of lies and deception, the polar opposite of true love.

And Holly deserved true love.

It was wrong to avoid her because of our past, and it was wrong to pursue her for that same reason. I needed to start looking at Holly as the girl right behind me, the one I first saw in the NYU bookstore in June of 2009.

"How do you do that?" Emily said. "Show me again!"

From the corner of my eye, Holly came into sight, her blond hair flying around her as she flipped backwards in the grass, landing perfectly on her feet.

I sighed to myself. This no-jealousy thing wouldn't be easy. Like so many other things in life, it was going to take time. And practice. And unfortunately, a few more screwups, knowing me.

"Like your little computer brain can't figure this out perfectly." Holly rubbed the top of Emily's head. "It's all about strength-to-weight ratio and physics."

"And fear," Emily said. "Or lack of fear, in your case."

Holly flashed her a wicked smile. "That's always been my greatest weakness."

I reached down to pick up more rocks as Holly did a series of three handsprings, landing dangerously close to my feet.

Don't be angry. Don't be in love. Don't be anything. "Staying in shape just in case?"

She shrugged. "Just messing around, I guess. You know, lack of television and Internet."

"And CIA missions," I added.

"That, too," she said. "What else is there to do?"

"Besides listening to Blake's awkward makeout stories?"

She laughed. "God, that was so freakin' weird."

I kicked at a rock with my shoe and kept my eyes on the grass. "So . . . I was wondering if maybe, since you don't seem pissed off at me right now, we could start over. Like I'm Jackson and you're Holly and . . . and that's it."

The amusement dropped from her face. "I can't do that."

"Why not? Why is it so important for you to know everything?"

She shook her head and let out a breath. "What else do I have control over now? Nothing. All I have . . . all *we* have to hold on to is what we *know*. I don't plan on forgetting anything anytime soon."

So much for new beginnings. I plopped down in the grass next to Emily and she mouthed sorry to me while Holly's back was turned. I nudged her shoulder with mine and smiled. "Are you gonna do some backflipping too?"

She shook her head fiercely. "No way. I'm not fearless enough."

"I think you're pretty fearless, Emily, maybe just a different kind."

"You, too," she said.

"We're finishing our project tomorrow morning," Holly said, giving me a knowing look.

Hopefully the rest of Blake's memory files would be more PG and less likely to cause Holly to go off on me again.

CHAPTER SEVEN

DAY 12. BEFORE DAWN

Blake and I were now sharing a cabin and I woke up to the sound of the shower running in the less-than-luxurious bathroom. I sifted through a large pile of clothes and found some black gym shorts, boxers, and a T-shirt that were fairly close to my size.

Blake gave me a real razor blade to shave with, and I was relieved that the severity of the shaking in my hands seemed to have lessened since yesterday. Grayson had told me last night that it would get better with time.

Blake had shaving down to a science, but it took me a little longer with this method. I was also not fond of the future toothpaste. It came in a tiny jar and was basically a clear gel that you spread onto the toothbrush. It was like eating five Altoids at once.

We found Holly in the supply-and-technology building before the sun had come up all the way. She was digging for breakfast. Blake opened a cardboard box and handed each of us what looked like a granola bar but tasted a lot like a PowerBar, only worse.

"Why is it you're keeping this information from everyone else?" I asked Blake when we had closed and locked the door on the reproduction room.

"Grayson knows most of it. And the others know their own version, which is probably similar," he said between bites of the nutrition bar. "And we're only keeping it a secret until we can actually form a plan that sounds remotely possible."

"What kind of plan? An escape?" Holly asked. "I thought you were just trying to prove to me that Eyewall is bad or something?"

"There's no escape," Blake said. "But there might be something worth fighting for if they move in again. If they come to pay us a visit."

"Are they going to do that?" I asked.

"It's happened before," Blake said. "But not often."

Holly and I looked at each other, noting in a wordless exchange that we were the ones who probably should be ready for a physical encounter with the enemy. I wasn't sure Grayson, Lonnie, or Sasha had any kind of experience with weapons or hand-to-hand combat. And I already knew that Blake didn't. Neither did Emily or Courtney.

Holly had brought a second chair today and she scooted it closer to mine so we could lean in and read the screen. "Later you can test out your hands again," she whispered. "See if they've gotten steadier."

"They have a little. But yeah, I'd like to regain my ability to use a gun."

Blake started up the recording again, and I followed the words moving across the computer screen.

SEPTEMBER 30, 2874.
AUDIO RECORDED BY HOST AND
MEMORY EXTRACTED FROM HOST.

I'll be honest and admit right here that I've been spending all my free jumps with Grayson in 1987, which is where I'm headed today. I always land after the date of my last jump to that year because then I don't have to retell him whatever we talked about during the previous visit. A couple of times I missed my mark and went back to my present, then had to wait a few hours before trying again. Since free jumps are for research and education, here are a few details I've acquired from my chosen research subject:

1) Grayson's in love with a man called Devin.
2) In 1987, there is no method of legally bonding two men or two women in marriage.

3) Grayson doesn't believe in God and neither does Devin. I'm not that surprised. There are people in my present who choose not to follow a religion, but it's always been a part of me, so I find it strange when others are completely distant from those beliefs. But then again, from what I can tell, God is a very different "person" in 1987 than in 2874.
4) Grayson defends his choice to stay in 1987. He doesn't think Thomas understands the fact that not everyone, special abilities or not, is made to save the world or even to see the bigger picture. He'd rather focus on what's around him.
5) Grayson secretly told me that he doesn't take the B-29 supplements stowed in the cabinet.

When I found Grayson at the hospital, he was thundering up the steps as I was running down them toward the lab.

"Blake! How are you? I'm heading up to do a delivery. Baby's coming a little early and faster than planned," he said, slightly breathless.

"Oh, I could come back another time."

He stopped before reaching the door to the third floor and grinned down at me. "Come with me. I want you to see this. Childbirth in 1987 is quite different from your present. It'll be very educational."

Before I could ask more questions or object, I was in a delivery room, my hands scrubbed raw, and blue paper covering my clothes, hair, and shoes.

"This is a very special student of mine," Grayson said to the distressed-looking middle-aged man and woman. A nurse put gloves on his hands and another tied a mask over his face. "Blake, this is Professor Kendrick and Professor Kendrick." Grayson turned to me, giving me a knowing look. "The first specimen that you assisted me with was baby Kendrick."

The one we supplemented with a Tempus gene carrier rather than using Professor Kendrick's specimen. So this child will be born with the Tempus gene. This child will be part of the reason the Tempus gene appears twenty-six years earlier.

The woman's screams kept me from marveling at this discovery, and I barely held on to my lunch or my consciousness as I watched Grayson literally extract the child from the woman's sexual organs. There was nothing pretty or beautiful about this delivery. It was messy, painful, and nauseating. But once they had the little girl cleaned up and wrapped in blankets, a cloth hat placed on her head, which seemed to have a strange shape like a cone, the situation improved dramatically. And I found myself walking over to the little thing as she screamed at the top of her lungs while everyone in the room smiled.

While Grayson listened to her chest, I caught one of the flailing miniature hands. The baby immediately squeezed my index finger and I stared at our hands—connected, even with an entire millennium between us.

And I decided right then that time travel really was a miracle from God even if Grayson didn't believe that.

"What's her name?" Grayson asked, when he finally got to hand her over to Professor Kendrick and Professor Kendrick.

"Lily," they said together.

The birth of Lily, all six pounds and two ounces of her, weighed heavily on my mind for the remainder of my stay in 1987 and in the days that followed.

"Kendrick," I mumbled, causing Blake to freeze the words on the screen and snap his head in my direction. "Holy cow."

"You know of the parents or the child?" Blake asked.

"Lily . . . Lily Kendrick. She's my Tempest partner," I said. "In 2009."

"She's okay?" Blake asked with urgency that came totally out of left field.

"She was okay when I left 2009, as far as I know. I had seen her a few hours before."

"I saw her, too," Holly added. "Probably twelve or so hours before . . . before coming here."

Blake leaned against the nearby wall and closed his eyes, letting out a breath. "All this time, for nearly two years, I didn't know." He jerked back to a full standing positioning and quickly composed himself. "I'm just relieved she's okay, that's all."

I lifted my eyebrows and glanced at Holly, who shrugged. "You could have told all this to my dad and he would have told you about Kendrick weeks ago."

"I'll remember that next time," Blake said.

Holly laughed under her breath. It was the first time we'd heard any trace of sarcasm from Blake and it didn't quite fit.

"Lily became my mission," Blake said. "She's the reason I ended up here. Not that it's her fault but because I witnessed her conception, her birth, and then found a way to keep seeing her."

OCTOBER 15, 2874.
AUDIO RECORDED BY HOST.

Today, during my training session at the White House, I asked Thomas and Dr. Ludwig about B-29. I told them about Professor Kendrick's yelling and then crying in 1987 during Lily's birth, and about the passion and chaos I had come to tolerate and eventually enjoy in that year. I asked if they thought B-29 might be inhibiting natural responses. Both Thomas and the very confident, always stern and fatherlike Dr. Ludwig dismissed this right away. This is the theory Dr. Ludwig explained to me by showing me the data and research.

THEORY: B-29 brings clarity to the mind, not submission. Alcohol, drugs, stress, fear, elation, and lack of security cause poor decisions. Individuals without B-29 deficiencies have been traced throughout history and in most cases have been a huge asset to society.

That was the end of our discussion on B-29, which led both Thomas and Ludwig to ask me about my own ideas for possible missions based on my free-time research. Since I've only been visiting one location, one year, and mostly one person, I had only one idea: to check in on the product of the Tempus gene experiment that I had seen born just days ago. If I could find her location and jump to a date later than her birth date in 1987, I would be able to report back to President Healy on whether or not she possesses special intelligence and possibly the ability to time-travel.

Luckily, Ludwig and Thomas thought this was brilliant. They said at my age, I'm always going to blend in easily with most years. People don't suspect a kid of being part of the government or a terrorist threat.

So, now I have my very own experiment to work on. I'm naming it: Project Lily.

OCTOBER 20, 2874.
AUDIO RECORDED BY HOST.

Day One of Project Lily is complete. I observed the subject in the year 1995. Age is approximately eight years old. She was playing with a few other children at a neighborhood playground in a place called Chicago, Illinois. I'd heard of this city during history class, but the merger with the country formally called Canada in 2245 relieved this city of its title. I missed the mark on the first try and Thomas had to lead me there. He left right away, which I was happy about since I wanted to complete this mission on my own as planned. Now that I'm familiar with the area, I don't think I'll have any trouble next time even with a different year.

Lily Kendrick appears to be slightly tall for her age, very slim. Before the other children arrived at the playground, she was reading a book that, after careful research, I have determined to be far more challenging as far as vocabulary and plot complexity than the average for a child her age in 1995; however, it would be standard level in my present. This is proof that the Tempus gene has expressed itself in her phenotype, but the ability to time-travel is not present at this time, though I didn't really expect it to be.

I also noticed unusual behaviors when the subject interacted with peers. During a game that seemed to have complex rules that changed frequently, the subject attempted to correct the other children or suggest a more logical rule and immediately backed off the second she was met with resistance. The timid behavior surprised me, given her superior intelligence. I wonder if it might be difficult for an individual with the Tempus gene to assimilate socially to this year? Maybe it's not God's intention to displace a natural product of evolution? But then why would time travelers exist if not to help advance the future?

Day Ten of Project Lily. I made a big mistake today. The biggest one you can make on a mission like this. 2002 affected me very differently than the previous years of observing the subject. I hadn't seen her older than eleven until now. I followed the fifteen-year-old Lily Kendrick while she walked her dog around the neighborhood and then stopped at a coffee shop and took up residence at a table outdoors. So, of course I did the same and this is what happened:

An older woman walked up to me, tapping her foot and holding a small tablet and a pencil. "What can I get you?"

I tore my eyes from Lily, who was bent over in her chair, tying the dog's leash to one of the table legs. "Um, nothing. But thank you."

The woman stared at me, her mouth hanging open, and then anger crept up in her expression. "You can't sit here unless you're going to order something."

"Okay, I'll have coffee." The words were out of my mouth before I realized that I hadn't planned on making any purchases in this year and didn't bring money that would work in 2002. This was a rookie mistake and I knew I'd get ripped apart for it later on. I'd have to vanish before needing to pay. That would guarantee me a week without time-travel privileges.

I must have looked as panicked as I felt because next thing I knew, Lily Kendrick was staring at me from the table beside mine, laughing lightly.

"You look like someone who forgot his wallet?"

I felt my pockets to go along with her theory. "Yes, and I think I've just gotten myself in a bind."

She nodded toward the empty chair across from her. "I'll buy your coffee if you sit here with me. I just need a small favor."

"Are you sure?" I should have been asking myself that question rather than her. Interacting with the subject was never in the plan.

"Uh-huh," she said, gazing out at the street. The waitress came and set down my coffee and Lily's chocolate milk, which was a much more appropriate choice than coffee considering the current summer temperature.

"We're on one check," Lily said to the waitress, who rolled her eyes but moved on without objecting. "I just need you to look really excited to sit here with me in about ten minutes, okay?"

"But I shouldn't look excited right now?" I asked, and couldn't help smiling.

She returned the smile, tossing her long brown hair over one shoulder. "That's totally up to you. I realize I'm completely pathetic but the boys' cross-country team comes by here almost every morning at this time and it's possible I might be trying to impress one of them."

"Impress them by buying me coffee?"

She sighed and leaned back in her chair. "Okay, maybe 'impress' isn't the right word. I guess I'm trying to make him jealous or just get him to notice me."

"Oh, right."

"I told you it was pathetic. After today, I'm quitting cold turkey, I swear." She smiled at me again and took a long drink of her milk. "Do you go to East View?"

Must be a school name. "No."

"Where do you go then?"

It took me a few seconds to reply, but finally I formed some sort of identity in my head to use for the remainder of this conversation because I was enjoying it far too much to end it now. "I do my studying at home. Home education."

She wrinkled her nose. "You're homeschooled? No offense or anything, you're not one of those religious nuts, are you? Do you have fifteen siblings and parents who force you to build houses and make your own clothes?"

I laughed really hard. "No, I have only three older brothers. And I can safely say we've never agreed on anything long enough to complete a project like home building together. That would be a disaster. Does believing in God make me a religious nut?"

"Maybe."

"Statistics show that 87 percent of this population believes in a higher power."

She shrugged. "I guess. I just don't see how you can believe the Bible and science at the same time, so I've chosen science."

I nodded, finally understanding her issues. "Well, I guess I don't believe in the Bible. You shouldn't have to choose God or Science. Mostly I believe in a creator and an afterlife."

"Well, I guess that's safe of you," she said, trying to sound objective but I could hear the skepticism behind her words. "That way if you end up being right, you don't have to go to hell after you die."

"I don't really think like that," I explained. "I don't think believing in God makes your afterlife better. For me, what happens to you after you die is a direct reflection of your level of moral integrity while you were alive."

Her eyebrows lifted and I could tell I had either intrigued or impressed her. "That doesn't sound too bad, actually. You aren't going to convert me, are you?"

I laughed again and tried to sip the revolting coffee. "No, it's a personal choice. I don't think there's a right or wrong. The outcome is the same either way."

That was just the beginning of three hours of conversation with the subject of my mission. She asked if she could call me or email and I told her I'd meet her at the same place, same time tomorrow. I know I shouldn't have, but some other force had taken over, and it wasn't alcohol or the coffee because I only had a sip of it and I spit most of it right back into the cup. Something else made me want to break all the rules and talk to Lily Kendrick every hour of every day.

"It's weird, all the connections," Holly said. "Like everything is so orchestrated."

"I know. I had no idea it was like that," I said. "I always wondered things like, who was the first time traveler or how did Chief Marshall and Dad find these Tempest agents I worked with. It's almost like Tempest was just chasing someone else's work the whole time, picking up stragglers and trying to make the best of a bad situation."

"How very noble of you," Holly said, rolling her eyes at me.

"He's basically right," Blake said.

I punched a fist in the air and then pointed a finger at Holly. "See? You're evil and I'm good. I knew it all along."

Holly cracked a smile. "That would be the ultimate cover, wouldn't it, considering you don't look even a little bit innocent and I can pull off the good-girl act fairly well."

"We'll have to use that to our advantage should the gods otherwise known as Eyewall pay another visit to Misfit Island," I said.

Blake opened his mouth to respond, but a loud bang on the door stopped him.

Holly and I both sprang up from our chairs. She reached the door before me and flung it open. It was Emily and she looked upset. She grabbed my hand and pulled me into the hall. "Come on, you've got to help!"

The three of us ran outside behind Emily, past the fire pit, past the cabins, and toward the grassy hill where we had first crossed inside the force field weeks ago. Rain had started to fall in a drizzle just like it had that day.

The first thing I noticed was Sasha, her olive skin and wild, curly hair standing out among the group of people. That and the fact that she was holding someone at gunpoint.

"Does she even know how to use a gun?" I mumbled to Holly and Blake.

"I was just gonna ask that," Holly said.

Blake shook his head, increasing his pace. "I highly doubt she does."

Finally, I took in the entire situation and realized that Dad stood several feet to the side of Sasha, also holding her at gunpoint. "Put the gun down, Sasha. She's not going to hurt us."

She?

I walked closer and got a better look at the person under Sasha's control and nearly lost my ability to stand. "Holy shit!"

"Oh my God," Mason said, approaching me from behind. "It's Stewart!"

From the corner of my eye, I saw Holly spring into action. She grabbed Sasha from behind, snatching her gun and tossing her into the grass in the process.

Okay, Commando Holly: 1. Sasha: 0.

Mason and I ran toward Stewart. She was covered in dust and

looked like she had been through hell to get here. I reached her first and grabbed her, pulling her into a tight hug. "What the hell are you doing here?"

She stumbled out of my arms and took in Mason. "What the hell are you doing alive?"

"Emily did it," I explained. "Probably around the point when you were off giving Healy truth serum, Emily was using her fingerprint advantage to read my diary."

"I knew I liked that kid," she said, reaching out to hug Mason.

It was Dad who broke the reunion. He grabbed Stewart from behind, turning her around and gripping her shoulders. "How did you get here? Who brought you?"

She let out a breath. "I can't tell you. I'm sorry. I really can't."

Grayson stormed up behind Dad, then surprised me by turning toward Emily. "Is she one of us?"

Emily opened and closed her hands, squeezing her fingers together and then releasing them. "No, she's not. I can't feel it."

"Can't feel what?" a few of us said at the same time.

"Emily can sense the presence of time travelers," Grayson explained. "She describes it as a buzzing in her head."

Okay, that's insane. But then again . . . "Wait?" I asked. "Is that how you found me and Kendrick in Central Park? Could you sense me?"

Emily only had a chance to give a tiny nod because Grayson was drilling Stewart. "Someone brought you here, then?"

"Obviously," Stewart said.

"That was Sasha's concern. We don't know whose orders she's here on. We both know how convincing Eyewall can be," Grayson said.

"Oh God, give me a break. I know what I'm doing," Stewart said.

Dad looked almost as crushed as he had when Courtney and I showed up. "You shouldn't have come. Whatever you were told isn't true."

She folded her arms across her chest, glaring at Dad. "You must have no faith in me at all. I'm here to get you guys out. I have a plan. A damn good plan."

"But the force field—" I started to say.

"We're gonna shut it down," Stewart said. "And then get the hell out of 3200."

CHAPTER EIGHT

DAY 12. NOON

"This sucks." I pointed my gun at the tree-stump T-shirt target. The slight tremble in my left hand still prevented me from actually firing.

"What sucks?" Holly asked. "The fact that you still can't shoot or the fact that we've just been shoved away like little children being excluded from the adult conversation?"

"You don't think they'll do anything to Stewart, do you?" Mason paused midreload and waited for Holly, Blake, or me to reply.

"Dad won't let them," I answered right away, hoping it was true. Like Dad, I didn't want Stewart trapped here either, but I couldn't say I wasn't the slightest bit happy to see her. Besides, she said she had a plan.

And I'd learned to trust Jenni Stewart in moments of stress. She had yet to let me down. I also knew she was strong enough to withstand any interrogation Grayson, Lonnie, and Dad might be throwing at her in the reproduction room right now.

"I don't think there would be any concerns about her safety if she'd just tell us who brought her here," Blake said.

"If she said she can't tell, then she can't," I snapped. But really, I wanted this information, too.

"And why does everyone insist on showing up unannounced with weapons?" Sasha said. "It's like they're asking to get killed."

Holly laughed under her breath and was then awarded with a killer glare from Sasha, who still seemed pretty bitter about the fact that Holly had tackled her to the ground. "Did you really think you would have hit her on the first try? Considering the fact that you've never used a gun before?" Holly asked Sasha.

"I can time-travel, unlike you," Sasha said. "I don't need firearms as a crutch to keep me alive."

Holly snapped the trigger into place on her gun, eyebrows lifting way up. "Really? How's that working out for you right now?"

Sasha grumbled something incoherent to herself and then Holly sighed and turned to face her. "I'm not trying to insult you, I'm just saying that learning to protect yourself might not be a bad idea, given the circumstances."

"She's right," Blake said, kicking Sasha's shoe playfully. "It couldn't hurt to have a better defense ready."

The wait was killing me. I had to do something constructive while Stewart got picked apart in private. "I'm gonna go chop some wood," I said before walking off.

"I'll go with you." Blake jogged after me. "Think Holly and Sasha will be okay without us?"

I picked up my pace, hoping to keep anyone one else from joining in on my distracting activity. "I think Holly will be okay."

We walked farther than I'd ever been on Misfit Island, all the way to the edge of the thick woods, the complete opposite end of the lake. Blake handed me an ax and picked one up for himself. Large pieces of tree trunks lay scattered around our feet. I picked a thick one to start on and hit it several times before making a dent.

"Was Holly correct the other day?" Blake asked after a good ten minutes of perfect silence, only the sound of metal hitting wood having passed between us. "When she said you're keeping stuff from her? About her?"

I threw something extra into my swing, splitting a piece of tree trunk into two perfect halves. "I'm keeping a lot of stuff from Holly. We were enemy agents, you know? It's not like she's told me much about her life in Eyewall."

"That's not what I mean." Blake stopped chopping and stacked up his firewood pieces. He already had a good-sized pile compared to my two pieces to contribute thus far. "I understand why she might feel entitled to have this information, but she can't possibly know what it's like to time-travel, like you and I do. She can't comprehend the anxiety it causes us to know things that happened a certain way and watch them change. It would be like if we had the ability to read minds and then we were ridiculed and hated for not telling people what went on in the heads of their own family members and loved ones." He wiped sweat from his forehead, staring off into the distance. "It isn't fair to accuse us of anything when we can't help having this God-given ability."

"Your ability might be God-given," I said, wiping my own sweaty brow. "But mine sure as hell isn't. I'm completely man-made."

"Regardless," Blake said. "The origin has nothing to do with you. You didn't ask for this."

"Those are all valid points," I conceded. "Why don't *you* try explaining that to Holly?"

As if it were that easy.

"I will," Blake said, looking dead serious.

Suddenly I felt that tiny bubble of jealousy boiling to the surface again, threatening to spill over. I didn't want Blake alone with Holly long enough for him to have this talk with her. I didn't want Blake alone with Holly at all.

"She was my girlfriend," I blurted out against my better judgment. "Before I went back and erased us. Then everything changed and what I did, the sacrifice I made to keep her safe, meant nothing. Her life went completely to hell and I can't just tell her, oh by the way, I've succeeded in getting two out of three versions of you to fall for me, so the probability that it could happen again is very high."

I channeled the aggression into chopping and split another large piece of tree trunk in half. Then I wondered what kind of hidden anger Blake must have to be so damn good at chopping wood.

"I'm not going to tell her," Blake said quietly after several long moments of silence. "And I already knew that you were in love with her. It's pretty obvious."

My arms were ready to fall off so I dropped the ax and lowered my hands to my side. "I want to deny that so badly, to tell you that I was in love with a different Holly in a different universe, but before we left 2009 there was something . . . something that made me realize that although she's different now, the core of her, the basic foundation that makes up a person . . . it's always going to be the same no matter what happens. And that's what I love. That's *who* I love."

"Thomas would disagree with you on that," Blake said. "And to some extent I agree with him. Holly's life might have changed, if she went from a normal eighteen-year-old in 2009 to being an Eyewall agent, but her childhood hasn't changed at all, has it?" I shook my head, knowing she had the same mother, the same house. "The way she was raised didn't change. But if that was altered somehow . . ."

I let that concept sink in for a minute or two, and then Blake and I were interrupted by Dad. *Finally.*

"Stewart is still insisting that she can't reveal her partner in crime or the plan will backfire," Dad said. "But she's ready to tell us her idea."

All eleven of us crammed into the small reproduction room minutes after Dad came to find us. Emily and Courtney sat on the floor. Stewart occupied the chair. She looked a little rattled but overall okay. The rest of us leaned against the wall. I took the spot next to Stewart's chair.

"I still can't believe you're here," I whispered to her. "What did they do to you?"

She shrugged. "I've had worse. And why the hell are they so serious about every damn thing? Are we starting a political system here? Will there be an election later?"

I glanced down at her and grinned. "I missed you."

"Of course you did, Junior."

Grayson clapped his hands together. "Agent Stewart, you have our attention."

It was very subtle and maybe only I could see it because of my proximity to her, but Stewart drew in a nervous breath before speaking. "The invisible field, the one that doesn't allow you to leave the area, it's controlled from only one location and that's on the other side of the woods—"

"Wait," I interrupted. "You mean the woods here on Misfit Island? Isn't that where the perimeters end?"

Everyone stared at me like I had brain damage. Which might be true. Then Courtney's face lit up and she looked over at Grayson. "He wasn't here. He wasn't conscious when you showed us the maps of the area."

"Right, Courtney. I forgot as well." Grayson pushed himself off the wall and started tapping buttons on the control panel. A map appeared on three different screens hanging on the wall at eye level. Everything was there. The cabins were clearly identifiable, and just beyond the thick section of trees, there was more grassy land and images of tents scattered everywhere. Around the tents were tiny black dots, some of them staying in place and some moving. Grayson's finger touched one of the screens and moved from the technology building through the woods, through the area with tents, and stopped just before reaching another thick mass of trees. "That's where the perimeters of the force field extend."

"The force field gets taken down more than you think," Stewart said. "But they hit you with memory gas to stop anyone from leaving. Think about it, they can cross into the area without taking the field down, it's just getting out that's the problem."

"So the controls are on our side?" Grayson asked.

I could already see him, Blake, Lonnie, and Sasha all exchanging glances, possibly believing Stewart for the first time. Then Grayson shook his head. "Even if we found this box, there's no way we could gain access. All the Eyewall workers have identity chips, fingerprint access—"

Stewart pointed her index finger at Holly. "Good thing we've got one of their team members to help us gain access."

Several people started talking at once, trying to disprove or encourage exploring this theory. I kept my mouth shut and my eyes on Holly, who also remained quiet.

"Okay, okay," Grayson said. "It's possible this could work. She *is* in the system. The retina scanner identified Holly as an Eyewall member. But Eyewall guards will teleport in as soon as the field drops."

"True," Stewart said, nodding and obviously stalling like she might be afraid to tell us the next part. "The electromagnetic pulse will go up as soon as the field is down. The only point of access for time travel is just outside the Eyewall headquarters. All we have to do is take out the guards who come charging in after the field is dropped, remove their identifier chips, implant them on our own bodies, walk to Eyewall headquarters, at least to the point of access, then time-jump the hell out of 3200."

"Is that all?" Sasha said, sarcasm falling from every word.

Grayson and Dad both kept their expressions as blank as if they were jacked up on B-29. Dad spoke first. "Let Grayson, Lonnie, and I discuss this more in-depth. There are some logistics to work out. It's a long journey to headquarters."

We all filed out of the room, knowing there wasn't any reason to argue or discuss it further until they made a decision. I grabbed Stewart by the shoulders from behind and gave her a squeeze. "Nice job. Honestly, I figured you had no idea what you were getting into. It's a good sign that they're even willing to talk about it."

Once we were outside, near the fire pit, Stewart turned around to face me, grief filling her expression. "It's my fault you're here. If I hadn't dosed Healy with the truth serum, Emily wouldn't have been alone long enough to start her little quest and Healy wouldn't have trapped you so soon. He would have waited longer and we'd have figured out that he was trying to trap you . . ."

I didn't know how to respond. I was sure there was some truth to what she was saying but still, so many factors led to this entrapment. No way could we pin it all on Stewart.

"Did you know Healy is the President of the United States in the future?"

Stewart's mouth fell open and I laughed, steering her toward a log to sit down on. "Let me fill you in on everything you missed."

"You don't think I have any good gossip to share?" Stewart said. "I was hanging out in 2009 for three whole days before coming here."

I sat down beside her on a log and Mason, who'd been listening in from Stewart's other side, joined us. "You can't possibly top Healy as President in the future."

"Okay, maybe not."

CHAPTER NINE

DAY 13. BEFORE DAWN

I tossed and turned all night in my bottom bunk, having dream after dream about Holly. Then suddenly, the scent of her hair fell right under my nose, dragging me from another amazing dream.

Cold fingers gripped the sides of my face, holding it tight. "I don't know where your hand is trying to go, but it's not gonna happen."

My eyes flew open and were hit with a bright flashlight. Holly leaned over me, fully dressed, shoes and all.

"What are you doing here?" I asked.

She released my face and took a step back. "Come on; Blake gave me the memory file. We need to hear the rest of it."

I shook the dream from my thoughts and stumbled out of bed, rummaging for shoes. It was pitch-black outside and the bite of cold in the air was even worse than ever. Holly shivered and wrapped her arms around herself.

As we crept as quietly as possible across the grounds toward the technology building, Holly kept glancing sideways at me, like she was about to bust out laughing.

"What?"

"Nothing," she said, and then she did start laughing. "Were you having a good dream? Anyone I know?"

Oh, God. What had I said in my sleep? "It's none of your business."

"Okay, whatever," she taunted. "But you do realize I know the name of every single girl you've ever dated or hooked up with? Some of them I even know addresses and phone numbers. It was part of my training."

Seriously? Why was my dating history a top CIA priority? Mason had the very same assignment and made a point to taunt me about it as soon as I joined Tempest.

"Like I would dream about some girl I could hook up with anytime I want," I said with a smirk. "Where's the fun in that?"

"So, it was a celebrity?" Holly asked, sounding slightly intrigued.

"Or a couple celebrities."

"Gross."

"You asked."

She reached out in the dark and gave my shoulder a hard shove. I caught her hand, holding it firmly, and felt a familiar buzz of electricity flow through my entire body. I heard her quick intake of breath and wondered if she felt it, too.

I rubbed a callus near her thumb with my middle fingers and took note of her pulse speeding up. "From your gun?"

"Uh-huh," she said.

We were stopped in front of the building now, Holly turning to face me. I released her hand and reached around her to open the door. Her entire body brushed against mine as she turned her back to me again and stepped inside.

I took the chair in the reproduction room and Holly stood beside me, playing with the controls, trying to remember what Blake had showed her about how to use the computers. Her leg kept rubbing against mine as she moved and I was thrown back into the memory of my dreams. I swear she was doing it on purpose.

"I'm just gonna let it play straight through. We don't have Blake here to drill with questions," she said.

"Sounds good to me."

DECEMBER 1, 2874.
AUDIO RECORDED BY HOST.

Thomas spent the night at Nora and Jean's place last night and Jean spent the night on our couch. I didn't even realize this until the morning when I woke up and saw her curled up and sound asleep in the front room.

Jean wouldn't give me any details but I already know how Nora feels about Thomas. It's pretty obvious she worships him. I know almost everyone does, but Nora really, really does.

When I asked Thomas about last night, he said it wasn't an impulsive choice. It's something he discussed with Dr. Ludwig. I can't imagine discussing plans for a romantic evening with Dr. Ludwig, but then it hit me . . . time travelers reproducing.

And now I can't help but wonder what Nora would think if she knew about this plan. Somehow, I doubt their feelings are on the same level. Thomas is too committed to his work to get wrapped up with a family.

DECEMBER 25, 2874.
AUDIO RECORDED BY HOST.

Thomas just told me that Nora is pregnant. She's only two weeks along but he wanted me to be the first to know. He's been staying with her almost every night for the past three weeks and they've spent every waking moment together. I'm starting to think I might understand what it feels like to be in love, but that's because of my frequent missions for Project Lily, not because I see this in Thomas. Around Nora, he's affectionate and attentive, but when she's not around, he's all business. They're going to move in together in January in a building across town. Which means I'll have my own place and so will Jean.

Today is Christmas Day and I was supposed to be allowed to visit my family. I guess there was a security breach at the White House last night and none of us can go anywhere today. I started missing them so much that when Thomas went to see Nora this afternoon, I did a time jump to five years ago and watched me and my brothers and Mom and Dad take a family picture outside. It's a tradition every year in my house and we all hate it except for Mom. I had to hide behind the house and watch from a distance.

If it weren't for Grayson and Lily, I think I'd really want to go back to my old life. Everything about it represents who I am now. No matter how hard I try to become this person Dr. Ludwig, President Healy, Thomas, and the rest of the world expect me to be, I can't shake Blake the little brother getting pinched in the back by three different hands during Christmas photos. Physically I'm the most resilient time traveler, Dr. Ludwig has told me this on several occasions, but mentally, maybe I'm just not cut out for this job.

JANUARY 10, 2875.
AUDIO RECORDED BY HOST.

I think Lily is on to me. She knows something is up. All my visits with her have been on weekday mornings during her summer break. She and Lexi (her dog) are at the coffee shop every morning. She's been pushing me for personal information like my phone number and address. I'm not sure I can brush her off for much longer, but I can't exactly tell her the truth, can I?

Today she asked me if I was homeless and I could

tell she already knew the answer. She's pretty brilliant and could easily put together the fact that the first day we spoke to each other is the only day that I haven't had money, not that I purchase anything more than a drink and sometimes a muffin or a sandwich. And I'm always dressed in different clothes, current to the year 2002. I look like I've showered and trimmed my fingernails and all that.

But she's just so pretty and smart and kind. Probably the most kind person I've ever met. I keep thinking about her playing with those kids in 1995 and how she never argued or told them they were wrong, even when they were. That's just how she is. She's not going to take hope away from another person who needs it more than she does. Lily doesn't have any problem debating issues with me, but that's because we're more intellectually matched. I haven't tried to kiss her or even hold her hand or anything remotely close to my wild night with Jean (an incident that we haven't spoken of since), but I feel like maybe I love her . . . maybe.

But can you love someone if they don't really know who you are?

FEBRUARY 15, 2875.
AUDIO RECORDED BY HOST.

Today was scary. The most frightening day of my entire life, actually. Besides the day I discovered I could time-travel. I only have a few minutes to get this information into my chip before the next meeting begins so I'm making a short list.
1) We were all awakened in the middle of the night

and brought to the White House for an emergency meeting.

2) Sasha, a girl very close to my age and also a time traveler, came from the year 3102 to tell Dr. Ludwig about the destruction and war that is ahead of us. She had pictures and everything. New York City, my new home, crumbled to bits. I've never seen anything less peaceful than those images.

3) Sasha sat in the meeting, right across from me, between Jean and President Healy. She grew more and more tense as the meeting went on but didn't seem quite as fear-stricken as the rest of us.

4) Fifteen government officials were present today to vote on a plan of action. This is the first time we've had major information from the future.

5) Everyone agreed that the most effective solutions would require more time-traveling manpower. The six of us (seven now counting Sasha) can only jump so much and so often. We need to explore too many years, events, and people to find the root of the destruction and stop it before it happens.

6) It was unanimously decided that the Tempus Gene Project has not been an effective method of increasing time-travel manpower in this year.

7) Dr. Ludwig and President Healy informed us that Ludwig had perfected a cloning formula that would use our DNA to create another human being and the process would replicate the time-travel ability we possess.

8) The clones' genetics could be altered just enough to ensure that the clones aren't identical matches

in appearance to any of us, and they will be born from artificial wombs and raised from birth by the government to fight this war on time.

9) Jean's and Nora's reactions of complete horror and shock reflected my own, but none of us said a word. We weren't there to give our opinions. We were only there to answer questions about our abilities to help implement this plan of action.

10) Nearly everyone on the committee voted no to the cloning, what Dr. Ludwig and President Healy called Project Eyewall, despite their impressive sixty-minute presentation. Frank, a longtime committee member, one who's always been the nicest to me of any of the navy-suit workers, was so angry about the presentation he left the room and didn't return for several minutes. He was more strongly opposed than anyone else.

11) I've never been more relieved than I was after the vote was final. I don't think I breathed the entire time, waiting for more hands to go up in the air.

12) All of us are due back in another long meeting in twenty minutes, in which the committee will evaluate each of our abilities based on past missions, and with Dr. Ludwig's help, come up with parameters for each of us and individual goals for research to help us learn about this future war. In other words, what's the maximum amount we can time-travel without its killing us. I'm afraid I won't be able to see Lily anymore and I'm really wishing that I had led them to believe she might be able to time-travel soon so that I could keep visiting her.

That's all for now.

I can't believe what's happening. I thought I could trust Thomas. And Dr. Ludwig . . . and President Healy . . . he's the President for Christ sake! I'm in 1988 with Grayson right now.

A few hours ago, I was in my present, in the White House. Dr. Ludwig put me under sedation to evaluate my brain waves like he's done a dozen times before, only I must have awakened early and Dr. Ludwig must have left the intercom on and I was alone in the lab and strapped to the brain scanner, not able to feel half my body, when I heard his voice and President Healy's coming through the intercom. They were having a meeting in Ludwig's office right behind the glass wall.

After I realized what they were discussing, I had to shut my eyes and do my best to lower my pulse rate to the slow, sedated level because if they knew I had heard them, I'd probably be dead or locked up somewhere.

They are going ahead with Project Eyewall! Even though the committee voted no weeks ago! The plan is to have Sasha (the girl from 3102) take Ludwig to that year. They are hoping that amid the war and destruction he can find a quiet place to make clones who can time-travel.

President Healy plans to insert himself into a political position somewhere in the year 2000 or 2003 so that he can make sure legislation is more open to these ethically controversial issues. Those were his exact words! And the whole time I heard them go through this plan, I kept thinking how would the President insert himself into a position hundreds of years in the past without the help of a time traveler not only to take him there but to make alterations to the past. Would Sasha do this too?

That's when I heard him. He'd been in the meeting all along. Thomas. The man who might be father to a time traveler in less than six months. My mentor. The person I had worked so hard to impress this last year.

He's part of the plan. Not only that but he has all these theories on how the time-traveler clones should be raised in Eyewall headquarters. He thinks nurturing children will hinder their abilities. They want to raise these children with no physical contact with humans at all. No emotional bonds. It's so wrong I can't even think straight. How could this be better than any war we'll fight in the future?

I never thought I'd get unhooked from that scanner. It took so long and I had to act calm and cool as Dr. Ludwig dismissed me. As soon as I got to my apartment, I jumped to 1988. Grayson is the only person I could think to tell what I'd heard. He's as upset as me, maybe more upset. He said he thought both Ludwig and Thomas were headed down a path like this one but never imagined President Healy would take this big a risk, go against the rest of the government. Grayson only agreed to aid with the Tempus Gene Project because he thought it might hold off the cloning for a while.

We were both very worried about the fact that I overheard this conversation, and Grayson said I needed to hide my memory files from them. He helped me place them somewhere that would be nearly impossible for anyone to find. Memory files are the personal items that an individual owns in my present and the three hundred years before that, and they're rarely used against a person by the government or any law-enforcement agency. It's stated in the constitution of 2515. Individual thoughts, opinions, and mental plans cannot be used as concrete evidence in any shape or form. We are free to think and feel whatever we like. Only our actions and choices outside of the mind can be considered fact. No one can deny the usefulness of memory files. They have changed the way the world is run. They have truly improved society. To be able to see your past thoughts and ideas . . . it's an invaluable tool.

But Ludwig constantly uploads data from my memory file as it's recorded. If he knew what I knew, he wouldn't use that file against me—he'd kill me to keep me from talking.

Lucky for me, Grayson is way smarter than he ever lets anyone see. Not only did he help me hide my memory file for safekeeping rather than destroy it like I wanted to the second I got to Grayson's lab, but he also created a false memory file. He said there are tons of people who have figured this out in my present, those who fear government conspiracy and memory erasing, who want to keep their thoughts, but keep them hidden.

Grayson told me I have to go back soon and I have to keep pretending that I don't know anything and follow whatever orders I'm given. Thomas knows me too well, I think he'll see right through me, but I don't have any other option, do I?

Thomas and Sasha took me to the Eyewall headquarters in the year 3197. Thomas told me he trusts me to understand why he made the choice to go against the President's committee and follow Dr. Ludwig's lead.

The city was destroyed and there were communes of faceless people, poverty-stricken and without any way to fulfill basic needs. We just sped past them; Thomas didn't even look at anyone. Sasha did, though. We were beyond her present year, and knowing that fact, I could guess that either: A) another time traveler beyond Sasha's time was discovered naturally and took her to this year or B) Dr. Ludwig was successful and had created a time-traveling clone that brought Sasha and Thomas to the future.

One jump beyond our farthest point with another time traveler is all we needed to have new, broader boundaries. I would now be able to travel this distance alone if I wanted to.

The Eyewall building was constructed so uniquely, one and a half floors are visible aboveground and at least half a floor sinks beneath the earth. Electric fences surround the entire place and beyond those perimeters, a dark forest encircles the building. We used a hover vehicle to fly over headquarters and land near the entrance. I had only seen hover vehicles in a museum. No one used them in my present, hadn't since around 2650, after teleportation devices become accessible to everyone.

Why wasn't teleportation an option in 3197?

I was too scared to even speak as Thomas led me inside the building. Men and women in brown coveralls moved swiftly through the hallways. I stuck close to Sasha's side even though I had no idea if she'd been here before, if this even fazed her. But I couldn't trust Thomas. I couldn't let him know how much I disagreed with his actions. Distance in this kind of situation was crucial.

"Twenty-two years," Thomas said as he opened a door at the end of the first hallway. "It took that long to build this project and generate successful products."

Sitting in the middle of a room full of technology I couldn't even begin to unravel, was a much older Dr. Ludwig. He had to be in his sixties by now. His skin looked worn and wrinkled. He smiled at me and the reunion was less awkward than I expected considering I'd only aged about two months since the last time he saw me and he was my grandfather's age now rather than my father's age.

He spoke quietly to Sasha, who left the room abruptly without another word. Thomas dimmed the lights and pressed a button on the wall. Dozens of hologram screens popped up in front of us, displaying identical rooms, bare white walls, beds, dressers, and in most cases, one individual per room.

I held my breath as my eyes scanned the images one by one. I saw girls and boys about my age, several small children, but no one much older than me. And that made sense . . . twenty-two years. I'm seventeen. They had to build the building, the machines, everything.

Thomas raised a finger, hovering over one of the rooms where a small girl with bright red hair sat on her bed reading from a handheld device. "This one . . . this one is my project," he said proudly. "She's completely unique, not a full-blood like the rest of them. She's a part copy of another experiment that showed promising results but failed in the end to be useful. The results so far have been exactly what I predicted. Her brain activity is superior to anything known in your present. She's fluent in every language we presented her with and she's only 2525 days old."

I watched her tiny legs, dangling off the side of the bed, while she read. "What's her name?" I asked Thomas, barely managing an audible whisper.

"We don't name the experiments. Too complicated. Some of them look too much alike," he said. "She's 1029. Part of the Untouched group."

"Untouched? Like she's above the others in ability?"

He shook his head. "No, she's never had direct contact with human skin. Any needed contact was performed with thick, rubber-coated gloves that reach above the elbow. And it isn't just physical contact, the experiments grouped in this area are given no rewards from humans at all. No verbal praise or positive words. They are given instructions appropriate to their age and gender and if instructions aren't followed, basic needs are taken away for a period of time without warning. There is no leader or teacher. No parent role. They are taught nothing but self-sufficiency and they know no other option except to complete tasks exactly as given. Safety is never in jeopardy because nothing can influence them to test their limits. So far, the theory is working exactly as envisioned."

I immediately pictured a headless body, holding an infant out at arm's length. A sick feeling washed over me. This was so wrong. And Nora, my friend, practically my family after everything we've been through, would be giving birth to Thomas's child soon, having no idea how little he valued this tiny girl's life.

And the others, what about all the others?

"1029 is predicted to be able to achieve proficient time travel around 3650 days old," he said.

Ten. She's going to start performing missions for Dr. Ludwig and Thomas at ten. This is not what God intended us to do with our mind power, with our abilities.

I knew what I needed to do first and foremost. Tell Nora everything. And get her as far away from Thomas as I can before he gets his hands on that baby.

The coldness of these manufactured humans sitting alone in their rooms was the polar opposite of watching Lily Kendrick run around her neighborhood playground at eight years old. Or the feeling I used to get as a child, racing my brothers or my friends to school, my mother tucking me into bed. My father leaning over me at the kitchen table, checking my schoolwork, rubbing the top of my head if I had done well and sometimes even if I hadn't.

My present wasn't as open to touching as Lily Kendrick's because of the Plague of 2600. But still, human contact, whether physical or emotional, was essential to growth and development. It's a fact. I learned that in school. The people who influence us and whom we influence represent the humanity in us.

Maybe that's what Thomas didn't want in these soldiers. Humanity. Would this really work to stop whatever war had caused this destroyed world? And even if it did work, what price would we pay after death for this moral corruption?

All I could do today was agree to help Thomas even though I knew I wouldn't ever consider being a part of this. I had to get back home and find Nora as soon as possible. Then I needed to do something to stop this. Maybe I can't fight it, but I have to at least let someone know. Someone who cares.

Nora is safe. My hands are still shaking, I'm so scared of what will happen when Thomas finds out she's gone. Grayson came here and took her to a year before the first time traveler was discovered. We decided that was best and also decided that he shouldn't tell me the year. It would be safer for me not to know. I paced the apartment for hours, knowing the time jump could kill the baby, but Grayson came back and told me Nora was just fine. He gave her a new identity and they didn't want to tell me that either, but he's already looked her up and she had a boy. A healthy boy.

After Grayson left, I had to report to the lab for regular testing. Frank, President Healy's committee member who was so openly opposed to project Eyewall when it was first presented, was there waiting for me.

My heart pounded as I watched Frank lock the door to the lab and turn off the surveillance systems. Did he know I had just aided in a time-travel escape?

"Listen carefully, son," he said, turning to face me. "I only have a few minutes. The President's committee has been infiltrated and only two members in opposition to Project Eyewall are left."

"You know what Thomas and Dr. Ludwig are working on—?" I started to ask.

"Yes, yes, of course I know. Dr. Ludwig has always possessed the type of ambition that would lead him to extreme measures such as these. It was only a matter of time," he said. "First of all, do you know where Nora is?"

"No," I answered honestly. "But I know she's safe."

He let out a breath. "Good. As you heard in the presentation several months ago, Project Eyewall crosses lines of ethics the government and the United Nations do not support in any way, shape, or form. We only listened to the presentation and voted out of courtesy to President Healy, who we now realize might be brainwashed."

"I've seen it," I said, looking at the middle-aged man who possessed nearly as much political power as the president himself. "Eyewall headquarters. I've been there. It's . . . it's the complete opposite of everything good in the world." Those were the best words I could use to describe the horror of this project. Adrenaline rushed through my veins as I finally realized that I had someone to help me, to take this burden off my shoulders. "We have to stop them, you don't understand how terrible—"

Frank held up a hand to stop me. "I know. I have a plan, but I need your help—your abilities—to put this in place."

"Just tell me what to do."

He checked the door and the hallway, using the computer system before continuing. Then he pulled up a file on his handheld labeled PROJECT EYEWALL. "Many lives were risked to acquire this information, so listen carefully because I'm going to have to destroy the evidence when we're done here."

I nodded and leaned over to see the screen. My legs were already shaking.

"Dr. Ludwig is not the brains behind the successful cloning. So many formulas were tried and all of them failed throughout history, except one young man's theory recorded in 1953."

I glanced at the information on the screen. *Andrew Melvin: April 5, 1953, basement of NYC Public Library.* "Who is he?"

"A very smart young man," Frank said. "I need you to pay him a visit."

"You need me to destroy his notes?" I asked, catching on to this plan.

Frank shook his head. "That wouldn't be enough. The theory is etched into his memory. He'll write it down again. I've already sent someone to talk to him, but it didn't work. Somehow Dr. Ludwig still got the information."

"Who?" I asked. "Jean? Lonnie?"

Frank hesitated for a moment, like he was debating telling me another secret. "There's another time traveler. I've kept him secret from absolutely everyone. I saw how all of you were going to be used and I knew we needed someone working on our side, the side that will not aid Project Eyewall in any way."

Another one of us. Except he didn't have to give up his life like the rest of us. Or maybe he did, but just in a different place, in a different way.

"This time traveler is much older than you. I think your age and your apparent distress in this situation could be enough to convince Andrew Melvin to keep his work a secret and not pursue it any further."

"I'll do everything I can," I promised Frank.

He touched a hand to my shoulder. "I know you will, son. You have always displayed the ability to do what's right. I respect that more than anything even if no one else does."

I'm pretty sure that was Frank's way of telling me that my so-called bad habit of showing nerves, excitement, and apprehension during training sessions and meetings showed that I was human more than anything else.

The jump to 1953 wasn't as difficult as I thought it would be. Frank had me memorize a map of the city in the 1950s. The access code he gave me to open the CIA-protected door worked perfectly.

What surprised me most about 1953 was Andrew Melvin. I hadn't expected to have this world-saving conversation with a skinny kid about my age.

"Andrew Melvin?" I asked, wanting to be sure I had the right person.

He pushed his glasses up on his nose and eyed me skeptically from his desk, which sat in a large room full of shelves of books, papers piled in every corner. "Who are you?"

"Blake," I said. "Listen . . . this is going to sound crazy, but just give me five minutes to explain."

I had to give him credit for his patience. He listened to me for ten minutes without asking questions.

"I don't know what theories you're talking about," he said when I had finished explaining my I'm-from-the-future story. "Probably a mix-up. Another Andrew Melvin think tank."

"It's not another Andrew Melvin," I said firmly. "And

I'm not asking you to admit to anything. Just don't write it down. Destroy it if you already have. Don't let anyone have that information inside your head. It will be the worst thing you'll ever not get credit for. Trust me."

I could see the debate in his eyes. The internal conflict as he asked himself, "What if this crazy fool is telling the truth?" Could I do anything more than that? Maybe one thing . . . "I have a good friend in 1987. I'm going to check up on you and make sure that you did what I asked you to."

I left him with those final words because I could feel the fatigue and stress dragging me down, lessening my power.

JUNE 11, 2875.
MEMORY EXTRACTED FROM HOST.

I collapsed into my bed the second I returned from 1953 and slept for fourteen hours straight. When I woke, Thomas was in the kitchen putting eggs on a plate. He glanced up at me and set the plate in front of an empty chair. "I made you some breakfast."

My eyes stayed on the plate of eggs and bacon, the glass of orange juice sitting beside it. "Um . . . thanks."

"I had a meeting with the presidential committee this morning," Thomas said, giving me no indication of his mood based on his tone. "Frank said you went on several missions yesterday for the committee, that they might have worked you too hard."

I nodded, unable to trust my voice, then I sat in the chair and started eating even though food was the last thing on my mind.

"I know you were trying to help find Nora. I appreciate your effort, Blake. I really do. But I think it's best if you don't put stress on your mind looking for her," he said.

I was literally holding my breath, not even able to swallow.

He sat across from me at the table, hands folded in front of him. "I'll admit, I had high hopes for this child, but obviously Nora and I didn't agree on certain aspects of parenthood. I just wish she would have spoken to me first. If she had been honest about her concerns, I would have listened."

I highly doubted that.

"I've told the committee to let it go, that she'll come back when she's ready and we should give her some space." He paused for a second, watching me carefully. "You didn't tell Frank what I've shown you in the future, did you?"

"No," I answered honestly. We hadn't actually discussed this in detail.

"Thank you. He'll find out soon enough," Thomas said. "That's what I wanted to tell you. The committee was impressed with the progress of Eyewall, though they were a little disgruntled with Dr. Ludwig's choice to go against the vote. Either way, they've forgiven Dr. Ludwig and given us their full support to continue the project. Frank, however, has chosen to betray the government since being outvoted. We've taken him into custody this morning, but we have evidence he's already formed a new agency specifically designed to act in opposition to Project Eyewall."

Grief and fear took over. I hadn't done it. I failed to convince Andrew Melvin that his ideas would eventually destroy the world. And now I'd lost the one person in my present who could help me. But had Frank really done it? Had he organized an opposition knowing they'd take him away soon enough? He seemed prepared, like he'd been planning every last detail yesterday.

All I could do was hope.

"I'm as disappointed as you are," Thomas said. "Frank has been a crucial member of the government for fourteen years. I trusted him, we all did. And I wouldn't worry about this opposition. He doesn't have time travel on his side. Only we do."

Hope sprang up inside me. *Yes he does. He has a secret time traveler.* Frank was smart. He knew exactly what he was up against. And this time traveler was skilled enough to steal files from Dr. Ludwig. I just had to figure out how to find him.

Deal with Thomas first, I reminded myself, *he still trusts you.*

Jean came through the front door before I had to verbally react to the information Thomas had just given me. "Oh good, he's awake."

Thomas looked from Jean to me, and then said, "I have a task for both of you. Something you'll be working on together."

I only got a few minutes to finish my breakfast and clean myself up and then Thomas, Jean, and I were in Central Park. In 1992.

The day was warm and people were everywhere. Thomas walked several paces in front of us, and Jean leaned into me and whispered, "What are we doing here?"

Finally, Thomas stopped and sat on a bench, pulling a newspaper from his back pocket, spreading it open to block his view. Jean and I guessed we were also supposed to stop and sit. So we did.

"If you look straight ahead, about two hundred feet away, you'll notice a young man and woman with two small children running around in the field."

I squinted in the sun, making out the outlines of two taller people and two little ones. I could see bright orange pigtails sticking straight out of one child's head.

"Those children are a creation of the Eyewall opposition organization," Thomas said. "They call themselves Tempest."

"Tempest," I said under my breath, memorizing it. Is this what Frank had done?

"Wait, so they're cloning in 1992?" Jean asked.

My head snapped to look at her, realizing Thomas's words . . . the creation of the opposition.

"No," he said. "The woman with them carried them, a surrogate. But they used the eggs of one of our products, a successful time traveler. They have two brilliant scientists working on their side. And they have a theory. They believe the half-breed method will create abilities stronger than the products of Project Eyewall."

"And you think they're wrong," Jean concluded.

"No," Thomas said, folding the paper back together. "I think they're right."

"So what do we do about it?" Jean asked. The eagerness in her voice scared me. She would follow Thomas anywhere. "We've got to destroy them, right? We can't have time travelers not under our control."

"Violence is almost never the answer, Jean," Thomas said. "And who says they aren't under our control? Or that we can't bring them to our side eventually? It's just a matter of showing them what they can be a part of. The importance their lives can hold." He turned to face me and Jean. "That's your mission. Keep watching the twins. Tempest calls them experiment Axelle. Product A is female and B is male. When and if their abilities present themselves, we need to be right there, ready to help them make the right choice, understood?"

"And what if they refuse?" Jean asked. "Look at the way they're being raised, it's not the methods used for Project Eyewall. What if we can't convince them to join us?"

Thomas looked out at the field again, watching the two little bodies chase a red ball around as it rolled through the grass. "If, and only *if* Plan A fails completely, we terminate them. We can't have that kind of power working against us."

I held in a gasp and glanced at Jean. She nodded solemnly as if she had already accepted this horrific task.

Suddenly the man with the children was walking toward us. He looked Thomas's age or maybe a couple years younger. He moved past our bench without making eye contact, but as soon as Thomas stood up, I knew this was a planned meeting.

"Follow me," Thomas said to us.

Minutes later, the four of us were hidden from the public eye by a small forest of trees.

"I thought we agreed, no backup," the man said, nodding toward me and Jean.

"They aren't backup, Kevin, just young trainees," Thomas said casually. "And our definition of trainee is very different from yours. They've never picked up a weapon in their lives or learned hand-to-hand combat. They're time travelers. Two of the originals."

Originals . . . that's what we were going to be called now that cloned time travelers were a part of society.

Kevin looked us over carefully, the disgust in his expression shifting to surprise maybe. It was hard to tell. He seemed to have composure as solid as Thomas's.

"I have a short message to deliver," Thomas said. "Dr. Ludwig and I are very impressed with your efforts toward scientific advancements. Even with the limited technology this year has to offer. I came to tell you that the experiment products—"

"Jackson and Courtney," Kevin said, speaking through his teeth.

"Of course," Thomas corrected. "Jackson and Courtney are in no danger. And we wish you and your team the best regarding the experiment's outcome. It's a brilliant concept, it truly is."

In that moment, I completely lost my head. I could feel something surfacing inside me as Kevin looked at us, grouping me with them. I couldn't stand it. Not for one more second. "He's lying!"

Thomas turned to look at me and so did Jean. "Blake, do you have something you'd like to say?"

"They're not safe!" I said to Kevin. Blood rushed to my face, flooding my judgment and thought process. "The kids, they'll never be safe."

Thomas rolled his eyes. "He knows that, Blake. And besides, it's not completely true. If the children present no special abilities over time, we won't have any interest in them at all."

Of course he knows that. I felt like an idiot right

then, trying to do something heroic and it wasn't even close. They're on opposite sides. Of course Kevin isn't going to take Thomas's message seriously. It's just a formality. Thomas is formal about everything. And he wanted Kevin to see us—me and Jean. To know that we were real and natural and maybe he wasn't working for the right side.

As Kevin walked away, leaving the three of us alone in the wooded area, I felt the weight of the entire world on my back. I couldn't fight it. I'd never win.

"Do you really think they'll be able to do it?" Jean asked. "The Axelle products? Even the Eyewall Project has suffered casualties."

"Failure is part of every experiment," Thomas said. "We made the subjects aware of the dangers of time travel and they made the choice to jump."

"Casualties? Some of the clones died trying to time-travel?" I asked.

"Yes," he said right away. "The earlier products, though I'm certain it will still happen now and again."

Oh God . . . this is worse than I thought. And what did he mean they made the choice? He told me they follow orders. They were raised to do everything they're told or basic needs are withheld.

"I want out," I said to Thomas right away. "I can't do this . . . not the mission, not the job. I've never been right for this."

"Blake," he said. "You've been through a lot in the past twenty-four hours. You haven't even had a chance to grieve the loss of Nora and Grayson. Perhaps we—"

"Grayson!" My stomach flipped upside down as I fought the urge to vomit. "What happened to Grayson?"

Jean chewed on her fingernail, keeping her eyes on the ground. She knew something. And she had kept it from me.

Thomas rested his hands on my shoulders, staring right at me. "Relax. It's a lot to absorb. Let's back up and take things one step at a time."

I could feel my legs trembling beneath me. "Just let me out, please. I'll never tell anyone about Eyewall or what you're really doing there. That children are dying . . ."

Thomas's eyes turned hard and cold, disappointment filling his expression as his hands dropped from my shoulders. "You've lost your head, Blake. You're not looking at the big picture. Plus, everyone knows you and what you can do. We can't exactly put you behind a desk without explaining things."

A small part of me thought maybe Jean would jump in and say she agreed with me and felt the same way, but I knew it wouldn't happen.

"I'll hide . . . let me go to 2002 or 2003 and stay with Lily . . . I can let you know if anything happens with her and I won't jump at all," I pleaded.

Thomas showed a rare sign of distress, rubbing his hands over his face for a few seconds. He glanced at Jean then back at me before taking a deep breath. "I wish this were easier, Blake. I really do." He pressed something against my neck and the whole world went black.

When I woke up, I was lying on the floor in a living room somewhere. There was a fire in the fireplace beside me. It crackled and popped as the wood shifted. I lifted my head, feeling the grogginess still heavy in my limbs. Jean and Thomas stood in front of a couch, leaning over it slightly. I jumped to my feet when I saw the limp hand hanging over the side.

Jean had latex gloves on and held a huge syringe in one hand. "The boy next?"

"Yes," Thomas said.

I glanced around the room, trying to figure out who the people who lived in this house were. Then I saw her . . . on the mantel . . . a photograph.

Lily.

This was her house.

"What are you doing?" I demanded.

Thomas touched the body on the couch. I leaned over and could now see it was two bodies. Both Professor Kendricks. Curled up together. Blue lips and faces. No rise and fall from either chest.

They were dead.

Thomas narrowed his eyes at me. "First it's them, next it's her. Unless you can find your focus again and never go near this subject in any year."

"Oh God, Lily," I muttered, then glanced up at the steps. "Carson! Not Carson."

Lily's much younger brother. The baby her parents never thought they could have. She adored him. Half of our conversations revolved around funny stories about Carson as a toddler, Carson in preschool.

I dove past Thomas and took off for the stairs, flying up them two at a time. Jean stood next to the bed in Carson's room. The sleeping boy looked older than preschool, maybe eight or nine years old.

"Stop!" I shouted at her. "Please, don't do this. Jean, it's wrong. You know it's wrong."

Thomas calmly stepped behind me, pressing

something into my back. I felt a shock of electricity go through my body and then complete paralysis. I knew what he had done and it was only temporary. Law-enforcement officers used these devices in my present.

I was completely powerless as I watched the little boy sit up, awakened by the commotion. His wide blue eyes froze on me and his mouth barely had time to form an O as he started to scream.

"Jean!" Thomas commanded.

Don't do it, please don't do it.

Her hands shook as she raised them. Her eyes glossed over and a tear trickled down her cheek when she stabbed the needle into Carson's neck.

His eyes rolled up in the back of his head and he slumped over. No tears could form in my eyes while paralyzed, but inside I was breaking into a million pieces. Then Thomas lifted me off the ground, tossing me over his shoulder. The stunner still pressed into my side.

He set me down outside in the frigid air and finally released me from the horrible paralysis. Jean seemed to have pulled herself together, her eyes no longer wet.

"I'm not angry with you, Blake," Thomas said, standing over me as I tried to pull my knees toward my chest in an effort to get up. "Lots of people make judgment errors as you have, and to be truthful, there isn't really a right or wrong for you to choose from. Take some time and think about what you'd like to do next. Come find me whenever you decide."

He grasped Jean's shoulder and they vanished right in front of me, leaving me alone in this unidentified year.

Headlights edged their way toward the driveway in the dark. I scrambled to my feet and ran to hide behind a nearby tree.

I saw her feet first, then her legs as she climbed out of the car, keys rattling. Lily Kendrick a few years older than I'd ever seen her before. I felt my chest caving in, pain crushing me as I watched her open the door, knowing what she was about to find.

I slid to the ground again, pressing my face against my knees and feeling tears come out so easily even though the last time I could remember crying was six years ago, when I dislocated my shoulder while playing soccer.

Maybe I could warn her or . . . something.

I did a quick jump back home and then right away jumped again to the day after the last time I had seen fifteen-year-old Lily.

The quick shift from night to late-morning sun blinded me for several seconds and then I could see her, sitting at our usual coffee-shop table. I started to run but then slowed myself, attempting to act normal.

"Lily!"

"Blake," she said, laughing at my volume.

I took a deep breath and fell into the chair beside her. "Sorry, I thought I'd missed you, got busy this morning."

The smile faded from her face. "Is something wrong?"

My feet tapped nervously as if a clock were ticking away at my minutes with her, her parents' and brother's minutes of life. I jumped to my feet. "I can't sit . . . I'm just . . . can we walk? Do you wanna walk with me?"

I glanced around and saw that her dog wasn't here today.

"Yeah, okay. Whatever you need." She stood up and we headed down the sidewalk, toward the park. "What's up with you today?"

Someone just killed your family.

But I couldn't say it. It didn't matter. She couldn't stop it from happening. Thomas would just pick a new date. I could feel us both hurtling toward this grief-stricken future and I wanted to hold on to her for as long as I could.

I reached out and grabbed her hand, squeezing it tight. Her cheeks blushed pink but she didn't pull away. In fact, I got the tiniest smile from her.

My breathing slowed as I forced myself to inhale longer and deeper. "Sorry . . . I had a bad day. A very bad day. But let's talk about something else . . . like anything."

She laughed nervously. "Um, okay. I've decided that Josh is an asshole."

Josh. The boy who ran by the coffee shop shirtless every day. I hated him. "Good. That's really good to hear."

Her eyebrows lifted as she glanced sideways at me.

"It's good because I like you," I said, spitting out the words with as much confidence as I could muster.

She smiled down at her shoes. "Yeah, I kinda figured you didn't hate me considering you hang out with me every day."

"True," I said, turning her toward the park and away from the street. "I guess it's not really a secret."

"You could tell me why . . ." she said. "That part is a secret."

I stopped under the shade of a large maple tree and turned to face her, still keeping our fingers laced together. "I like you because you'd rather be kind than superior."

Her face turned a deeper shade of pink, but she was brave enough to look up at me. "That's not completely true. You haven't really seen my competitive side."

"You're not as selfish as me," I said. "I know that for sure."

"How are you selfish?" She laced her fingers through my other hand and tugged me closer, removing the gap of space between us.

Heat flowed through my entire body. I leaned in, knowing today would be the day I was finally brave enough to kiss Lily Kendrick.

It was also the last time I'd ever come back here.

CHAPTER TEN

"I don't believe in God," Holly said after silence had fallen over us for far too long.

"Me either," I mumbled, my thoughts still glued to Blake and his memory of watching Kendrick's family murdered.

"How are we supposed to feel that overwhelming urge to fight Eyewall if we don't believe in God?" Holly chewed on her lower lip, and when she leaned over me to turn the screen from blue to black again, her hair fell onto my shoulder and I inhaled the scent. "Obviously, that's what drove Blake to want to inform us. To tell us how unethical the world would become."

"I knew about Kendrick's family already," I said, dropping my gaze to my hands. "She's the one who found them."

Holly released a heavy breath. "Damn . . . I can't even imagine . . ." She shook her head, unable to continue. And she didn't need to finish. I was perfectly capable of filling in the blanks. The thoughts of Lily Kendrick and her family, of the future of the world, weighed so heavily on us, I think we both had sought out a distraction the moment that recording had finished.

One of her legs was practically wedged between mine as she stood, half in front of me, half beside me. If I reached out only six or seven inches, I could grab her waist and pull her onto my lap and—

Stop!

I closed my eyes for a second and then opened them again, holding my breath as I spoke. "Just because . . . just because we don't believe in God doesn't mean we aren't morally good."

"Maybe *we're* good, but we don't have that external drive to serve people we don't know. To fix the world or whatever."

"I don't think it's God. I think it's *guilt*." My gaze was glued to Holly's waist again, which showed perfectly through the formfitting blue tank top she wore under her sweatshirt. My eyes shot to the white hoodie lying in the corner of the room where she had tossed it twenty minutes ago. Then my gaze followed all the empty floor space we could fill with additional articles of clothing. I swallowed back the images and cleared my throat before pulling myself to a stand. "That's it, right? We finished all of it? We should probably go back and talk to Blake about all this and . . ."

My voice trailed off when Holly reached behind her and brushed my hand before grabbing on to it. "It's this room, isn't it? Something about the confined space and proximity."

I had no idea what she was talking about, but I heard the invitation in her voice. She wanted me to move closer. So I did. Just one step and my body was brushing her back.

Maybe Blake's last memories were so intense neither of us could mentally process them right away. Or maybe it just felt like the end of the world would come even sooner now that we'd heard how awful things would get and this was the time to give in to these impulses.

Holly leaned into me and flipped my hand over so it was palm up and moved her thumb across the center.

Did she really want this? Did she want me to do something? Make a move? I hadn't told her anything about us. Nothing. But maybe . . . maybe it was just meant to be.

My free hand snaked around her waist. My nose touched the top of her hair and moved down toward her cheek and then her neck while her thumb continued to move inside my hand. I barely touched my mouth below her ear and I could already feel her pulse racing at a similar speed as mine.

I couldn't convince myself to do anything more than graze lightly over her skin, like she might crumble to ashes at my feet if I did.

Or beat me to a pulp.

Slowly, she released my hand and pressed more firmly against me before turning around. My pulse pounded from my heart all the way to my feet. Our eyes met for only a second and then I felt her fingers gliding under my T-shirt. Over and over the images of our shirts falling to the ground played in my mind until I realized she was lifting mine over my head. I held my breath as her fingers trailed over the scar from being stitched back together after having my lung uncollapsed.

"Does it hurt?" she whispered, her eyes focused on my chest.

"No." If it did hurt, I wasn't feeling it at the moment.

My hands found her waist again and rested there loosely, waiting for the fantasy to be shut down by some outside force. Inch by inch, my fingers crept under the bottom of her shirt. She raised her arms slightly and I took the hint, lifting the tank top over her head. It was still cool in here but the second her skin hit mine, there wasn't anything to be felt but intense heat.

I tightened my arms around her waist and just like that, we were kissing—hard and intense, like she'd spent half the night dreaming about me the same way I'd spent it dreaming about her. I lifted her off the ground and set her on the counter, avoiding the keyboard.

Maybe all that time Agent Holly and I had spent together, when I was moaning and groaning about my poor broken heart, might have actually been getting to her. In a way that she had skillfully hidden. I hadn't even considered that possibility.

Until now, anyway.

She kept tugging me closer, eventually wrapping her legs around me, molding our bodies together. And I could hardly grasp a single solid thought other than the realization of how good and perfect and right it felt to kiss Holly.

I was right to doubt myself that night with Stewart. There was no comparison and there never would be.

"Jackson?" She tilted her chin up toward the ceiling, allowing me to kiss the front of her neck. "Do you think . . . is it possible . . . ?"

"What?" I asked, breathless and brain-fogged.

I had just gained enough focused coordination to finally unhook Holly's bra and I allowed a few inches of space to come between us while she slid it off her shoulders. "Do you think we've been set up here?"

My arms went around her back, sliding her toward the edge of the countertop, pressing us together again. I rested my forehead against hers, catching my breath before speaking. "Like here inside the force field? Or here inside this room?"

"This room." She kissed me again, gripping my face and holding it tight like she had when she woke me up this morning. "Like they're trying to get us to do exactly this. Maybe it's a gas or the lighting?"

I closed my eyes and sighed, raising my head to the ceiling, letting Holly kiss my neck so hard she would probably leave a dozen hickies and I didn't care, not even a little. "The lighting is nice . . . really nice . . ."

The haziness in my mind cleared a little and I held Holly's head in place and leaned back to look at her. "Oh, I get what you're saying now. But it's not like the room has magical powers or that reproduction is even possible with our pants still on . . ."

Her eyebrows slowly lifted like she was considering all the absurd possibilities. "Right. Keep our pants on. Easy enough."

I smiled at her before letting my eyes close again, leaning in to kiss her. But a loud bang on the door stopped our mouths from making contact again. We stared at each other for a whole three seconds and then both of us dove to the floor, Holly crawling under the desk to retrieve her tank top and me snatching my T-shirt from the ground and pulling it on inside out.

Both of us were standing by the time the doorknob began twisting, but Holly was caught in her sweatshirt. I yanked the bottom of it and her head emerged, hair tangled around her face. The door opened, directing our attention that way.

"Shit!" Holly said when our eyes fell on her white bra lying at our feet.

I snatched it from the ground, trying to stuff it in my pocket, but Dad was already inside the room, looking us over carefully, eyes scanning us head to toe, pausing at the bra dangling from my left hand.

"Are you gonna wear that?" he asked me.

Holly started laughing right before me and then neither of us could stop. Eventually, I shoved her out the door and followed her, yelling to Dad that the room was all his.

When we got outside, I handed Holly her bra and watched as she skillfully put it back on without taking anything off again.

"I need to avoid him for a few hours," I said. "Should we go practice shooting?"

Holly's laughter faded. "I'll shoot, you watch, and then maybe we should give your hand-to-hand combat skills a test run."

Nerves fluttered in my stomach, thinking about the tremor in my hand that had yet to go away. "Okay, and then we'll talk to Blake. I have a few questions for him."

"Me, too," Holly said, heading in the direction of the lake.

As I followed her, I couldn't help but wonder, what the hell had just happened?

DAY 13. MIDDAY

"What were you doing?" Grayson asked.

Blood gushed from my nose and down the back of my throat at such a heavy rate, I couldn't speak at all. I sank onto the bed I'd spent way too many days and hours in. Courtney sat beside me and rubbed my back with one hand and held a towel under my nose with the other.

"He was just . . ." Holly stuttered from the other side of the room. The guilt on her face grew more intense as my blood loss increased. "We were fighting. The training kind of fighting. I might have kicked him in the face."

"It was an accident," Courtney said, before I could attempt to answer.

Grayson tilted my head up slightly, examining the bridge of my nose. "It doesn't look broken."

Several big globs of blood flowed down the back of my throat, gagging me. Nausea swept over me and I couldn't shake the image of having a pool of blood sloshing around in my stomach. Cold sweat trickled down my neck and back and I knew I was seconds away from getting sick.

Courtney caught on quickly and reached for the basin beside the bed, holding it in front of me. My stomach spasmed and I tossed up the cups full of blood. Courtney turned her head quickly the second the sticky red liquid made its reappearance, and Grayson stepped back, out of the way. From the corner of my eye, I saw Holly close her eyes and shudder.

The whole puking up blood concept just made me heave even more and it took a while to get it to stop.

"Can't you do something?" Courtney said to Grayson.

I wiped my mouth with a clean towel while Courtney set the bloody basin out of sight.

"I'm gonna have to do something." Grayson dug through a cabinet, pulling out supplies. "I can't stop the bleeding and he's going to need transfusions. Soon." He glanced at Holly. "Do you know your blood type?"

I couldn't hear what she said, but I saw Grayson shake his head and sigh in frustration.

"I'm pretty sure we've got the same blood type," Courtney pointed out.

Grayson turned slowly to face both of us, holding some kind of plastic bag. "True . . ."

"I'll go get Dad," Courtney said, knowing we needed him if this was going to involve both his kids.

Holly held Courtney back before she reached the door. "Stay with your brother. I'll get Agent Meyer." She took off before anyone could object, not that they would have.

"And Blake!" Grayson shouted after her.

While we waited for Grayson to get whatever supplies he needed ready and for Holly to come back with Dad and Blake, I stood over the sink rinsing my mouth with the bottle of water Courtney had given me a few seconds ago. I swished and spat until the bright red turned to a lighter pink. Being careful to keep my head leaned far enough forward so the blood stopped running down my throat, I sat back down beside Courtney, who had taken over the job of pinching my nose closed with the towel again.

"He looks pale," she said, glancing at Grayson. "Really, really pale."

Grayson worked hard to get an IV in my arm, while I fought to stay conscious as Courtney tossed bloody towel after towel onto the floor and replaced it with a clean one.

Eventually, I couldn't hold on to consciousness and the last thought to drift through my mind was that Holly hadn't even kicked me that hard. I just ducked a little too late in our hand-to-hand combat training and the bottom of her shoe made contact with my face but nothing too intense. It didn't even hurt much.

DAY 13. 1:30 P.M.

When I woke up again, Courtney was asleep beside me, her hand resting on a stack of clean towels. Blake sat in a chair next to the bed. A dark red IV line traveled from his left arm to my right arm.

"One of the benefits of looking like Thomas, huh?"

He turned his head in my direction, looking up from the book he'd been reading. "Yeah, not just the Tempus gene thing but we have a closer-than-average genetic bond."

"Closer than me and Courtney?" I wiggled my nose a little. The inside burned really bad but it seemed to have stopped bleeding.

Blake glanced wearily at the redheaded lump passed out beside me. "I'm not sure. I think Grayson thought it might be . . ." He blew out a breath, looking away from me. "I'm not sure."

Panic flapped its way around my insides. This had something to do with Courtney's health, I was sure. Did Grayson think she needed all the blood her body could hold?

"He had to cauterize some of your blood vessels," Blake said. "It might hurt a little."

I felt my nose with my free hand and then shook my head. "I don't even want to know what that means." I pulled myself up to a sitting position, swinging my legs over the side of the bed.

"I suffered a similar injury," Blake said.

"A girl kicked you in the nose, too?" I laughed, remembering how incredibly hot Holly looked when she went all bad-ass agent on me.

"Not the nose thing," Blake said. "I mean when I time-traveled to this year. That's why I don't have any memory files from my jump here. Grayson had to save me, too."

This was news to me. Why hadn't anyone said anything before now? "But your hands work just fine; does that mean the trembling I have will go away eventually?"

"I don't know." Blake glanced at Courtney again, like he was checking to see if she was really asleep, then his eyes shot to the closed door. "That's why I had Holly wake you up this morning to let you hear the rest. What happened to you . . . what happened to both of us . . ." He angled himself so he faced me now. "The damage is permanent. Grayson doesn't know if our brains will survive any time jumps let alone multiple ones. It sounds like they may have agreed to let us risk the escape plan—"

"Really?" I sat up straighter. "When did they decide this? You're talking about Stewart's plan, right?"

"Yeah." He leaned forward, closer to me, and I saw for the first time that intensity Holly had mentioned earlier about feeling compelled to save the world. "Once we get off Misfit Island, if we jump back right away, to wherever we go, that might be it for us. We aren't going to be able to come back."

I shrugged. "I can live with that."

Blake shook his head fiercely. "No, you can't. This could be our only chance to do something about Project Eyewall. If you and I tell everyone we're jumping back and then we let them go and we make the trek to headquarters and then we . . ."

"What?" I asked, leaning forward, hanging on his words.

His mouth formed a thin line as if to say he was already a hundred percent sure of his course of action, it was just a matter of changing mine. "We destroy it. It will take them another twenty years to rebuild, assuming we aren't able to take Thomas and Dr. Ludwig down with the building."

My heart was already racing just from hearing this plan. Did I have the same fight in me that Blake had? I imagined Dad's and Courtney's reactions if I stayed here without telling them.

And it was like Blake plucked the thought right from my brain. "If we do everything right, we can get you back to where you came from, we could even time it so it's only seconds after the others get back and they won't even know."

"Won't know what?" Courtney stirred beside me and rolled on her back, examining me. "You look much better."

Blake's face returned to the impassive look he had talked about in his memory files. "I think my job is done here. I won't have to give him all my blood."

Blake skillfully disconnected the IV from his arm, pressing a piece of gauze to it. Then he did the same with mine, and I wondered when he'd had time to learn this somewhat-more-than-basic medical procedure.

The past two years, I guess.

"I'm going to go help Grayson," Blake said. "He and your dad had to rush out to fix the power in the technology building."

The second he was out the door, Courtney turned sharply toward me. "I know what you guys were talking about."

I swallowed the dry prickliness in the back of my throat. "Courtney . . ."

"The dots." My stare must have been completely blank because she let out a frustrated breath and explained in more detail. "The dots on the map. The one Grayson showed us. I know what they mean. I figured it out last night."

"You did . . . ?" I said slowly, still totally clueless as to what the hell she was talking about but at least she hadn't actually heard my conversation with Blake. We should have never been discussing Blake's memory files anywhere near Courtney, sleeping or not.

"People," she said firmly. "Lots of people. I want to know why we've been kept away from them or why they haven't wandered over here to us."

"The dots are people . . ." I mumbled, pulling the image up in my head. "What kind of people?"

"That's what we need to find out." Courtney reached out and pulled my bloody T-shirt away from my skin. "I brought you some clean clothes."

"Great." I stood up and waited a full ten seconds before the room stopped spinning. "I think I'm going to have to scrub myself from head to toe. There's dried blood almost everywhere."

She stretched her arms and yawned before standing and handing me a stack of clothes and toiletries. "Go shower. I'll see how Dad is doing and ask Grayson what you're supposed to do now that you're almost normal again."

I took my time under the water, forcing soap into every crevice of my body despite the cold temperature. Then I spent a good five minutes brushing my teeth and my entire mouth to wash out all traces of blood. My lips were probably blue by the time I came out of the bathroom wearing jeans that were a little too long and drying my hair with a towel.

Holly was standing near the bed, holding a large cup filled with some kind of orange liquid in one hand and the shirt I must have dropped in the other. I stopped several feet away from her, frozen with the memories of this morning.

Her eyebrows lifted as she held out the cup and looked me over. "I'm supposed to stay and make sure you drink all of this."

I took the cup from her hand. Her fingers brushed mine and heat crawled through my veins instantly. I examined the light orange drink and then chugged it quickly. The salty taste was pretty revolting but not so bad that I couldn't keep it down. I wiped my mouth with the back of my hand. "Nasty . . . what is that stuff?"

Holly shrugged. "Something they give babies when they have diarrhea."

I decided not to ask any more questions about the drink since it was already in my stomach and obviously Grayson wanted it to stay there for whatever reason. "So . . ." I said, returning to rubbing my hair with the towel.

"So . . ." Holly picked at her fingernail before glancing up at me again. "I'm going to get a new training partner. I need someone who won't bleed to death after a tiny little kick in the face."

I felt myself smiling. "Really? Like who?"

"Stewart, probably." She reached out and pulled the towel from my hands, then I watched her calves flex as she stood on her toes, laying her hands in my hair and smoothing it down. I closed my eyes for a second, wanting so badly to hold myself in this exact spot for as long as possible.

"Holly," I mumbled, as my brain scrambled for ways to ask what the hell we were doing and if she liked it as much as I did.

Her fingers tangled into my hair and then she pulled her mouth to mine. I barely noticed her walking backwards, still kissing me as we moved toward the door. She rested her back against it and reached up with one hand, fumbling to find the lock and turn it. It was just like this morning—reckless and hot, our hands all over each other with no hesitancy.

But somewhere in the middle of Holly's shirt falling to the floor for the second time today, the words *cheap thrill* drifted to my frontal lobe. It wasn't a cheap thrill for me, though, at least it didn't feel that way. But what about her? Was it just a random desperate hookup for Holly? Was this physical gratification enough for me?

Stop thinking so hard!

As her fingers touched my lower back, pulling me into her, our bodies and mouths pressed tightly together, my mind wandered far from this moment, remembering lying in the grass in Central Park with 007 Holly. I could practically smell the scent of burning wood and fall air that I'd inhaled that morning. The weight pressing against my heart was so heavy as I remembered what it felt like to lie next to her, nothing but our fingers touching and feeling so complete and perfect, if only for a few minutes. But still, she had opened herself up to me. And when that happened, it was like nothing I'd ever, experienced before. Or maybe Holly had always been an open book and it was me that had been closed off?

Slowly, my mind returned to the present, feeling the pressure of Holly's lips against mine and my fingers in her hair. She looked as beautiful as ever, but no amount of physical contact would break down that wall between us. Holly was damaged and I was an asshole for ignoring that fact.

And I wanted that feeling back again, the lying-in-the-grass-with-only-our-fingers-touching-and-yet-closer-than-ever feeling.

With great effort, I pulled my mouth from Holly's, closing my eyes and resting my forehead against hers as my speeding-train pulse tried to slow down.

"What?" Holly said, breathless and confused.

I exhaled and opened my eyes, staring into hers, searching for some kind of connection. I lifted my hand to her face, gently moving my thumb across her cheek. Her body stiffened immediately and she pressed harder against the wall. Her eyes were wide and still swimming with confusion.

"What's wrong?" she asked. "Why did you—"

"Nothing," I said quickly. I rested my other hand on her other cheek and touched my mouth to her forehead. She stiffened even more, her muscles flexing like she was ready to pounce on something or someone. "Nothing's wrong . . . I just . . . I don't . . . I don't want to . . ."

"What?" she demanded, squeezing her eyes shut tight.

It was obvious I'd made her uncomfortable so I dropped my hands from her face and stepped back, putting a small distance between us. "Maybe we should talk about this, or at least figure out what's going on? I thought you hated me."

Okay, maybe I should have left out that last part.

I reached for her hand and held it between mine. This seemed to make her squirm and her eyes looked anywhere but right at me. Suddenly, more memories flooded back to me. Memories of a conversation right before we got stuck here. My heart started racing all over again, but this time it was from anger and fear as words formed in my head. Words Agent Carter, one of Holly's superiors in Eyewall, had said the night he, Holly, and I had had a showdown in the NYU Library. The night he accused Holly of being a double agent. I'd shot him. Killed him in an instant, not just because I knew he would have killed Holly but because of what he'd said, what I'd thought he had done to her. How did this memory get forced so far back in my head?

"You know that little game we play in our division?" Carter had said. *"The point system?"*

"Cut the bullshit, Carter," Holly had said. *"I know the point system. And I know what you're going to tell me. So, which is worth more? Turning in a double agent or killing a weak trainee?"*

"You know what got me the most points so far?" A sly grin had spread across his face. *"Nailing a virgin spy. Apparently it's off the charts. Easiest points I ever got. Poor Flynn, your best friend's dead. Need a shoulder to cry on? How about a few drinks, too?"*

My hands were trembling with rage, but I pushed it away for now and focused on easing her into the subject. "I know things kinda sucked for you in Eyewall and I don't want to screw you up even more."

She jerked her hand out of my grip and folded her arms across her chest. The impassive-agent face had returned. "Don't you think it's incredibly arrogant and self-righteous to assume that you're *important* enough to screw me up?"

I scrubbed my hands over my face. This was not going well. I should have kept kissing her. "I don't think I'm important enough to do anything. Okay, not exactly that, I just—"

She let out an angry breath and shoved me out of the way before stepping past me and snatching her shirt from the floor, throwing it on in ten seconds flat. "Forget it. This isn't worth the effort. You're probably a few seconds away from bleeding to death all over me. I doubt anyone wants to see that happen."

So many emotions overtook me as her hand reached for the doorknob, turning it quickly. *Don't do it . . . don't say it. Not yet.* "What happened with Carter, Holly?" I blurted out. "What did he do to you?"

Shit.

She froze for a second then spun around to face me, her expression calm. "It sounds like you already know everything, Jackson. I'm screwed up, remember? Your words, not mine."

"Holly—" I tried reaching for her again but she pulled away so fast.

"Don't talk to me about Carter," she snapped. "From what I can see, you're pretty fucked up, too. We all are. So quit trying to help me or whatever the hell you're doing. Find another hobby. Like keeping yourself out of this makeshift hospital for starters."

And with that, she was gone. And I was pretty sure we wouldn't be engaging in any more impulsive makeout sessions. I'd taken the affair to a level Holly wasn't willing to go. She and I had been on this wild up-and-down roller coaster ever since I got out of this bed a few days ago. Maybe I just needed to back off, like she had asked.

After taking a few minutes to ward off the blood-loss-induced dizziness and level out my anger, I stormed out the front door and headed toward the technology building. Holly's blond hair shone in the distance, near the lake.

Everyone besides Holly was either inside or huddled around a giant closet full of wires and electrical stuff right across from the reproduction room. Courtney stood next to Mason—a little too close—and held several tools in her hands, palms open, waiting for him to reach for one. I opened my mouth to comment on their close proximity, but Dad popped out from behind what looked like a water heater. Relief filled his face when he saw me and he started to reach for me, then glanced at his hands, covered with black smudges.

"You look so much better," he said.

"Did you drink the solution Holly gave you?" Grayson's voice emerged from behind the big cylinder thing.

"Yep," I said. "What's going on here?"

Dad's attention was jerked back to the problem at hand, whatever that was. Stewart leaned against the wall at the end of the hallway, drumming her fingers. She came to life when she saw me and headed our way.

"He survives again," she said. "We should start calling you 'The Boy Who Lived.'"

Courtney laughed and I rolled my eyes. Stewart nodded toward the exit, and said, "I've been standing here for over an hour and they haven't needed me yet. Let's go do something else . . . get out of the way."

Stewart and I headed outside. I stopped her from going toward the lake to avoid another encounter with Holly. Instead, we sat near the fire pit and let the almost setting sun beat down on us.

"So that's it?" I asked. "They made a decision to go with your . . . *idea*?"

Stewart nodded and pulled back her long dark hair with a rubber band that had been around her wrist. I noticed she had new clothes on today. A pair of sweatpants that were rolled at the waist several times and a giant red T-shirt, the bottom tied up in the back with another rubber band.

"Surprised the hell out of me," she said. "Especially after my warm welcome."

I scooted closer to her and lowered my voice. "Are you worried?"

"Yeah." She caught my gaze and plucked the next question right from my head. "No, I'm not going to tell you who brought me here, so don't even bother asking."

"Okay, sorry."

Stewart pulled two of the disgusting energy bars from her pocket and handed me one. We ate in silence for a few minutes and I kept my eyes on the lake to make sure Holly stayed there. "You were there for three days, right? In 2009, after I left?"

She swallowed a big bite, making a face after catching the bitter aftertaste. "Uh-huh."

"Was Kendrick okay when you left?"

"She was fine." She stared at her hands. "But Freeman and Parker are dead."

I sucked in a breath. "I knew about Freeman. I saw him, but not Parker."

She finally lifted her eyes to look at me. "And Healy, he's dead, too."

"Why didn't you tell me before? Last night when we were talking, I mentioned Healy and you didn't say anything."

"It didn't seem like the right time."

Hadn't I seen it happen? In my weird half-jump dream while I was dying. Marshall . . . Marshall shot Healy before shooting the other me.

"What's up?" Stewart asked, probably reading the many emotions flickering across my face.

I relayed my story to her about the dream or half-jump. She listened carefully and then shrugged like she really couldn't trust the memory since even I didn't know if it was real.

"I don't know who killed Healy," she said finally. "I saw the bodies piled up in that weird warehouse place, but it was the aftermath."

My heart pounded. "Did you see him there? The other me?"

Some of the color left her face. "Yeah."

"So then it *is* real," I said. "Marshall killed the other me and Healy."

She diverted her eyes from mine. "I don't know. I really don't know. And I don't think we have a division to get back to anymore. Everyone is dead. I'm not even sure what the point of escape is."

"Then why are we doing it?"

"Because we're supposed to." She exhaled heavily. "I want something to fight, you know? Not this sit-around-and-survive shit. I *know* we can't change anything by staying here, I'm not even sure we can change things if we make it back to 2009. But if we don't at least try . . . then what? We wait to be killed and for Eyewall to take over the world?"

Her questions left me with a fire under my skin. An itch to do what Blake suggested and blow the Eyewall headquarters and all those clone-making machines into a million pieces.

I stared right at her. "What if we escape and we don't go back right away? Like we do a little mission first. Give you that fight you're looking for."

Stewart's eyebrows lifted. "What are you talking about?"

"Exactly how big is your save-the-world complex?"

She leaned in closer. "I'm listening."

I pulled her to her feet and dragged her all the way to the hospital room so no one would overhear us if they came out of the technology building.

Then I told her everything. All the information from Blake's memory files and the plan he had to make the others think we were jumping back and then to not go and the part about how he and I might be too damaged already to make a return.

"Wow, so Kendrick had a love stalker from the future," Stewart said. "Kind of pervy, don't you think? Considering he watched her get pushed out of her mom's lady parts."

"I hadn't really thought of it that way, but maybe a little. I don't know, I've heard worse. Blake doesn't really seem like the pervy type to me." I scratched at the scab on the back of my head. "What do you think about the fact that my time-travel powers might be done for for good, even if we do get out?"

"I heard Grayson talking about that earlier. I wasn't sure if you knew so I didn't want to say anything." She paused and shook her head. "So, are you going to do it?"

"I didn't want to at first but now I think . . . I think I want to see that place go down. Especially now that I know the horrible stuff they've done to the experiments. The cloned children, I mean."

"Me, too." Stewart stood up and dusted off the back of her pants. "So yeah, I'm in."

There wasn't a hint of doubt in her voice, like there had been in mine when Blake first presented the idea. And Stewart's confidence confirmed my decision. Now we just had to keep anyone else from knowing.

Let the others get back safe and sound.

Mason came bounding into the room, interrupting us. "Hey, dude! Still alive. Good job."

I rolled my eyes at him, but held my sarcastic remark when I saw Stewart's face go a little white. She was probably thinking about Mason's being blown to bits on the night of Healy's ball in 2009.

"We're going on a hike at 0500," he said, a grin spreading across his face. *Guess Blake isn't the only one itching for a mission.* "We're gonna check out the other side of the island. See if we can access that electric box like Stewart says we can."

Stewart glanced at me, eyebrows lifted. "Here we go."

CHAPTER ELEVEN

I rubbed my hands together, bringing them closer to my mouth, and attempted to warm them by blowing hot air on them.

"Damn, it's freezing."

Dad nodded his agreement as his eyes scanned the forest in front of us. We were both early to arrive and waiting on Stewart, Mason, and Blake. The rest of the crew was staying back since this was a test run. An exploration of the potential point of escape.

"Still feeling okay today?" Dad asked, looking me over as carefully as possible in the dark.

"Yeah, I think so. Other than Holly's being ticked at me. *Again.*" I removed the gun from the back of my pants and aimed it at the forest. My hands trembled slightly and I let out a frustrated sigh before putting it away again. "I really wish she could have been kept out of this."

Dad shook his head. "Me, too."

"Do you think she was already in the CIA—like part of Eyewall—when we were doing Tempest training and you were getting updates from your secret source?"

"Absolutely not," Dad said firmly. "Somewhere between my last contact with my source and the point when you first saw Holly in that NYU bookstore, the world had been altered. Not enough change for us to pick up on right away, apparently. But that's because it was all a carefully orchestrated plan. Eyewall was born right in front of our eyes and we never saw it coming."

I could barely wrap my head around that concept because my time-travel experience had rarely been so circular. But that was what people thought of as the normal method of time travel.

A wave of grief swept over me. "If only Holly could have been kept out of all of this. It would be so much easier to live with."

"Speaking of Holly . . ." Dad cleared his throat and glanced back at the cabins. "I haven't had a chance to ask you what was going on yesterday morning in the technology building?"

"Nothing." I shook my head, releasing another frustrated breath. "Absolutely nothing."

"Didn't look like nothing."

"I guess it *was* something," I conceded. "But not the something I want from her. Not that I deserve anything from *this* Holly. I have no claim on her, no past with her. I just . . . she won't even talk to me. She's got a lot of shit to deal with and she won't talk about it."

He inhaled a long, slow breath and nodded. "I'll take a stab at it, okay? Grayson thought she might have some issues, too. He's worried about her. Especially if we're going to give her the responsibility of taking down the force field with her fingerprints. Grayson doesn't like to force anyone to do anything. He's pretty serious about all of us retaining our free will while we're trapped here, as much as we can, anyway."

"Well, I'm all for that," I said, hoping I could stay as true to this conviction as Grayson had. Holly deserved it. More than anything else, she deserved free will.

Stewart, Blake, and Mason joined us, passing around the disgusting meal bars we had boxes and boxes of here. We had just started talking strategy and looking over the map Blake had drawn when we heard arguing coming from the cabin area.

A flashlight pointed at us from a couple hundred feet away. Dad squinted and then Blake shined his own flashlight at the people approaching. My stomach did a few flips when I saw who it was.

"Holly's coming with us?" I muttered to Blake.

"Yeah, I thought you knew," he said. "We need her to test out the access."

"Aren't we just looking at it?"

"I'm going with you," I heard Courtney say to Dad.

Dad shook his head. "No." His tone was firm, like the time he denied her pleas for a fifth hamster.

"I tried to tell her that," Holly said.

I glanced in Holly's direction and tried to meet her eyes. She looked away, keeping her agent face on. Blake handed out flashlights to everyone while Courtney and Dad continued their argument. Eventually, Stewart cut in and ended it.

"Grayson said there was nothing dangerous," Stewart told Dad. "I don't see why she can't come. They don't need her help back there."

Dad narrowed his eyes at Courtney. "If I tell you to go back, you *will* without a word of protest, understood?"

"Yes," she said.

I watched my sister's gaze travel to Mason, and I didn't miss the triumphant smile she flashed in his direction. I glared at the back of his head and pushed my way to the front of the group as we entered the woods.

"Mason and I will take the lead," I said. "Courtney . . . you stay in the back with Holly."

"Who put you in charge?" Courtney muttered, but she did what I said and stayed next to Holly.

I gave Mason a shove from behind, putting a good amount of distance between us and the others. Stewart joined me on the opposite side of Mason.

"Are you conspiring with my sister now?" I snapped at him.

He held his gun at his side, glancing in every direction. "She won't shut up about those stupid dots. I just figured if she came with us, she could see whatever it is she wanted to see."

"That's great." I glared at him, pulling my own gun out. "Let's drag the untrained, unarmed, fourteen-year-old girl into the woods to an area we haven't even explored yet. Seems like a fabulous idea."

"Blake is untrained *and* unarmed," Mason said. "And your sister can kick some ass. I showed her a few moves. She's good, really good."

Complete and utter rage went through me at the idea of Mason's wrestling with my sister, and I nearly pummeled him right there in the woods but Stewart must have sensed my mood and jumped between us.

"Not now," she snapped at me.

"We wouldn't have a problem if Mason would do what I told him to do," I said.

He lifted his free hand up in surrender. "I didn't touch her!"

Leaves crunched under our feet as we walked with only the glow of flashlights to guide us.

"Like hell you didn't," I said, leaning around Stewart to point my light at Mason's face. "*Oh Courtney, let me show you some self-defense moves.* Everyone knows that game, Mason."

"Just because you were a sleazeball at seventeen doesn't mean I am, too."

I dove around Stewart, reaching for Mason's shirt, but she jumped between us again, gripping the front of my jacket and shoving me backwards. "Enough! Get in the middle with Blake."

Staring right at Mason, I said, "We'll finish this conversation later."

I shuffled next to Blake, who looked mildly amused. "I'm starting to get the impression you don't play well with others."

"Not when they keep insisting on messing around with my sister. She's freakin' fourteen. Seriously." I glanced at Blake and then shut my mouth, remembering his weird relationship with Kendrick at several different ages. At least I never had to encounter an infant Holly or even any version younger than seventeen. Blake looked over his shoulder and then back at me. Holly and Courtney were quite a ways behind us. I could hardly make out who was who. Dad was even farther back, bringing up the rear.

Blake reached a hand toward my ear and then quickly stuck something inside it. He lifted his eyebrows. I opened my mouth to respond and then I heard Courtney's voice coming through my ear.

He'd bugged my sister? When? Maybe Blake has more skill than I realized. And maybe this was a less violent method of finding out what was up with Mason and my sister. Of course, leave it to Saint Blake to come up with the peaceful solution. Then again, he did express a desire to cause a deadly explosion at Eyewall headquarters. *That totally doesn't count as peaceful.*

"I don't care if Jackson's pissed off at me," Courtney said. "He needs to chill out. He's, like, so intense all the time. I don't know where it's coming from. My dad's being overprotective, I can understand, but not Jackson."

"Uh-huh," Holly said dismissively.

"Do you have any brothers?" Courtney asked. "Or sisters?"

"Nope, just me."

"Maybe you're lucky then. It's like he exists for the sole purpose of agitating me," Courtney said. "You know, he used to make these Lego dynamite minefields and steal my dolls and then leave ransom notes in my room. Not to mention the fact that he killed my hamster. Now he's taken up the hobby of controlling my life. As if I don't already have a parent to do that."

Blake kept his eyes straight ahead, watching Mason and Stewart as if he was giving me privacy while I invaded my sister's.

"Didn't look like you hated him all that much yesterday when you were cleaning up after him, watching him vomit buckets of blood," Holly said, her voice low and free of any emotion.

"You're right. I didn't mean that." Courtney was quiet for several seconds, then finally spoke again. "So what's going on with you and my brother?"

"What's going on with you and Mason?" Holly's response was

such a quick reflex, it was like she couldn't turn off her inner agent anymore.

"Mason is . . ." Courtney said, and my hands balled up inside my pockets. "Really interesting. I don't think I've ever met anyone like him before. He's super smart but not about everything."

Yeah, like believing me when I say that I'm going to kick his ass if he messes with my sister.

"So Jackson's overreacting about you guys?" Holly asked.

"Totally," Courtney said. "Now tell me what's going on with you and my brother? Don't say nothing. I know it's not nothing."

How did she know?

"It's not nothing," Holly said.

"I knew it!" Courtney squealed. "I've seen how he looks at you. I don't care what he says, it's more than friendly."

"That's how guys look at you after they've seen you naked," Holly said.

What?

"What? When?" Courtney asked.

Finally, some emotion broke through Holly's voice and she laughed. "I'm kidding."

"Okay, not funny." Courtney laughed, too, though. "But seriously, he's pretty cute, right? He plays guitar, too, like really well. And sings."

What the hell is she doing? Fixing me up with Holly? The irony was almost hilarious.

"I'm sure he's a regular rock star," Holly said. "I wouldn't expect anything less from Jackson."

Hmm . . . not sure what that means . . .

"You should see him at fourteen. He's kind of short, but my best friend, Kelly, has a megacrush on him. I'm paranoid every time she sleeps over that she'll sneak into his room and steal some underwear for her shrine to Jackson or something."

Uh . . . what?

"Kelly," Holly mumbled. "She lives in the building on Eighty-seventh Street, right? Blond hair, big boobs . . ."

"Yeah . . ." Courtney answered slowly. "Maybe not the big-boobs part."

"Well, she'll get them," Holly said. "She'll buy them, actually. And if you do make it back to your present, you can tell Kelly to hold off on the shrine because Jackson will come around eventually. May of 2007, if I remember right. They'll hook up and it'll last about two weeks."

Shit. She wasn't bluffing yesterday when she said she knew my history.

"Oh. My. God," Courtney said, enunciating every word. "You have to tell me more! What else do you know?"

"Apparently not everything," Holly said with an edge to her voice. "Hold up a sec, Courtney . . . you've got something on your back."

I heard the plastic crunch against the ground and then a high-pitched squeal ripped through my ear. "Fuck!"

Blake's head snapped in my direction and then Mason and Stewart stopped in front of us, turning quickly and pointing guns at every empty space. I yanked the spy gear from my ear and pressed it back into Blake's hand.

"Sorry, stubbed my toe," I said to Stewart and Mason.

Stewart rolled her eyes at me and then continued on with our hike. I rubbed the hell out of my ear, trying to get rid of the ringing sound. She knew. Holly knew I was listening that whole time. Great.

"Game over," I mumbled to Blake.

He glanced wearily at me. "Maybe it was a bad idea anyway."

We walked in silence for a good thirty minutes. Just as the sun was starting to lift over the horizon, allowing us to conserve our flashlight power, Dad, Courtney, and Holly caught up to us. Holly walked between me and Blake, keeping her eyes forward, giving no indication that she'd caught us spying on her and Courtney. "It's too quiet, Jackson, you should sing us a song. I hear you're pretty good."

"He's too busy telling everyone what to do," Courtney said from my other side.

I decided to keep my anger under control because Holly had made a good point earlier. I tossed my arm around my sister and gave her shoulders a squeeze. "I never did say thank you for yesterday, for cleaning up my bloody mess and staying with me."

Her shoulders relaxed like she couldn't hold on to her anger either. "You would have done it for me."

I closed my eyes, fighting a dozen emotions, knowing that I was never brave like that at Courtney's age. She should know that. Why did she make it sound like I was this great person when I wasn't? I hadn't been then, and now . . . *I'm still a work in progress.*

Since I couldn't confirm Courtney's declaration, I pulled her closer and kissed the top of her head. "I'm sorry," I whispered into her hair.

She looked up at me, questions in her eyes . . . *sorry for what?* I shrugged and shook my head and she didn't ask me anything else.

Dad's gaze was on us, I felt it without even looking over. Then he cleared his throat and pointed through the trees. "This is the end of the forest here. Let's scope it out before we walk any farther."

Without any warning, a gunshot rang through the silent morning air. All of us dropped to the ground. Instinctively, I reached for Holly, tossing an arm over her.

She threw my arm back at me. "I'd kick you in the face again but I don't think Blake's had enough time to grow more blood."

Holly glanced around and then sprang to her feet after seeing Stewart and Mason doing the same.

"Idiot civilians," Stewart said, looking right at Blake and Courtney. "Stay behind us." She turned her eyes to me. "Think you can hold that gun steady, Junior?"

"Steady enough to scare someone."

She exchanged a look with Dad. He nodded, allowing me to stay up front with the big kids. From the corner of my eye, I saw Holly angling her body so it was directly in front of Courtney's.

"A lot of them don't speak standard English," Blake said, moving forward. "Better let me communicate."

I froze to my spot. "Wait . . . *them?*"

Courtney was right. I noticed nearly everyone else staring at Blake, waiting for him to explain.

"Usually they hide . . ." he said, stuttering through his words. "They're harmless, seriously."

"They?" Dad said, through his teeth. I could tell he was more than pissed about being sent on this mission without all the information.

"Basically, they're rebels but Ludwig calls them rejects." Blake tugged on his ponytail. "To him, they're failed experiments. Ludwig keeps them inside the force field, too, but they have implants under their skin to prevent them from entering the forest."

"Did Ludwig give them guns, too?" Mason snapped.

"It's probably just a flare."

I wasn't sure what to think about this new revelation but there were a hell of a lot of dots on that map Grayson had showed us the other day.

The sky was nearly all the way lit up now as we approached full morning light. The forest came to a dead stop and a huge clearing of dirt and grass stood before us. We stepped out of the forest and into the wide-open world again. Tan-and-green-colored tents stood off in the distance, patched in various places. It occurred to me right then that it was a very strong possibility we were in a future version of Central Park.

As we walked, putting the trees and woods behind us, there was no sign of anyone. Not even the slightest sound of movement despite the flare we had clearly heard only minutes ago.

"Do you think it was a signal? Maybe to tell everyone to hide?" Courtney asked Blake.

"Probably." He pointed in the distance, where I could just make out a small hill if I squinted hard enough. "That's where the controls are."

Dad scanned the area and then did a once-over of our group. "Holly, come with me, we'll test out those fingerprints of yours. Blake, you, too. Stewart and Mason, follow behind and position yourself at the base of the hill, stay on the lookout." Dad turned to me and Courtney. "You two stay right here—"

"I'm going with you and Holly," I said immediately. "Stewart can stay with Courtney and Mason can be on his own at the bottom of the hill."

"We don't need a huge entourage crowded around the control box." Dad lifted his eyebrows, communicating silently with me.

Oh, right. He had said earlier he was going to talk to Holly. Did he mean right now? Was this really the best time?

I shrugged and took my position next to Courtney. I had to trust him, he knew what he was doing. Courtney and I watched as everyone headed away from us. She sat down right in the dirt, stretching out her legs. After a quick glance around the area, I plopped down next to her.

We had only been sitting in silence for about five minutes when Courtney tugged on the sleeve of my shirt.

"Jackson," she whispered. "Look."

I peeled my eyes from the direction of the hill—my current focal point—and caught sight of what had startled Courtney. "Holy shit . . . is that . . . a *baby*?"

CHAPTER TWELVE

DAY 14. JUST AFTER SUNRISE

Okay, so maybe baby wasn't an accurate description considering it was walking, but it wasn't a kid either. Emily's a kid and this . . . little person . . . was less than half her size.

I quietly rose to my feet and Courtney did the same beside me. We walked in its direction, abandoning our post. The baby continued to wobble toward us, still about two hundred feet away. It wore a T-shirt and sand-colored cloth over its backside as a diaper. Blond hair stuck out from the sides of its head and its skinny little legs and feet were bare despite the chilly morning air.

"Where'd it come from?" I whispered to Courtney.

She pointed off in the distance, toward one of those tents I'd seen earlier.

"You watched it walk all the way from there and you're just now getting my attention?" I hissed at her.

She pressed a finger to her lips and glared at me to be quiet.

I glanced over my shoulder, toward the hill, hoping to see Blake and Dad emerging soon. Why didn't we have coms units? I scanned the area everyone else had walked toward, squinting into the sun, trying to spot Stewart or Mason. When I turned my attention back to the baby, a little blond girl had emerged from the bushes. A giant T-shirt covered her all the way to her knees, but her feet were also bare. Courtney and I both stood there stunned as she swiped the baby up in one swift motion and took off for the tents in the distance.

What the hell just happened?

"Did you see that girl earlier, too?" I asked

"No, she must have been hiding in the bushes the whole time we've been here," Courtney said. "Maybe she's the one that set off the flare. Maybe the baby came looking for her. They could be sisters? Or brother and sister?"

"Courtney. Jackson." Dad's voice came from the distance. Seconds later, he appeared at our sides with Blake, Holly, Stewart, and Mason.

All of us were now shielding our eyes from the sun, which had quickly turned very bright, heating up the air around us. I still hadn't gotten used to this weird day-and-night weather.

"We need to head back," Blake said. "It's getting hot really quick and we didn't bring much water."

Dad peeled his eyes from the tent area and nodded his agreement. "Come on. Let's move out!"

"But Dad, we just saw—" Courtney protested.

I shook my head slightly, hoping she'd get the hint. We could discuss this when we got back to camp, where we had access to plenty of water and wouldn't shrivel up like raisins.

We entered the woods quickly and began our journey, drifting between the trees. "Okay, so what's the report? Is the control box there like Stewart said?"

"Yes," Dad answered. "And we tested it out. Holly's fingerprints scanned perfectly and she stepped through the force field without setting off the alarm."

"And you came back?" I asked, only joking.

"What was I supposed to do?" Holly snapped. "Walk into Eyewall headquarters and put on a uniform?"

"So what's the plan for escape day?" I wiped sweat from my forehead with the bottom of my T-shirt. I caught Holly staring at my stomach. Feeling self-conscious, I quickly dropped my shirt, covering the big ugly scar I was pretty sure she'd been looking at.

Her cheeks flushed and she turned her head, facing forward again.

Dad opened his mouth to respond to my question but Mason interrupted him. "Are we not going to talk about the big elephant in the room?"

"What elephant?" Courtney and I said at the same time.

Mason kept his eyes on Dad as we walked. "The fact that Jackson left his post and dragged Courtney with him. What the hell was that about? You can't do that shit when we're walking into some strange place. You didn't see me and Stewart moving from our guard spots. We weren't even watching the area between the woods and the hill. You left us wide open for an attack from behind."

Wow, that's a very anticlimactic elephant. Obviously Mason is digging for things to pin on me. Or maybe he has some irrational paranoia about being attacked from behind.

Dad shot a glance at me, lifting his eyebrows. "Mason's right, Jackson. Everyone has to be able to trust you in these situations. You cannot, under any circumstances, leave your post."

Okay, guess Dad's going to patronize this irrational concern of Mason's. I rolled my eyes. "We walked like thirty feet away. I wouldn't exactly call that abandoning our post."

"A baby wandered right up to us," Courtney said. "What were we supposed to do? And there was a little girl hiding in the bushes. She's probably the one who set off the flare."

Mason had clamped his mouth shut the second Courtney had started talking. *I guess if it's Courtney's fault, he isn't going to whine about it.* Our walking pace had increased significantly as if the urgency of the oncoming heat wave pushed us forward faster.

"And I'm pretty sure I saw more people out there where those tents are. How come those people can't come into the woods or our area?" she asked Blake. "You said they couldn't pass through here but we can?"

He scratched the back of his head, diverting his eyes from Courtney's. "They have trackers embedded in their skin. They'll get shocked if they pass through the invisible boundaries."

"What? Like a dog collar?" Courtney stared at Blake incredulously as if to say, *you've got to be kidding me.* And I couldn't help agreeing with my sister. It seemed very inhumane.

Blake opened his mouth and then shut it again quickly, not sure how to respond.

"Well, we're going back, right?" Courtney asked.

"To escape?" Dad said. "Yes, but probably not for a couple days. We have to wait for—"

"No, I mean to help them." Courtney looked from one of us to the other as if her point couldn't be more clear. "They probably need food and clothes. That baby had almost nothing on."

"Courtney," Dad said. "We don't know what they have. Just because your brief assessment provided one scenario—"

Courtney jumped in front of us, stopped walking, and turned to face the entire group. "You didn't see it either!" She turned to me, looking totally desperate for help. "Tell them, Jackson!"

There wasn't much to tell other than what she'd already stated, but I was pretty sure my silence would further her frustration. "Um . . . yeah, there was a baby and . . ."

Courtney folded her arms across her chest and I could see she was seconds from stamping her foot and throwing a tantrum right here in the woods. Because despite my sister's heart of gold, there was no way to shake the privileged, spoiled kid out of her. And Courtney was far more spoiled than me. She had almost always gotten her way with Dad.

"Then we can all go back and get a more accurate assessment right now," she demanded.

Holly shrugged and turned to Dad. "I'll go back with her if that's what she really wants."

"Me, too," Mason chimed in. "We can get some pictures."

"No one is going back there, understood?" Dad said sharply. "We're returning to Grayson, Lonnie, and Sasha and we're going to finalize our plan to get out of this year."

Courtney didn't budge from her spot. "We have tons of food, clothes, water, medical supplies. If we're leaving and we're going out that way, then we should bring them the supplies. We're not going to need any of it, right? We don't even have to go all the way over to the tents. We can just leave some stuff in the field for them to get, can't we?"

"I don't know, honey," Dad said. "We don't know anything

about what you saw. Let's see what Grayson and Lonnie think, all right?"

"You're just saying that so I'll shut up about it. I can tell you're not going to do anything and neither is anyone else. There are babies, Dad. Babies!" She was so determined, I could see the tears about to show themselves. "I don't care what you say, I'm getting some stuff and I'm going back there. Jackson will come with me. This is just like . . . just like . . ." Courtney closed her eyes, her tongue resting on the roof of her mouth. "The green . . . the green hair . . ."

"Green hair?" I said.

It was Holly who leaped toward Courtney first as her eyes rolled up in the back of her head. I felt my heart stop, the only sound in my ears was the rush of blood and a dull ringing as my limbs went numb.

All I could do was watch as Holly and Dad caught my sister in what seemed like slow motion, lowering her to the ground. I hadn't seen this happen the first time and neither had Dad. Courtney had been in gym class and I'd been clear on the other side of the school building, in Geometry. I heard the buzz in the hallway, the slightly abnormal sounds of something going on during class. A girl who had sat behind me got a text about Courtney's seizure and told me what had happened even before the principal came in to say that they had already taken her to the hospital and that my dad was there and I was supposed to go meet him right away. But I never had to watch this. By the time I saw her, she was almost normal again, despite the horrible news Dr. Melvin had delivered.

Through the roar of blood in my ears, I watched her body shaking in that horrifyingly scary way and fought the urge to cover my face and pretend it wasn't happening. I heard Holly's voice break through the numbness as she spoke to Dad, "What do we do?"

Dad closed his eyes for a second, his face filled with so much pain, it was as if he'd just been stabbed with a knife. "Nothing . . . wait for it to stop."

Mason shrank back away from me and Dad, obviously not wanting to get in our way.

Blake knelt next to Holly and leaned over to loosen the top buttons on Courtney's shirt. I felt someone's hand on my arm and then saw Stewart from the corner of my eye.

After the longest sixty seconds of my entire life, Courtney finally stopped shaking. Her breathing was erratic, her eyes wide open, totally frightened as she stared up at the trees. Dad touched her cheek and then lifted her head, pulling her into his arms.

"What happened? I don't feel good . . . my head hurts . . . really bad." She buried her face in the front of Dad's shirt and started crying.

"I know . . . I know . . . it's okay." Dad stood quickly, as if he weren't holding a hundred-pound girl, and walked briskly and with purpose back to camp.

I, on the other hand, couldn't seem to get my legs to work and Stewart had to tug my arm to start the moving process. Even if I could have offered to carry Courtney, I knew Dad wouldn't let me.

All any of us could do was follow him.

DAY 14. MIDDAY

I leaned against the outside of the makeshift hospital. I'd been standing in nearly the same spot for hours. Finally, Grayson came out the front door and headed right toward me. He took his time speaking, first leaning against the wall next to me and then offering me one of the horrible meal bars, which I took but didn't open. The idea of eating right now was almost unfathomable.

"I don't have access to MRI or X-ray machines," he said, staring straight ahead at the fire pit. "All I have is the timeline your dad gave me based on when her symptoms began and when she . . . when she . . ."

"Yeah," I said. "I get it."

"I don't have chemo. I don't have radiation machines," he said. I kicked the dirt with my toe. "Not like it would help, anyway."

"True."

This was already so painful, I didn't know how I would make the next move, but I had to. "Can I go in now?"

Grayson nodded and then patted my arm before walking toward the technology building, where I'm sure everyone else had been waiting for his arrival so they could recommence the planning phase. They had even grabbed Emily to ask her some questions after she had stood next to me for nearly an hour, doing nothing but holding my hand.

I took a deep breath before opening the front door and walking inside. Dad's voice came from the same room I'd nearly bled to death in yesterday . . . *happy family memories*. The door was open and I stopped to listen before letting either of them see me.

"Dr. Melvin found the tumors the first time. He did everything he could but nothing worked," Dad said.

"Maybe something else will work?" Courtney said. "Maybe there's something Dr. Melvin didn't know about? Something brand-new?"

I rested my forehead against the wall beside the door, taking in deep, shaking breaths, but finally succumbed to letting a few tears fall from my eyes. And Dad. This was killing him and he just sat there beside her and told her everything all over again.

"I'm sorry, sweetheart. I'm so sorry. I wish I could tell you we can fix it, but I can't."

"What about Jackson?" Courtney sniffed. "Is he okay? Does he have tumors, too?"

I squeezed my eyes shut, my gut twisting into a million knots, and I thought I might get sick right then. Sick from pain, from grief.

"No, he doesn't have any."

"Good," she said. "I'm just . . . I just . . . I don't want to die . . . I really don't. Not like this."

That was it for me. I couldn't take another second of it. I couldn't believe we were about to go through this all over again, and this time I'd get a front-row seat to my sister's death. The image of Courtney lying in a casket popped into my mind and I had to stop and hold my breath until it dissolved.

I flew out of the building and headed straight toward the lake, not caring if the sun was insanely hot. I didn't know how much time had passed before anyone found me. All I knew was I'd tossed about thirty handfuls of rocks into the lake, failing at each attempt to skip them more than two times.

"Well . . . the good news is that it looks like we're gonna get out of here."

Never had I imagined it would be Holly who came to find me first. That was the only reason I halted in my rock throwing, at least for a few seconds.

"That's great," I said. "Now you'll be able to go back to your Eyewall buddies in 2009."

She grabbed the rocks from my hand and tossed them on the ground. "Don't be an asshole."

I swallowed back the lump in my throat. "Sorry, I didn't mean that."

"I know." She took a step closer to me. "Grayson said your dad told her everything. How did she take it?"

I had to work hard to keep my voice steady. "Not well."

"I can imagine." Holly let out a breath. "How did she take it the first time?"

"The first time . . ." I picked the stones back up and tossed another at the water, watching it hop twice before vanishing. "She was told things were bad, but they would fight it and fighting it would probably make her very sick. She wasn't told she was going to die. Today, my dad said those exact words to her and I don't know how he did it. How can he sit next to her and watch? I must be a self-centered bastard to be out here and not in there."

"You probably are," Holly said. "But if you think it's more noble to head back in there and talk about dying, then that's what you should do."

The word "noble" struck a chord in me and I turned quickly to Holly. "That's it!"

I dropped the rocks back into the grass and walked toward the technology building. Holly had to jog to catch up with me. "What are you doing?" she asked.

"I'm getting some food and water and stuff," I said, feeling as confident as Courtney had sounded in the woods. "You know, to leave in the field for Dr. Ludwig's rejects or whatever Blake called them."

"Right now?"

I shrugged and kept walking, increasing the length of my stride. It felt good to have something important to do. "Yeah, right now."

"Can I come with you?"

I stopped for a second, turning to Holly to see if she was joking. She wasn't. I could tell by her expression. "Um . . . okay. We'll be able to bring more stuff if there are two of us, right?"

"Uh-huh," she said. "But just so you know, I still hate your guts."

"You aren't the first girl to tell me that."

CHAPTER THIRTEEN

DAY 14. LATE AFTERNOON

Weighed down with supplies, we were fifteen minutes into the woods before I spoke again. "What do you miss most from 2009?"

Only the sound of dried leaves crunching under our boots answered me as Holly shifted the heavy weight of her backpack. I tightened my grip on the straps of my own pack and wished she wouldn't be pissed off if I offered to carry the load for her.

She looked sideways at me before answering. "I don't even know where to start. Coffee? Real food besides fish and those disgusting meal bars, jeans that actually fit me? Having more than one bra? My mom . . ."

I remembered her standing in that hellhole of an apartment that Marshall had given me while I held her at gunpoint, shocked to find out Holly had become part of the CIA and had broken into my place on an Eyewall mission. She'd pleaded with me, thinking I was about to kill her, to let her call her mother . . . *I just want to hear her voice,* she'd said.

I wanted to reach out and touch her arm or take her hand, but I could already sense her shrinking away from me as if she'd said too much. "Remember that night I caught you snooping around my apartment?"

"I remember," Holly said, not letting an ounce of emotion leak through her voice.

"Did you mean it when you asked to call your mom? Kendrick and Stewart were convinced that was code for something, like you were trying to get help from Eyewall in case they happened to be listening in."

"Nobody was listening in." Holly kicked some dirt up with her tennis shoe. "I was sure you were going to kill me and yes, I wanted to call my mom."

There were so many things I wanted to say right then, so many important and probably extremely sappy things, but I didn't because it wouldn't have the impact I wanted it to have.

"I miss Central Park." I used my foot to force a broken tree branch out of our path. "The 2009 version. I miss thinking the world is much smaller."

"Me, too." Then with another glance in my direction, she added, "I'm sorry about Courtney. This must be so hard for you to go through all over again."

I adjusted the straps on my very heavy backpack. "It's different this time, though."

"How so?"

I watched Holly's face carefully for any sign of sarcasm or anger, but she looked fine. Curious, even. "I wasn't there the first time. I was so scared. Not just scared for Courtney, but scared of watching someone die, scared of realizing my own mortality. I know it's selfish—"

"You were fourteen," Holly said, as if this excused everything.

"Yeah, true. But then I went back to see her not too long ago and I watched it happen." I let out a breath, fighting off the emotion threatening to take over. "It was a half-jump so it didn't change anything but I needed to be there." *And you were the one who helped me see that,* I wanted to say, but couldn't. "I realized something after that. I think when you're actually about to die, you accept it. You're not afraid anymore. That fear of death is the strongest of any fear and it's also a gift. It means it's not your time yet. And when it is my time, I'll know and I'll stop being afraid. I'll stop wanting to fight it."

"So like, if a bullet hit you in the back of the head in the next five seconds, you'd be ready for that?" Holly asked, her eyebrows arched, her voice skeptical.

"I've thought about that," I said carefully. "Like the people who die suddenly in an accident or something." *Like Mason blowing up.* "I have a theory if you want to hear it . . . ?"

Holly shifted her body so she faced me more than the path. "Okay?"

"I think time slows down. Like you're dying quickly to the people around you or even instantly, but in your mind, it takes longer for it to happen. And it works the other way, too. Like with the terminally ill, like Courtney. You're probably mostly gone before you're actually gone in the physical world."

Holly turned her eyes back to the path in front of us. "And then what?"

I laughed under my breath. "I haven't figured that out yet."

"But you think it will be easier?" she asked. "With Courtney this time?"

"Not easier. Just that I'll be focused on being sad, on grieving, and less on fearing my own mortality. And I'll be sad for my dad this time. Before, I couldn't shake the thought that he wanted it to be me instead."

"That's not true," she said right away. "You didn't see him when you were—"

"I know."

"I like your dad," Holly added. "He makes me wonder about my own dad. I've never met him and it never seemed like a big thing, but now . . . now I kinda want to know more."

"Have you asked my dad about that?" She shook her head. "You should. It's possible he might know something."

We had reached the edge of the forest now and both of us stepped into the brighter sunlight and examined the field between here and the tents. We left the clothes, blankets, stacks of meal bars, and all the water we could carry halfway between the tents and the woods.

The second we got into the woods, Holly stripped off her backpack and rolled her shoulders and neck out. "At least it's a lighter load on the way back."

Without thinking about it, I stepped behind her and started rubbing her shoulders with both my hands. She stiffened immediately under the weight of my touch, but I didn't let go this time. "What can you possibly gain by being stubborn right now?"

She looked over her shoulder at me, eyes narrowed, but must have had no argument to win over mine because she relaxed under my hands and stayed put.

"Jackson?"

I ran my thumbs along her shoulder blades, carefully working over all the places that I knew were sore on me from carrying that bag. "Yeah?"

"Lonnie wants to take Emily," she said, letting all the words out so quickly I knew it must have been something she wasn't supposed to tell me. "When we escape and most of us jump back to 2009, Lonnie is going to a different year, with Blake and Grayson, and she says Emily will fit in better there and be easier to hide."

My hands froze on Holly's shoulders. I wasn't sure what to feel at that moment. Emily was tied to me in this way I couldn't explain and yet . . . "If they think she has the best chance of surviving with them, then I guess . . . I guess that's good."

Holly stepped out of my reach and started moving forward again. "I thought you'd be upset. With what's happening to Courtney and everything. Plus, she seems really attached to you."

"I think it's the other way around," I joked.

Before Holly could respond, I felt something in the air shift and panic churned in my veins. "Oh shit. Not again."

The last image I saw before the metallic scent filled my nostrils was Holly, walking backwards, away from me toward a tree, her back hitting it as she slid down to sit on the ground.

It felt like the forest floor was being pulled from underneath me and I fell so fast, the blur of Holly's body below me, out of my reach.

Unlike the last time we got hit with memory gas, I knew what was happening right from the beginning, but all I could feel was the falling sensation and that's why it took me so long to react. Finally, I fumbled for my shirt, pulling it over my nose and holding my breath as the world swirled below me until it changed to the green and brown and black of the woods.

I shook my head, trying to turn the world right side up again. The first thing I saw was Holly, still sitting on the ground soundless, knees pulled to her chest, face pressed into her knees, her entire body trembling.

What did she see? Was it Adam?

"Holly?" I approached her slowly, remembering how she'd yelled at me the last time. She didn't respond, but I could see her back rising and falling with each deep breath. "Holly . . . ?"

I touched her back, barely resting a hand on it, and she didn't move or lift her head. She was lost in something, somewhere I couldn't bring her back.

All I could think to do was sit down on the ground beside her, waiting for her to snap out of it. Slowly, with several instances of hesitation, I put my arms around her, pulling her all the way against me while she kept her face pressed against her knees.

After several long minutes, her muscles relaxed, her breaths got a little bit deeper, and she leaned into me, her arms dropping from her knees.

"Don't move, okay?" she whispered, without lifting her head. "I feel really nauseous. It'll pass, I'm sure. Just don't move."

I froze, not even allowing myself so much as a wiggle from one of my fingers. Sweat trickled down her neck and through her hair. Her skin felt clammy under my fingers. Eventually, she uncurled her legs out in front of her and they overlapped one of mine. Her cheek fell against my chest and her eyes opened.

"Better?" I asked, and she nodded. I pushed the sweaty hair off the side of her face and tucked it behind her ear.

Her eyelids fluttered shut again. "I thought I was going to puke a few seconds ago and now I feel like falling asleep. Are you okay?"

"I'm fine." I pressed my face against the top of her head, closing my own eyes and holding on to the fact that she was here, in my grip, not free-falling ahead of me. If I didn't let go of her, I wouldn't have to face that memory a second time, even if the gas did hit us again.

"For someone who was just acquaintances with another version of me," Holly mumbled into my shirt, "you seem very comfortable cuddling up to me. We've ended up like this, how many times now? I haven't seen you having hug sessions with anyone else."

I was too relieved to hear some semblance of normal returning to Holly's voice to worry about covering up my behavior. I rested my chin on the top of her head. "I do this with everyone in private. I cuddled with Stewart for an hour yesterday and then Mason this morning."

She laughed. "Now I know you're lying. Stewart is the least cuddly person in existence and Mason . . . well, I don't think he's exactly your BFF right now. And I would totally move if I could. It feels like I've just finished a marathon. Plus, I'm freezing."

I pulled away from her a little and lifted her chin, examining her face carefully. Pink now covered her cheeks and the sweat was gone. I picked up one of her hands and felt it shaking in mine. "Have you eaten anything today?"

She sat up straighter, eyebrows lifting. "No. I haven't actually."

"You look dehydrated. Feverish, too." I pulled the remaining meal bar from my bag along with a bottle of water. I opened the water first and handed it to Holly, who was now leaning against the tree again. She took several long sips and then handed it back to me.

"Have *you* eaten anything today?"

"Not much," I admitted, taking a long drink before holding up the meal bar. "Should we split this? It's protein-flavored. Hard to resist."

Holly nodded, wrinkling her nose. "It'll be a miracle if I can manage to choke down half of it."

"Me, too."

"Jackson!" a voice called.

Holly and I both squinted into the nearly dark trees before jumping to our feet.

"Holly!" a second voice called. *Blake.* Of course he was the one to go searching for Holly.

I rolled my eyes in her direction. "Your BFF is here to save you from me."

She mustered some strength despite not looking too well at the moment and shoved me hard enough to cause me to stumble into a tree as Dad, Blake, and Mason appeared in front of us.

Dad's dark hair and forehead were covered in sweat and his face reflected that of an extremely pissed-off agent. "What the hell were you thinking?"

"You can't leave without telling anyone," Mason added, though he didn't have any of the edge that Dad had in his voice.

Blake's eyes bounced between me, Dad, and Holly, then he nodded toward the path ahead. "Want to walk back with me?" he said to Holly, who scrambled to his side, following quickly, probably wanting nothing to do with this domestic dispute.

"You go, too, Mason," Dad said, his eyes still focused on me.

Mason threw a glare in my direction and then jogged to catch up with the other two. I dropped my gaze to the forest floor and kicked a few sticks. "What's his problem?"

"Mason?" Dad folded his arms across his chest. "He's speaking on Courtney's behalf. She's pissed off at you for getting everyone worried."

I felt like I was eight again, facing Dad after watching Courtney's rodent pet commit suicide. "I was doing what she wanted to do. Drop off supplies to those poor people. All the little kids."

"I figured that," he snapped. "But you have no idea what you're dealing with. And neither does Courtney, no matter how badly she wants to help. I can't keep doing this with you, Jackson."

I finally looked up at him. "Doing what?"

He scrubbed his hands over his face. "Dealing with this fear of letting you out of my sight. Every time I do, I have to wonder if you're going to do something stupid and get yourself killed."

I balled up my hands and then released them, letting out an

angry breath. "Fine. Whatever. I'll stay under your careful watch from now on 'cause God knows I can't be trusted to keep myself alive—"

The metallic, rusty smell invaded my nostrils, cutting me off. I groaned loudly, closing my eyes. "I hate this shit."

This time, my mind sifted through a dozen images, each holding itself still for only a millisecond. *Adam bleeding. Holly falling. Courtney taking her last breath.* I pushed the memories aside. The world around me returned to normal so fast I wondered if I'd imagined it. I had my answer the second I opened my eyes.

Dad's arms were now uncrossed, his face blazing with anger. His pistol pointed right at my head. "Do you have any idea how long I've wanted to be in this exact position? How long I've wanted to watch you die right at my feet?"

My heart took off on a full-out sprint, my hands lifting in the air. "Dad, please . . . *don't.*"

He took two long steps toward me, leaving only five feet between us. "I want you to feel a few seconds of that fear I've lived with every day for seventeen years. But this isn't just for me. It's for my father, for Eileen. For the years I've spent waiting for you to hurt Jackson. I want you to feel it right now. I want it to be the last thing you feel before you take your final breath."

I was feeling the fear. That was for certain. "Dad, it's me, Jackson! It's just the memory gas!"

His face twisted with rage and before another word was uttered, he pulled the trigger. But instead of squeezing my eyes shut and waiting for the inevitable, my vision zoomed in on the bullet, a tunnel forming around it, the speed quickly decelerating, until it become clear to my conscious mind that my next move was to dive to my left.

My body hit the hard ground with a thud as my left shoulder landed on a giant tree root. I waited—heart pounding and lungs constricting—to feel the sting of a bullet. To feel my world collapsing around me. Dad had been too close to miss. Too close to allow any human enough time to move before getting hit. But there was no sting, no bullet lodged in my body.

I had dodged that bullet. And I had no idea how the hell I'd done it.

CHAPTER FOURTEEN

"Oh God," Dad whispered. "Jackson, please tell me I didn't really fire."

I peered up at Dad, seeing his face transform right before my eyes. He had snapped out of the memory and was left with an aimed gun he couldn't remember drawing. I slowly rose to my feet as he looked over at me in horror.

"No," I lied. "You didn't fire."

"Thomas," he muttered. "I saw Thomas."

"I know, Dad." I edged closer, trying to assure him I was unharmed. "Well, at least I figured it was him you saw."

Something like realization snapped onto his face and suddenly he looked cold and distant. He swallowed hard before asking, firm and direct, "Did I fire at you? Did I actually pull the trigger?"

"I'm totally fine."

He shook his head, hands moving quickly as he opened the gun and counted the bullets. He stalked across the forest until he found the hole his bullet had put in an oak tree behind me.

After I'd dodged it.

Yeah, I hadn't forgotten about that part yet.

He walked toward me again and held his gun out to me. I stared at it, not sure what to do. "Take it!" he demanded.

"Dad, you didn't know what you were doing." My eyes met his, and there was so much sadness beyond the cold, agent face he'd formed since coming out of the memory-gas trance.

"Take the damn gun, Jackson," he said more softly, yet somehow forceful and eerie.

I reached out and lifted the weapon from his palm, holding it loosely in my hand. "It's okay. You couldn't help it. I know that."

"It's not okay," he snapped. "Now get out of here. We're not walking back together."

The sky had turned completely dark, throwing a blanket of black over us, leaving him in a shadow cast by a tree behind him.

"Dad," I argued. "Come on. Let's just go back. I shouldn't have left without telling you. It's my fault all of this happened."

"Get out of here now," he repeated slowly, emphasizing each word.

There was nothing I could do to shake him from his terrible guilt so I turned and did as I was told for once, leaving him alone in the woods, my own guilt at the thought of leaving him in that state eating its way through my empty stomach.

There was no arguing that he'd scared the hell out of me. My hands and legs were still shaking. But what scared me even more was the fact that it had been a perfect shot. Assuming I hadn't performed miracles in the form of superhuman movement.

I spent the thirty-minute walk worrying about Dad's mental state, my ability to slow down bullets, and what was coming for Courtney very soon. But my introspection was short-lived. The second I reached the campfire circle, Lonnie was running toward me, the fire blazing behind her. I glanced quickly over my shoulder to see if Dad had changed his mind and followed me anyway.

He hadn't.

"What?" I asked immediately. "Is it Courtney? Is she okay?"

Lonnie shook her head. "It's Emily."

We were already walking briskly toward one of the cabins. "What happened?"

"We don't know," Lonnie said. "She's been like this for hours. Grayson and I thought maybe you'd seen this before from her."

"Seen what?" I asked, frustrated with the lack of information. Was she bleeding to death? Levitating? Dodging bullets?

The cabin door creaked as we stepped inside and took in the situation. The light from a couple candles illuminated the entire room. Holly stood beside Blake, chewing on her nails. Grayson,

Stewart, and Sasha were on the other side, wearing identically concerned and confused expressions.

Emily lay on her stomach on the cabin floor, loose pages from a notebook strewn all around her, her face paler than usual, her right hand moving furiously as she scribbled neat loopy writing that looked very familiar. Tears streamed down her cheeks as she muttered nonstop under her breath, switching from English to Farsi to Russian.

"Emily?" I approached slowly, kneeling beside her. "What are you doing?"

"She won't answer," Grayson said, after we all remained silent for a good ten seconds. "She's filled over a hundred pages and won't stop."

I glanced at the papers, picking one up and bringing it close enough to read. I recognized it immediately. Words stolen from the Tempest Agent Training Diary I'd kept. She'd mimicked my handwriting, my crossed-out words, and the spacing exactly as I'd written it.

"It's my journal," I said finally. "She read it before we came here."

I reached over and gently placed my hand on top of the page she was currently trying to fill. Her little fingers froze for a second then she shoved my arm out of the way with more force than I thought possible from such a tiny person.

"I need to finish," she said, her eyes still locked on the page.

"Finish what?" Grayson asked before I could. "Emily, take a break and talk to us."

"It's been four hours, kid," Stewart added. "Give it a rest."

Emily shook her head furiously. "I. *Can't.*"

Holly stepped closer, kneeling on Emily's other side. "You can't stop thinking about things that you don't want to think about, right?"

"Yes." Emily lifted her head for a split second, looking at Holly like a savior before sliding a page across the floor and ripping a blank sheet from a spiral-bound notebook. "Can I give it to you? I have to give it to someone. I can't keep it. I just can't anymore."

More big fat tears rolled down her cheeks and she sniffed back a sob. Catching her off guard, I reached for the pen, removing it from her grip before she could stop me.

She sprang to her feet, panic all over her face. "Give it back! Give it back, Jackson!"

I tossed the pen across the room to Blake, who snatched it out of thin air without even batting an eyelash. Emily took off toward Blake but Holly caught her around the waist, holding her back.

"Explain what you're writing," Holly said gently, reminding me instantly of my 009 Holly and the voice she used on her six-year-old campers. "And then we'll give you back the pen and all the paper you need."

I stood there helplessly as Emily fought Holly, trying to break away. "Please, give it back. I need to . . . I need to . . . there's too much . . ."

"This isn't helping," Sasha said, throwing a disgusted glance in our direction before stomping toward the cabin door, calling over her shoulder, "Guess I'll be the responsible one and check on the fire."

Grayson completely ignored Sasha as he moved closer, studying Emily's face carefully. "I think she's overloaded. She copies everything. Remembers everything. If I had access to a brain scanner . . . I bet every region of her brain would be lit up—"

"Is that what's wrong?" I asked Emily, desperate to help her calm down so I could figure out where Dad was and check on Courtney. I had more than enough to deal with already. "Have you been reading too much or thinking too much or something?"

From the corner of my eye, I spotted Stewart, picking up a trail of papers, sorting them in a stack, eyes scanning each page quickly before picking up the next one.

"Did you have access to the Eyewall systems before you left?" Grayson asked Emily. "Did you copy information from the system and now you're overloaded?"

Holly glared at him. "God, she's a kid. Not a computer." Then she moved back a little, gripping Emily by the shoulders and looking her right in the eye, blocking Emily's view of the pen resting in Blake's right hand. Emily's head moved from side to side as she tried to see around Holly. "Look at me, Emily!" The little girl's eyes finally paused on Holly's face for a second. "Good. Now close your eyes. Take a break."

I was pinned to the spot, mesmerized by the intensity radiating off both of them. Emily stared hard at Holly, ready to pounce any second.

"It's not what you know that's overwhelming," Holly said. "It's what you're feeling. You can't get rid of that. Putting it on paper won't get rid of it."

More tears slipped down Emily's cheeks and a sob escaped. "I have to. It's too much."

"You just need to feel something else." Holly's voice stayed calm and steady. I completely bought into whatever act she was pulling, but Emily wouldn't. No way. "Fill your head with something else. A poem, maybe? A book?"

The storm calmed in Emily's eyes and she looked as though she might actually be trying to do this. Her voice emerged, tiny and youthful as she muttered under her breath again. The tension began to visibly roll off her shoulders. She looked like she was waking up from a nightmare.

"Those people out there," Emily said to Holly, her voice shaking with more tears. "I've been with them. I got away and I couldn't come back to help them."

"What people?" Stewart said, looking up from the page she'd been reading.

"The ones in the woods that Courtney and Jackson saw today." Emily spoke directly to Holly, not moving her eyes to anyone else in the room. "Thomas . . . Thomas took me there and left me because I wasn't right. Not for him. Not for the experiment. And when I'm older . . . I'm supposed to tell Jackson to leave you, and then another Holly is going to be hurt and then Adam will die and nothing can save Courtney. I couldn't get the blood samples from Lily's parents either."

"Lily Kendrick?" Holly asked, glancing briefly at Blake, who looked stricken by the mention of my Tempest partner.

Emily nodded. "Lily wanted to know what killed them. I need to go back and bring her samples and in my head I keep doing all these things and then watching the effects on the future and it's turning out all wrong. I can't fix it!"

She was breathing so hard, her chest rising and falling rapidly.

My heart completely broke and I knew everyone in the room felt it, too. That weight piled on top of this child was so heavy she'd started to drown in it. But I understood. I understood in a way that I was afraid to admit because I'd felt the same crushing guilt and grief so many times I'd lost count.

But I wasn't eight years old. I wasn't a child who'd never experienced love and had seen nothing but evil and destruction.

"Calm down," Holly said. "You're going to lose your grip again."

Emily sank to her knees, hitting the floor with a thud and falling into Holly's lap, who willingly held her, letting her half cry, half whisper furiously to herself.

While Emily's face was hidden, I tried to communicate silently with Holly. She met my eyes and then nodded toward the door. Slowly, I rose to my feet and tugged Stewart and Lonnie's arms, directing them toward the door and waiting for Blake and Grayson to follow behind us.

The cool night air hit me in the face and I couldn't help glancing out toward the woods, wondering if Dad had returned.

"The child has unmatched intelligence and memory capabilities," Grayson said. "Psychologically, it might just be too much to handle."

"Maybe that's why Thomas ditched her?" Stewart said.

Lonnie just shook her head. The situation was obviously painful for her and she probably didn't want to speak scientifically just yet. Blake stared out at the campfire, lost in thought. "She's not supposed to care. He was banking on her not caring. The caring takes up too much space and time. Literally."

He was right. It went with everything Emily had said to me about Thomas and Ludwig hating that she was like me. And it went with Blake's memory files. The day he went to the future and Thomas told him about his special experiment. When he'd stolen my hair, my DNA, he'd gotten more than he'd wanted from me.

"This is exactly what we'd all been afraid of," Grayson said. "It's why I knew Ludwig and Thomas shouldn't mess with nature."

Just then, I saw Dad emerge from the woods, his gaze met mine for a split second before he turned his back to me and headed toward the lake. I sighed with relief but left him alone because he obviously wasn't ready to talk yet. I walked toward the hospital building instead, hoping the sight of Courtney, still breathing, would help calm me down.

When I walked into the room where I'd slept the first ten days of my stay on Misfit Island, Mason nearly fell out of his chair, his hand dropping to his lap too quickly to not reveal guilt on his part. He was holding her hand. *God, talk about inducing both anger and nausea all at once.* I glared hard at him then turned to Courtney, whose eyes were wiggling open.

I only had to point to the doorway and then Mason scrambled to his feet, exiting without a word of protest. I shut the door and then sat on the side of the bed, waiting for Courtney to unleash some of that anger Mason had mentioned earlier.

"How's Emily?"

I looked at my sister and then let out a heavy sigh before twisting my body and lying beside her, our shoulders touching. "She's messed up, like the rest of us." I hesitated for a second, and then added, "Dad tried to shoot me in the woods."

Courtney bolted upright, staring down at me. *"What?"*

I kept my eyes on the ceiling. "He didn't mean to. It was the memory gas. I don't know what I did, but I dodged the bullet. It was almost like what you did when we first got to this year and we were fighting off those ugly, faceless dudes and you kept vanishing. I slowed down the bullet. Or maybe I slowed down time. And then I fell out of the way."

"Could life possibly get any stranger?" She sank beside me again. "What did Dad say?"

"He took it pretty hard," I admitted, even though Courtney had enough to worry about at the moment. But maybe she'd know what to say to him to make this all right. "He handed over his gun and made me leave him in the woods."

Her mouth hung open. "You didn't, did you?"

"I had to. But he's back already. Avoiding me, but safely returned."

She sighed and reached for my hand. "It's his worst nightmare, Jackson. He's not going to let it go and move on."

"I know." I suddenly felt so exhausted I could hardly keep my eyes open. "I'm going to sleep now," I mumbled, my eyelids fluttering up and down. "Stay here, okay? Don't go."

I never heard her answer, but some part of my mind registered Dad's presence as he took the chair Mason had abandoned earlier.

CHAPTER FIFTEEN

DAY 15. DAWN

I woke up to Courtney's arm thrown across my face, her body taking up seventy-five percent of the bed and mine shoved into the other twenty-five. I was reminded then of why I'd forced her to sleep on the floor of my room all those nights when storms had spooked her.

I carefully moved her arm from my face and extricated myself from the bed, giving my sleeping dad a quick glance before quietly slipping out of the room. We'd have to talk. I knew that. I just wanted to give him more time.

Outside, I stood on the porch of the medical building and looked over toward the lake, where I could make out Sasha and Stewart using a tree trunk as a table to clean fish. Mason had a headset on, gun aimed at the makeshift target, but he wasn't firing yet. Holly stood closer to the lake, her back to me. She had taken up my pointless activity of tossing handfuls of rocks into the water one at a time, attempting to get them to skip. That's when I noticed Blake off to the side of Holly, who seemed completely unaware of his presence as his body moved in a blurred form, over and over again, snatching the rocks she was throwing out of thin air, then tossing them into the lake himself.

Why was no one else seeing this? This was Blake, the guy who didn't have the hand-eye coordination to be confident enough to shoot at a target even once.

An idea formed quickly, but I had to be discreet. His words kept repeating in my head over and over. He'd suffered a similar injury to mine when he landed on Misfit Island. Grayson had to save his life just like he saved mine, and now I'd seemed to develop a few new tricks.

I walked closer to Sasha, the smell of dead fish filling my nostrils, wanting to test my theory on another time jumper first. I removed my key chain from my pocket, and said, "Sasha, catch!" before tossing the keys close enough for her to attempt to grab them but too far for even the most advanced human to actually succeed. Her fingers missed by an entire foot, and she glared at me before walking forward and then bending over to retrieve the keys from the grass.

"What are these for?" she asked.

Stewart's eyes were on me now, too, waiting for some big piece of information. I took the keys out of Sasha's hand, stuffing them back in my pocket. "Nothing. Just saying good morning."

Blake and Holly had stopped their contemplative rock tossing/catching activity and were now watching this exchange. I made sure to catch Blake's eye as I held my hand out to Stewart. "Can I borrow that knife for a second?"

"Want me to clean off the fish guts first?"

"Nope." The knife landed in my palm, the wooden handle slimy from fish blood, the blade aimed at the grass. I flipped my hand around the knife, holding Blake's gaze, my heart beginning to speed up from the adrenaline rush. And then in an instant, I lifted the knife and threw it hard, aiming right at Mason's back. The adrenaline made my vision sharper and that was probably the reason that I saw Blake's body move in a blur of dark hair, red shirt, and blue jeans.

The second I registered the knife in his hand, before anyone could make a move, I snatched Stewart's gun from the back of her pants, and as soon as Mason dove to the ground, I fired at Blake.

One bullet. Two bullets. Three bullets.

He shifted left, then right, then left, the bloody knife still clutched in his right hand, the bullets piercing a large maple tree fifty feet behind him.

Finally, I lowered the gun to my side, ears still ringing from the shots. A second passed, giving me the chance to absorb the shocked faces of the four individuals watching, Mason shouted a string of swear words while peeling himself off the grass and then Stewart was barreling into me, pinning me to the ground.

"What the hell is wrong with you?" she screamed right into my ear, her voice amplified from the ringing in my ears.

Within ten seconds, Mason and Holly stood over me, guns pointed at my head. Sasha took off running, probably to get help, but Blake stood in the same spot near the water, looking completely stunned.

"What just happened?" he muttered, staring right at me, not appearing in the least bit concerned with the fact that I'd attempted to take his life.

"He tried to fucking kill both of us," Mason said, glaring down at me.

"Is it memory gas?" Holly asked, looking at Stewart, who had been standing closest to me.

Blake finally moved toward us. "How did you know I could do that? How do you—"

"I did it yesterday." I grunted out the words, Stewart's weight pressing on me and constricting the air flow to my lungs. "My dad shot at me under the influence of memory gas and he was only five feet away, aiming right at my head, and I saw the bullet clear as day, saw it in slow motion and I fell to the side. I shouldn't have been able to dodge it."

"Okay, but that totally doesn't give you the right to use Blake as your test subject," Holly said.

"You threw keys at Sasha and knives and bullets at Blake?" Stewart asked, but she let up a little, giving me room to sit up.

"No." Blake shook his head. "It's because of our brain damage." His eyes lifted to meet mine. "If you had told me, if you had even hinted at it . . ."

"You couldn't have done it," I finished for him, nodding and feeling a bit of relief that he understood. "I saw you catching the rocks Holly was throwing."

She glanced at him, confused. "You were catching the rocks? But you weren't close enough—"

"Exactly," I said.

Both Holly and Mason lowered their guns and Stewart moved away, sitting back on her heels.

"Maybe you couldn't warn him," Stewart said, "but you could have warned the rest of us."

I shrugged. "I would have talked myself out it. It was completely impulsive."

When I stood up, my hand brushed against Holly's, sending a jolt through my stomach. I laid my hands on her shoulders and turned her body about fifteen degrees. "Don't move."

I walked out farther in the grass, making sure I was lined up with the maple tree in the distance. "All right, now shoot me."

"No way," Holly said, looking disgusted. "Get Mason or Stewart to be your lab partner."

"Gladly," Mason said, already lifting his gun again.

"You have the best aim, Hol. Can't have bullets ricocheting off the trees."

"Do it," Blake instructed, surprising me. "He'll be fine."

"This is so stupid." Holly shook her head but she was already lifting her gun, pointing it at me. Which wasn't the first time I'd been in this position with her, unfortunately. We'd been meeting like this a lot in World A.

As Holly pulled the trigger, I spotted Dad and Sasha running toward us and then pulled my eyes back to focus on the bullet heading straight for my forehead. I stepped two feet to my left and watched the bullet in slow motion as it floated past me and then penetrated the surface of the tree.

"What the hell?" Dad shouted.

"Again," Blake said, staring at the side of Holly's face. "Do it again."

She followed orders and fired four more bullets at me, relaxing a little as I dodged each one. Finally, she lowered her gun, shock filling her expression. "I'm out of ammo."

Dad stopped in front of us, letting out a breath and rubbing his temples. "What is going *on*?"

"Your kid is no longer human and neither is Blake, apparently," Stewart said, then her eyes snapped to me. "And Blondie does not have better aim than me."

"I think we're time-traveling," Blake said, getting everyone's undivided attention. "Inside the electromagnetic pulse. But it's such a small jump, somehow it works. And that explains—"

"Emily," I said, following his train of thought, astonished at this realization.

"Are you sharing a brain now, too?" Mason asked.

"She said she was with the other people on the island," Blake said. "Thomas left her there to rot along with them."

"She told me when I found her in 2009 that Thomas and Ludwig said she wouldn't be able to escape but she did. Somehow, she made it out," I finished.

Holly tucked her gun away. "Well, at least there's hope for two of us getting out of here."

She walked off toward the cabins without an explanation. I was about to call after her but Dad stopped me. "This is what you did yesterday, isn't it? In the woods? You dodged that bullet."

I nodded warily, afraid to say anything else about those freakish few minutes.

Dad closed his eyes briefly, drawing in a quick breath of air. "So you're not quite as vulnerable as I thought then."

"Guess not."

He clasped his hand to my shoulder and gave it a squeeze. "Good." Then he turned to Stewart. "Come with me to explain this new *development* to Grayson and Lonnie. I'm sure they heard the gunshots and will want to know what's going on."

Sasha jogged behind them, probably wanting to make sure her

side of the story was reported accurately. After they were out of sight, Mason picked up the bloody, fishy-smelling knife and pointed it at the shooting target.

"Think I can do it, too?" he asked. "Want to throw this at my head again and see if I move quick enough?"

"Sure," I said at the same time Blake said, "No."

Mason dropped the knife into the grass and shrugged like I hadn't just offered to throw another weapon at him, and then he walked off toward the medical building.

"You *are* going to lay off him eventually, aren't you?" Blake bent over to retrieve the knife from the grass and then stabbed the blade into the tree trunk beside the beheaded fish.

"That depends." I wiped the remaining fish blood onto my jeans and tried to breathe through my mouth to avoid inhaling the re-volting smell. "If he stops looking at my sister like . . . like—"

"Like how you look at Holly?" Blake said quietly.

"No," I snapped. "He's all lust and impure thoughts."

Blake snorted back a laugh and I couldn't exactly blame him. I sounded like an angry, overly protective father. "And you know this for a fact?"

I eyed him suspiciously. "Why? What has he told you?"

"Nothing." Blake shook his head. "But I have eyes. I watch people. And you around Holly, that's about as desperate, lustful, and in-love as anyone can look at someone."

My mouth fell open to respond but we were interrupted by Holly's returning with a box of bullets in one hand and her gun in the other.

Holly's eyebrows shot up. "Discussing something important? More Jackson Meyer secrets to bury?"

"No," I said. "We were just talking about Mason and Courtney."

Holly spun the gun around in her hand, stepping closer to me. "I'm getting sick of your martyr routine. You refuse to tell me any-thing that resembles the truth. That's fine. Whatever. But quit fucking looking at me like you'll die if I die."

Blake's eyes dropped to the grass as he coughed loudly, too polite to say, *I told you so.*

"I'm not trying to look at you in any particular way. It's probably accidental."

"Right." She rolled her eyes. "You're a trained agent, Jackson. You're telling me you can't conceal your thoughts from invading your expression?"

"I don't—" I started, but she lifted a hand to stop me.

"You're like one of those girls in high school that goes on and on about how she likes someone but then won't tell you who until you bug her ten thousand times," Holly said, her eyes staring hard into mine. "You're doing it on purpose, aren't you? Dangling it in my face until I beg you to tell me the big secret you're keeping from me."

"You have no idea what you're talking about." I moved my gaze from her face and started to walk away.

"Don't I?" She reached out and grabbed my arm. "You're doing it right now." She turned to Blake, but still gripped my arm tight. "You can see it, too, can't you, Blake?"

Blake's eyes widened and he shook his head. "No. Not really."

We both heard the lie in his tone and Holly's pointed expression aimed at me silently said, *See? I told you.*

She released my arm from her grip. "Either tell me the big secret or quit playing the attention-seeking-high-school-girl role and act like a grown-up and keep it to yourself."

I was suddenly so pissed off I couldn't see straight. Not at Holly. Not really at anyone. Just at the situation. No matter how much I wanted to, I couldn't seem to do the right thing.

"Why is it so important for you to know?" The anger in my voice must have surprised her because she took a tiny step back. "What difference does it make what happened in another time that doesn't exist anymore?"

She closed the gap between us. I could feel someone else approaching, maybe two someones. Or three. But I was too pissed off to care about who listened in.

"Because it's about me," Holly challenged. "You're keeping details about me from me and relentlessly reminding me of this secret info."

"Not you." I shook my head. "I keep telling you it wasn't you. It was a different version of you. Why is that so hard to wrap your head around?"

"Because I remember!" Holly shouted at me.

CHAPTER SIXTEEN

Everything stilled.

My insides froze. My heart stopped. Her words punctured the surface and sunk beneath my skin and then everything was in motion. My brain sifted through theories and my hands reached out and gripped her shoulders, my head leaning in close to hers, bending down enough to be eye level. "What, Hol? What do you remember?" I demanded.

She squeezed her eyes shut, her breath and voice coming out shaky. "Paint. I remember red paint. And kissing."

007 memories. It was happening to her like it had happened to Stewart and Dr. Melvin. And Adam. In that note he'd left me, he said he was seeing visions of himself younger and that he knew me because of those visions.

I had forgotten that we weren't alone. Forgotten that this wasn't 007 Holly. "You remember that?" I couldn't believe she had those memories. It felt like a blessing. Like seeing an old friend again for the first time after a long absence. Even her expression seemed to change and evolve into a look 007 Holly might have worn.

My hands slid from her shoulders to her face, the heat from her mouth hitting mine even before my lips made contact with hers. She melted right into me, her fingers lifting to touch my hair, her tongue dancing with mine.

I don't know how long we stood in that spot kissing and breathing each other's air, but eventually the need for outside oxygen became too great to ignore and our mouths broke apart. Her forehead rested against mine, eyes closed, both of our chests rising and falling with the same rapid rhythm.

"I'm sorry I left," I whispered, without thinking about who I was actually talking to.

The spell broke immediately and her hands were on my chest, shoving me back. She stared at me in disbelief, wiping her mouth with the back of her hand. "What the hell . . . what are you doing to me?"

I reached for her again, but she jerked away. "Listen, Holly, I didn't know that was happening to you, I'll tell you stuff now. I'm sorry."

She shook her head, anger quickly shifting to fear. "You mean it was real? What I'm seeing? That really happened?"

I nodded. "It was a different timeline. You were younger then. I was trapped in 2007."

"2007," she muttered under her breath.

"Let me explain it better—"

Her eyes were huge as she raised her hands in surrender, stepping back away from me. "No, that's okay. You were right. I shouldn't know this. I shouldn't know any of it."

She spun around quickly and then took off running.

"Holly!" I shouted after her, but Dad stepped in front of me, holding me back.

I hadn't even noticed him standing so close. "Let her go," he said. "Give her some space."

Grayson moved to stand beside Dad. I hadn't noticed him in the vicinity either. My nerves were on edge, my hands shaking, but I tried to focus when Grayson said, "We need her calmed down. Tomorrow morning we're going to attempt to make our escape."

CHAPTER SEVENTEEN

DAY 16. BEFORE DAWN

This time, all of us, even Courtney, who had recovered from her seizure, tramped through the woods again before sunrise, the tension of today's mission driving everyone to silence. I kept watching the back of Holly's head, feeling like I should say something to her. What if we didn't survive this escape?

We reached the edge of the woods in no time and everyone looked out toward the tents, watching for movement or babies running around like we'd seen before. This trip we came fully equipped with supplies—food, water, backpacks with tents, extra clothing, basic medical supplies—to get us through the three-day journey to Eyewall headquarters. Some of the stuff that Grayson, Lonnie, and Blake had produced from the technology building left the rest of us completely speechless. A portable toilet and shower that could be set up by remote control. It was like being in a wizarding world or magical realm. Was this how people from the year 1500 would view 2009?

The part that Blake and I hadn't discussed since that first time was whether or not we would execute our secret plan to take down Eyewall headquarters before jumping back to where we came from. We also hadn't discussed Stewart's involvement in this plan. To me, and probably to Blake since it was his idea, it almost seemed more likely that we would succeed since discovering our newfound abilities. That was also a good reason why it needed to be us and not everyone else.

Emily had been walking beside me the whole journey so I was the first person to notice her stop in her tracks, just past the forest, her forehead wrinkling, hands pressing against the sides of her head.

I knelt in front of her. "What's wrong?"

"My head," she whispered.

I glanced at Dad and Grayson, who were closest to me. Hopefully we weren't about to see another episode of Emily's information overload. "She says her head hurts."

"It doesn't hurt," she explained. "It just . . . it's loud."

Oh boy. Loud voices in her head? This poor kid was in need of some psychiatric assistance we didn't seem to have available despite the fact that we had toilets and showers that folded up into a backpack.

Grayson didn't look nearly as concerned as he had two days ago when Emily had freaked out. He squatted in front of her. "It's all the people who can jump. The buzz just got louder, that's all."

Emily nodded and let out a breath. "I know, but it still makes it hard to think."

I looked from Grayson to Dad, and then Dad spoke up, "Because she senses the presence of time travelers? It's more prevalent if she's around more of them?"

"Yes," Grayson answered.

"But wasn't she with them before?" I asked. "She said Thomas dumped her there."

"I'm guessing that's why she had to leave," Grayson said, and Emily nodded. "That's probably what gave her the strength to do what Ludwig thought impossible. She truly had to get away from it."

I scooped her up off the ground and held her upright in my arms. "Let's get this done so you can get rid of all that noise, okay?"

Emily buried her face in my shoulder, and whispered, "Thank you."

No other words were spoken, as most of us hadn't seen the communication box that Dad and Holly had checked out the other day and we were all anxious to see how it worked. The box sat on top of a long, concrete pole like an old-fashioned pay phone.

Grayson stepped forward and opened the metal box, pressing a few buttons before turning to face the group. Everyone else's eyes seem to shift toward Holly.

She took a deep breath and moved beside Grayson. "Can we

review the procedure one more time before I pass through the retina scanner?"

"Of course," Dad said, because he had been the one to draw out the exact plan, CIA-mission style. "You'll open the access and we'll all cross through the barrier. Three minutes after, Eyewall agents will teleport directly to the barrier line, at which time we'll need to incapacitate them before they have a chance to alert headquarters of our escape. Within a few minutes, we'll need to remove the tracking chips implanted behind their ears and attach them to ourselves."

"Wow, that sounds pretty daunting when you say it like that, Dad," Courtney said.

Lonnie took Emily from my arms. "You're gonna need your hands free."

Blake and I were to be on the front line, so to speak, and Dad wasn't too happy about this; but for everyone else, given the recent discovery, it was a no-brainer.

I held my breath, pulse pounding in my ears as Holly pressed her fingerprints into the gray box, accepting the red light flowing past her pupils. Blake did the honor of crossing the line first, and when he walked through, there was an immediate release of air from everyone's lungs. I walked through next.

The rest crossed through after me. I half expected the scenery to change or some big alarm to sound because we'd finally ended up on the other side of the force field. If this was a revelation for me, I could only imagine what it felt like for Grayson, Lonnie, Blake, and Sasha, who had been here for years, not days.

Thirty seconds passed as we walked farther from Misfit Island. My stomach flipped over a dozen times, my anxiety hitting a peak. I could feel Holly's presence beside me and instinct took over. I reached for her hand, tugging on it to get her to look at me.

"Holly," I said quickly. "I want you to know—"

She yanked her hand from mine and pointed to something in the distance. "Look! Someone's out there! There's a tent."

Sure enough, we all squinted into the rising sun and could just make out a tent much like the ones we'd packed. The blur of a dark-haired figure sat in front of a fire.

"Ninety seconds," Dad whispered.

"Do you think they're waiting for us?" Mason asked, nodding toward the tiny tent in the distance.

As if to answer his question, the figure stood up. He lifted a hand to his head as if to shade his eyes so he could see us. And then he started sprinting in our direction.

Those of us with guns drew them immediately, but the guy stopped. That was when the men and women in dark blue coveralls landed right in front of us. It was a flashback of what had happened in Heidelberg, Germany, when we'd been invaded by a greater number of EOTs than we thought existed.

And that was exactly when my panic, my nerves, completely left and I switched on my months of training, diving to take down a stocky dude who outweighed me by nearly a hundred pounds. I got him on the ground and wrapped an elbow around his neck until his eyes fell shut and his body stilled.

I left him there, my heart thudding as cries of pain rang out all around me. From the corner of my eye, I saw Holly kicking some dude in the chest, sending him flying backwards, giving Dad the chance to leap on him, giving him a blow to the temple that knocked him out.

Stewart had gone down on my other side and I took off after the guy that had pressed something to her back. He aimed some kind of weapon at me that looked like a laser gun, but I dove for his ankles before he could hit me. He crashed onto his back but when I lifted my head, I saw a stream of something drift through the air and knock Mason right in the chest. He fell to the ground, landing in a heap.

"Mason!" I shouted, but then I turned my attention back to my attacker, knocking him out quickly by hitting his temple like Dad had done.

Five minutes later, all the blue-coverall people were down

(obviously Dr. Ludwig and the rest of the Eyewall experiment team were too busy playing Dr. Frankenstein to teach his experiments any form of hand-to-hand combat skills). I went to Stewart and hovered over her, checking her pulse, listening to her breathing. She was out cold but still appeared to be okay.

"It's a temporary, chemically induced coma," Grayson said. "Might last a few hours or a few days."

Mason, Stewart, and Sasha had all been hit. Lonnie stood over Sasha. Blake, Emily, and Courtney were all checking on Mason.

When I looked over at Grayson, I saw him grit his teeth, remove a pocketknife, and slice into one of the Eyewall dude's skin.

"Get the tracking chips out and then we'll worry about our fallen soldiers," Grayson instructed, looking slightly annoyed that he was the only one slicing open skin at the moment.

Dad pulled out a pocketknife, while Courtney turned her head. "I can't watch this."

Lonnie suddenly leaped to her feet, snatched Mason's gun from his limp fingers, and pointed it at the guy we had seen before with the tent. "There's another one!"

Holly had been staring at the figure ever since we'd finished our three-minute battle and now she was limping toward him. Did she get hurt during the fight? "Stop!" she yelled at Lonnie. "Don't shoot!"

I was on my feet again, trying to figure out what she was seeing. *Or who.* I took several long strides in her direction. My mouth fell open. Shock filled every bit of my body.

"Holy shit," I muttered. Then I turned quickly and yelled over my shoulder, "Dad, it's Adam! Adam Silverman!"

CHAPTER EIGHTEEN

DAY 16. EARLY MORNING

"Adam!" Holly shouted.

He ran toward us, staring in disbelief before throwing his arms around her. "Oh my God . . . what the hell?"

"I thought you were dead," Holly whispered loud enough for me to hear. "What are you doing here?"

He looked at me from over Holly's shoulder, and I literally had to hold myself in place to keep from hugging him as hard as Holly had. I didn't know which Adam this was.

"It's *the* Jackson Meyer," he said, whistling under his breath. "No wonder things have gotten crazy lately."

"Who is this?" a voice demanded from behind me.

Lonnie stood with Mason's gun pointed at Adam. I quickly shifted to face her and put myself between them. "It's okay, we know him. He worked with Holly."

"Did you know to not enter the force field?" Holly asked him, dropping her arms and stepping back. "Or wait, are you the source Stewart mentioned?"

"I have no idea what you're talking about," Adam said. "I've been undercover, working at Eyewall headquarters for the past six months, getting information by being on the inside. Until they were on to me. I took off before things got scary." Adam nodded at me. "I had this feeling that it might be you they had trapped here. But I never thought Holly would be here." He turned to her and stared in disbelief. "How did this happen? Agent Collins and I purposely kept all the info from you so you wouldn't end up in this time-travel mess, too."

I couldn't attempt to wrap my head around how he got here, I was just so elated to see him that I didn't care. And this time I couldn't stop myself from grabbing him and giving him a giant hug. "You remember me, right? You've had flashbacks of us being friends?"

He seemed startled but didn't resist. I dropped my arms soon after, moving back a comfortable distance. After having watched him bleed to death, I just couldn't stop the grin spreading across my face.

Adam was my constant.

"Yeah, I remember," he said, laughing. "Though I really need to know how you know about that?"

Lonnie kept the gun pointed at Adam and grabbed him by the arm. "Let's go see what Kevin and Grayson think of your story before we let down our defenses, all right?"

"Yeah sure," Adam said, then he turned to Holly. "Hey, Hol, grab the little handheld computer from my tent. I think it'll help prove my case."

She headed toward the tent we'd seen earlier from a distance, limping noticeably. I followed after her. "Are you okay? You're limping."

She waved me off from over her shoulder. "I'm fine. Just twisted my ankle."

"Well, stop and let me look at it," I said, but she had already entered the dark blue, rectangular tent. Before I could go in after her, the metallic scent hit my nostrils so fast and so strong there wasn't time for even one word of warning to escape my lips before the scenery dissolved and I stood facing my sister's dead body lying in a plush casket.

"No!" I yelled, backing away, but an invisible force held me in place, lifting my eyelids, preventing my eyes from shutting tight as they had done at Courtney's real funeral.

My stomach churned and my eyes blurred with tears, both from grief and the cold April wind that had been present on the day of her funeral. Her face appeared so discolored, her red hair falling all around her. It was anything but peaceful.

"It's not real, it's not real," I muttered to myself over and over again until the trees formed behind the casket and eventually the casket disappeared altogether. I sank to my knees, clutching my stomach, and literally tried to shake the image from my head. I hadn't even looked that carefully on the real day of Courtney's funeral. But somehow that image had stuck itself into my brain and emerged with the help of memory gas. *That's what they wanted.* To see all of our weaknesses. To know what could be thrown in front of each of us to get us to follow their orders.

I thought my body wouldn't cooperate enough to stand until I heard Holly's voice, shouting through the fog of false images. I was on my feet in seconds, ripping open the flap to the tent. The moment I saw her thrashing, fighting some invisible force, when I heard the words she was saying, I knew with complete certainty exactly what was haunting her. Clarity came quickly, along with a rage I'd never experienced before. A desire to murder someone who had already lain dead at my feet. As my hands balled up, my pulse pounded, I imagined killing him a hundred thousand more times and I didn't care if using time travel to do this would eventually kill me.

But Holly's voice, the intense fear in it, snapped me back to worrying about her. I lay on the ground beside her and tried to pull her into my arms. She fought hard against me, kicking and throwing her elbows into my face and chest. Just the thought of what she was reliving made me sick to my stomach and broke my heart all over again.

"Holly, it's okay," I said, finally pinning her arms down. I wouldn't let her be alone this time even if she screamed at me to get out and called me an asshole. If she could just talk about it, maybe this wouldn't keep happening. Maybe she'd move on to a different memory, the way Blake and Grayson had theorized. I pulled her closer, her face pressed against my chest. "I'm not going to hurt you, Hol. You're okay, I promise."

I kept whispering the same words into her ear over and over until she eventually stopped fighting me. Then she was crying so hard her entire body shook with sobs. I lay there and held her tight, stroking her hair and rubbing her back. I couldn't convince myself to be anywhere else despite the turmoil going on around us. Despite Adam's and everyone else's presence not too far from us.

"Please don't tell Adam," Holly whispered after she had calmed down, though her voice was hoarse and still thick with tears.

"Okay," I said, not wanting to take any chance of upsetting her more. "Whatever you want."

She rolled away from me, lifting the bottom of her shirt and wiping her eyes and nose with it. I waited patiently while her gaze stayed focused on the ceiling of the tent. "He'll blame himself."

I turned on my side, propping myself up on one elbow so I could see her better. "Why would he—"

"Trust me, he will."

I couldn't help myself, I leaned down and kissed her forehead before tucking some loose hair behind her ears. "Hol, we need to talk about what happened with Carter."

She let out a breath and squeezed her eyes shut for a second before opening them again and looking at me. "I know."

"We could get hit with the gas again any second. It happened in the woods with my dad, just minutes after you and I were dosed. Maybe if you talk about it, you won't have to see it anymore . . . ?" I suggested.

Her eyes stayed focused on mine. "I'm sorry I got so pissed at you yesterday. I freaked out because the weird visions started making sense and before, I'd honestly just thought I'd been given memory-modification drugs."

"That's what Stewart thought, too," I said, remembering when she'd first had 007 visions. Her hand lay between us, so I slid my fingers over and covered her hand with mine.

"I don't remember what happened to me." Her voice had turned from shaky to steady as if she had fully committed to telling me this story. The real question now was whether or not I could handle hearing it. "I got some sort of vibe after . . . after it happened. I knew I stayed at his place. I knew there was clothing removed.

I remember him kissing me. And then nothing. I think subconsciously I ignored the physical evidence." She shook her head like she was angry at herself, at her own brain's ability to deny something like that had happened. "Obviously, there was evidence."

I tried to draw in a slow, calming breath but all I could do was fight the urge to punch something.

"You heard what he said though, right?"

"You mean before I shot him," I said through my teeth. "I remember."

She pulled her hand free and rested it across her stomach. "That was when I knew we'd gone much further than I realized, but it wasn't until the memory gas hit that first time that I figured out it wasn't . . . it wasn't consensual. He drugged me and I still fought him but he still . . ." She covered her face with both hands and took a deep breath to regain composure. "So when you had these memories that I didn't have, in a way it felt the same. I don't really want them, but part of me needed to push you and see if—"

"Oh, God, Holly. It's not like that, I swear." I reached for her hand again, picking it up and squeezing it. "You have no idea how badly I want to kill him all over again."

Her gaze shifted back to the ceiling, her voice turning almost casual. "So we were together? You and me?"

"Yeah, a couple different versions of you."

"Did you love me?"

"Yes," I said without hesitation. "We loved each other." Her eyes widened, her head turning to me in surprise. "But listen to me, okay?" She nodded. "What I just saw you relive, I'd do anything to take that away, to make sure you never had to feel like something like that could happen to you against your will, without your being able to choose. I want you to have freedom more than I want you to love me back. Sometimes I forget my goals and I cross the line, look at you the way I used to when we were together. But I do want you to be able to choose, more than anything. That's why I didn't want to tell you about us."

She stared at me for a long moment. "You're not lying."

It wasn't a question. She knew I meant it. Her agent training had provided her with that much at least. "And I feel terrible for messing around with you in the reproduction room—"

"And then again in the hospital room," she added, giving me a half smile.

"You're my friend, Holly. Whether you like it or not," I said. "We've been through too much together and I'm talking about *this* version of you. You can stop pretending that you don't care about me and everyone else in our little commune."

She laughed a little. "I guess I can live with that."

My thoughts snapped back to reality. "Shit! We should go help."

We both jumped to our feet, but before we left the tent, Holly stood on her toes, wrapped her arms around my neck, and gave me a huge hug. I squeezed her so tight, her feet left the ground.

"The computer thing," she said, remembering the reason she came in here in the first place. I waited while she swiped a tiny black device from the floor. "And just so you know, I didn't exactly hate making out with you."

"Really?" I asked, following her back outside.

"Really."

Both of us were quick to shift gears, scanning the area and counting heads.

"You all right?" Dad asked us when we had reached the group again.

"Yeah, we survived." I glanced at Adam then back to Dad. "Is everything cool? With Adam?"

Holly handed over the black device Adam had requested from his tent and he hurried over to Dad to explain. "So, I've got pretty much every file in the Eyewall system copied here. All the experiment data, all the results, and everything they've done to build their utopian world—"

Dad lifted a hand to cut him off. "It's okay. We've actually got most of that already."

Adam's jaw dropped open. "How? I went through hell to get this and I was on the inside for six months."

Dad glanced at Emily, and that was when I remembered her scribbling down data not just from my journals but also from the Eyewall systems. "It's a long story," he said with a sigh.

Grayson jogged over to us and proceeded to tape a tiny metal chip to the inside of both our wrists. I recognized the device because it was identical to the memory card Blake had extracted from his foot days ago. From the corner of my eye, I saw Holly wrinkle her nose. I wasn't too thrilled about attaching something that had been under another person's skin to my body either but at least we didn't have to insert it under our skin, just close to a major vein to allow it to register a beating heart.

"You can tape it to your chest if you prefer, just do it quick," Adam said from Holly's other side. He lifted his T-shirt to display the tiny metal piece resting over his heart.

The metal poked my wrist and I immediately decided the chest was better.

"Here, let me help," Holly said, taking the supplies from my hand. "Hold your shirt up." She gently moved my free hand aside and I lifted my shirt again. She managed to pull the tape off without too much pain. A shiver went up my spine when her fingers pressed against my chest, finding my heartbeat before securing the tape in place. Pink crept up from her neck as her fingers continued to drift over the scar on my chest. "It looks good . . . I mean, it's healing really well."

Holly's eyes met mine, her face even more flushed than a few seconds ago. She wasn't Agent Holly right then, she wasn't looking at me with the same scrutiny and skepticism as her trained-agent persona would. But it wasn't 007 Holly either.

She was just Holly.

Adam cleared his throat, causing her to withdraw her fingers from my skin and me to drop my shirt back into place. I stepped away from them and walked over to Dad. "What's the plan?"

"Set up camp over by Adam's tent," he said, glancing at Stewart's sleeping body. "Not much choice with comatose team members. We'll have to wait until they come to."

A couple hours later, I sat in a newly set-up tent with Adam, Holly, and Courtney, waiting out the hottest part of the day in the shade.

"Wow, you weren't kidding," Adam said, sifting through a pile of notebook papers Emily had filled up the other day. We'd brought them along at Emily's insistence. "That kid must really be overloaded. Apparently another version of me wrote notes in Jackson's journal?" I nodded to confirm this. "And Emily's copied my handwriting perfectly."

Holly and I both reached for the page Adam had just discarded beside him. Our fingers brushed and she slid it in my direction and reached for another page. I recognized the journal entry right away. It was mostly my handwriting, but experiment results were written across the bottom in Adam's writing using his code. I slid beside Adam as I scanned the page.

I laughed. "Oh God, I remember this experiment."

He leaned in and read over my shoulder. "So what happened? My other self didn't record any definite results."

Before I could answer him, Holly jumped to her feet, looking a little spooked or just jumpy for some reason. "What's wrong?"

"Nothing." She shook her head. "I'm gonna get some water."

Courtney stood up, too, brushing dirt from the back of her jeans. "I'll go with you."

I turned my attention back to Adam, who appeared to be eagerly waiting for my answer. "Do you get the whole half-jump concept?"

"Bits of it," he said. "But not completely."

I went on to explain how my body stays in the present, how hardly any time passes in the present even if I'm years in the past and hanging out there for hours at a time. And how sensations like pain and heat and cold are dulled in the half-jump.

"Once, I missed the target and ended up in the middle of traffic," I explained. "This semi ran right over my leg and I heard the bones break. It was so nasty and it hurt like hell. Of course, I jumped back right away and was practically dying, but my leg ended up being fine."

Adam pushed his glasses up on his nose. Sweat from the noon-hour heat had caused them to slide. "Seriously, dude?"

"Well, I had a faint purple bruise for a few days but that's it."

"That's insane." His forehead wrinkled with that look of deep concentration, and it was so familiar it made me feel like I'd gone back in time and everything was how it used to be. "So it's not complete invincibility, right?"

I laughed. "Right. And that's exactly what your other self was so fascinated with."

He flipped furiously through more pages. "Okay, tell me about this experiment."

This morning's fight and the emotional drama with Holly had taken a toll on my body. I stretched out across one of the sleeping bags, resting my hands behind my head. "After I survived the leg-crushing incident, we both had a few new ideas that included putting me through physical peril of some kind in a half-jump just to see what I came back with in the present."

It was so strange to think about those months experimenting with the original 009 Adam, hooking up with Holly, and feeling almost completely carefree. I had virtually no responsibilities, no real life-or-death concerns other than figuring out what the hell was wrong with me. But meeting Adam, messing around with time, hanging out like I wasn't a freak, made this worry dissolve pretty early on.

I remembered this experiment more clearly as I recounted it to Adam now. It had been mid-August of 2009. We were sitting in the TV room at my apartment. Dad was working so we were alone. Having swiped a bottle of Crown Royal from Dad's stock, both of us were failing miserably at our attempt to beat our previous high scores on Halo and that was when the more colorful ideas began to evolve.

Adam had tossed his game controller and picked up the newspaper. "This is awesome!"

I glanced over at the article he'd been reading. "Eighty people got food poisoning from bad sushi in the East Village. What's awesome about that?"

It only took me a few seconds to catch on to his train of thought. By that time, we'd been doing this type of thing for nearly five months and I knew how Adam thought. Well, mostly. "When did this happen?" I asked.

"Between seventy-two and forty-eight hours ago."

I jumped to my feet and started pacing in circles around the coffee table. "I can't do seventy-two hours yet, but I can manage forty-eight."

"Dude, we gotta do this!" He had already retrieved the notebook from my camp bag and was jotting down theories and details.

"No one died, right?" I asked.

"Not so far." He shrugged. "I think they puked a lot."

"Okay, so I go back two days, eat the tuna roll at the joint in the East Village," I recited. "And then what?"

He looked up from the notebook. "I guess you'll have to wait since food poisoning isn't instantaneous. What do you have going on tomorrow, just in case?"

I flopped down on the couch and started up another game of Halo. "The Mets game with Holly. I can cancel."

"Don't cancel," he said, and something in his tone made me look away from the game for a second before turning back.

I shrugged. "Holly's cool. She'll be fine with it."

"Uh-huh." He leaned down closer to the notebook page as if his drunken haze made it harder for him to read his chicken-scratch handwriting.

"What?" I asked. "You know she's not going to get pissed and go all crazy girlfriend on me. She's not like that. *We're* not like that."

"Exactly," he said.

"That whisky is messing with your head, man." But somewhere in my head I knew what he was trying to tell me, I just hadn't wanted to put it into words out loud. Not yet, anyway. "So I won't cancel, then. Besides, I'm sure I'll be fine."

I'd had no problem making the two-day back-in-time half-jump and no trouble getting my spicy tuna roll down, but the following morning, about two hours before Holly was supposed to come over so we could go to the game, my head was buried deep in the toilet. I was so sick that I couldn't even leave the bathroom to retrieve my phone and call or text her to warn her not to come over. Which is why when she walked into my bedroom and heard me barfing for like the hundredth time, my entire body had been covered in sweat and yet I lay on the bathroom tiles shivering, my head spinning.

"Oh my God," she'd said. "Are you hung over?"

I'd managed to shake my head and croak out a few words. "Bad sushi."

My eyes barely stayed open as she flushed the toilet, grabbed a washcloth, wet it, and pressed it against my forehead. Taking care of each other wasn't a usual kind of date or activity for Holly and me. "You should go," I said. "Don't think I can make it to the game."

"No kidding," Holly said. "But I'm not leaving you like this."

I couldn't protest because I was too busy clawing my way back up to a sitting position so I could hurl into the toilet again. I managed to stand and lean over the sink, fumbling with my toothbrush, trying to get the vomit taste out of my mouth, hoping that would help my subconscious to stop thinking about puking again. The second I started to sway, Holly wrapped an arm around my waist to steady me.

I could only barely remember the details of her helping me to my bed, putting a small trash can beside me that I could wrap my arms around. Eventually, I talked her into retrieving my phone so I could call Dr. Melvin and tell him that I needed him to come save me from my sushi poisoning. Holly sat beside me, pressing the cloth to my forehead, not making even one comment about how only spoiled rich kids have doctors who did home visits.

Dad had shown up before Dr. Melvin, and at that time, Dad made Holly pretty nervous so she left shortly after.

"So, you do have results for that experiment?" Adam asked after I'd finished the story.

"Nothing factual." I laughed under my breath. "It turns out that three days before I started getting sick, I ate at this burger joint that turned up as having some kind of *E. coli* outbreak. So there's no way to know for sure."

"You could have done blood work or stool samples!" Adam protested. "If it was *E. coli,* it would have showed up."

"Yeah, I was too sick to call you for like a couple days and Dr. Melvin gave me an antiemetic and an antibiotic shot right away. The meds worked so he didn't need to investigate further. Maybe he did draw blood while I was out of it. We could ask Dad but unfortunately none of that happened to this version of Dad."

Adam grinned at me sheepishly. "I'm guessing you didn't feel like trying again?" I shook my head. "Yeah, I don't blame you. My other self must have been too drunk to gather the proper preexperiment data and make sure there wasn't any potentially spoiled food in your three-day history?"

"That would have been hard to know for sure, right?"

"Probably." He set the loose notebook pages aside and his face turned more serious. "So, like the thing with your not being able to ask your dad because he's never had that memory, it's the same with Holly? She's never lived that day either? You lost all that?"

I sat up and looked down at my hands. "Right."

"Does Holly know about this stuff?"

I relayed the events of the last couple weeks to him and explained (leaving out what happened with Carter because I promised her I wouldn't tell) how she'd been having the flashes of 007 Holly memories. Then I had to explain 2007 to him.

"So that's the visions I've had!" he said. "World B. That's been confusing the hell out of me."

"Not just you," I said. "Even Stewart thought she'd been given memory-modification drugs."

"I had a feeling time travel played a part in those visions but I had too many missing pieces to fully understand the different types of jumps," Adam said. "It feels really good to have the rest of the puzzle."

"I'm sorry you got all wrapped up in this Eyewall, time-travel, world-destruction shit. I never wanted this to happen." I looked over at him. "But I'm glad you're here, despite the circumstances."

Adam tossed a meal bar in my direction, smacking me in the forehead. "Like before when you were screwing around with Holly, drinking and partying way too much?"

I threw the bar back at him, laughing harder than I had in a long time. "You were one hundred percent on board with my life choices."

"Yeah, that does sound awesome." He leaned back against the side of the tent. "Well, not the screwing-around-with-Holly part. Would have been cool to actually make it to college, especially MIT. Seems kinda trivial now, doesn't it?"

"Unfortunately."

We were interrupted by someone's arm poking through the flap of the tent. We both watched as Jenni Stewart fully emerged. "I'm awake, bitches! What'd I miss?"

Her eyes traveled from me to Adam then back to me. "Okay, apparently quite a bit."

I scrambled to my feet and rested my hands on her shoulders. "You okay? Are Mason and Sasha waking up, too?"

"Yes and yes," she said, nodding toward Adam.

"Right." I turned around to face him. "Adam this is Jenni Stewart. Stewart, this is Adam Silverman, my friend from many time-lines."

"Glad you're not dead," she said before snapping her attention back to me. "Explain. Now."

Before I could even open my mouth to speak, shouting from outside the tent stopped me. The three of us looked at each other and then tumbled out the entrance and into the stifling heat.

Dad and Holly both stood with pistols pointed at the same target. My gaze traveled outward, finally identifying what had sent them reaching for defense weapons.

Chief Marshall.

CHAPTER NINETEEN

DAY 16. AFTERNOON

I raced to get in front of Dad and Holly, my gun raised toward the man who'd managed to deceive me like no other. My hands held steady, no sign of trembling at all. The need to protect Holly, Dad, and the others destroyed any trembling weakness left in my body. I gave one second's thought to obtaining information from Marshall versus risking the people behind me. No contest. My training kicked in and I aimed. One to the head. One to the chest. My finger touched the trigger.

"Stop!" Stewart leaped in front me, her lean, dark arms spread wide.

At my touch, the bullet left the gun, now heading straight for Stewart. I jumped, taking her body down, shoving her out of the way. The dry dirt puffed around us.

"What the fuck, Jackson," Stewart said, coughing at the dust.

I rolled off her to my knees, looking for Marshall.

He'd moved and appeared unhit and unresisting.

"Wait. Let Chief Marshall explain."

"Damn it, Stewart, he was your trusted source?" I trained my gun again.

Adam ran forward. "Wait."

Chief Marshall sauntered closer, his arms resting at his sides, no weapon in sight.

"Don't move," I said.

Chief Marshall stopped. "I orchestrated this escape plan."

His hated voice reminded me how much I had never liked him, and that was before I'd seen him murder an alternative version of myself.

Dad's weapon stayed up and his gaze flitted to Stewart. "He's your secret source? I trusted you! We all trusted you! What were you thinking?"

I stared at Adam, who'd placed himself in front of Marshall. "Not you, too."

"He can time-travel," Adam explained.

"Yeah, I kind of figured that when I saw him vanish after murdering the other me and Healy," I snapped.

"He can time-travel like the originals." Stewart pointed toward Grayson and Blake, who had just appeared outside in our little battleground. She climbed to her feet, swiping at the dust on her pants, then proceeded to point at Lonnie and Sasha as they too emerged. "He's one of them."

"Shit," Mason said, joining us from one of the tents, his voice still groggy from the laser-induced coma he'd been in. "Marshall." He drew his gun and moved to Holly's side.

He can time-travel like the originals? This means . . . "So Thomas and Ludwig figured out the secret formula for perfect, synthetic time travelers," I said.

Dad shook his head at Stewart. "He's talked you into leading us right to them. Right to Eyewall headquarters." He sounded pissed at her and at himself.

"There's probably some kind of weird-ass experiment being performed on us right now," Mason added. "Like this whole journey is testing us so they know exactly what we're capable of, what we can potentially do for them."

"He's not an experiment! He's an original," Adam shouted.

Grayson shook his head. "Impossible."

"There's no record of any others," Lonnie added.

"That's not completely true." Blake stepped up and held out his hands for everyone to calm down. He looked right at me and then at Holly. "Frank. Remember Frank? He was on Healy's committee. He had another time traveler working for him. Before he was thrown in jail, he'd set something in motion. A project to fight Eyewall."

"Something he named Project Tempest," Marshall said, moving closer.

"Don't move," Dad snapped to Marshall, who paused. "Who the hell is Frank?"

"He worked for the government when time travelers were first identified," I explained.

"When Frank figured out that Ludwig had done something to Healy to get him and the committee to agree to support Project Eyewall, he sent me on a mission to find Dr. Melvin in 1953 and try to convince him never to write down his cloning theory," Blake explained.

Grayson scratched his head. "I remember that part. But I don't remember the part about any secret time traveler."

Blake's eyes dropped to the ground. "I thought maybe you knew already and that's why you wanted my memory files hidden in a new location."

Grayson stepped forward, looking more angry than I'd ever seen him. "But you had no problem letting those files play aloud for these two?" He nodded at me and Holly.

"Only because it didn't matter anymore," Blake said. "Either we'd still be trapped inside the force field or we'd get out and then I'd . . . I'd . . ."

Grayson's eyes narrowed. "You'd what?"

"Blow up Eyewall headquarters with the bagful of explosives I brought along," Blake finally answered. The guilt dropped from his voice. Only pure defiance remained. He was obviously dead set on this plan and I had no idea explosives were among the supplies we'd carted across the boundary lines this morning.

Everyone except Stewart and I started talking at once. Stewart already knew about Blake's plan, though I don't know how this worked into her secret source we'd all been counting on. Marshall. Jeez, Stewart.

"Enough!" Dad finally shouted to stop the chatter. "Obviously, there's a lot we need to piece together. Holly. Mason," he ordered. "Restrain Chief Marshall so we can question him properly."

Marshall didn't resist as Holly and Mason gathered supplies and then tied his hands behind his back and his ankles together. If only we had an ocean to dump him in. And a couple of cement blocks.

After Holly had finished her job, she turned to Adam, her defenses way up despite her earlier elation at seeing him. "Why are you defending him? What do you know that I don't?"

Adam's exasperated sigh made it seem like the answer should be common knowledge. "He's the one who put me undercover at Eyewall headquarters. How the hell do you think I got to the year 3200?"

That was a very good question. One that got interrupted before I could interject.

Courtney and Emily were the last to join the makeshift court trial, and to everyone's surprise, Emily was more than delighted to see Chief Marshall. She ran to his side. "You came! I knew it was you helping Jenni! I just knew it."

"Why do I feel like I know absolutely nothing?" Dad whispered to me.

"You and me both."

"Are you actually planning on giving me the opportunity to explain myself, Agent Meyer?" Marshall said, and it was like we were back in France again, performing a simulated training mission, Marshall pacing in front of us, giving orders and warnings, never glossing over the bad stuff.

Dad tucked his gun into the back of his pants as Holly and Mason ushered Marshall into a portable folding chair and strapped him to it. Dad moved in front of the bound man and crossed his arms over his chest. "Fine. Explain."

"First of all," Marshall said, calm as anything, "you should all know that President Healy—Senator Healy to some of you— had been gone for some time before I finally put him out of his misery. He was merely a vessel left for Ludwig to control and use."

My mind flashed back to the last time I saw Healy, before the vision or half-jump, before I came to the year 3200. It was like someone was inside him, trying to claw his way out. I had relayed this to Dad and Grayson after waking up from my near-death experience.

"*They got me . . .*" *Healy had whispered.* "*Mind control.*"

Marshall's eyebrows lifted as if he knew I was remembering Healy's strange behavior, his mention of mind control. Did he know about the perfect utopian future and the conclusion I'd drawn about the peace that emanated from every one of those people?

"Cloning isn't the only invention Project Eyewall has perfected," Marshall said.

I faked calm, like a good agent. "That doesn't explain why you killed the other me. Or why you were Healy's right-hand man."

"I'm sure you're familiar with the term '*double agent,*' son," Marshall said. "I agreed to help Healy, which meant I was essentially helping Ludwig and Thomas. I provided a time traveler to perform alterations for them and they agreed not to ask who aided me."

"But it was just you doing it, right?" Mason asked.

"Correct." Marshall looked at Emily. "And this child."

My fists tightened and I put the safety on my gun before I acted on my anger. "You used a little kid for your missions? That's twisted. You're as bad as Thomas and Ludwig."

"It wasn't like that," Emily protested. "I found him. I wanted to help."

Dad rubbed his temples and sank onto an empty chair. "This is getting way too complicated. I have no idea what the hell we're doing."

Tension settled on top of everyone after hearing Dad's confession. He had a point. A very good point, but we were all so used to Dad's holding it together. Maybe he'd just done this too long. I felt like I'd been fighting this battle forever so I couldn't imagine how exhausted Dad must be.

"Let me start at the very beginning, Agent Meyer," Marshall said. "I was born the same year as Thomas. However, my time-travel abilities emerged even earlier than Blake's. I was eleven years old. My schoolteacher contacted the authorities and Frank showed up. Grayson and Lonnie had already been discovered by that time and made into public figures. Unlike Blake and many of the others, I had no family to my name. I'd lived almost my entire life in a military-academy school as a scholarship student. Before that, I was in foster care. Frank took one look at me and he couldn't bring himself to take me into the capital. He couldn't turn me in to the government at my age, with no family to help me make the choice to leave.

"Frank explained what the government would expect of me if I turned myself in as a time traveler and threw out my options. I could go to the capital or he could erase what happened and help me hide. I wanted nothing to do with the government after years in the foster-care system and then more years training for the military. So for me the choice was easy. In the end, Frank adopted me and enrolled me in another school.

"He didn't ignore what I was though. He taught me everything he knew about the future, about the fight ahead. When I was finally ready, I began my own search, my own missions into the past. I found Agent Meyer, a young boy who'd stumbled upon the existence of time travelers in the 1950s, and saved him from a deadly fate. After learning of Dr. Melvin's discoveries and the scientific advancements that a young Scottish woman named Eileen Covington had made regarding time travel and genetics, I brought them on board and formed a team in the late eighties. Frank continued to pass along information to me that he'd received in his committee meetings. His early concern came from the Tempus Gene Project. I kept an eye on each and every child from the project and made sure to bring them on board before the other side tried to use them. Agent Sterling and Agent Kendrick were among those children."

"Wait, what?" Mason said. "I'm a product of something?"

We all ignored him for now because Marshall's story was getting too interesting and making too much sense to deal with Mason's whining identity crisis.

"My number-one goal, above anything else, was to keep my ability a secret," Marshall said. "The second I revealed myself, everything would crumble." He glanced at Emily. "I know that because of Emily. She paid me a visit when I was eighteen and said those exact words. She also informed me that Jackson would suffer an injury when traveling to this year. Then when I came across Mr. Silverman sneaking out of Eyewall headquarters, he's the one that hypothesized with me, coming to the conclusion that I had to eliminate the other version of Jackson trapped in this timeline in order to keep the Jackson sitting here with us today from dying."

My mouth fell open. "What? Adam, you told him to do that? Why?"

"Yeah, I haven't exactly had a chance to explain that to them yet," Adam said to Marshall, then turned to me and Dad. "It's a long, complicated theory that I'll refrain from explaining but it came partially from data Thomas acquired from Eileen Covington."

I knew how much Dad was probably hurting, hearing Eileen's name dropped several times into the conversation like a piece of history or data and not a person he loved.

"The other piece of information I acquired from Emily is the role this young lady played in nearly every one of your near-deadly screwups." Marshall turned his gaze to Holly and then back to me. "Which is why, after you took matters into your own hands and traveled back three months in the past to erase your relationship, I decided to make sure she wouldn't be a threat to your future missions. Same with Mr. Silverman."

"What do you mean?" I asked, moving closer to Marshall.

He looked me right in the eye, no fear or hesitation when he said, "I orchestrated her involvement in the organization trained to kill you. Same with Mr. Silverman."

Red. Red was all I could see in front of me and behind me and all around me. He did that? He put Holly and Adam in the CIA? It wasn't Thomas or Ludwig or Healy. It wasn't even the enemy.

I lunged for Marshall, knocking him backwards in his chair and wrapping both my hands around his throat. He was completely defenseless against me with his hands and feet tied up, his body strapped to the chair. The pressure I put on his neck caused his dark skin to redden, his eyes to bulge.

Stewart and Adam both jumped on me, trying to stop my attack, but they had nothing on the intense fury I felt. It wasn't until I heard Dad's voice above the pounding blood in my ears, "Jackson, no! Not like this," followed by Courtney's heart-wrenching plea, "Jackson, don't! Just stop," that I finally loosened my grip. Adam and Stewart both tugged me away and pushed me toward Holly, who just stood there, mouth hanging open.

Dad was the one who stepped forward and returned Marshall to his former upright position. Marshall didn't look shaken at all, but his voice came out strained when he spoke again. "Agent Meyer has never been able to see what I clearly could from a very early age. He raised a selfish, spoiled, hardheaded boy who would develop powers strong enough to destroy the world. Do you know how dangerous you are, son? The cage in that warehouse was probably the safest place for you."

"It was your choice to allow him to join Tempest," Dad said, his voice furious. "He would have stayed away completely if it wasn't for your permission."

"And leave him to run off with Silverman, opening portals into another timeline with their experiments. Not to mention involving Holly, another innocent civilian. At least I made sure she had skills to defend herself. You and I both know he wouldn't have stayed away."

I stared at Marshall for a long time, replaying so many events that had happened since I made that first jump to 2007, while questions flew from everyone else's mouths.

Dad was guilty of some of the same things Marshall had accused me of, except his job had been to protect me at all costs. My job had never been to fall in love with Holly and to be part of her life or even to protect her or get myself trapped in the year 3200 to be able to see my dad again. Everything I'd done had been personal. Even opening up the alternate universe, World B, had been because I couldn't bear to watch Holly bleed to death in 2009. And when I finally made it back to 2009, I didn't have to take Holly on a little romantic weekend to Martha's Vineyard. I could have ditched her and taken off. Kept Thomas from ever throwing her off that roof.

Then in the NYU bookstore, I told myself I'd gone over to the aisle she had been in just to make sure she was okay, but really I wanted to see her again. I didn't have to engage in more conversation with her at Healy's ball either, after that fifty-thousand-dollar dance. I didn't have to climb inside Adam's car and steal his CD, stupidly leaving my fingerprints behind.

"He's right," I said, interrupting a verbal feud. I sank into the empty chair Dad had occupied a few minutes ago and rubbed my hands over my face, removing sweat and dirt in the process.

All eyes turned in my direction. I dropped my hands and looked up again. "Marshall's right. I would have given in eventually. If I hadn't run into Holly again in New York, something else would have triggered it and I would have inserted myself right back into her life again. Adam's, too." I turned to face Holly. "I'm so sorry. I know this doesn't help, but for what it's worth, if I could fix it right now, if I could go way back before we ever met, I think I'd finally be strong enough to let you go."

Dad's hand landed on my arm, "Jackson . . . ?"

I shook my head, wiggling out of his grip. Before Holly could do anything more than gape at me, I swallowed the lump in my throat and turned my eyes back to Marshall. "We do need you. I get it now. I can't see the big picture and you can."

"It's not that you can't see it," Marshall clarified, "it's that you choose to put your personal concerns above the big picture."

I nodded. He was right. "Blake wants to blow up the Eyewall headquarters and I want to help him. Is that big picture enough for you?"

"Yes," he said.

My eyes met Dad's.

"Are you sure?" Dad asked.

"I'm sure." I paused and swallowed. "We need Marshall. Let him go."

"Untie him," Dad said to Mason and Stewart. "Unless anyone else objects?"

We waited for a few moments, and when no one spoke, Marshall was freed and stood in front of us like he'd done so many times during training. He shook out his arms and shrugged his shoulders. "Let's pack up and make our way to headquarters. We'll formulate a cohesive attack plan on the way."

Thirty minutes later, we were hiking through a giant field, the hot sun beating down on us. No one jogged too closely to Blake and his bag of explosives. I adjusted the heavy straps of my bag and took the bottle of water Courtney passed me. After the lukewarm wetness hit my throat, I took another bottle and carried it over to Blake. After the short break, Marshall, Dad, and Grayson took the lead and I hung in the back, mentally drowning in my own world of self-doubt.

"If we'd had a little more time, I would have gotten around to telling you more," Adam said.

I looked sideways, only just realizing he was beside me. "It's all right. I understand. You couldn't tell anyone about Marshall. Keeping it a secret was more important than staying on my good side."

"True," he said. "But that doesn't mean I don't think the guy's a total robot. He is. And a lot of good wouldn't have happened if you or your dad were like him. It's just the way it is. That's the system that has to exist in order for us to succeed. We each have our own mission, our own stake in this."

"I guess." I shook my head, kicking dirt up as I walked. "I still wish I could have managed to keep you and Holly out of this."

Adam spread his arms out wide, turning sideways to grin at me. "Well, I'm here, so deal with it."

I managed a short laugh. "Okay, okay. Fine."

"Thank God!" Adam said, lifting his hands to the sky. "Your brooding, brokenhearted-lover routine was getting a bit annoying."

I shoved him hard, watching him stumble forward into Stewart, who turned around and caught Adam. "Junior could win an Oscar for his brooding."

I rolled my eyes. "Shut up, Stewart. Besides, you know we share the loyalty curse."

"True," she said with a sigh. "Very true."

"But we'll get to test that theory soon, right?" I pointed out. "No failing at the destroy-Eyewall mission to save my ass."

"Don't flatter yourself, Junior. I'm not that fond of you."

My eyes traveled to Dad and Courtney and eventually to Holly and my stomach was already twisting in knots. Was I loyal enough to this mission to risk survival? Would I screw up again to make sure Holly or Dad or Courtney or Adam or Emily was okay? I guess there was only one way to find out.

CHAPTER TWENTY

DAY 19. LATE EVENING

I stood outside Eyewall's electric fence, huddled in the evening cold with Blake and Marshall. I was trying hard not to think about Dad, Holly, and Adam right now, tiptoeing their way to the gate and gaining access for all of us after Adam performed his computer magic and hacked into the system. We were all counting on the Eyewall guard chips attached to our bodies to help us fly under the radar for a while. Adam and Emily had both said it wasn't uncommon for Eyewall guards (aka time-travel-clone experiments) to teleport somewhere and have to return to headquarters on foot due to their brains needing a rest—something I could totally relate to from my own time-jumping experiences.

Three days of planning this mission, three days of walking and sleeping outside, and we were all mentally and physically fatigued, not to mention battered and bruised. I knew Holly had sprained her ankle during that fight when we first stepped outside the force field, I'd seen her limping toward Adam, but she refused to admit the injury existed and had kept on walking with a determined pace for the past three days. Adam said it was the former gymnast in her that knew how to push through the pain. She and I had hardly spoken since I'd given my guilt-ridden public apology, but there was no more tension. She'd sat with me and Adam and Stewart or me and Courtney and participated in conversations with none of the hot-and-cold mood swings I'd seen since arriving in the year 3200. Maybe it was the last memory-gas episode or Adam's arrival that finally got her to break through that barrier between her and everyone else.

"Any minute now," Marshall said.

The building was just as Blake had described in his memory file—one and a half stories aboveground. A fence surrounded the perimeter about fifty yards away from the building. Trees were planted all around the fence as if to conceal the building.

"I hate this place," Blake muttered from my other side. "It's everything that's wrong with the world contained in one single architectural structure."

"So what's the deal with the explosives?" I asked, keeping my voice low. "They've just been sitting on Misfit Island for all those years for what reason?"

"Actually," Blake said, staring through the trees at the building, "I made the bomb myself from supplies in the technology building."

"Seriously? How do you know it will work?"

He shrugged. "Guess we'll just have to wait and see."

I groaned to myself but didn't complain otherwise. Now wasn't the time, and if Marshall, Grayson, and Dad had agreed to this plan, then they must have had faith in Blake's ability to build weapons. Even though he couldn't fire a gun to save his life, nor did he fit the prototype for garage bomb builders. Quite the opposite.

We squatted behind the trees for another couple minutes. Only our pounding hearts and uneven breathing invaded the eerie silence. When I felt a tap on my shoulder, I literally jumped into action; Blake reacted the same from beside me. I had the newcomer pinned facedown into the dirt and pine-needle-filled forest floor in half a second.

"Jesus, Holly!" I said when I realized my mouth was full of blond hair. I released her immediately and helped her up as she dusted off the front of her shirt.

"You guys are freaks," Holly said, still breathless and spitting out dirt. "I didn't even see you move and then I was eating dirt."

"Quiet," Marshall hissed, before glancing at Holly. "They're in?"

"Yep, Adam's messing with the computers now and Agent Meyer's guarding the door." Holly scooted between me and Blake and sat on the ground, looking out at the building. "I passed the east-side entrance on my way back here. Stewart, Grayson, and Sasha are in position. Mason's ready to follow them inside."

I already knew that Lonnie, Emily, and Courtney were hiding out in the woods, waiting for us to return, much to Courtney's disgust.

"Good," Marshall said with a nod as he glanced at the stopwatch in his hand. "The thirty-minute mark passed four minutes ago . . ."

"Right," Holly said. "I got held up after leaving the south entrance. Memory gas."

I turned my gaze to her, my stomach plummeting. We hadn't run into memory gas since the day we found Adam. "You okay?"

She met my eyes, giving me a sad smile. "Yeah, I'm okay. It was just like you said, I moved on to something new."

Part of me felt relieved and part of me panicked that maybe she'd moved on to something worse and that would be my fault for getting her to talk about it. "Better or worse?" I asked finally.

"Better, I guess," she whispered. "I broke my neck when I was fourteen. I fell off the uneven bars at gymnastics camp."

"Shit." I shook my head. "Want to talk about it?"

She laughed a nervous laugh. "Maybe later."

I stared out at the building again, letting her words sink in. What if we didn't have later? What if this was it? I leaned in closer to Holly and inhaled the scent of her hair. "Why does your hair still smell the same?"

"The same as what?" she asked. "007 Holly? The other 009 Holly? Me before getting trapped in 3200?"

"All of it," I said. "It's always the same."

Marshall glanced at his stopwatch. "Fifteen more minutes."

Fifteen minutes of Dad on the inside and us stuck helplessly out here would feel like an eternity. Fifteen minutes of Holly's uneven breathing beside me, her body heat colliding with mine. I wanted to take her hand and tell her I loved her. I wanted to hug her and make her go hide out in the forest with Lonnie, Courtney, and Emily. But instead, I just sat in silence trying to convince my own heart to slow down.

"Time's up," Marshall said finally.

"Who's testing the fence?" Holly asked.

I reached my hand out, but Marshall swatted it away and wrapped his fingers around the fence.

Nothing happened.

Blake stood and tossed the bag over his shoulder. "We're in."

Holly started up the fence first, climbing twice as fast as the rest of us. I stayed close behind her and landed on the concrete ground inside the perimeter about twenty seconds after she did. We waited another minute for Marshall and Blake to touch ground. The darkness made me squint and wish for night goggles.

"You two head that way." Marshall pointed toward my right. "Holly and I will let the others know they can cross through."

Before I could take off with Blake, I reached out and squeezed Holly's hand. "Be careful, Hol."

She gave me a tiny nod but wouldn't meet my eyes. I had no choice but to follow behind Blake as we ran around the dark building and entered through sliding doors. Under Adam and Emily's directions from earlier today, Blake and I dove into a small closet full of brown coveralls. We both quickly stepped into a pair and fastened them closed. I reached for the doorknob.

Blake grabbed my arm. "You know that ring Emily brought to you in 2009?"

"How do you know about that?" *And why the hell are we talking about that right now?*

"I read about it in your journal last night," he admitted. "The replicated pages that Emily made."

"Maybe we can talk about it later." I moved for the door again, but he stopped me.

"Do you have it with you?"

"It's in my bag," I said. "With Courtney and Lonnie."

"Describe it," he demanded, squeezing his eyes shut, his face so intense it scared the hell out of me.

I took a deep breath. "It's a gold band with a small diamond in the center and then two tiny diamond studs beside the larger center stone embedded into the band."

"Is there an engraving inside?"

"Yes." How the hell did he know about this? "It says J + H forever. You don't . . . you don't know where that came from, do you?"

"I do." He finally opened his eyes again. "It's Lily Kendrick's mother's ring . . . Jacquelyn and Henry."

I stared at him in disbelief. "What? Why do I have it—" I shook my head. "Forget it, we gotta get moving. I'll think about that later."

He slung the bag of homemade bombs over his shoulder again. "Promise me you'll give it to Lily? I know she'd want to have it."

My hand froze on the cold doorknob. She did want to have it. She'd told me that once. But I needed to focus on the mission so I told Blake what he wanted to hear. "Sure, I'll give it to her."

We shuffled out into the hallway, passing a woman in brown coveralls. I held my breath as she gave us a curt nod and continued on. I exhaled, moving with more ease down the tiled hall. A shrill alarm pierced the air. Red lights flashed. An automated voice shouted a warning. "Doors closing. Please verify and account for presence of all experiments."

"Shit."

Blake took off in a jog and I followed behind him. "They know we're inside. They know the system's been penetrated."

He looked over his shoulder for a second, probably taking in the panic on my face as I searched around for signs of Dad, Adam, Holly, or any of the others. "I'm fine, Jackson. Go look for them if you want."

I shook my head and kept following. Blake pointed his finger to the right, counting doors as we ran. Finally, he stopped in front of a door with a huge red warning sign—DANGER HIGH VOLTAGE. He grabbed the door handle and swung it open. *Of course, we're going in this room. The only one that screams: Enter and you shall die.*

"Stand guard at the door while I set up?" he asked.

"Yeah, go." I stood in the hallway while he went in. Suddenly, people in coveralls rushed into the hall, doors flew open along the length. I removed my gun and held it behind me. I spotted Dad and Stewart way at the far end of the hallway, but before I could make eye contact with either of them, someone appeared behind me, pressing something into my back, causing my body to freeze, my brain to fog over.

"Jackson."

I recognized the voice

The hard object dug deeper. "Of *course* you're right in the middle of this," Thomas said.

I opened my mouth to warn Blake of Thomas's presence but I wasn't sure any sound came out. I did, however, take in the image of Stewart kicking the hell out of Thomas and then Thomas, hunched over on the ground obviously in a great deal of pain, vanishing before he could finish me off and probably Blake, too. The world swirled around me and it reminded me of the time I tried ecstasy at a party when I was sixteen. The only illegal drug I've ever used in my entire life. I processed images and blurred movements all around me, but I couldn't bring myself to care, let alone take action. Yet somewhere amid the haze, a thought formed in my mind. Maybe Blake would blow up this place with Thomas in it. That was a bonus we hadn't counted on.

I knew time was passing but I was unable to react. The alarms kept sounding, people kept running, and I leaned against the door and stared into space.

"Is it under his nose?" Adam asked.

Something cold and metal tickled the inside of my nostrils and then I heard a clank as metal hit the tile floor. Seconds after the device was dropped to the floor, I finally felt a sense of urgency. My body sprang from the wall, my gun aimed at nothing but readied regardless.

"It worked!" Stewart said.

I shook my head and looked back and forth between the two of them. Stewart had a huge bruise on her cheek and blood running down her face from a cut on her forehead. Adam had dirt all over his face so I couldn't tell if he'd been in a fight or not. "What happened? Where's everyone else?"

"We don't know," Stewart snapped. "We need to get out of here. Now."

"They've got guns," I accused, aiming my words at Adam. We had not counted on anyone at Eyewall having a gun.

"I never saw a single weapon while I was here, I swear," Adam said.

As if on cue, gunshots sounded from the floor above us. "Get out of here! I'll get Blake."

Stewart looked at me for a long moment and then grabbed Adam's arm and took off, dragging him along.

I found the door Blake had disappeared through and saw him bent over some complicated device full of wires. "Blake, we gotta go! Plan's changed."

He stood up and looked right at me. "Go ahead, I'll catch up."

My heart raced as I heard more gunshots coming from unidentifiable locations. Where were Dad and Holly? Did they leave already? I could only hope. "You don't even have a gun, come on!"

I grabbed on to his sleeve but he shook out of my grip, yanked up the leg of my pants, and swiped my spare gun. "Now I do."

"You don't even know how to use it," I snapped. "Let's just go."

I waited while he reached into the back of his jeans and removed a white envelope, holding it out to me. On the front, in careful script, was a name: Lily.

When I didn't reach out to take it from his hands, he lifted my shirt and stuffed it inside my waistband before stepping back farther into the small room. "I'm not leaving, Jackson. I was never going to leave."

Something twisted in my gut and my heart sped even faster. "What the hell, Blake? Why can't you set the damn thing and go?"

"They'll find a way to turn it off and we won't get another chance."

"No, no way." I exhaled and squeezed my hands shut. "Give it to me, then. I'll do it. *I'll* do it, Blake. You go."

He gave me a sad smile. "I'd never let you do that, Jackson. This is my fight. This is my chance to make amends for what happened to Lily and her family. You'll get your turn soon enough."

A high-pitched scream erupted from the hallway. I skidded out the door and saw Emily being carried deeper into the building by two men, a woman trailing behind them. She fought and kicked, trying to get away. Blake was right behind me, watching over my shoulder.

"Get her and get out of here," he said firmly. "You've got exactly three minutes."

I felt like my chest had caved in. I had no idea what lay outside this building. Had anyone else made it out? Regardless, Emily was here and I could save her. I knew I could.

I spun around to face Blake. "Look—"

"Go!" He pointed toward the screaming Emily. "I know you'd never let anything happen to her, Jackson. Go! Just do what I asked, for Lily?"

I let out breath and looked over at Emily. "Okay . . . *okay.*"

That was it. My decision had been made and all I could do was take off toward the men and woman trying to stuff Emily back in that room again or worse, "eliminating experiment 1029" as Thomas had basically tried to do by dumping her in the wilderness with the rebel experiments.

With my adrenaline rush and my newfound superhuman powers, I kicked one dude to the ground, knocked out another with my elbow, and shot the woman in the thigh with my pistol. Emily screamed as she and the woman fell. The woman clutched her leg, red seeping into her brown clothing. Before I could scoop Emily up, half a dozen more people appeared in front of us, guns aimed at the tiny little girl with flaming red hair. Her eyes bulged and her entire body froze. I dove forward, reaching for her waist, and barely took in an unfamiliar blurred figure, someone much younger than the other Eyewall workers, who seemed to stumble forward, accidentally flinging himself in front of the six bullets that released simultaneously, hurtling in Emily's direction. I had no idea what exactly had just happened but regardless, relief swept over me.

I grabbed Emily, jumped to my feet, and ran faster than I've ever run in my life, not taking a second to glance back. We burst outside into the cold night, Emily's face buried in my shoulder, and her fingers digging into my back. The second we passed through the gate connected to the electric fence, the entire structure exploded behind us in a cloud of fire, dust, and smoke. I forced the thought of all the people inside out of my mind and focused on my feet hitting the ground over and over again. The woods were so dark I could hardly see a thing, but they were miraculously free of the choking smoke. Emily lifted her head and pointed at several people, off to the right, standing frozen, watching the explosion. I slowed my pace, setting Emily down, clutched my sides, and tried to catch my breath.

My eyes zoomed in on the waiting people . . . *Courtney, Adam, Lonnie, Marshall, Stewart, Mason* . . .

"Oh thank God!" Dad shouted.

Before I could even begin to panic, Holly was right in front of me. She threw her arms around my neck, nearly knocking me over. She had caught me by surprise, so much that I almost cracked a joke about her being my enemy. But I felt her shaking, tears landing on the side of my neck. I froze for a second and then wrapped my arms around her, squeezing her tight.

I turned my head, burying my face in her hair, running my hand over it. "Blake made me leave him," I whispered. I needed to tell someone. "He wanted to set off the bomb himself. To make sure they couldn't stop it. He wouldn't leave, I couldn't . . ."

She lifted her head, eyes meeting mine. "Maybe he planned it that way all along?"

I fought off the blurriness in my eyes, the lump in my throat, and finally released Holly, stepping behind her, and got pummeled right away by my sister.

"I would have killed you if you didn't make it out," she said, crying much harder than Holly. Dad was bent over, like he was still trying to catch his breath from making his own run out here.

Lonnie had already picked up Emily. She looked at me, eyes still a little hopeful. "Blake?"

I just shook my head and watched as tears filled her eyes. "Where are Grayson and Sasha?"

"They were shot before we got out," Dad said. "I'm not sure who shot Sasha, but Grayson went after Thomas . . . he just took off, and there was no stopping him. Believe me, I tried."

I knew exactly what he meant. Blake had been just as hard-headed. We turned to face the smoke and fire that used to be the Eyewall headquarters and stood in silence. My arm was slung around Courtney's shoulders when Holly brushed up against my other side. Our hands collided and our fingers linked together. We all stayed there for a long time until Marshall broke the silence.

"The smoke will start drifting this way more heavily. We should move farther away and set up camp or decide to jump back."

I let go of Holly's hand and withdrew my arm from Courtney's shoulders. "Lonnie?" She turned around to face me, both her and Emily looking right at me. "Are you still going somewhere with Emily?"

"Only if that's okay with you?" She set Emily down on the ground again and I knelt in front of her.

"I'm gonna miss you, kid."

She was already wiping tears from her cheeks, sniffling from the drama of what had just happened, the smoke and the future ahead. "Me, too."

I leaned in closer, and whispered, "Do you know anything about that ring you delivered to me the first time I met you? Is it for Lily Kendrick? Are you still going to bring it to a younger me when you're eleven?"

She shook her head. "I think we've changed too many things for that to happen, right?"

I found my backpack on the ground and patted the front pouch. "So you don't know why I have this ring?"

I briefly explained Blake's conversation with me while the others talked and made plans.

Emily listened carefully, and then finally said, "Maybe Blake gave it to an older version of me? I don't know, but I guess it doesn't matter so long as she gets it."

I glanced at the wreckage again and sighed. "I guess not."

She put her arms around my neck and gave me a squeeze. I hugged her back and then had to ask one more question before she left me for good. "So that pet chicken you mentioned . . . where exactly—"

"With the people in the tents," she said right away. "The dots on the map."

"The electromagnetic field is down," Marshall said. "I can feel it."

I could, too, like a buzzing in my fingertips. I could jump right now. "Let's get out of here. I don't want to wait." *I don't want to think about Emily jumping so far away from me, about Blake being gone . . . yeah, let's get out of here quick.*

Emily touched my cheek, trying to get my attention again. "Chief Marshall is the best time jumper. You don't have to worry about anyone's getting hurt, okay?"

I knew she said that because it was obvious everyone thought I'd overexerted my mind on the jump here trying to protect Holly from injury. Maybe I had, but then again, I'd just done a half-jump to the 1950s prior to my excursion to the future and was pretty spent.

"And remember, Courtney can time-jump, too, so you'll have plenty of help getting everyone back safely," she added.

That's right, Courtney can time-travel. I'd almost forgotten about our arrival in 3200, when those faceless men had attacked us and before any of them could touch her, she kept vanishing and then reappearing like a magic trick. But based on how shocked she was by her own movement, I wasn't convinced she'd been put in the expert time-jumper category just yet.

"Thanks. I'll remember that." I gave Emily another squeeze and whispered good-bye before releasing her.

I stood between Dad and Courtney as we watched Lonnie take Emily's hand and vanish, heading to a time way beyond my present but far from this destroyed future.

The smell of smoke grew stronger and flakes of ashes floated through the air, so we quickly moved deeper into the forest. Even though I was ready to leave right that second, Dad and Marshall both agreed it would be best if we rested for at least a few minutes. Stewart and Mason set up some chairs and started a fire and we passed around bottles of water in silence. Holly came and sat beside me while Dad, Marshall, and Adam were deep in discussion about exactly which point each of us left in 2009.

"Hey," she said, handing over her half-empty water.

I took a long swig and then handed it back. "What's on your mind?"

"What isn't?" She glanced wearily at me. "I just can't believe they're gone—Grayson, Sasha . . . *and Blake.* I knew he was on a mission and all but I didn't realize . . ."

"Me either." I kept my eyes straight ahead, fighting off tears. I could still feel that moment in the room with him. I could have dragged him out. I could have done the job for him.

"I keep thinking about what he said in his memory files, the descriptions of the rooms full of kids. They're all gone now." Her voice shook. She paused and took a breath. "We did that. We . . ."

"I think that's the bigger picture Marshall was talking about. We managed to blow up that building, knowing there were experiments . . . *children* . . . inside and despite it all we still had the instinct to survive. Maybe this proves that Blake is a better person than all of us. *Was* a better person."

"Yeah, maybe," Holly agreed.

Courtney joined our conversation and I could tell she wanted to say something so I looked up at her and waited. "I'm so sorry about Emily getting in."

There were so many questions and blanks still to be filled in from the last couple hours. "How did she get away from you? And it was just her, not you and Lonnie?"

Courtney shook her head. "It was awful, Jackson. She saw some guy and took off running. We couldn't get her before . . . before they did. I don't know what she was thinking. Maybe she thought it was you?"

I patted Courtney on the shoulder. "It's okay. She's fine now. We all are." I looked at my sister, remembering what Emily had just mentioned. "Do you really think you can do the time jump back? Does it feel like something you know how to do?"

She managed a half smile or maybe more of a smirk. "My brain damage is worse than your brain damage and you know what that means, right?"

"What?" Holly and I both said.

"I'm accessing the area that allows for time travel to a much greater degree than you are." The smile faded and I knew she'd just recited something Grayson had probably told her. Maybe they talked about it the other day after she'd had her seizure and he'd examined her.

Not wanting to cast another shadow over us right before our big moment, I grinned at my sister, and said, "You think you're better than me? Game on, then. We'll see who comes out on top when we get back home."

Holly gave a little smile then gnawed on her lower lip. "But there's still so many doors open when you're dealing with time travel, right? What are the reversal possibilities? When will we know if changes are permanent?"

"Well that's just lovely to think about," Stewart mumbled.

"Don't think about it," Dad snapped. "I think it's best we focus on moving ahead, which for us means heading back in time."

I stood up and reached for my backpack, tossing it over my shoulder. "Let's do this. I'm ready."

"You sure?" Dad asked, concern filling his face.

I knew this had to be difficult for him after witnessing my near death from time travel not too long ago and Grayson's warnings about my possible brain damage, but so far, ever since Dad tried to shoot me in the woods, I'd had these ultrasharp senses that I could literally feel coursing through my body. Maybe that was the buzzing that Emily described when she was in the presence of time jumpers.

"Something we all need to be aware of," Marshall said. "Because our returns might not align perfectly with our points of departure, you may encounter duplicate versions of yourself."

Holly's eyes went wide with fear. "And what exactly do we do if that happens?"

Marshall's gaze traveled over Holly's head, not making direct eye contact. "We'll cross that bridge when we come to it."

"Great," Stewart and Mason both mumbled under their breath.

The impending time jump provided a good distraction from looking at each person around me and analyzing the possibilities of duplicate selves and the impossibilities due to horrible things that happened before the jump to the future.

We'll cross that bridge when—and if—we come to it. For once, I was one hundred percent supportive of a Chief Marshall plan.

"We are returning to the exact day and location that Jackson left 2009 because that is the most natural time jump for him to make with the lowest probability of his sustaining a fatal injury. Those of you who were deceased on that day or left on another day, we will take extra precautions for you after we arrive and head to either Agent Meyer's place or the underground Tempest headquarters, understood?"

We all nodded a yes and then I looked around at everyone, suddenly remembering one other very important detail. "We were all being held up by Eyewall agents when we left. They would have watched us vanish."

"Dude! That's right," Mason said. "Holly was our hostage."

Tension filled Marshall's face. "All right then, better play the hostage role, Agent Flynn. Everybody, have your weapons ready. Hopefully, the element of surprise will give us a few seconds to react before they do."

I drew my gun but turned the safety on. I didn't want it to fire accidentally if my brain exploded or something. My legs were shaking but I tried to play it cool and reached for Holly, pressing her back against my chest. "Let's go, Hostage, assume the position."

She laughed but I could feel the nerves leaking through. "Are you scared?" she whispered.

I leaned down so my lips were touching her ear. "Incredibly."

"We don't have to stay enemies, you know," Holly said. "Even if I am an Eyewall agent."

A lightness filled my chest, relieving me of some of the more recent pain. "I know. We'll figure it out."

After that, I opened my mind, focused on the time and space between here and home. Focused on the moment we left— smelling it, tasting it, breathing it. The world vanished and pulled me into a new oblivion.

CHAPTER TWENTY-ONE

Two things were immediately apparent as we landed back in the present:

1) My brain didn't explode.
2) The Eyewall firing squad wasn't waiting there for our return.

I knew we'd hit the mark just fine. I felt myself rejoining with the exact millisecond that I'd left 2009. I also knew that hitting this mark was the most natural form of time travel for my brain to handle. I wasn't sure exactly what I had expected to find. Possibly the parade of Eyewall agents that had been holding us all at gunpoint when we left? Maybe Senator Healy or my dead body lying outside that cage they'd kept the other version of me in for months.

After making my initial assessment, I released Holly and was immediately bombarded by Dad, Courtney, and Holly, who took turns lifting my sleeves, checking for bruises, and looking at my ears to check for bleeding. Dad produced a flashlight and shined it in my eyes.

"You're okay?" Dad asked. "Any pain at all?"

I knew the answer was important, and since I hadn't noticed myself dying the first time around, I took a second to step back to shake out my limbs and slowly go through each section of my body piece by piece. There were some sore places that I'd had before I left 3200, but nothing new.

I looked up at him, my eyes wide with relief. "I'm . . . I'm fine. Really."

He sighed and laughed at the same time and then hugged me. Courtney joined in until we were finally interrupted by Mason's asking the most important question of the day, "Okay, so, where's Eyewall? Are you sure this is the right time?"

"I'm positive." I stepped back from the group hug and drew my gun, ready for whatever happened to be on the other side of that door. "Is everyone else okay?"

"I'm fine," both Stewart and Mason replied. Marshall, of course, survived with no problems at all, and Dad, Holly, and Courtney appeared unharmed.

I elbowed Courtney in the side, feeling light with relief. "My jump was totally better than yours. I'm pretty sure I landed a couple milliseconds before you."

She snorted a laugh. "Did not."

As the eight of us braced ourselves for a fight, tentatively stepping through the door of the small room and into the hallway, passing the warehouse cage that the other me had been held in, all we found was eerie silence and no trace that anyone had entered this building for quite some time.

"There's dust on the floor," Stewart pointed out.

Dad leaned over and examined the untouched ground in front of us. "No footprints."

"Do you think it's different because we destroyed future Eyewall?" Adam asked.

Holly exchanged glances with him and I could see the questions silently arising—what would that mean for them? Were their lives altered, too?

No one had an answer. Not even Marshall. When we left the building and walked outside into the warm summer air, it became apparent that the changes to 2009 extended far beyond the absence of Eyewall. The streets were nearly silent. Only a couple cabs passed by, no buses, no people on the sidewalks. Which was why the sound of running footsteps caused everyone but Courtney to raise their guns and point them at the lone figure of a man approaching us in the darkness.

"Agent Collins?" Holly said, lowering her weapon. Adam did

the same, stepping toward the man who had been their Eyewall superior. But I knew Agent Collins wasn't on Eyewall's side—not after he warned me about protecting Holly when I interrogated him in Tempest headquarters before leaving 2009. Maybe we had landed a few minutes early and they were just now preparing to rush into the building? But that didn't explain the dust, the lack of footprints, the absence of Healy and the caged version of me.

Marshall held his gun steady but also moved toward the middle-aged agent who, I noticed, hadn't drawn a weapon and didn't appear surprised to see the eight of us here.

"Dr. Melvin sent me," Collins said, lifting his hands and facing Marshall. "We shouldn't discuss too much out here. There are a lot of government personnel monitoring this area."

Dr. Melvin's supposed to be dead, so either something is off or he's taking orders from a dead man.

"Which government personnel?" Dad asked, looking Collins over. "And why are they monitoring the area?"

"The virus." Collins's eyes were wide as if he was afraid to tell us the truth. "Because of the virus."

Marshall looked around, taking everything in. For the first time ever, I watched the careful composure drop from Marshall's face and form something other than anger or greed. I'd seen both of those looks on him before. But this was different. The expression that filled his face right then was a cross between wonder and panic. Neither of which was too reassuring. "Deludere Virus," he said under his breath.

Collins's expression was grim but he gave a nod to Marshall. "We need to get underground."

"Is it contagious?" Courtney asked. "Should we hold our breath or something?"

"No one knows exactly how it's transmitted." Collins turned his back on us, pulling out his own weapon and heading down the street, eyes darting around as we all followed behind him.

"But you know, don't you?" Holly said.

Collins looked over his shoulder at her and then faced forward again. "Dr. Melvin has a theory. I'll let him explain."

"Melvin's alive?" Stewart asked.

Collins took a moment to assess her question before finally answering. "Yes."

I forced back the sickening and gut-wrenching image of Dr. Melvin lying dead on the floor of his office, sheet white and cold as ice. *He's alive. That's all that matters.*

"This is totally going to turn all *I Am Legend,* isn't it?" I whispered to Adam, who was now beside me. "The crazy monsters are going to come flying at us any second trying to eat our flesh."

Adam's eyebrows lifted. "Deludere. It's Latin for—"

"Delusion," Stewart finished. "A false belief."

We all fell silent at that revelation. I had no idea if this was connected to the merging timelines and the delusions Holly, Stewart, and Adam had all experienced along with Dr. Melvin.

The entrance to the underground CIA headquarters was in a desolate subway station. Agent Collins glanced around before opening a heavy brown door, revealing a concrete staircase, with rusty metal railings and paint peeling from the walls. The stench in the air was similar to the smell you'd find after leaving sweaty gym clothes zipped up in a bag for a week. We trudged down several flights of stairs; Holly's arm brushed mine a few too many times to be accidental. I had envisioned our return to 2009 as the moment she'd stop relying on me, take off on her own, and go back to her life, but even without any words from her, I could feel them floating across the space between us—I'm not done with this. I'm not done with us yet. Even in light of the looming mysterious changes to 2009, I felt a tiny surge of hope simply walking beside her, watching the walls slowly crumble between us.

It took about twenty minutes to reach headquarters, which were still located below the NYU Hospital, despite all the changes. We found Dr. Melvin in a lab with Lily Kendrick. Of course, like an idiot, I ran up and hugged her. Instead of leaping with joy at my reappearance, she stiffened in the way you might when a relative you don't remember tries to hug you. I released her and stepped back.

"Um . . . this is new," she said to me before looking at Stewart and then Mason. "Where the hell have you two been for the past three months? I thought you were dead! We all thought you were dead."

"Uh . . ." Mason stuttered.

"Oh my lord." Dr. Melvin had wide, crazy eyes as he moved toward Courtney. "I can't . . . I mean . . . how?"

Our group had now grown to eleven members and we were huddled in the lab, everyone looking confused until Dad stepped into the middle of the room and held his hands up.

"All right, obviously we are *not* where we expected to be, so before anyone has a heart attack or draws weapons, let's assess the situation, get our bearings." Dad nodded toward Marshall, who walked to the giant whiteboard and picked up a dry-erase marker.

"Collins, you first," Marshall said. "State your name, position, and year of recruitment."

Collins snapped to attention, obviously recognizing Marshall as his boss, which was another strange phenomenon since he's been an Eyewall leader before we left 2009. "Agent Mike Collins. Graduate of Dunston Academy's early CIA recruitment program. Tempest Agent. Official CIA recruitment in 1989. Joined Tempest in 1996."

Dunston Academy? The teenage Agent Meyer Senior in the 1950s had told me he graduated from that school, too, as well as his father.

"Tempest?" Holly and Adam said together.

Marshall let out a frustrated breath and then grabbed Courtney's arm, shoving another marker in her hand. "Okay, in addition, state which individuals currently in this lab you recognize and have interacted with in person and under what circumstances. Kid A will record those responses."

Courtney glared at him but uncapped the marker anyway. "*Kid A* happens to have a name."

Collins let his gaze drift around the room as he listed off his answer. "Dr. Melvin, met him on my first day with Tempest. Chief Marshall, also met him on day one. Agent Kendrick, I oversaw her training beginning in 2008. Agent Sterling and Agent Stewart started working under me in 2007. Haven't seen them since they left for a mission in the Middle East three months ago." His eyes fell on Dad. "Agent Meyer is my superior and the man who recruited me from my former CIA division."

Marshall nodded toward Holly and Adam. "Do you recognize those two?"

"No, sir."

"Maybe he always worked for Tempest," I heard Holly whisper to Adam. "A double agent."

Marshall rested a hand on Courtney's shoulder while she wrote responses as quickly as possible. "And Child A?" Then he pointed at me. "Or Child B?"

Collins glanced wearily at Courtney. "I know them as Agent Meyer's adopted children . . . but . . . well . . ."

Courtney turned around and rolled her eyes. "I'm dead. We know. That's why I'm mysteriously three years younger than my twin even though I was born first. Okay, moving on . . ."

"Why is no one talking about the fact that Stewart and I are fucking MIA?" Mason interrupted. "Are we dead or what?"

"What he means," Stewart clarified, "is that . . . unlike Junior and Blondie here, neither Mason nor I returned to the point where we left, so . . ."

"There might be duplicates," Kendrick finished.

I raised my hand but spoke before anyone called on me. "I think I can eliminate a few individual assessments assuming that in this current 2009, neither I, nor Holly nor Adam have joined the CIA, which is why Collins and Kendrick know Courtney and me only as Agent Meyer's kids, correct?" I waited a second to get a nod from both Collins and Kendrick. "Marshall is the boss of Tempest, Dad is a subboss, and so is Collins. Now, have any of the people who didn't just time-travel from the year 3200 ever heard of Eye-wall?"

Dr. Melvin slowly lifted a hand in the air. "The child. She's the reason I knew you'd arrive today and where you'd arrive and that none of you have any idea of the danger involved in returning to your former homes."

"Emily," Stewart and Holly both muttered.

"Can we just get to explaining that whole deadly viral outbreak thing?" I asked.

Kendrick stared at me. "Why did you try to hug me? I've never interacted with you in person."

I had to admit, that stung a little. I valued Kendrick's friend-ship even more than I'd realized. "We were partners in Tempest. I guess you could say we were friends."

She must have read some of the disappointment in my face be-cause her expression turned less hard, making her look more like the Kendrick I had known.

I clapped my hands together. "Okay. Virus. Danger. The world is different. Let's talk about that."

"I second Jackson's suggestion," Adam said.

"Me, too," Holly said.

Honestly, I had expected Dr. Melvin or Marshall to start ex-plaining first, but it was Dad who cleared his throat and started talking, his voice low, carefully concealing his emotions. "It was a theory of Eileen's . . . creating an alternate world . . . the one Jackson calls World B . . . might eventually cause—"

"Convergence," I suddenly remembered from a chat in Dr. Mel-vin's office that seemed like five centuries ago.

Dr. Melvin nodded. "It's not a clean break; splitting off to cre-ate this World B might not be completely separate. The virus most likely started from time jumps to World B. Any tiny alteration that Jackson made in that world which is different from this world causes delusions to occur in any individual who might have been affected by those changes."

"And Jackson would have no idea of the chain reaction he'd created. It would all seem subtle," Kendrick chimed in.

Dad's hand landed on my shoulder, squeezing it tight. My heart was already racing, my palms sweating. Could I really have caused this viral outbreak and to what extent?

"The affected individuals then see two possible paths to every one journey," Dr. Melvin explained. "They lose the ability to differentiate reality from delusion, or at least in the eyes of the U.S. government and the United Nations, the alternative paths they are seeing or remembering are viewed as delusions. But *we* know it's reality, just not this reality."

"Wait," Holly said. "You mean you haven't shared this information with the government? Or the UN? Isn't that a little extreme, keeping your time-travel information a secret when there are people going crazy out there?"

"If we thought our information would help with finding a cure, of course we'd share it," Dr. Melvin said. "But everything we know does nothing but confirm the fact that there is no cure and it's only going to get worse."

"Jackson isn't the only one who jumped to World B," Courtney announced. "He might have opened the door, but all those cloned time travelers have been bouncing off that other world and probably making all kinds of changes."

"Well . . ." Dr. Melvin said. "That explains the severity of the outbreak. What all of you have to realize is that these chain reactions aren't instant. Maybe something one of those cloned time travelers did caused a person to not get on a train or a bus or to jump into a different cab and thus it affected something two years, ten years, or a lifetime down the road . . . the possibilities are endless. It's like a domino maze that goes on indefinitely."

"Why didn't we notice the virus before?" I asked. "This is the same night we left in 2009, yet we've come back from the future and everything has changed. Why?"

"The time jumps to World B must have increased while you

were all trapped in 3200," Marshall said. "It has created an alternate 2009 even though we're still in the same timeline. There has been an irreversible alteration. Future events have altered the past and caused the outbreak of this virus to speed up. But it *was* present before you left, if I'm remembering right, Agent Meyer?" Marshall was looking at me and not Dad so I nodded, knowing that Stewart, Dr. Melvin, and Holly had all experienced delusions.

"But if it's just delusions," Mason said, "how is that dangerous?"

"They're causing widespread panic," Collins answered. "Worldwide panic to be more specific. The delusions have resulted in people's no longer being able to grasp the concept of cause and effect or irreversible consequences. Currently, the virus is affecting about 25 percent of the United States population and 12 percent of the total world population. Those numbers go up on a monthly basis. There isn't enough space in hospitals to hold everyone who's infected. Of course, there are probably hundreds of thousands of people who are aware of early signs of it but are in denial. Over half of our division is currently locked up in the mental ward five floors above us."

Silence fell on the entire room. From the corner of my eye, I saw Holly back away toward the door. "I'm infected, right? I know you're all thinking it. I'm going to go crazy, aren't I?"

She didn't wait for anyone to correct her or to agree with her. She spun around and headed out the door and down the hall. Adam immediately started to follow her, but I held my arm out to stop him. "Stay here. You can explain everything to me later."

There were all kinds of classrooms and restrooms, labs and rooms with regular army-style beds and some with hospital-style beds, lots of supply closets and offices full of computers and other machines. This was why it took me a good twenty minutes to find Holly sitting in the dark on the floor of a room that had a twin bed, white dresser, white walls, white bedding, a small closet, and a bathroom with a white bathtub and shower curtain with white towels hanging on a rack.

"I have a feeling this is exactly what my new home will look like," Holly said, glancing up at me. "The only things missing are the padded walls and straitjacket. Did they decide already? How long before they take me up to the fifth floor?"

"If they take you, I'll fake delusions." I leaned against the door-frame, allowing my mind to focus on the positive, not the hope-lessness we'd heard. "We can be roommates."

Holly surprised me by laughing. "I'm not really as scared as I seemed in there. I just needed to get away. If Courtney can handle her fate with such bravery, I can handle mine."

"It might not get any worse." I stepped all the way into the room and walked over and sat down beside her.

Holly gave me a tiny smile. "Promise you won't tell anyone I said this?"

"I have to promise in advance?"

She rolled her eyes. "Once I'd heard all the facts and knew what we were dealing with, I kind of felt okay with it. I mean, I thought we were going to die a few hours ago, and now I'm back in 2009 and Adam's here and you and me are okay. And all I can think about is whether 25 percent of the population's being infected would cause all the Starbucks in the city to close because I'd love to have some coffee. And maybe the hospital has a cafeteria and we could, like, get some pasta or something that isn't fish cooked on a campfire or those meal bars. Maybe a piece of fruit or some vegetables? We're all probably on the verge of scurvy right now."

I stared at her in disbelief, hanging mostly on one tiny part of her speech. "You and me are okay? Really?"

The smile dropped from her face and she took a deep breath. "Do you want the honest answer or the vague one? Because I've been thinking about this a lot over the past three or four days."

"The honest one," I said without hesitation.

"Did you ever see the movie *50 First Dates*?"

"The one where the girl loses her memory every day? With Adam Sandler?"

The urge to touch her, to pull her into my arms, was so strong I had to fight to keep my hands off her. Every time we got closer and then came apart, I had to constantly reevaluate my status. Was I someone who was allowed to touch Holly whenever I wanted or was it just certain moments? We'd had nothing but a hot-and-cold relationship, which was why I couldn't believe she'd said we were okay.

"Yeah, that movie. It's all I can think about right now," she said. "Do you think it's possible to make someone fall in love with you every single day?"

I laughed. "I know it's not possible. Not every day. You can tell someone what they should feel or even what you know they've felt before but you can't make them feel it."

She was looking at me again, studying my face. "Okay, so that's what you're worried about, huh? That's the expression you're always wearing on your face that kind of scares the shit out of me. You want to know it's real? That it's really coming from *this* version of me?"

I hesitated before nodding. "Wouldn't you?"

"Yeah, I would." She turned her body, angling it toward me. "Since you asked for the honest answer, that's what I'll give you. I think you're one of the most interesting, compassionate people I've ever met. You're vulnerable and flawed and I love how you get so pissed off about Courtney and Mason and how you wanted to hate Blake but you couldn't help liking him even though you were fighting this urge to break his nose every time he got too close to me."

I pushed aside my grief for Blake and held my breath, unable to move a muscle while Holly's voice totally captivated me. Her face was so bright and beautiful, I didn't even want to blink. Somehow in the last few days, she'd dropped the agent facade and had just been Holly.

"And I love how loyal you and Stewart are to each other," she continued. "And how you tell your dad everything . . . and the way you looked at me when I told you about Adam that night when you caught me searching your apartment. I knew he meant something to you like he did to me, but I couldn't let myself see it then, not completely. I love how you are with Emily. She's just this ball of glass waiting to shatter and you always know exactly what to say to her . . . and I love how many times you've managed to tell me you're sorry." She looked down at her hands, drawing in a shaky breath. "But I don't know if I love you or if I'm too screwed up to be as close to you as another version of me was. I realize I've seemed more than enthusiastic on at least two occasions, but I don't think I would have been able to take it much further than what we did. And I had confidence from the delusions, as weird as that sounds. When I tapped into that other Holly, it all felt familiar and my own fears vanished, I guess because she didn't have those fears."

"Holly—" I started to say, finding my voice.

She cut me off, touching her fingers to my mouth. "But without a doubt, I can totally see why and how other versions of me have fallen for you."

I shook my head. "I was not the same guy the first time we met. Trust me."

"I know myself pretty well, and I think I would choose potential to be amazing over someone who's just plain great," Holly said. "And I like sitting here with you as me . . . just me . . . I like that I can see you filtering out those versions and deciding if this version is good enough for you. I think it's a good start, don't you?"

I wanted to kiss her probably more than I've ever wanted to kiss anyone in my entire life, but I couldn't ruin the moment or the progress we'd made. She was right, it had taken me a while to start seeing this Holly as this Holly. I smiled at her and nodded toward the door. "Want to go on our first date?"

"Where to?"

I got to my feet quickly and reached out a hand to help her up. "If I can dig into my memory, I should be able to gain the access code for the elevator and we can check out that hospital cafeteria."

"Just us?"

"Just us," I said, leading her out the door.

CHAPTER TWENTY-TWO

Holly dumped a few more Skittles into her hand, tossing them quickly in her mouth. "Well, vending-machine junk food still beats what we've been eating lately."

"Agreed." I leaned back on the bench, closing my eyes, enjoying every bit of my Snickers bar. After taking the final bite, I turned and grinned at her. "What next? What other 2009 experiences should we have tonight?"

Holly crumpled the candy bag and her face turned serious all of a sudden. "I want to go home, see my mom. I know they'll tell us we can't. We don't even know what my life is supposed to be like in this redesigned 2009, but I don't care about any of that."

One look at the desperation and intensity in her eyes and I knew she was dead serious, and there was nothing in the world I wanted more right now than to make Holly happy. I knew we shouldn't do this either, and I knew Dad and everyone would be worried about our disappearing, but I didn't really care about any of that either. "Okay."

Surprise filled her face. "Really? We can go?"

"Yeah, but we should go now because if they don't want us to do this, they'll start watching us or say something meaningful enough for us to realize our stupidity and I'm kind of in an ignorance-is-bliss mood, how about you?"

"Totally."

It took over an hour to get to Holly's house, and all the sitting around on the train caused me to grow a little anxious and nervous about leaving without telling anyone. It wasn't like we had working cell phones or anything either.

It was obvious right away from Holly's face and the missing vehicle that her mom wasn't home. Still, she found the hidden key and unlocked the door, letting me follow her inside and to her bedroom. I watched as she walked to the closet, lifting the sleeves of several different shirts to her nose and inhaling before throwing a big smile in my direction.

"It's a little different than Agent Holly's room but it still feels like me, like my stuff," she said. She glanced over at me right then, hope filling her expression. "Do you think this is the normal Holly's room?"

There was a framed picture lying on the nightstand. I held it up for her to see. Her eyes widened, and she said, "Oh my God! Do you think I'm still dating David? I was with him, right?"

I set the picture down and turned slowly to face her. "How do you know about that version of you?"

She busied herself, burying her face in a dresser drawer. "You know how Emily went all crazy and started writing a bunch of stuff down?"

I rolled my eyes. Of course I remembered.

"Well she wrote down Normal Holly's diary and I swiped some of the pages while you and Adam were looking over your experiments or whatever."

So that's why she bolted from the tent that day. "Why do you call her Normal Holly?"

She shrugged. "What do you call her?"

I laughed. "Um, I called her Holly. Then I called her 009 Holly after I'd met 007 Holly and needed a way to distinguish the two when I explained stuff to Adam. Now . . . well, I don't know what to call that Holly because I sort of went back to her but it was before the date I left and everything was different. I just don't know. The diary I've seen was from the first Holly that I met. That much I know for sure."

She stared at me, her mouth hanging open. "Wow, that is so freakin' weird."

"Yep." I lifted up the mattress and yanked the blue velvet diary out. Holly snatched it from my hands before I got a chance to open it.

"Oh look, David and I broke up two days ago!" She flipped back several pages and sank down onto the bed, reading.

I wandered the room, searching for familiar items, opening drawers. My fingers froze on a pair of purple thong panties resting in Holly's underwear drawer.

"Jackson, you're such a stud."

I dropped the panties, slamming the drawer shut, then glanced at Holly, expecting her to reprimand me, but she was still staring at the diary.

"This is the party in Jersey you were talking about at Healy's ball, the one with the fire and camping and beer kegs. It was Adam's party. I can't believe you went to that." Holly's eyes were still on the diary in her hands but she patted the spot beside her.

I sat down, leaning in to read the page she was currently engrossed in.

> Jackson looks comfortable and at ease chatting with Terri.
> Figures.
> I'm trying not to listen in on their conversation and what playboy method of flirting a guy like Jackson might use, but Terri's voice carries so much, I can't help but overhear.
> "Oh my God! I love French poetry. I can't believe that's your major," she squeals. "I totally would have picked that, but Brown isn't the best school for it and my counselor told my parents I could never have a career with that major."
> "I'll keep that in mind," Jackson says, with amusement in his voice. I guess it doesn't matter if he makes any money in the future. Not like he needs it. "I'm also majoring in English lit, like your friend Holly Flynn is planning on doing."
> "Right," Terri says, looking in my direction. "I forgot you're going to NYU."
> "Yep."
> Terri turns away from me and back to Jackson. "I'm dying to get into this lit class at Brown called Why Gatsby Makes the Perfect Husband. Don't you just love that book?"

"Gatsby would never make the perfect husband," Jackson says, sipping his beer.

"Oh come on. He's amazing and mysterious and so . . . devoted to one woman."

"The guy's a nutcase. Mentally unstable and shut down," Jackson says. "But maybe it's an improvement for some people."

I laugh and he glances in my direction. "Holly's a sucker for Shakespeare."

Just the way his eyes are zooming into mine gives me goose bumps and I run my hands up and down my arms. Jackson pulls a sweatshirt out from behind him and tosses it at me. "You look cold."

"Thanks," I say, and then roll my eyes. "I never said I liked Shakespeare."

I slide my arms into his shirt and he motions for me to move closer. And I actually do. Maybe because I'm bored or possibly because I'm a little too curious.

"Forget what I said, Terri," Jackson corrects. "She likes sword fights."

Terri giggles again and then sighs. "I love Romeo and Juliet . . . and Hamlet."

"Hamlet's awesome," Jackson tells her. "Death, suicide, incest . . . what's not to like."

I laugh again and Terri glares at me. I'm not trying to be mean, but I totally can't help it. It takes a halfway smart guy to actually remember what the story's about, but to know it well enough to make fun of it, now that's pretty freakin' cool.

"Actually, I did like one line in the play," he says. "I know a hawk from a handsaw."

"That's a very useful line," I joke. "Any metaphors? Or theories on the hidden meaning?"

He turns to me and pulls the borrowed sweatshirt over my shoulder. "I turned in a ten-page paper about how that line represented the male preoccupation with size and got an A. But really it was a complete load of crap."

"That I believe," I say.

He leans in closer and my voice stops dead in my throat. I don't know why he's moving so close and why my heart is racing and why I'm totally frozen. Then he whispers, "Are you going to scream if I tell you there's a bug in your hair? I'm just asking because it would ruin my chances of hooking up with this chick."

"In that case, you'll thank me later," I say through my teeth. "But please remove the bug."

He reaches a hand in my hair and pulls something out before tossing it behind us. A shiver runs down my spine and Jackson smiles, and says, "It was just a beetle. No big deal."

And then it's like his face changes. He's staring at me with such an intense look and I can't look away. Then his free hand moves over my hair again and he tucks it behind my ear. "All clear now."

"Thanks," I say, and somehow I just know if he keeps staring at me like this, we'll keep moving closer, and it feels like the most natural thing in the world. And suddenly, I'm fighting this urge to touch his face. There's a tiny bit of stubble on his chin and I'm dying to run my fingers over it. Instead, I take my free hand and sit on it.

He says something in French and it pulls me from my daze.

"Huh?"

He shakes his head and smiles. "Sorry, I meant to say that in English." His eyes unlock from mine and dart in Terri's direction and then back to me. "That was just one other Hamlet quote I can handle without gagging."

"Which one is that?" Terri asks, although she's supposedly fluent in French. Guess she forgot.

"I have heard of your paintings too, well enough; God has given you one face and you make yourself another."

"Yeah, I like that one, too," I say. "So many ways to interpret it."

Terri gets up to get another beer and I nudge Jackson in the shoulder. "Seriously, don't hook up with her . . . I mean, do whatever you want . . . but I know her pretty well and she giggles and squeals way too much . . . Of course if that's your type?"

Now I'm babbling like an idiot and Jackson grins at me. "It was a joke, Holly."

I can't help but love the way he says my name. It just sort of rolls off his tongue like the double R's I can never pronounce correctly in Spanish. "But you and Terri have so much in common."

He smirks. "Like French poetry, right?"

"Yep, something I know nothing about."

"Me either. I just pretend," he whispers dramatically. "But don't tell anyone."

"Can I ask you something?"

"Sure," he says.

"Why do you have a job . . . I mean it's not like you need the money?"

With the blazing fire in front of us, his blue eyes really stand out. More than usual. "Well . . . I used to be a camper . . . and me and my sister loved it so I thought it might be fun to do the whole counselor thing."

"Your sister?" I ask.

He looks at something over my shoulder and then jumps up. "Sorry, I almost forgot. Adam's got a little . . . project for me . . . I'll talk to you later."

"Um . . . okay."

"Keep the sweatshirt," he calls over his shoulder. "Happy graduation."

I lean back and watch him retreat toward Adam, standing near the woods. What the hell are they doing? Maybe "doing a project" is polite, rich-kid code for finding a place to pee outside?

And then I see the shadow of a third person behind them. Someone following him? Or he has a bodyguard? I've never asked him what his parents do for a living, but the dude who always picks him up after work has this thing in his ear, like the Secret Service wear.

I wrap Jackson's sweatshirt tighter around me and press the sleeve up to my face, inhaling the scent. That one little whiff of his cologne must have done things to my head because I got into my tent with David last night and had the most amazing and totally hot dream about another guy. Now I'm trying to figure out how to contact Jana while she's on a cruise. I need some girl advice in a major way.

Love,

Holly

We'd reached the end of the second page and Holly looked up at me. "You remember this, right? You weren't really trying to hook up with that Terri girl, were you? I remember her fairly well and she's obnoxious."

I was almost too stunned to answer. We'd somehow landed back in the 2009 I thought I'd erased. My head spun trying to figure out how we got back to this point, and I couldn't come up with a solid explanation. Although this story wasn't exactly how I remembered it, but it could have been Holly's translation.

"No, I wasn't trying to hook up with her, I thought she was obnoxious, too, but before my life turned crazy, I often entertained myself by having random conversations with annoying or weird people. Especially while in Jersey."

Holly scooted back and turned her body toward me. "But you were totally trying to steal me away from David, right? Because it really seems like you did a good job of that. I had no idea you were such a flirt."

That got me to laugh. "Yes, I was a flirtatious coworker but no, I wasn't trying to steal you from David, though I toyed with the idea for a little while. Until I met him and decided he was a better guy than me."

She held a hand to her heart and gave a dramatic sigh. "So tragic. But I told you there was potential, the fact that you didn't steal me away, it's like a soap opera, isn't it?" She eyed me curiously. "You've been in my bedroom before, haven't you?"

I laughed again and rubbed my eyes. We'd been awake for probably twenty-four hours. "Yes, I have, but that happened much later than today's date. July or August, I think."

Holly snapped the diary shut and jumped up, grabbing random items from her closet and heading toward the bedroom door.

"What are you doing?" I asked.

"I'm getting my own clothes, taking a shower with my own shampoo, and then I'm going to climb into my bed and go to sleep." She shrugged like I should have guessed this myself. "Don't worry about everyone else. Trust me, Adam knows me well enough to guess where I went. I'm sure they'll be pissed off, but nobody is going to think we were kidnapped or anything."

"What about your mom?"

"She's out of town," Holly answered from behind the bathroom door now. "It's in the diary. And I guess this means I'm in the clear with the duplicate-Holly issue. She doesn't seem to be hanging around anywhere."

While Holly was in the shower, I picked up her diary and flipped through it quickly. I could tell there were changes from the version Stewart had discovered, the same one Emily had read and begun recording on paper, back at Misfit Island. There were entire entries devoted to updates about Deludere Virus. In mid-May, she wrote an entry about having gotten into NYU and how the housing situation was up in the air. If they didn't find a cause for how the virus was transmitted, they wouldn't be able to offer student housing in the fall. And the camp I'd spent practically all of my childhood summers at was no longer busing kids out to the woods. Instead, everyone stayed in the newly secured YMCA building with hired security officers at the doors. But Holly still worked there and so did Adam and I, apparently.

Holly's mom hadn't wanted her commuting to New York every day and she had to promise to be home by dark. She even mentioned a few classmates who had been hospitalized and never returned to school.

"Finding anything juicy?"

Holly's pajama pants and tank top seemed to fit better than any of the Misfit Island clothes she'd been wearing. She looked too happy for me to destroy that by explaining the differences between her life and the other original 009 Holly's life. I inhaled slowly. "I remember that shampoo."

The contrast between Holly's cleanliness and my less-than-clean self gave me an excuse to escape to the bathroom and compose myself mentally. I decided to use her toothbrush without permission. I also found a washcloth and removed the dirt still left on my hands and face after the Eyewall explosion. It took me a while to return to Holly's room mostly because I couldn't shake that sad feeling that I kept getting hit with every time I thought of my life before all this. My time with the first Holly I ever met was truly gone. I'd never get it back.

"You look cleaner," Holly said. She tossed me a T-shirt from her second drawer. "This should fit you."

I yanked my dirty, long-sleeve shirt over my head and dropped it onto the floor. Before I could put the other shirt on, Holly moved closer, examining the scar on my chest.

"Maybe we should get tattoos," she said offhandedly, her finger now tracing the scar. "Well, a second one for me, a first for you." Her eyes lifted to meet mine. "Why don't you look excited?"

I forced a smile. "I'm excited, totally. Tattoos, diaries, clothes that fit, candy bars, it's awesome."

The grin fell from her face. "What's wrong? We can go back if you're worried about your dad and everything. Of course you're worried. I'm sorry, I should have—"

"It's not that." My eyes focused on the T-shirt in my hands and not on Holly's face.

"What is it, then? What 2009 thing do you want to do? Just tell me. Whatever it is, I'll do it."

I glanced around at the room, feeling myself smile a little, for real this time. Then I put Holly's shirt on and sat down on the bed. "I think this is exactly where I'd like to be. It's nice here."

She folded her arms across her chest, staring me down. "You just feel sorry for me because I'm infected. My bucket list is more important than yours, right?"

I laughed and looked her right in the eye. "My bucket list has items that you don't want to hear me say out loud, trust me."

"Oh, I get it." She plopped down beside me. "You had other things on your mind when I mentioned hanging out in my room. Of course you did, you're Jackson Meyer the flirtatious co-worker."

"Exactly." I stretched out on the half of her bed next to the wall and let my eyes close, enjoying the idea of sleep.

I felt Holly's head rest on the pillow beside mine. "Tell me the truth, why are you really upset?"

"I can't explain it in words, it's just that feeling you get when you know something good is over and you can't have it back," I admitted, despite my desire to keep her happy.

"Me? That's what you're upset about? The Holly you met before?" Her voice was calm, not judgmental or defensive, which I took as a good sign.

"It's not that exactly." I opened my eyes and turned my body to face hers. "I can tell you're afraid of me, being close to me like this. And the other Hollys were never afraid, and I hate thinking about the things that happened to change that for you. Mostly one thing."

She was quiet for a long time, and then finally said, "I'm not afraid of you, Jackson, not even a little bit."

I reached out and touched her wet hair. "I wouldn't ever hurt you, you know that, right? I'm not capable of ever doing what Carter did to you."

"I know that."

"Then ask me again what I really want to do tonight." I rested my hand on her cheek, barely brushing her skin with my fingers.

"What do you want to do tonight?" she whispered.

I scooted closer, moving my hand from her cheek to her waist, and then I leaned in. "This is just for this *you*, okay?"

She gave a tiny nod before her eyes fluttered shut and our lips collided gently. I kissed her probably a thousand times until we both fell asleep, our limbs tangled, our chests pressed together.

"Jackson?"

Tiny cold hands gripped my arm and shook me gently. I peeled my eyes half-open, squinting in the dark, catching only a flash of red hair. "Courtney?" I looked closer, catching more details.

I shot upright. "Emily!"

She reached out and clapped a hand over my mouth. "Shh!"

Then I felt the empty space beside me. "Shit! Where's Holly?"

"She's in the living room watching TV. Actually, I think she's asleep."

My vision had started to become clear and I realized that this wasn't the eight-year-old Emily that Lonnie had taken away from me. "What are you doing here? How old are you now?"

"Twelve . . . almost thirteen." She sat beside me on the bed. "I've been with Lonnie for a while now. Where we went, it's just amazing. We have this cabin in the woods. I think it's what you'd call Upstate New York. The town is really small but I know everyone there. There are no time travelers yet but the technology is far more advanced than 2009. I've also been to New York and it's amazing. It's the UN capital in 2522—"

"There's a UN capital in 2522?"

She smiled and nodded, giving me a chance to really study her. The oldest I'd ever seen Emily in the past was eleven and that was the first time I ever met her, though not the first time she'd met me since she already knew me then. Now that she was closer to Courtney's age, the difference between the two of them had become more apparent. Emily was smaller—shorter and skinnier, less developed. She also had not only my eyes, but my nose. She looked ten or eleven instead of almost thirteen. I vaguely recalled my own growth spurt happening much later than my sister's and a time, before middle school, when Courtney had gained an inch or two on me in height. Emily clearly possessed more of my genetics than my sister's despite the matching gender and hair color.

"What are you doing here if 2522 or whatever is so awesome?" I asked.

Her face fell. "I have to show you something."

"Uh-oh . . ." I rubbed my temples, already preparing for the worst. "Half-jump or full jump?"

She exhaled heavily. "Half-jump."

I was sure the cry of pain that escaped my mouth as the splitting-apart sensation ripped through me had to be more than loud enough to wake Holly from the living room. But there was nothing I could do about that because we were headed to another time.

We landed right in the middle of a busy hospital hallway. NYU Hospital. A man in a white lab coat smacked into us from behind, dropping the clipboards he'd held in his arms.

"How did you two get in here?" he asked, as Emily and I snapped around to fully face him.

"Sorry," Emily said, tugging my arm. "We were just leaving."

The man considered stopping us but I think he must have decided picking up his clipboards was more of a priority. I followed behind Emily as she rounded a corner and then stopped in front of room 512. There was a name written on the whiteboard beside the door.

FLYNN, HOLLY M.
PATIENT #35724
INFECTED: DELUDERE

I sucked in a breath, feeling my heart race, my stomach tie in knots. "Holly . . ."

"I'm so sorry, Jackson," Emily whispered, her arm brushing against mine as she stood beside me. "I came to find you as soon as I found out."

"When does this happen? Is there going to be a cure?" Before Emily could answer, my gaze traveled to the tiny window into the room on the other side of the door. An empty bed sat to one side of the room, white sheets and blankets flipped back, and then I saw someone's feet.

Dangling feet.

"Oh God!" I reached for the door handle, shaking it, not registering the security-code box above the handle. "Help! Somebody help!" I shouted down the hallway, hoping a doctor or nurse would hear.

Emily finally caught on to what I was seeing and her hands flew to her face. "Oh no! Jackson, I didn't know! I swear I didn't know!"

Ignoring her, I rammed my shoulder against the door, trying to open it. My heart thudded in my ears. I raced down the hall and grabbed a metal chair sitting near an observation window. Skidding back across the tile floor, I smashed the leg of the chair into the window, shattering the glass. I tossed the chair aside and crawled through.

Holly dangled from what looked like shoestrings. Her blond hair falling all around her, concealing her face. The checkered hospital gown reached almost all the way to her ankles, just ghostly white feet sticking out. A chair lay tipped over on the ground.

I hurdled over the fallen chair and grabbed her legs, lifting her and taking the weight off her neck. The sound of her choked breaths echoed through the room.

Who did this to her? I'll kill them. Whoever it is, they're dead.

"Somebody help!" I shouted again. A red emergency button on the wall caught my eye. I lifted my foot, scooting sideways, and kicked it with full force. A bell rang through the room and suddenly a crowd of doctors and nurses rushed in as the door was finally flung open.

"What the hell happened in here?" one of them shouted, taking in the broken glass and exposed window.

I held Holly's legs tight as the dresser was slid over and a doctor stood on top, releasing Holly's neck from the confines of the string. She fell into my arms, her eyes rolling into the back of her head, her face a mixture of dark red and blue.

"Put her on the bed."

I laid her down on the white sheets and stood beside the bed, frozen, as half a dozen people crowded around, jumping into action.

"Who left her with shoelaces?"

"Airways clear. She's breathing, but irregularly."

"At least we're not cleaning up a pool of blood this time."

"Sedate her again until we can consult her family again. I don't care how opposed they are to restraints, she's just going to keep doing this over and over again. One of these times we'll be too late."

One of Holly's arms was flipped over, a needle inserted into it. My eyes traveled the length of her biceps down to her elbow and then I gasped, seeing the streaks of red scabs, scars two to three inches long, covering her forearms. Cuts. Slit wrists.

Slowly, I backed away from the bed. My chest was caving in. *I'm dying. I can't breathe. I can't think. I can't see this anymore.*

"Jackson! Jackson!" I barely registered Emily, still trapped in the doorway, blocked by the crowd of people. "You can't change this. It's just a half-jump!"

My feet started to move in her direction, my hand reaching out until I grasped her fingers.

CHAPTER TWENTY-THREE

DAY 2: 2009

I knew that Emily had pulled us right back to Holly's room in 2009. I knew that my body hadn't really left and the horror I'd seen seconds ago was only a mirror image of reality, but I still couldn't gather a single thought or a word.

My legs shook and I told myself to sit down, only to realize that I was already seated on Holly's bed. I'd never gotten up.

"Why . . . how . . . ?" I managed to sputter before adding, "When?"

Emily's voice wavered as she spoke and her hand landed on my arm, gripping me tight. "It's the virus, Jackson, it's spreading. That's why I had to leave 2522. I woke up one morning and everything had changed. Lonnie was gone. The destruction happens much earlier now."

I should probably have been crying after what I'd just seen. But the shock, the panic was too great for tears. "When did *that* happen?" I emphasized *that* so I wouldn't have to say the words out loud.

"A year from now," she whispered.

One year. One year and the world would be a horrible place. Not a hundred or two hundred. *We'd all need a bucket list at this rate.* It wasn't crumbled buildings and piles of remains. It was the fall of sanity. The one thing we were allowed to keep no matter how bad the environment became around us.

"One year," I repeated aloud, resting my head in my shaking hands.

"I went to see Eileen," Emily said, quickly brushing a few tears from her cheeks.

I lifted my head to look at her. "That's right, you did go to see Eileen because she knew about . . . about Courtney . . ."

"There might be a way to fix this. A theory she had."

Already, based on Emily's reluctant tone, I could tell this plan was either very unlikely to work or very dangerous. Or both.

"We have to get her notes," Emily said. "And then figure the rest of it out."

"Does that mean you're staying here with me?" It was selfish to want her here when I knew that she'd had a better life with Lonnie in 2522, but I couldn't help it. Emily had become such an important part of my life.

"Yes, I'm staying."

There was a finality in her tone that scared me, but suddenly all I could think about was Holly in the other room. I got up and opened the bedroom door, gesturing for Emily to follow. The TV blared, playing an early-morning repeat of some Food Network show. Holly had her feet up on the coffee table, a knitted blanket with frayed edges thrown over her and her head falling sideways as she slept.

All it took to wake her were a few creaks as the wood floor groaned beneath our weight. Holly's eyes bounced from me to Emily then she rubbed the sleep from them before looking again.

The blanket was tossed aside. "Okay, Emily, right? But not the same Emily . . ."

"Same version, just older." Emily emerged fully from behind me and rushed over to Holly, plopping down and hugging her.

Holly hugged her back and glanced up at me, her eyes full of questions. "Just tell me if we're leaving again? Like, leaving this year or this timeline or whatever. That's all I want to know."

"No one's leaving," I said finally.

Holly sighed with relief and Emily stood up again, moving toward the kitchen. "I'm going to get some water."

I took Emily's spot beside Holly and turned my head to face her. "Couldn't sleep?"

She shrugged. "I did sleep for a little while and then I just wanted to walk around my house and look at everything else and then I wanted to watch TV. It just seemed so . . ."

"Normal," I finished.

"Yeah, normal." She eyed me carefully then lifted a hand to rest it on my cheek. "Oh boy. Those are some big, big secrets you're wearing, Jackson Meyer."

I leaned in, resting my lips against her forehead, and closed my eyes. "I'm just now beginning to realize that my life resembles a very difficult game of chess. Keep this piece, sacrifice this one. Move this way and twenty moves from now . . . *checkmate*."

She pulled away from me and lifted my arm around her shoulders, then curled up against my chest. The emotional walls between us had clearly been knocked down in the past twelve or so hours and I couldn't think of either a better or worse time for this to happen. Instead of thinking, I sank farther into the couch and pulled her a little tighter into my arms and just tried to breathe . . . in . . . and out.

Emily eventually returned and stood in front of us, waiting for someone to make a decision. Holly yawned, and mumbled, "A few more hours of ignorance, please? We shouldn't go anywhere in the middle of the night, right?"

Emily took the spot on the couch beside me and we all sat in silence watching episode after episode of *Iron Chef* until the sun began to rise and drift through the space between the blinds in Holly's living room.

Around six-thirty in the morning, after both Holly and Emily had drifted off, the doorknob to the front door twisted. My senses were immediately alert, but I relaxed after watching the intruder's obviously noisy and amateur method of entering the house. It wasn't anyone who shouldn't be here.

Katherine Flynn stumbled through the door, tugging a rolling, carry-on-sized suitcase. She froze the second her eyes landed on me. "What—?"

Her voice must have pulled Holly from her sleep because she jerked awake and was on her feet so suddenly it startled me and Emily. I figured she'd rush into an explanation about why I was here while her mom was out of town. Once, with the original Holly, we'd been caught in a more-than-compromising position when her mom had been out for the day and returned about five hours early to find us asleep in Holly's bed, clothing spread out all over the floor and the awful casserole we'd concocted for lunch, and then forgotten about, literally on fire in the oven, smoke filling every room.

But today, Holly didn't start explaining or even mention me at all. She just fell into her mom's arms, hugging her like she hadn't seen her for weeks, which honestly was about right. Katherine looked extremely startled but squeezed her back anyway.

"What's going on, Holly? What happened?"

My chest ached and my throat tightened. This was too hard to watch. Seeing Holly's future a year from now had nearly killed me and *this*? This show of emotion was like stomping on a soldier who had already fallen to the ground.

"Nothing," Holly mumbled, her voice shaking as she sniffled. "I just . . . I mean . . ."

I cleared my throat. "There was a security breach at work yesterday. It was pretty scary and Holly didn't want to come home alone." I glanced at Emily, who nodded her encouragement. "And I'm taking care of my *cousin*. So we just thought we'd hang out here with her until you got back."

"You work together?" Katherine said over Holly's shoulder. After I nodded my answer, she pulled back and got a good look at her daughter for the first time. I braced myself for the reaction. "Did you . . . did you cut your hair?"

Holly laughed and quickly brushed away a few tears. "Yeah, I cut my hair. It was just too long."

"You look thinner. Did you forget to eat all week or something?" Katherine turned Holly around and guided her toward the kitchen. "You're eating every bite of breakfast that I make you and taking every single vitamin I set in front of you, understood?"

Katherine shook her head, sighing, but I could tell she didn't mind taking care of her daughter, maybe even enjoyed the opportunity. "I knew you should have gone to Indiana with me. Grandpa insisted you were old enough to stay on your own. Shows how much he knows, right?"

Emily and I followed them into the kitchen and sat at the small round table with Holly as her mother shuffled around, quickly putting a meal together for her allergy-ridden, vegetarian daughter.

After the basic introductions, with Katherine's back to us as she cooked, we answered casual questions as best as we could.

"How old are you, Emily?"

"Twelve," Emily said.

Katherine spun around to look her over carefully. "Older than I would have guessed. Reminds me of someone else I knew at that age . . ." She tossed a grin in Holly's direction.

A plate of cut-up melon, apples, pineapple, and strawberries was placed in the center of the table. Both Holly and I looked at it, wide-eyed, before diving in. Emily reached slowly for a piece of fruit, obviously not reacting like it was foreign as the two of us were.

The fruit was followed by piles of scrambled eggs, orange juice, toast, and fake sausage that tasted much better than I'd anticipated. Holly was given more vitamins than I knew existed but she swallowed each one without complaint.

Katherine sat down with us, taking only small portions of everything. Holly shoveled the food in as fast as I had but she never took her eyes off her mom. Like maybe she wanted to memorize every movement, every characteristic just in case they ended up apart again.

"Is this what's going to happen when you live in the dorms this fall?" Katherine said to Holly. "You have to be responsible. You have to take care of yourself."

Holly set her fork down, letting it clank against her plate. "You're right. I'm probably not ready for that. I want to live at home."

This was the most bizarre conversation I could possibly imagine at the moment, but luckily we were interrupted five minutes into Holly and Katherine's verbal list of the pros and cons of her living in the dorms at NYU in the coming fall.

The doorbell rang at around eight in the morning and Katherine rushed to answer it, Holly quickly on her heels. A few seconds later, Adam and Stewart stood in the kitchen, trying to hide that they were clearly pissed off at us, how shocked they were to see a twelve-year-old Emily, and the relief that we were still alive.

"How's it going?" I said to Adam. "You guys still freaked out about that whole security thing at camp yesterday?"

Adam's eyebrows lifted. "Right . . . yeah . . . that was . . . *man* . . ."

"Insane," Stewart filled in for him.

Holly's mom stuck her hand out to Stewart. "Katherine Flynn, and you are?"

"Jenni Stewart," she said, shaking hands and then nodding toward Adam. "Adam's girlfriend."

"So you work at the camp, too?" Katherine asked, her eyes bouncing between Adam and Stewart as if just looking at them several times would help her figure out how this unlikely pair had become a couple.

Adam looked nervous as he awkwardly tossed an arm around Stewart's shoulders. "Yep, she's a counselor, too."

Stewart turned her head and grinned up at Adam. "That's right. I just love little children."

Adam coughed back a laugh. "She has amazing patience. And tolerance."

"Are you guys hungry? I've got plenty of eggs left," Katherine said, gesturing toward the table filled with plates of fruit, toast, and eggs.

Pretending everything was okay and that I hadn't seen the worst event possible take place just hours ago was making me feel caged and claustrophobic. I stood up and grabbed Emily's hand, pulling her to her feet beside me. "We've actually got to get back to the city. They came to pick us up."

My eyes locked with Holly's and I waited for her to speak. "I'm staying here," she said.

I hated leaving her but I knew there was no changing her mind. She just wanted to sink into her old life and I wanted her to be able to do that. More than anything.

Despite the fact that Holly hadn't established any relationship with me from Katherine's point of view, I still leaned in to kiss Holly's cheek before leaving.

"I'll call you later, okay?" I whispered into her ear.

She gripped the front of my shirt, holding me in place. "Do I even have a phone number? Do you?"

Adam overheard her and nodded, indicating that he'd taken care of this already. Maybe he'd retrieved his own phone and already had Holly's number programmed in it? Did that mean that he didn't have the duplicate-self issue either? Or worse—the *I'm supposed to be dead so I can't show my face at home* issue. He looked too happy at the moment to have encountered any problems with going home so everything must be okay on that front.

Holly met my eyes again and then gave me a quick kiss on the mouth, even with her mom watching and Adam and Stewart watching. "Thanks for staying over last night."

"Sure." I stepped away from her and headed toward the door with Emily. "I'll see you later, Holly."

The second we were out the door and down the block, Adam and Stewart both dropped their facade and turned to me, looking royally pissed off.

"What the fuck were you thinking?" Stewart snapped. "Do you know how worried your dad and Courtney were?"

I stared at the sidewalk ahead of us, and muttered, "Sorry."

"What's the deal with the kid?" Adam nodded toward Emily.

Emily's hand landed in my palm as she walked beside me,

matching my stride perfectly. I couldn't say it out loud. Couldn't speak the words that would explain why she came back and what we had seen. All I could do was keep walking, heading toward the station and the train that would get us back to the city and force us to make the next move as the clock ticked on this horrible game of chess.

CHAPTER TWENTY-FOUR

DAY 2: 2009. MIDMORNING

After standing in silence while Dad chewed me out for leaving, while looking way more relieved to see me than angry, I snuck away from the group and sat on the floor in the room Holly had occupied the previous night.

Finally, I allowed myself to absorb what I'd seen and within seconds my entire body was shaking, my stomach in knots. My chest tightened with that familiar panicky feeling, but this time the dread was a whole notch higher. Sweat trickled down my neck and back.

When the door flew open, I nearly jumped out of my skin. Courtney stepped inside, slamming the door behind her.

"Do you have any idea how much I hate you right now?" She had her arms folded over her chest, foot tapping with more than the average annoyed-with-my-brother body language. Her eyes met mine and all the anger dropped from her face. "Oh my God, what's wrong?"

She sat in front of me, resting her hands on my knees. I drew in a shaky breath and then allowed a few tears to fall out of the corners of my eyes before pressing the heels of my hands to my face, covering them. "Holly . . . Holly's . . ."

My composure was completely gone and losing my shit like this wasn't exactly a regular occurrence for me. Courtney had to have been shocked but she hid it well, scooting closer to wrap her arms around me, her head leaning in close to mine.

"What happened to Holly, Jackson?"

I shook my head, sucking in a breath and finally pulling my voice to the surface. "Not yet . . . nothing yet but next year . . . she's going to try and kill herself . . . over and over again."

My eyes stayed hidden behind my hands as I relayed everything

Emily and I had seen to Courtney. She was eerily quiet and still as a statue, her hands frozen on my back.

"I don't know if I can keep fighting this battle," I mumbled. "It keeps getting bigger and more hopeless."

"Jackson . . ."

I lifted my head, wiping my eyes on the T-shirt Holly had loaned me. "I want to stop trying. I want to spend time with you, with Dad, Holly, and Adam, and Emily. I don't want to take it for granted that we're together right now. I want to be selfish and not think about the rest of the world anymore. I'm not ready to start missing you again."

"Or Holly," Courtney choked out through her own tears. "You stayed with her last night? Like all night?"

Despite the emotions still flowing freely in my head and my heart, I managed to roll my eyes. "Like you'd ever give me the details of your secret makeout sessions with Mason."

I had meant that to be a joke so it caught me off guard when Courtney rested her own face against her knees and started crying really hard. I stretched out my legs and put my arms around her. "What happened with Mason? You can tell me. I won't say anything to him or Dad."

She sniffled and wiped her eyes. "It's not that . . . it's just . . . stuff like this makes me miss you . . . the other you. The one who was going through the same thing as me at the same time . . . and then it just . . . makes me really sad because now I know what it was like for you . . . after I was gone."

"It was awful," I admitted. "I felt like part of me died, too."

Courtney wiggled out of my arms, scooted back, and sat up straighter. "You're right, Jackson, we're here now. Let's figure out how to make the most of it."

I nodded slowly, and the sadness of giving up swept over me.

"But you know," Courtney added, "Emily would never have showed you what she showed you if there were absolutely no hope of fixing it."

"Yeah, I know." I closed my eyes, drawing in a deep breath. I had thought of that already, but how many people would we have to lose while trying some long-shot plan that had almost no chance of success? How many hours, days, or months would we waste on this mission, whatever it was? How many days did Courtney even have left before the cancer would take her life all over again? Probably two or three months at best.

I opened my eyes again and stared at my sister, letting her see the resolve written on my face. "What's the first 2009 thing you'd like to do?" I asked, attempting a smile.

"Go home," she said immediately.

"You and Holly both." I paused for a second, thinking. "Do we even know what the status of our building is and everything?"

"Dad went there early this morning," she said. "He thought you might be there. I don't know if it's exactly how you remembered it in 2009 but we still live there, so . . ."

"Good enough for me." I stood up and held out a hand for Courtney. She grabbed on but when I pulled her to her feet, she wobbled and nearly fell over. I caught her with one arm. Her eyes squeezed shut and she held her breath. "What's wrong?"

Her forehead stayed tightly wrinkled and her breath came out jagged as she shook her head, then leaned against me, face pressed into the front of my T-shirt.

I shook her shoulders gently, panic hitting me again. "Courtney, tell me what's wrong!"

I watched her fingers curl up around my shirt, gripping it tight. "Dizzy," she sputtered. "Head . . . hurts . . ."

"Helpless" was the best word to describe how I felt in that moment. My sister had tumors all over her brain and all I could do was stand there and keep her from falling over, unable to take any of the pain away. Her head pressed harder into my chest and her hands tightened around the fistfuls of shirt locked in her grip. The pain was getting worse. "I'm gonna pick you up, okay? I'll find someone to help."

"Just go and come back."

I took two seconds to think that over, recalling the image of her convulsing on the floor of the forest and decided against leaving her alone. "I'm sorry, I have to."

She groaned as I lifted her into my arms, her eyes still shut tight. I jerked the door open and rushed into the hall, spotting Mason at the end of the corridor.

"What happened?" He was already running toward us, concern filling his face.

"Go get Dr. Melvin!"

Courtney's fingernails dug into my chest, her hands squeezing around my shirt. Mason didn't turn around to run toward the lab where I assumed Melvin was. Instead, he flung open a door closer to the far end of the hallway.

"Bring her in here!" he shouted, and for some reason I actually listened to him. The room was large and cold. After scanning it quickly, I recognized it as an operating room. "Set her down on the table."

I laid Courtney down on the cold metal table and watched her curl up in a ball on her side right away. "Go get Dr. Melvin," I snapped at Mason, who seemed to be busy digging through a supply closet.

What the hell! Is he planning on operating or something?

"He's at Lenox Hill Hospital." Mason snatched several bags of pills from a shelf and stood in front of Courtney.

"What the hell is he doing across town?" I blew out a frustrated breath as Courtney's breathing got more jagged, indicating that the pain was getting even worse. "Go get my dad, then! And maybe Kendrick?"

"They're all the way up on the ninth floor." Mason leaned close to Courtney, pulling her hand away from her face. "How bad does it hurt? On a scale of one to ten?"

"What the fuck, Mason? Go get someone who can tell us what's wrong with her." I reached out to pull him away from Courtney, but he moved quickly out of reach.

Mason glanced at me for a second before returning his eyes to my sister. "Scale of one to ten?" he repeated.

"Eleven," Courtney said with a whimper, then after attempting a deep breath, corrected her answer, "Nine . . . it's a nine."

He stepped away from the table and sifted through the bags of pills he'd removed from the closet. He took two round orange ones from a bag and held them in his fist. "Do you feel nauseous?"

Courtney gave a tiny nod and Mason looked through the bags again, removing two longer brown pills. Part of me wanted to shove him out the door and force him to get some real help but the fact that he seemed to have some kind of specific plan caused me to stay rooted to my spot near Courtney's feet as I gripped her ankle, wanting to stay connected as long as possible.

Mason found a paper cup and filled it with water before lifting Courtney's head and getting her to swallow four pills at once.

"You better know what the fuck you're doing," I said as the pills entered her system.

Mason ignored me and began digging in a drawer, removing two tennis balls and a package of those hospital footie socks. He stuffed the tennis balls into the sock and then tied it tight at the end. When he put them on the operating table and then laid his hands on my sister to roll her onto her back, I almost yanked him away from her. But curiosity stopped me. I had no idea what the hell he was doing but it seemed like something very specific. The sock of tennis balls rested behind her neck. He lifted one of her hands, massaging the space between her thumb and index finger. His other hand landed on her forehead and he turned to glance at me. "There's a red button behind the door. It should set off your dad's cell phone and tell him to come down here."

I stared at him in disbelief. "Now you tell me."

After the red button had been pushed, I returned to holding

Courtney's ankle while Mason massaged both her forehead and hand at the same time.

"The pain meds are sixty percent muscle relaxers," he said gently to Courtney, using such an intimate tone that it caused my anger to spike. "If you can do some of that relaxing on your own, you'll get some instant relief. Mind over matter, right?"

Courtney visibly tried to relax and the wrinkles in her forehead smoothed out.

"Good, just like that." Mason's fingers continued to move over her face. "This is what Dr. Melvin meant last night when he said you needed to take the pain meds all the time. You have to stay on top of it or it's not going to be tolerable, okay?"

"Dr. Melvin examined her last night?" I asked.

Mason nodded, his eyes staying on Courtney. "He did an FMRI, too, in order to see the progress."

"And . . . ?"

Courtney inhaled and then slowly released the air from her lungs before saying, "Two months."

I suddenly felt dizzy and disoriented hearing the truth spoken so bluntly. And seeing Mason holding it together, calm and in control, not even hesitating for a second at the idea of getting close to Courtney. As much as it killed me to admit it, Mason couldn't really be held to the label I'd given him—hormonal flirt with the sole mission of getting in my sister's pants. Because honestly, who would do that with a girl who only had two months to live?

Unfortunately, my desire to kick his ass hadn't faded a bit.

He pressed more firmly into the space between her thumb and index finger. "Better?"

Courtney took a few breaths and then sighed with relief. Tears escaped her eyes, rolling down the sides of her face. Mason quickly wiped them away with his fingertips.

"How's the nausea?" he asked.

"Tolerable," Courtney whispered, lifting a hand to touch Mason's face. "Thank you. I'll take the pills from now on, I promise."

"What did you give her?" I asked, deciding that I needed to acquire whatever knowledge Mason had so I could help her next time.

Mason opened his mouth to answer but the door burst open and Dad, Stewart, Kendrick, and Emily charged into the room. Mason glanced over his shoulder at them and then held a finger to his mouth. "Keep the volume down, she's fine. Just learned an important lesson in pain management."

Dad stalked over to the table, causing Mason to release his grip on Courtney's hand and back away. Kendrick lifted the plastic bags one at a time, reading the labels. "You gave her forty milligrams of the oxycodone, right?"

Mason nodded.

"And the promethazine?"

"Yes," Mason answered, rolling his eyes.

"Good boy." Kendrick gave him a smile and then patted his head. "And the tennis ball trick, somebody got an A in home remedies."

Dad pulled up a chair beside Courtney, taking one of her hands and squeezing the pressure point like Mason had. "Just try to relax, sweetheart," he said. "You'll feel better in a few minutes." Dad glanced at me for the first time since entering the room. "Was it only pain? No seizure?"

"No seizure," I answered. "I think she got dizzy first and then the headache."

Courtney nodded her agreement and then wiggled her eyes open. "Dad, I want to go home."

My hand froze around Courtney's ankle. Kendrick still held the bag in her hand, having only zipped it halfway closed. Emily stood near the door, her eyes on me, and Mason held the paper cup of water above the garbage can, obviously distracted by this request.

Dad lifted Courtney's hand to his face and closed his eyes briefly. "Okay."

"Really?" Color finally started to creep into Courtney's cheeks again. She had gone completely white since her episode started a few minutes ago. She squeezed her eyes as if hit by another wave of pain.

"Let's wait until the medicine kicks in," Dad said.

"She wouldn't have to go through this if she'd let us put in a central line," Kendrick said.

Mason glared at Kendrick. "She said she didn't want one. Quit bringing it up."

Kendrick just shrugged. "She also said she didn't want pain meds last night so I thought maybe her opinions had changed after this episode."

Courtney opened her eyes again, looking at me then Dad. "Please don't let her put a tube in my chest . . . please, Dad . . . Jackson . . . ?" Her look of desperation hit me right in the gut. And she and I had just established the fact that we were going to spend our time doing what we wanted to do. Not necessarily what was the best thing to do.

I cleared my throat. "It should be her choice, Dad."

This confession would have been noble had it not been my only action since Courtney started suffering some pretty intense level-nine pain.

Dad's gaze stayed focused on the wall behind the operating table. "Yes. It's her choice."

Courtney sighed with relief. "I can't wait to sleep in my own bed."

The entire room froze again and I figured out right then why this had happened the first time. I took a breath that cut through the silence and caused everyone to look at me. Maybe this would be my contribution since I hadn't been able to help Courtney before.

"Courtney . . ." I waited for her to look at me. "Um, your room isn't . . . I mean, it's not how you remembered it. It's not your room anymore. It's empty now."

Her face fell but she nodded slowly. "Right, yeah, that makes sense. But everything else is still there, right? It's not, like, completely different?"

I attempted a smile. "It's still home."

"I just don't get why you like this movie so much. It's the most depressing story ever." I tossed a few pieces of the popcorn Courtney had barely touched at the TV screen as poor Jack's frozen corpse was released into the ocean.

"It's romantic," Courtney muttered from her spot on the couch in our TV room.

"Rose could have made room for him on top of that piece of debris. Kind of selfish of her, don't you think?"

Courtney laughed. "You're not even watching, are you?" She pointed at the stack of books on the coffee table and then the one currently spread across my lap.

The whole situation earlier had freaked me out so much that I asked Kendrick for some medical books to read. I didn't know how much I could comprehend but I did have that photographic memory thing going for me. Not to mention the motivation of not allowing Mason Sterling to be more valuable to Courtney than me.

"All right. I'm taking a reading break." I closed the book and set it on the coffee table. "What should we watch next?"

"I think I should start working through the list of movies that came out after April of 2005," she said with a yawn. I didn't move or speak and finally Courtney rolled her eyes at me saying, "Stop it. You said we we're going to do bucket-list stuff so let's get on with it and cut the crappy I'm-too-sad-to-enjoy-myself faces."

"You're right." I stood up and began searching our extensive shelf of DVDs for movies released after early 2005. "Looks like we've got two Harry Potter movies to tackle."

She still looked exhausted and possibly in pain but her face lit up. "Perfect."

As I was putting the DVD in, Courtney sat up halfway, angling herself to face me. "You met Eileen, right?"

"Yeah, kind of. She took those memory drugs after so it wasn't exactly a two-sided meeting."

"What is she like?" She returned to curling up on her side, eyes on the TV again. "I mean, we were an experiment to her . . ."

"She's different from everyone else in Tempest," I said, thinking carefully about what words could best describe the woman who was sort of our mother. "I think she's as selfless as Dad, and that's saying a lot."

Courtney pulled the blanket off the back of the couch and spread it over herself. I grabbed the ends and helped cover her feet. "I think you're pretty selfless, too, Jackson."

I shook my head. "Not like her. Not like Dad."

"I bet he misses her."

The menu screen had popped up on the TV, playing the familiar Harry Potter theme song. I hit PLAY before saying, "I know he does."

I made it through about an hour of the movie before falling asleep sitting up, wearing nothing but gym shorts, my hair probably sticking up from the quick post-shower towel dry I had done prior to watching *Titanic*. I vaguely recalled Dad's lifting a sleeping Courtney off the couch and carrying her out of the room.

CHAPTER TWENTY-FIVE

DAY 3: 2009. 2:00 A.M.

After what felt like several hours of sleeping upright in a less-than-comfortable position, I woke up when I felt the weight of someone sitting on my lap. I peeled my eyes open, secretly hoping I hadn't dreamed the soft hair tickling my cheeks. Sure enough, Holly was seated on top of me, her mouth dangerously close to mine, one knee placed next to each of my hips.

"Hey," she whispered. "You know, I think we should just be friends."

My brain was too fogged with sleep to absorb the shock of this situation. I rested my hands on her lower back, feeling the exposed strip of skin above her jeans. "This is friendship? Sure, I'm in."

My vision finally cleared enough to look into her light blue eyes and watch the mischievous smile spread across her face. "Repeat after me . . . Sweetheart . . ."

Her fingertips landed on the sides of my neck and I closed my eyes again, letting out an involuntary sigh. "Sweetheart . . ."

"Baby . . ."

"Baby," I repeated.

"Honey . . ."

"Honey." My hands slid higher until I reached her hair and tangled my fingers in it. "Is this a new game all the kids are playing?"

"Is this room really soundproof?" she asked, leaning in closer.

"Okay, I'm totally down with this game." I opened my eyes again, wanting to see if she was still real. "And yeah, it's . . ."

A conversation I'd had with 007 Holly came tumbling back to me right then. We had been right here on this exact couch, her feet in my lap, her eyes fighting to stay open while a movie had played on the TV.

283

"The surround sound is really loud," 007 Holly had said. *"Don't the neighbors complain about the noise? It is an apartment building . . ."*

"This room was made for media," I had said. *"It's soundproof."*

007 Holly had lifted her head and raised an eyebrow, probably wondering if I'd taken advantage of the soundproofed space with anyone else.

The Holly currently seated on my lap also arched a blond eyebrow. "I figured out something this morning before you left my house. Things you say and certain places and objects are triggering the visions. I walked in here and I remembered the sound-proofing conversation and then I thought maybe we could experiment. Since we dated, I figured you must have called me something—some corny term of endearment—but nothing triggered any memory."

I shifted her hair to one side and rubbed the back of her neck. "I'm sorry, did you say something? I've lost the ability to concentrate on anything besides your current position on top of me."

She rolled her eyes. "Grow up."

"Unlikely."

She laughed. "Okay, fine. I'm not really here, you're dreaming."

"That sounds about right." I dropped my hands to my sides and allowed myself to get real about this odd wake-up call. "What are you doing here, Holly? I thought you were going to stay home with your mom?"

She ignored my question and her nose touched my cheek and then the side of my face, causing a shiver to run down my spine. "You must have shaved yesterday. Whatever you use to shave, I remember the smell. Aftershave or shaving cream?"

"Shaving cream." Her eyes met mine again, causing all the horrible panic of yesterday to come rushing back to me. Those memories, that stupid World B and 007 Holly's life would eventually ruin this Holly's mind. The process had already started.

"Oh no . . ." Holly rested her hands on my cheeks. "Not that face. You just turned about five shades lighter. I thought maybe if

I made my entrance distracting enough, we could avoid the guilty, hopeless Jackson Meyer sad face."

I tried to smile, but I'm sure it looked forced. "So that's why we're sharing a couch cushion when there are four perfectly available cushions for you to occupy?"

"Exactly." She pulled back, looking me up and down. "You still have the face."

I took a deep breath and tried to shift her sideways to sit beside me but she held her spot firmly. "Look, Hol, there's something I have to tell you."

Her finger touched my lips, cutting me off. "I already know. Courtney told me a little while ago while you were sound asleep."

"You already know?" A tidal wave of grief washed over me. I moved her finger from my mouth but held on to it tight. "Everything?"

"Yes. And you're still looking at me like I'm an egg about to crack. I thought I had a year before that happens?" She shifted and I thought that was finally the end of my little lap-dance fantasy, but instead she seemed to slide her hips closer until she was completely pressed against me. I sucked in a breath, wishing that I wasn't the only shirtless one in the room. A smile spread across Holly's face. "That's better. Anyway, I went to Mike's gym yesterday. I walked through the whole place and there were memories hitting me left and right and then after I got home, I realized something very important."

"What's that?"

"How I feel when I see those things are really coming from me."

"What do you mean?"

"I mean, before I couldn't help wondering if what I felt around you was just implanted into me from another version of me, but it's not. The connection I get when I'm around you comes from my reaction to how you were with the other me. Like if someone had told me stories of the love you lost and how important that person was to you, I'd like you more because of that. Combine that with what I've seen myself . . ." She touched her lips to my cheek, causing me to sigh again. "So you can stop worrying about me giving up my right to choose or whatever the hell it was that kept you up at night."

I reached up and held her face in my hands. "I can't believe Courtney told you everything."

"I think she wants you to be able to live—however long that is—and not carry this huge weight around." Holly closed her eyes and drew in a deep, shaking breath, showing something other than amusement for the first time since waking me up. "I'm glad I know. I'm glad she told me, but I don't want to spend all my time thinking about it."

"What do you want to spend your time doing, then?" I asked.

"Hanging out with my friends—Adam, Jana, and David. Assuming David doesn't hate me after the breakup we apparently just had. I want to have Lifetime movie marathons with my mom every Saturday like we did yesterday. Maybe go visit my grandparents in Indiana. And . . ." She dipped her head, barely touching her mouth to mine before pulling back again. "And I want to be with you. I want to let myself fall in love with you. Again."

I closed my eyes, feeling warm and happy but incredibly sad all at the same time. I drew Holly's mouth to mine again, letting myself get lost in kissing her. It was much hotter and more intense than the other night when we had lain in her bed, allowing our legs to entwine but keeping a conservative distance between the rest of us. I felt the freedom she was granting me now and I took it without hesitation.

Holly paused between kisses, resting her forehead against mine, both of us struggling to catch our breath. "Now you look happy."

I laughed. "Again, consider where you're sitting." I smoothed her hair back behind her ears.

"It's really nice here, actually." She moved my hands to the bottom of her sweatshirt. I took the hint, slowly lifting it over her head, leaving her in just a skintight tank top.

She sank back on her heels and my thumbs unraveled from her belt loops and traveled the length of her, grazing over her stomach and ribs and then pausing under her breasts. "So, I'm assuming you remember us making out on this couch?"

"Uh-huh." She laughed. "I remember your stopping and making up some excuse about getting a drink and the look you gave me before pulling your hands out from under my dress was almost painful. Was that your first stab at self-control?"

"I believe it was." I wrapped my arms around her waist and hid my face against her stomach. "Holly?"

"Hmm . . . ?"

"I love you."

I had to say it but I couldn't bear the awkward pause or silence that might have fallen, so I quickly lifted my head again and started kissing her, then eventually succeeded in shifting her off my lap and stretching us both out across the couch.

A while later, after the tank top had joined Holly's sweatshirt on the floor, after my hands succeeded in covering at least eighty-five percent of her body, I stopped abruptly, my fingers frozen on the waistband of her jeans. I didn't miss the tiny flinch she tried to conceal. She opened her eyes and looked at me questioningly.

"I should check on Courtney. She was in lot of pain earlier." I started to crawl over Holly and stick a foot onto the white carpet but she laid her hands on my back and held me in place.

"Courtney's asleep," Holly said, eyeing me carefully. "Your dad gave her pain medication and sleeping pills, she's completely out. What's wrong, Jackson?"

I blew air out of my cheeks and relaxed into the couch again, resting my head beside hers. "I don't know . . . it's just . . ."

"Carter," she whispered.

My jaw tightened at the sound of his name. "I don't want you to think about that . . . you know, with me."

"I don't think I will."

The sound of the doorknob's turning jolted us both and we immediately raised our heads. I grabbed the blanket from the back of the couch and tossed it over us. Holly wiggled around underneath me until we looked more cozy and less in the middle of something NC-17.

Never in a million years could I have been prepared to see Stewart and Adam stumble through the door, laughing, hands all over each other.

"Holy shit," Holly whispered into my ear.

I clapped a hand over her mouth, wanting to give them a second to realize we were in here. Apparently neither of them had their agent brains turned on. Holly's eyes went really wide when Stewart gently pushed Adam's back against the wall and then leaned in to kiss him. And he totally kissed her back.

"It's the reproduction room all over again," I muttered before coughing loudly, finally jolting them apart.

Adam's face was beet red, but it seemed more likely to be from his seeing Holly's top lying on the floor than us catching him because he quickly covered his eyes with one hand. Stewart snorted and yanked his hand back down. "God, don't be a baby. There's no underwear on the floor, not even pants. Junior has issues closing the deal."

Holly raised her head, eyes darting between me and Stewart. "Wait . . . what?"

I managed to extricate myself from the couch without uncovering Holly and I grabbed both Adam and Stewart and shoved them toward the door. I left Holly alone to put her clothes back on and went into my room, where Courtney was sound asleep in my bed. I glanced at the couch and saw Mason stretched out on his back, his mouth hanging open and a book barely still clutched in his hand. When I opened my dresser drawer to retrieve a T-shirt, I noticed Dad yawning and stretching in the recliner on the other side of the bed.

"You let Mason sleep in here?" I asked.

"I'm armed," he reminded me, pulling the lever to lower the feet of the recliner. "Courtney told me what happened with Emily. Actually, she told Holly at the same time. Holly's okay? You talked to her, right?"

Wouldn't exactly call it talking . . .

I glanced out into the hallway then quietly shut the door before sitting on the floor near Dad's feet. I scratched the back of my head, trying to find the right words. "Can we have a father-son talk? The kind that involves girls and sex?"

Dad's eyebrows lifted. "I was honestly hoping we were done with those years ago but apparently not."

I took that as a yes. "I think Holly's pretty serious about not being treated like an egg ready to crack, as she explained it, but after what Carter did, I just feel like an asshole for even wanting to be that close to her and then I feel like an asshole for treating her differently *because* of that."

Sympathy filled his expression. "You have to stop comparing *that* to your being with Holly. Carter wanted to hurt her. You love her. It's different."

"I know that," I said. "It's just . . ."

"Someone like Holly," he continued. "I think she wants to feel normal again. To be in control of what happens to her. You'll never try to take that from her. So you don't need to feel guilty."

I stood up and rested my hand on the doorknob. "We do get to shoot Mason if he attempts to add this particular item to Courtney's bucket list, right?"

"Absolutely." He returned to reclining, his eyes trained on Mason as if he might sleepwalk into Courtney's bed any second. "Life was much easier when you two were five."

"Or even thirteen," I agreed.

Dad laughed. "You were easy at thirteen." He nodded toward Courtney. "This one was a pain in the ass. Every friend's crisis was her crisis. We weren't saving enough wildlife. God forbid we put an egg carton in the garbage and not the recycling bin."

I smiled at the sleeping Courtney. "I used to put soda cans in the Dumpster outside when she wasn't around. Just to maintain some power over my own garbage."

Dad looked at me and his face turned serious. "That's the important stuff, Jackson. Relationships aren't about idealistic love and happily ever after. It's those things that bug the shit out of us about each other and yet eventually we find ourselves wishing we could go back and do it all over again."

I couldn't help laughing. "That's the last thing you told me in our official sex talk when I was twelve, the part about relationships not being based on idealistic love. I think I took it to mean something entirely different at the time."

He looked puzzled. "Huh?"

"I didn't really do the girlfriend thing much. I thought that's what you meant, like people my age who did that were just pretending or playing a modified version of husband and wife. That's what it always seemed like to me. I didn't get it."

"Until you did."

"Right." I nodded. "Until I did."

He leaned back and closed his eyes again. "Me, too . . . me, too."

When I walked into the kitchen, Holly was already there, dressed and talking to Adam and Stewart like nothing had happened.

"Give yourself a minute, Junior?" Stewart said.

I shoved her toward the dishwasher. "Shut up." That was when I got whiff of her. I leaned in closer, just to be sure. "You guys are drunk."

Holly stood behind Adam, nodding, and mouthed, "Trashed."

Adam was oblivious to this exchange and he clapped his hands together looking genuinely excited. "I want to see the secret room."

I exchanged glances with Stewart, who shrugged like she didn't care either way. I started to walk toward Dad's bedroom and felt the three of them following closely behind.

"Where's Emily?" I asked.

"In the lab with Kendrick," Stewart answered. "Dr. Melvin

wanted to run some tests. He's worried about her immune system and something about natural antibodies being different."

"She has your nose, too. I didn't notice that on the little version of her." Holly's hand drifted down my arm until her fingers landed in my palm.

I don't think anyone was more fascinated watching my fingerprints open the trapdoor and reveal the secret room between floors than Adam Silverman. The room with the electromagnetic field that prevented time travel in or out of it.

Despite his drunken state, Adam was the first to venture down the rope ladder, bounding into the room with uncharacteristic energy. "Dude, this is kick-ass."

"I think Adam should have been raised in a fallout shelter in the fifties," Holly said.

While Adam explored and Stewart followed behind him, putting everything he had lifted up back in its place, I grabbed Holly and pulled her into the center of the room, wrapping my arms around her from behind.

"So you and Stewart had a little fling, huh?" she said, more teasing than angry.

I pressed my face into Holly's shoulder and groaned. "Do you really want the details? I'll tell you everything but honestly, I'd rather just forget it. That's what I was trying to do that night. Forget you."

She turned her head to look at my face. "Did it work?"

"No, not even close." I smiled and leaned down to kiss her. She was taking this very well. "Look up."

She tilted her head, resting it back against my shoulder. "Your dad wrote this stuff?"

"And Eileen." I buried my face in her neck, kissing the space behind her ear.

"Why?"

I lifted my eyes to the low ceiling again. "I don't know. I guess it's romantic. We can ask him if you want?"

She scanned the quotes for a few minutes, and then asked, "What would you write?"

"I'd stick with Shakespeare." I chanced a glance in Stewart and Adam's direction. They were occupied with something on the floor, under the small kitchen rug. "Maybe something like, *Love all, trust a few, do wrong to none.*"

Holly shifted over about a foot to read some of the other quotes, pulling me along with her. "I'd pick something like, *Hell is empty and all the devils are here.*"

I pressed my cheek against hers and laughed. "Morbid, Hol, very morbid."

"I like Hemingway better than Shakespeare," Holly said. "We had a poster at my old gym in Indiana, right behind the uneven bars. Whenever I'd swing around the high bar, it was my focal point, a Hemingway quote . . . *Never confuse movement with action.*"

There was something so tranquil about standing in this spot with Holly, reading words my dad and Eileen shared with each other and shutting the rest of the world out. "Supposedly, Hemingway's most beloved piece of writing was a story he told in six words."

"Hmm . . ." Holly relaxed against my shoulder. "Do you know the story?"

From the corner of my eye, I saw Stewart look over at us and then move closer. *"For sale: baby shoes. Never worn,"* she said before I could answer. "I think me and Junior took the same American Lit class at NYU."

"Professor Paulson?" I asked.

Before Stewart got a chance to respond, we were distracted by the bottom half of Courtney's body emerging down the rope ladder. She was followed by Dad, then Mason, then Chief Marshall, and finally, Agent Collins.

"Nine is a bit of a crowd for this space, don't you think?" I said, releasing Holly and moving beside Courtney. "How are you feeling?"

She turned to me and smiled. "Much better."

I put an arm around her and we both watched in silence as Dad moved around the room, almost trancelike, his fingers gently brushing over items. Chief Marshall and Collins were in deep discussion about the electromagnetic field when Dad slowly pulled out a record and placed it on the record player, lifting the needle to start the music. It was the same Frank Sinatra album that Kendrick and I had listened to before the big jump to Misfit Island.

"I knew there was something weird about this floor tile!" Adam looked up at all of us, triumphantly holding up a perfect square piece of tile and revealing a hole in the floor.

Of course the eight of us all rushed around Adam, trying to see what was inside the space. What we found was a stack of eight spiral notebooks filled with pages and pages of writing.

"Those were *not* there before I left 2009 to go to the future," Stewart said. "I searched that hole myself."

"I'll take those," Marshall said, holding his hands out to Adam. "Looks like we've got a lot of reading to do."

As everyone started to head upstairs again, the promise of something that resembled a lifeline in those notebooks, I grabbed Adam by the back of his shirt, allowing the others to vanish out of sight before asking, "Did you know those were down here? Did Emily tell you?"

"She hinted at it."

"What do you think is in there?" I asked.

"I don't know, maybe nothing."

I rubbed my eyes and stifled a yawn. "This is *exactly* what I was afraid of. Tiny shreds of hope that either require actions that have impossible odds or consequences that are greater than the benefits."

"But we have to keep trying, right?" Adam said, sounding surprised by my lack of enthusiasm. "We can't give up and let this virus invade the world."

I sighed and sat down on the bed. "Maybe not, but right now I just can't do this anymore. I'm tired of fighting these battles that just get bigger and bigger and we keep coming full circle right back here and every time I return, the world is a little bit worse than the last time."

Adam's eyes were wide as if he couldn't believe my defeatist attitude. He glanced up the rope ladder and back to me. "It's gonna happen to me, too, Jackson. What happened to Holly."

I inhaled a sharp breath. "When?"

"Remember, I started having visions even before Holly," he said. "I don't want to be locked up and helpless in solving this problem."

My heart increased in speed, adrenaline killing my calm buzz. "When is it going to happen?" I asked again. "And how do know? Did Emily tell you?"

"Yeah, she told me. I cornered her in the hospital a few hours ago and she told me everything. I've got six months." The color drained from his face and he sat down beside me. "It's worse than Holly, Jackson, way worse."

I laughed under my breath, but there was no humor in it. "What's worse than hanging yourself after dozens of previous brutal suicide attempts."

He stared at me, hard and fierce. "Killing five other people before succeeding in suicide."

I'm sure there was nothing but horror and panic filling my expression. "Six months?"

He nodded. "I don't want to be a murderer. Not ever. I swear to God I'll tell you the second I feel like I'm slipping but you have to keep this between you and me, please?"

"I promise, I won't tell anyone. I trust you. I've always trusted you."

"Maybe you shouldn't." He stood up and shook his head. "But I don't want to turn into a monster. We need to fucking fix this merging timeline. There's got to be a way."

No matter how much Adam seemed to doubt his ability to hold on to good judgment, I didn't doubt it one bit. In another timeline, Adam had been dying but he *still* made it a priority to give me a message about not screwing up the world with time travel and that he knew Eyewall was bad. In his last moments, he cared about everyone but himself.

I stood up and clapped a hand on his back. "I won't let you do anything you'll regret."

He let out a breath of relief. "Thanks."

"Besides making out with Stewart," I added, getting a shit-eating grin in return from Adam. "Seriously, what's up with that?"

He shrugged. "No idea. But I sure as hell enjoyed it."

CHAPTER TWENTY-SIX

DAY 3: 2009. 6:00 A.M.

Holly closed the notebook she'd been poring over for the last hour and rubbed her eyes. "I gotta head home before my mom gets up."

Everyone who had crammed into the small underground room was now either seated around the kitchen table or leaning against a counter, searching Eileen's notebooks for some answer to saving the world from its inhabitants. Except for Courtney. She was making pancakes.

"Do you want me to go with you?" I asked Holly.

She shook her head immediately. "It's light out now. I'll be fine."

"Actually"—Chief Marshall looked over at us from across the table—"Agent Sterling has an assignment to fulfill in New Jersey. He can ride back with you."

Mason was clearly not happy with this plan but didn't protest; nor did anyone elaborate on the assignment. Holly shrugged, and mumbled, "Whatever," like she didn't really think she and Mason combined was all that different from her alone, but it made me feel a little better.

"I'll walk you out." I stood up from my chair and followed Holly toward the front door while she waited for Mason to gather his things. "Call me in a little while, okay?"

"I will." She gently tugged my face toward her and kissed me until we heard Mason shuffling behind us.

I leaned closer to her ear, and whispered, *"The course of true love never did run smooth."*

"More Shakespeare?"

I nodded. "That's what I would write first on the ceiling."

She smiled and pinched one of my cheeks. "Your charm is deadly."

Mason brushed past us to open the front door, making an obvious effort to roll his eyes in our direction.

When I returned to the kitchen, Courtney rewarded me with a giant stack of pancakes. Adam was already inhaling his, probably an attempt to sober up. Stewart looked ready to pass out right on top of the red spiral notebook she was currently in possession of. I steered clear of the Eileen's notes and instead leaned against the counter beside Courtney.

"So, what do you want to do today? What's on your list besides Harry Potter movies?"

She grinned at me, flipping a pancake in the process. "Central Park Zoo? Is it still open? With the virus and all?"

I was temporarily distracted by Adam. His fork had frozen in his hand and his face turned completely white again as he read a page in the notebook lying in front of him. Even from across the room, I could see the vein in his neck pulsing, indicating his heart rate had suddenly sped up. I watched as he discreetly glanced at Collins, then Dad, before dropping his eyes to the page. He took about three seconds to pull himself together, then closed the black notebook.

"Nothing in this one," he said, faking disappointment.

My gaze drifted across the table and landed on Marshall, who was studying Adam carefully. Had he seen what I had?

Marshall's eyes met mine for a brief second and then fell on Dad. "I'll accompany them to the zoo."

Dad looked up at him, clearly confused and surprised. "You're going to take Jackson and Courtney to the zoo?"

Marshall stood to his full height, impassive expression plastered on. "Someone needs to accompany them given the fact that you and Agent Collins are scheduled to report to the mayor's office in a few hours for the strategy meeting."

"Right," Dad said.

"Stewart can go with you and take notes," Marshall ordered.

"No way. I hate the secretary gig," Stewart said.

Marshall glared at her and she shut her mouth immediately. "And Agent Silverman will go with me."

Adam seemed lost in thought and barely gave a nod as he reached for another notebook to open. Dad walked behind Courtney, rubbing her shoulders gently, and whispered, "Be careful, okay? Take your medicine and don't overdo it."

"She'll be fine," I told Dad.

At exactly fifteen minutes before the zoo opened, Marshall, Adam, Courtney, and I exited the building and crossed the street toward Central Park. Nothing outside looked too altered except the way people moved, hurrying to their destination with an even greater speed than usual for New York City. And there were no tourists in sight. Living in the city my entire life had made spotting tourists and their cameras and T-shirts, showing off where they'd been already, an easy task.

The four of us walked in silence until it was obvious that Marshall had headed in the wrong direction.

"It's this way," Courtney said, pointing to a path behind us.

Marshall stopped at a table secluded in the woods of Central Park. "We're not going to the zoo. Have a seat, please."

Courtney opened her mouth to protest but I pulled her down onto the bench beside me before she could object. I didn't know what Marshall had planned but he had obviously orchestrated the exact people he wanted to hear whatever information or news he had for us. And I had figured it was about Adam and what he knew about himself six months from now. Maybe Marshall already knew it and wanted to keep it secret from the others?

"Mr. Silverman," Marshall said. "Care to tell us what you discovered in Eileen Covington's notes this morning?"

Adam's face turned pale for the third time today and he shook his head fiercely. "No."

Marshall wrapped his large, dark-skinned hands around the end of the picnic table, leaning forward. "You have the missing piece, don't you, son?"

Adam swallowed hard, continuing to shake his head.

"You read what I read, the timestorm formula, and then pieced that with knowledge of your own and figured out the solution, didn't you?" Marshall pressed, leaning closer to Adam.

"No," Adam said. "I only reacted like that because I didn't have the information. It just felt more impossible than before, that's all."

Even I could see that Adam was lying, so he had no chance of Marshall believing him.

"What's going on?" Courtney said. "What's a timestorm?"

Marshall hesitated for a long moment, as if forming a new plan, then he slid into the spot beside Adam, folding his hands on top of the table and giving Courtney the most sympathetic expression I'd ever seen Marshall wear, which wasn't saying much given his uncanny coldness.

"First of all, young lady, that tumor pressing on the back of your skull"—he reached across the table and touched a spot under Courtney's ponytail—"is going to rupture in two weeks. The radiation you had early on the first time you experienced this prolonged your life by a month or two."

Adam dropped his face into his hands. I swallowed the lump that had suddenly formed in my throat and scooted closer to my sister, laying a hand on her shoulder and watching her eyes fill with tears.

"Two weeks," she croaked.

"Can she have the radiation now?" I asked desperately.

Courtney shook her head, sucking in a breath and trying to steady her voice. "I don't want it. Lily said the side effects are terrible and I'd be miserable longer." She quickly swatted away the tears that had fallen. "Does . . . does Dad know?"

"He would if he had gotten through all the notebooks before I swiped the pages giving us that information." Marshall removed several torn pages from the back of his pants. "Which brings us to Mr. Silverman . . ."

Courtney's gaze moved to Adam but I couldn't take my eyes off my sister. My chest felt constricted, as if the walls were caving in on me from all sides. Two weeks. That was all I had left with her. Six months with Adam and one year with Holly. Could I really stick around to watch everyone I loved fall one at a time? It would be worse than dying. Far worse.

"The timestorm formula is so complex and the code completely foreign, I expected to be the only one to grasp it after reading it a few hours ago," Marshall said to Adam. "And then when I saw your face, I knew that you had the location. Am I correct?"

I finally looked away from Courtney and saw that Adam's head was still in his hands. "Adam?" I said. "What's going on?"

"Eileen solved the problem," Marshall explained. "If the alternate world began to merge with the original universe, the solution was to create a timestorm. A time jump from a very specific point in the world that has the power to destroy the World B that Agent Meyer unintentionally created, a location that Agent Silverman has known for a very long time."

"So let me get this straight," I said, attempting to shake the five tons of emotion from my head. "A time traveler stands in this one spot and does a jump to somewhere and then poof . . . bye-bye World B?"

"That sounds way too simple," Courtney agreed.

Adam finally lifted his head. "You'll drown," he croaked. "Maybe after you pull it off but maybe not."

"The location is underwater?" I asked. "Where? The bottom of the Hudson?"

"I volunteer." Courtney lifted her hand in the air. "I'm dying in two weeks anyway. Might as well save the world right before I check out."

"No!" I stared at her in utter horror. "No way."

Courtney snapped around to face me. "Why not, Jackson? Why the hell not? Because it'll make you feel guilty? It's not your fault I have cancer."

"You're not even an experienced time traveler. You've done it like twice." I looked away from her and faced Marshall. "I'll do it.

I'm ready right now. I'm the one who opened the portal and caused this mess in the first place."

"It won't work," Adam spat.

"Why not?" Courtney and I both said together.

"It won't work," he repeated. "Unless all three of you do it. At the same time."

That put the lid on our sibling feud instantly. Marshall, however, didn't look in the least bit shaken. "That's the other missing piece of information that I needed."

Adam glared at Marshall. "I never said I'd tell you where. You want to go on a death mission, figure it out yourself."

Marshall stared at him, a calculated expression drifting into his features. "And I thought you were smart, Mr. Silverman. Surely logic works in your head as well as it does in mine. Everybody on the planet, or three people with a dangerous gift, one of whom has an incurable and fatal disease."

"We can't tell Dad," Courtney whispered to me. "We have to leave and not tell him."

My heart was beating furiously, the weight of this discussion hitting me like a subzero gust of wind. Adam looked at me, something desperate in his expression, like he knew Marshall had a point, but since it was about me, his friend, he couldn't face the logic.

"He's right," I managed to say, faking calm. "We're supposed to do this. Eileen told me herself that Courtney and I were made to do something great, to make a sacrifice that Dad would hate. This must have been what she was talking about."

My insides were numb. Numb and cold and heavy with a sadness that had so much weight, and yet part of me felt light. I wouldn't have to watch them die after all. Maybe I could fix things for Holly and Adam. Me and Courtney together.

And Marshall.

I'd never felt an ounce of compassion for Marshall since the first time I met the guy, but I had to respect the fact that he didn't even flinch upon hearing this news, as if he too had always known he'd be making a huge sacrifice like this one.

"There's no way to be sure it will work," Adam said, holding on tight to that desperation.

"But there's a chance?" I asked.

He hesitated before nodding.

"Where are we headed, Mr. Silverman?" Marshall asked for what felt like the hundredth time.

Adam sighed heavily, and there was concession in his sigh as his face transformed to the genius-on-the-verge-of-explaining-a-great-discovery expression I had come to know so well. He was shutting down emotionally, and I needed to do the same or else I'd never make it through this last mission.

"I couldn't figure it out at first," he said. "Obviously, Eileen didn't have the answer either, but she knew a timestorm would destroy the alternate universe. She also knew that time travel affects weather patterns. Whenever a time jump is performed, air pressure in the location the time jumper lands is instantly altered. When it's more than one time jumper, the change in air pressure is even more drastic. We also know that an electromagnetic pulse shuts down the part of the brain that you use to time-travel. Eileen discovered something I don't think Tempest was aware of until today. That certain elements of weather give off the opposite of an electromagnetic pulse."

"So, like, time travel during a tornado could be easier or more effective?" Courtney asked.

"That's the idea," Marshall said, taking over for Adam. "But Eileen didn't have the benefit of test subjects and advanced equipment to study major elements of weather throughout history as Mr. Silverman did during his six months at Eyewall headquarters."

I turned my eyes to Adam. "That's what you did there?"

He and I had talked about so many things during the three-day walk from Misfit Island to Eyewall headquarters, but this apparently wasn't one of those subjects.

"Yeah, they wanted to find ways to increase the cloned time traveler's power to equal the level of the originals. Emily was the only subject who exceeded the originals. No others even came close to matching them."

"But why didn't they just copy the experiment they used to create Emily?" I asked.

A grin spread across Adam's face. "They did. Thomas and Dr. Ludwig nearly went insane trying to figure out what was different about her. They'll never figure it out because it goes against everything they believe."

"What?" Courtney asked. "What's different about Emily?"

Marshall looked right at me, his face completely impassive. "She uses her power the same way that Jackson does. She feels her way through it. It's emotionally driven. She began using her power at eight years old. Since her brain was still developing, it easily adapted and expanded to allow her to hold on to her superior intelligence and more powerful time-travel skill in addition to an uncanny ability to feel the change in air pressure, the buzzing she describes when she's around me or other jumpers. Unlike the others, she's going to fight the emotional overload you described before forever. It might get easier, but it will always be a battle for her. She was altered about five years into the experiment. Someone showed her a side of life she hadn't known before. One that includes love and hate."

"Who?" I asked. "Who altered her?"

Adam shook his head. "We don't know. I thought maybe it was Blake but you said he hadn't met her before Misfit Island, right?"

"Right," Courtney answered.

"Blake would have told us if he'd known Emily before. We were all trying to understand Emily's breakdown." I sat there in silence for a few seconds, mulling over the fact that Emily was like me in more ways than I'd realized, only she had never known a normal life. She'd always been a pawn in someone's big plan. Even when she'd been helping Marshall by showing up and giving me information and answers, she was a pawn in *his* plan. I understood why, I just couldn't help but want her to get the opportunity to live. To truly live. "Emily isn't going to have to go on this mission with us, is she?"

Marshall looked to Adam, who spoke up immediately. "Eileen's formula calls for two original time travelers performing simultaneous jumps. Since you and Courtney are half-breeds, you count as one."

"And I count as two," Marshall said firmly. "The child has been through enough. She'll be left here."

As opposed to the bottom of the Hudson? I really needed Adam to get to the point now. "Where exactly are we going to hold hands and time-jump?"

"A maelstrom," Adam said. "That's the weather element that provides the most powerful time-travel source. There's an invisible current that will multiply the force of your time jump to such a high level, it'll create a timestorm and thus destroy World B."

"Ending the delusions that people are already having before they reach potent levels," Marshall finished.

"A maelstrom? Like a whirlpool?" I asked.

"Totally not the Hudson then," Courtney muttered.

"Yes, it's a whirlpool." Marshall turned to Adam again. "And if we aim for the most powerful maelstrom, we have an even better chance at success."

Adam nodded, glancing wearily at me and then Courtney.

"Like the Loften Maelstrom," I said. "From 'A Descent into the Maelstrom' . . . that Edgar Allan Poe story. That's Norway, right?"

Courtney's eyes widened. "Norway!"

"Saltstraumen is the most powerful," Marshall said. "Also off the coast of Norway."

This was all getting too insane for me to grasp. I needed it broken down into simple terms so that I could begin mentally preparing myself. "So, we're going to head on over to Norway, paddle off the coast in our North Face jackets, follow the signs that lead to the giant swirling whirlpool, and then do a time jump? To where?"

Marshall didn't even attempt to put it gently and at this point, I appreciated the straightforward approach. "We won't be time-jumping from the boat, we'll be actually jumping off the boat. If I'm understanding everything that Eileen and Mr. Silverman have laid out for us correctly, we'll need to jump from the most power-ful access point and that will be as close to the bottom of the ocean as we can get. As far as where we'll be aiming for, it needs to be the largest, longest jump possible. Since I've seen the point the world ends, I will pull us toward that year and date. Just before we leave the boat, I'll describe this location to you in enough detail that you'll be able to use your own mind to search for it."

"Great." I pressed my forehead against my hands and tried to breathe normally. "When exactly have you had time to go and visit the end of the world? With leading a division and signing up my friends and loved ones for the CIA . . ."

"Eileen provided me with the dates based on her theories and I performed the action to provide that data for her research. Trust me when I say this," Marshall added. "Your brain will not survive the jump this far into the future. You won't bleed to death and be-come covered with bruises and experience the incapacitating pain you experienced when jumping to 3200. The lack of oxygen from being underwater prior to jumping combined with the distance of the jump will be enough. We'll all be dead upon arrival."

I stopped breathing.

Courtney's leg pressed against mine. Her breath caught in identical fashion to mine. There was no denying the fact that I was scared shitless. My hands shook and I balled them up into fists to hide it. I didn't want Adam or Courtney to know I still had doubts.

Marshall stood up, looking almost relaxed, or at least, the same as he always looked. "We'll leave tomorrow at 0400 hours. I'll ar-range the flight and the boat upon our arrival in Norway. I will also see to it that no one is in any condition to try to stop us from completing this mission. Mr. Silverman, I trust that you'll keep this information under complete lock and key?"

"What about after?" Adam managed to croak.

"What you tell Tempest Division agents after our mission is of no concern to me whatsoever." Marshall angled himself to face me and Courtney. "Take the rest of the day to fulfill any last-minute tasks of your choosing."

He made it sound like he was leaving us time to pick up travel-sized toiletries. Not to say good-bye to everyone. Good-bye to life itself.

The second Marshall was out of sight, Courtney covered her face with her hands and started crying. She leaned against my chest and the crying turned into shaking sobs. I sat there with my arms around her, my eyes completely dry, and waited until she could breathe again.

Adam's head was down, his fingers dragging furiously through his hair over and over. "I hate this. I hate knowing these answers. I hate knowing the bigger picture."

I looked over his way, desperate for a guarantee and assurance that it would all be worth it. "Will it really work?"

He lifted his eyes to meet mine. "I wish so badly right now that I could tell you no or even that I don't know, but it makes so much sense."

Courtney stopped crying and used my sleeve to wipe her face. "Then we're doing it. We have to."

Grief sat heavily on my heart, but this type of grief came with a complete lack of guilt, which I welcomed. I brushed the remaining tears from Courtney's face and nodded.

"We have to avoid Dad if we can," Courtney said. "It'll be so hard . . . God, I just want to say good-bye, but he'll know. He'll see it on our faces and try to stop us."

"I think Marshall must be planning on drugging everyone

tonight or something," I said. "So then Dad'll wake up and we'll already be—"

"Gone," Courtney finished for me.

She started crying again and all I could do was hold her and let her fight this emotional battle in her own way. That was all we could do at this point.

CHAPTER TWENTY-SEVEN

DAY 3: 2009. 1:20 P.M.

I was rifling through a medicine-supply closest in the underground hospital when Holly bounded into the exam room.

"Fancy meeting you here." She grinned at me, waiting for some clever response, and then kept talking. "So, I was thinking that since my mom is working all day, maybe we could hang out today."

I stared at Holly, a bag of pills hanging limply in my hands. I hadn't planned on seeing her. I hadn't planned on even talking to her, fearing she'd change my mind, but looking at her now, I knew I wouldn't chicken out. Not if chickening out meant Holly slitting her arms with razors and hanging herself in a hospital room. And now I wanted more than anything to be with her for a little while.

My smile wasn't even forced. It was genuine. "Give me a few minutes to get some more medicine for Courtney?"

"That's perfect because Dr. Melvin wants to scan my brain, so I'll be in the FMRI center." She opened the door again and called over her shoulder. "Come find me when you're done."

I turned my attention to the closet and removed the small scrap of paper I had written medication names on. I was pretty sure Marshall wouldn't want us drugged up and loopy for the actual mission but I sure as hell wasn't about to sit on a seven-hour flight doing nothing but thinking about what would happen after we arrived at our destination. I wanted to be out cold the second I sat down and not wake up until we got there.

I read the list carefully and filled a few empty bottles, which I stuffed into my backpack. I added plenty enough for Holly in case we ended up in the same place tonight. If anyone was going to prevent her from waking up and stopping me from leaving in the morning, I wanted it to be me and not Marshall.

After I finished in the supply closet, I headed up the elevator to the FMRI room. Even before seeing Holly, I had planned on going in there to finally give Kendrick the letter and ring I had promised Blake I'd pass along.

Kendrick was seated in the control room alone while Holly's head disappeared into the tunnel. I knocked on the window and Kendrick buzzed me in.

"Holly," she said into the microphone. "You're going to hear a lot of clicking. That's normal; try to breathe and keep your heart rate from fluctuating."

"How's it going?"

Kendrick's eyes were glued to the computer screen as Holly's brain image lit up in a multitude of colors. "Not too bad. Her scan looks great so far. Mason had some slight damage and Stewart, too. Nothing major. But your dad and Holly look like they didn't actually jump to the year 3200. It's amazing how resilient the two of them are."

It was a relief to hear this about Holly, and I already knew Dad was a survivor. "That's good. I was worried about her."

Kendrick glanced sideways at me and smiled. "So tell me about this partnership we had in another version of this world?"

I released a nervous laugh. "Right. We had an interesting dynamic, that's for sure. I was all antisocial, I'm the job—"

Her eyebrows shot up. "You, antisocial? I can't even fathom that. Not that we've ever socialized much but I read plenty of reports."

"Yeah, yeah, so I've heard." I rolled my eyes. "Anyway, I was focused on work and avoiding getting too personal and you were constantly like, *'Let's hang out, let's talk about our feelings. This is where I want to have my honeymoon someday. Where do you want to have yours? Why haven't you thought about this before? Are you having fun yet, Jackson? Isn't this great? Let's be friends.'* And our introduction came after I'd spent over two months going neck and neck with Stewart, throwing daily insults at each other. Needless to say, I was very confused by your approach and pretty much backed away with my hands in the air."

She laughed and shook her head. "You make me sound like one of those talking dolls where you pull the string on the back and they say a total of five different phrases. I'm so not like that. In any version of this universe."

I shrugged. "Hey, I'm just repeating the facts. I do have a photographic memory and you did say all of those things at one point or another."

Her eyes narrowed and pink rushed to her cheeks. "This was a platonic partnership, right? I mean you did hug me when I first saw you the other night."

"Actually . . ." I wiped the amusement from my face. "We were passionate lovers and you had three of my babies."

Her glare faltered for a split second, and then she released a breath and turned her attention back to the computer screen. "Real funny, Jackson. All right, so I drove you crazy with my friendliness and then what happened? Eventually you caved?"

"My dad disappeared. He was supposed to be on this mission with Marshall and we came back to New York without either of them. And none of the agents except Dad and Marshall knew that I could time-travel. Then I found out about Holly's being an agent and that Adam was dead. I couldn't get through it alone." I raised my gaze to meet hers, remembering all this made me wish for that Kendrick again so I could thank her. "And you were there. It was some of the worst moments of my entire life and you were there for me. That's not something I can easily forget, even if you don't have those memories right now."

She turned to face me, silence filling the room for several long seconds while she absorbed everything I'd just revealed. "Well, I'm sure if I was there for you, it probably went both ways. You must have helped me out, too."

This was the perfect window into what I'd come here to talk to her about. What I needed to give her. "Maybe a little. You told me about your family. I think you needed to say it out loud. Probably to someone who understood that kind of loss and I did. In a lot of ways, you reminded me what it was like to be human again. To feel things. I hated you for that, but at the same time, I appreciated it."

Shock filled her expression. "I told you about them? I never tell—"

"I know. But the circumstances were extreme. I know we're not close in this version of 2009 and it's weird to hear stuff like this from me." The memory of Blake, looking so intense and determined, invaded my thoughts, hitting me hard. "But I promised someone I'd do this . . ."

"Promised who?"

I stared right at her, letting out a breath before saying, "Blake." I removed the ring from my pocket, the one that had been the source of so much confusion for me. "I had this forever and I didn't know it was for you—the J and H engraved in it—I thought it meant Jackson and Holly. But all along, I've had it so that I could give it to you. So you'd have a piece of your parents."

Kendrick's mouth fell open, her eyes immediately tearing up as she took the ring from my finger. "My mother's ring. How did you get this?"

I laughed a little. "It's a really long and complicated story. But that night, when you told me about your family, I remembered your saying that you wished you had your mother's ring."

She quickly swatted away the tears from her cheeks. "Thank you."

The envelope with the letter from Blake addressed to her was in my other hand. I held it out for her to take and she did, looking up at me again with wide eyes, like it was a priceless, breakable antique.

I left her alone to read the note and to grieve or remember or whatever it was Blake thought she might need to do upon seeing this ring and I went for a walk around the hospital, giving Holly enough time to finish her test and dress in her normal clothes again.

"I'm completely unharmed," she said with a shrug as we headed into the elevator. "Hard to believe, huh? Given the crazy brain explosion *you* had."

"You're more resilient than me." I took her hand and smiled. "Where do you want to go today?"

"Take me somewhere you went with the other me, the younger one. I want to try out my new trick again. See if I remember."

I replayed moments with 007 Holly in my head before landing on a memory that we could easily recapture.

We stood in the exhibit area just past the lobby of the Metropolitan Museum of Art, Holly spun around slowly as if trying to catch a glimpse of 007 Holly's memory, while I watched her. She stopped suddenly and closed her eyes.

"Were you wearing a hat?"

I laughed, still amazed and horrified by this phenomenon. "Yeah, a Mets hat."

Holly flashed me a smile. "Okay, where to next?"

"You don't want to look around?"

She shook her head and grabbed my hand, heading toward the exit even though we had just paid our admission to get in. Not that I cared in the least. I followed the same route through Central Park that I had walked with 007 Holly.

When we reached the playground where 007 Holly had scared me to death by climbing on the swing set, I waited for her to jump up there and do the same thing, but she just stood in the grass, looking from the ground to the swing set.

"I don't get it," she said finally. "How is remembering this going to make me insane and suicidal?"

It was a rhetorical question so I didn't answer. I'd seen it with my own eyes so there was no doubt to be had. Instead, I tried to remember exactly what I'd felt lying in the grass with 007 Holly. That moment where I turned the entire world off and let myself be happy. That's exactly what I needed to do right now. Not allow the crushing pain of leaving Dad and knowing what it would do to him, losing me and Courtney at the same time. This was different than the grieving I had needed to do when I returned to Courtney's hospital room in a half-jump to be with her in those last hopeless moments.

I had to keep reminding myself that this wasn't hopeless. Until this morning, when Adam and Chief Marshall put their giant brains together, life was hopeless. What would happen after we left tomorrow morning was a solution. I had to keep telling myself that over and over.

"I'm starving. Wanna get something to eat?" Holly asked, breaking me out of my trance.

I pulled myself together, flashing her a smile. "Yeah, sure."

By the time we made it back to my place, it was nearly eight at night and Dad and Courtney were sound asleep in the TV room, a movie blaring in the surround sound. I wondered for a second if Dad had already been drugged but then I shook the thought from my head because I needed to focus on the solution and incapacitating Dad was an inevitable part of the solution.

I didn't want to see anyone else tonight. Just Holly. I pulled her by the hand into my room and locked the door behind us. Not that I'd planned what we'd do in my room with the door locked, but I knew what everyone else would assume and they'd most likely leave us alone.

She kicked off her flip-flops, her white summer dress swishing as she drifted around the room, picking up my things and studying them. "How many days do you think we've spent together? Like . . . if you added them all up from all the versions of me."

I sat down on the end of my bed, watching her move. "Hundreds."

She turned to me and lifted an eyebrow. "Really?"

"Maybe it only *feels* like hundreds. Probably over three hundred." I dug through my mind, adding and calculating as much as possible. "Well, I met the first version of you on March 15, 2009, and I didn't leave to meet another version of you until October 30, 2009, so that's seven and a half months. Then I spent about six weeks with the seventeen-year-old you, then a few days with the original version of you. And I've known this version of you fifty or sixty days, I think."

"What do you think would have happened with that first Holly if she hadn't been shot and you hadn't jumped to 2007?" She had set down the trophy she'd been studying and turned fully toward me.

I shook my head. "I don't know. That day changed me. Both good and bad."

"But if it hadn't happened," she pressed. "If it hadn't changed you?"

This was something I'd never thought about much before. I don't think my mind could ever get past the need to undo Holly's getting shot.

I let out a deep breath. "I think we were either on the verge of breaking up or becoming something more."

She laughed. "Isn't everyone?"

That got me to laugh. "I've completely lost sight of what everyone is doing or anything that's considered normal. I've kissed three versions of you in separate timelines. That's a far cry from normal."

"But seven months of knowing the first me? That's a long time." Holly returned to viewing the items on my trophy shelf. "You don't have to answer this if you don't want to. If you do, I swear I won't judge you or be mad or anything."

I scratched the back of my head, wary of ruining this evening. "Okay, what?"

She kept her back to me. "I know you were a commitment phobe during that stage of your life and you and that version of me didn't really establish your relationship or call it anything, but did you . . . were you with anyone else while you were dating that Holly?"

I almost smiled with relief. "No."

"But you didn't tell her that? You didn't actually come right out and say that she was the only one you were with at the time?"

"No," I admitted. That had been a bit of sore spot between Adam and me because I think he knew the answer to that question and he also knew that Holly had worried at times and he wanted me to tell her and I couldn't bring myself to say those words. It was too personal, like laying my heart on the table for her to take. It scared the hell out of me. I didn't understand why we couldn't just be together and not worry about all those details. And now, it was so hard to believe that was the kind of drama that had occupied my life. I'd take that life back in a heartbeat.

"But do you think *she* did?" Holly asked, slowly turning to face me again.

My eyes met hers. "I don't know. I honestly have no idea. The Holly that I knew then took her time. She wouldn't have met some random guy in a bar and made out with him but there was someone before me, so I suppose . . ."

"David?" Holly finished for me.

I nodded. "Even if she did cheat or whatever we'd call it since we didn't say we were exclusive, it wouldn't have been because she didn't want to be with me, it would have been because she was probably so scared of holding on too tight. I think right before she . . . you and I got together, she was confused, and probably screwed up a lot of things to figure out what she really wanted. I think what I went through after 009 Holly got shot and I couldn't get back to her, she experienced in a much more subtle form when she broke up with David. That realization that you want more, that you're willing to risk your heart for it, is something she hadn't known with David because he was safe."

Holly moved on to the items on my desk. "So really, your only problem was that your timing was off. She grew up before you did."

"I guess that's a good way of looking at it."

"In my version of junior year," Holly said, "the version in my head—not the one we've landed in—I never had that moment with David. I don't think about him like that. It's weird, isn't it?"

I laughed again. "I thought the same thing when I met him in 2007. I just didn't see the chemistry. Of course, I didn't *want* to see it, but I think that actually made me even more in tune with his every move."

She moved closer to me and nerves flickered in her expression for a second and then faded. But it was long enough to cause butterflies to start flapping around inside my stomach.

"I read about your first time with original Holly," she said, her voice dropping almost to a whisper. "It was in the pages that Emily wrote down."

I covered my face with my hands and groaned. "God, that child has to be the most morally corrupted kid on the planet. Not that it's her fault or that it's affected her negatively but man, eight-year-olds do *not* need to read about some eighteen-year-old losing her virginity."

"Did you ever read that entry?"

I shook my head. "I tried to read as little of that diary as possible. It felt like an invasion of privacy and I'm kinda pissed at that version of me for being an idiot."

Holly gave me a tiny smile. "Why did you have such a hard time going through with it after you found out it was her first time?"

I reached for Holly's hand and held it in mine. "It seemed too big, too important for me to be involved. I just wanted it to be fun. But then I got it. I got that she wasn't asking me for a ring or anything. She just had to tell me before I figured it out and then it would have been even more weird."

"The thing is . . ." She leaned into me, resting a hand on the back of my neck and pulling our foreheads together. The heat, the tension built between us. "I want to be able to write a diary entry like that one. That's what I want to envision when I think of being close to someone like that. I'm not saying it has to be today, but I am saying that you looking at me like I'm a wounded, fragile girl who you can't dare go crazy with isn't going to bring on the steamy journal entries and . . . I almost avoided telling you this because it's really hard to say out loud, but I kind of think we're past the point where we hold back important information and expect that we'll have the opportunity to say it later on."

I swallowed back the lump in my throat, knowing exactly what my face must look like. Sure enough, Holly pulled away and sighed. "See? There you go again. The sad Jackson face. It's so heavy, it's like you're suffocating me with all that guilt and grief and regret."

"I'm sorry." I reached for her, but she backed farther away. After a two-second hesitation, I made a decision to ditch the concerns from last night and take my dad's advice, and most of all, leave Holly knowing what it felt like to do this with someone who loves her as much as I do.

My heart was already racing, anticipating what would come of this revelation, and maybe I wanted it for me as much as I wanted it for Holly. I left her hanging in the middle of the room, while I walked over to my iPod and speakers and started looking for a song to play.

"Jackson," Holly said, sounding slightly frustrated. "You can't play the same song and pretend I'm the other version of me and that'll fix everything."

I hit PLAY and then turned around, grabbing Holly's hand and pulling her against me before she could object again. "I'm not playing the same song and I'm not pretending you're someone else. This is the version of you I want to be with, okay?"

Her eyes met mine, her arms circling around my neck. "Okay."

Until the moment I started kissing Holly, right after her arms tightened around me, I hadn't even realized how much of my self-control I'd used up in all these days of keeping my distance from her and drawing these invisible barriers between us. Knowing they were gone sent every concern I'd had over the past sixty days flying from my head, my mind focused on one thing and only one.

Holly was right there with me, pulling at the bottom of my shirt, tugging it over my head before crushing her mouth against mine again. I reached for the tie around the waist of her dress and pulled it quickly apart before sliding down the zipper. One of my hands was tangled in her hair and the other carefully slipped inside the opening at the back of her dress when Holly lifted her head suddenly and closed her eyes, her own hands pausing in their movement. "Good song . . . but I'm trying not to read too much into it."

Good.

I slid my hands to the back of her neck, and whispered, "Don't think too much. Not now."

After a few minutes of insanely good kissing, we ended up stretched out on my bed, both of us in our underwear and both of us completely breathless and absorbed in the moment.

"Condoms," Holly whispered into my ear, her leg wrapped around me, my fingers running up and down that bare leg. "Do you have any?"

I lifted my head and looked right at her. "I have no idea."

This wasn't usually a detail I skipped over. In fact, I'd been a pro at condom preparedness. Dad had stressed it from age twelve, years before I ever needed that lecture. I reached over Holly and opened the bedside drawer. Nothing but a couple books and a flashlight. I rolled over and brought her with me, yanking open the other drawer on the other side of the bed. I stared into it and let out a short laugh, causing Holly to look at the contents from over my shoulder. There were at least thirty condoms lying in the bottom of the drawer, a couple issues of *Popular Science* half covering the supply.

"Whoa," Holly said, laughing. "That's some wishful thinking, huh?"

I left the drawer open and turned back over, pulling Holly on top of me, kissing her and running my hands all over her body until she was the one reaching into the drawer and making the next move.

Her hand shook as she dropped the red-foiled package between us. I caught her wrist and pulled her hand toward my mouth, kissing her palm. "Are you sure?"

"Yes," she said. "I trust you."

There wasn't a trace of doubt in her eyes to cause me to hesitate, so I didn't.

CHAPTER TWENTY-EIGHT

DAY 4: 2009. 12:01 A.M.

"Maybe your dad put the condoms in the drawer," Holly suggested.

"Maybe." I rested my chin against her chest, looking over every inch of her skin from the shoulders up, memorizing the scars and the marks that made her Holly. I was trying my best not to let the sadness consume me, to remember that I'd made the right choice. She combed her fingers through my hair and I pressed my forehead into her chest, closing my eyes briefly, inhaling the moment. I almost wished this was the bottom of the ocean and I could just die right here like this.

I lifted my head when Holly's fingers slowed down and eventually her hands lay heavy on my head. Her eyes were fluttering shut. I leaned in and kissed her, lingering with my mouth against hers long enough to get her eyes to open all the way again.

"You're falling asleep on me," I said, smiling.

"I'm sorry." Her lids started to drift closed again, but she gave me a lazy smile in return. "I'm just happy . . . and that makes me tired."

"But you haven't told me yet," I said. "Is this going to make a hot diary entry?"

She laughed but her eyes stayed closed. "I think maybe it's just too perfect to put into words. We'll see."

I got up and put on the jeans I had worn earlier and went to the kitchen, my heart heavy and beating hard as I got a glass of water and dumped in the clear powdered solution that I knew would ensure Holly's inability to keep me, Courtney, and Marshall from leaving in a few hours' time.

Luckily, her eyes opened when I returned to the room and she gratefully took the glass from my hands and chugged half of it. That would be more than enough. It was almost too easy.

I pulled her into my arms, her cheek falling against my chest, her heart thudding slow and steady against my skin. I waited until the heaviness of her body against mine increased and I was sure the drugs had kicked in. It wasn't until then that I finally allowed a few tears to fall and my emotions to completely consume me.

I lay awake until a quarter to four, then slid out from under Holly, covered her with a blanket, and folded her clothes neatly, setting them on the bed beside her. Courtney's gentle knock on the door sent my heart racing again, but I hadn't changed my mind. I leaned in to give Holly a quick kiss on the forehead and then left the room, shutting the door behind me.

DAY 4: 2009. 6:40 A.M.

"I can't believe we're taking a commercial flight," Courtney whispered into my ear as we took our seats in row thirty-five, seats E and D. "And coach? Seriously?"

Chief Marshall leaned over from his seat at the end of the middle section. "It was the only way they wouldn't catch up to us. Once we get to Norway, we'll have to lie low for about eighteen hours before we get on the boat."

The word "boat" sent my heart into a full-out sprint. Courtney squeezed her eyes shut beside me and drew in a slow breath.

We had both been provided with passports identifying us as Landon and Marie Robertson. I'm not sure what Marshall's name was but the fact that we hadn't even traveled under our own names would mean it would take a while for Dad and anyone else to catch us.

It wasn't fear that consumed me and forced me to reach into my bag for the heavy sedatives, it was the thought of Holly and Dad waking up to find us missing. To know that we weren't coming back. Ever. Adam would explain it all eventually. It killed me to think about what they would feel in that moment. No way in hell could I sit on a plane for seven hours absorbed in those thoughts.

I held the bottle out to Courtney, offering her a pill. She shook her head and patted a book in her lap. "I've got some things to do."

My head started falling toward my sister's shoulder over the next few minutes and I was out like a light long before takeoff.

The small cabin Marshall had rented near the coast had the most amazing views. I couldn't even fathom how this much beauty could exist in moments as dark as this one. Since I'd passed out on the flight over, only waking when Courtney shook me for a full five minutes after the plane had emptied, I was a bundle of nerves now, watching Courtney sleep in the bedroom we were occupying with two twin beds and creaky wooden floors. I'd already forced myself to eat a sandwich and take a shower and there was nothing left to do but sit in the dark and think about what would happen the next morning.

I nearly fell right off the bed when Courtney's pink cell phone buzzed loudly from somewhere in the bag lying at the foot of her bed. She stirred and then woke up, her eyes first meeting mine, wide with panic.

"I'm sorry," she whispered as if the caller on the other line might hear us talking. "I had to bring it in case I wanted to call at the last minute."

I squeezed my eyes shut. "Just turn it off, please."

She fumbled around in her bag and finally powered off the cell phone. That seemed to instantly increase the distance between us and everyone else we loved. I needed that distance if I was going to make it through this. "It was Mason."

My eyes opened again and I tried my best to look sympathetic. "I'm sorry. It must have been hard leaving him."

She nodded, her eyes glistening with tears. "But it's not like you and Holly. I'm fourteen, Jackson. I like him a lot but I don't think I'm capable of that kind of love yet, you know?"

"Yeah, I do." If she was even twenty percent like me at age fourteen, then I totally understood why she wasn't there yet.

"Honestly, I've only really loved two people in my life—you and Dad." Her voice trembled more with every word. "And there's part of me that feels like I've always known it would just be you two and that I wouldn't get older. Not like you."

I didn't know if that was true or not but it hurt so much to hear either way. It wasn't fair that I got more years to live than Courtney. We were twins. It should have been equal.

Courtney must have seen my face because she quickly added, "I didn't mean it like that, I really didn't. I'm so happy you had the time to become *you* and be in love with Holly. It's like you got to be a man. At least for a little while."

I smiled and then stood up, walking across the room and sitting beside her, giving her shoulders a squeeze. "I missed you so much. All those years, it was like I couldn't be a whole person again. Maybe it's best that we're doing this together so one of us doesn't end up alone without the other."

She leaned her head against my chest, tears dripping off her nose and onto my hand. "Do you ever think about what's on the other side? What if it's just the same thing all over again?"

"Like reincarnation?"

"Maybe." She sighed heavily. "If it *is* like that, then I want you to promise me something, just in case I'm not there or another version of me doesn't know what I know."

"Okay, what should I promise you?" I wiped the tears from her face with the sleeve of my sweater. "Should I get married to Holly Flynn and have six kids?"

She glanced up at me, her eyes wide and amused. "How did you know I'd say that?"

I laughed. "Because you told me that before, when I visited you in the hospital."

"So maybe we have nothing to worry about then," she said, laughing with me. "Sounds like all the versions of me think alike."

Marshall opened the door then, interrupting our conversation. "Jackson, can I see you in the other room please?"

I shrugged when Courtney gave me a questioning look and then headed across the hall into Marshall's room. He had a white plastic bag in his hands and a roll of packing tape.

"Raise your shirt," he ordered. I did as I was told and then turned around, my back to him when he gestured for me to do so. "This bag contains two capsules with a potassium cyanide solution in the event that you arrive at our destination with your heart still beating and your thoughts intact."

"Is that going to happen?" I asked warily.

"It's highly unlikely but to not send you prepared would be barbaric," Marshall said. "Your sister's survival is impossible but there are two capsules just in case a miracle happens. Do not swallow these whole, crush them between your molars. Brain death will occur within minutes of consuming the poison and then your heart will stop beating shortly after."

I held still while he firmly taped the bag to my back. It would be hell to rip off if I did need the suicide pills. When he was finished, I turned around to face the man I had once considered a murderer. And even knowing the truth, I still couldn't see a good person. Not exactly. "Are you scared?"

"Fear is not something I allow myself to feel," Marshall said.

"What do you feel, then?" I asked. "You must feel something or else you wouldn't be able to do this. You wouldn't care."

He shuffled over to the dresser and fiddled with a stack of papers. "That's where you're wrong, son. I'm just another Thomas given a direction and a purpose that I feel is the only right way. And I plan to do everything in my power to ensure the outcome is the one I wanted. The difference between him and me is that I was shown a different path early on. The same path that you happen to be on yourself." He looked up at me then, taking in the stunned expression I hadn't tried to hide. "Don't mistake my choices for nobility. I'm playing a chess match, just like Thomas, only we have different strategies, different endgames, and different teachers. My teacher, Frank, believed in free will above all things. Thomas's teacher believed in peace above all things. Do you see where our lines cross?

"And Agent Meyer? He believes in love first. The goal of a good leader is to find what drives his soldiers and feed that need. I let him have you and your sister, and Eileen, too, before she was killed. He exceeded every expectation I ever had for him. If it weren't for Eileen, you, and Courtney, he would have been good . . . above average . . . but not the great agent that he is today. We wouldn't have made the progress we've made toward this goal of stopping Dr. Ludwig and Thomas."

I couldn't even begin to wrap my head around the complexity of his thoughts and the tremendous difference between him and me and how we viewed the world and people. And just the simple reminder of Dad and how much he loved me and Courtney caused a lump to form in my throat. I cleared it away quickly before asking, "What if I can't? What if I get there and I just can't make myself . . . you know . . . take the plunge?"

Marshall opened a dresser drawer and removed a gun and held it out for me to take. "You might need this. And to answer your question, I have no doubt you'll follow the plan precisely just like you jumped off that rooftop without hesitation to save Holly."

I tucked the gun into the back of my pants and nodded. He was probably right, but there was no way to know for sure until the time came.

Courtney was asleep again, her cheeks bright red with a brewing fever. She had to be in so much pain right now. It killed me to think about it. Instead, I lay on my bed for a couple hours, sitting on my thoughts and good-byes. I hadn't really gotten a chance to talk to Adam after the big moment in the park and making our plans. He was the only one I really needed to say good-bye to since he knew what would happen to me and Courtney and I hadn't said a thing to him. Without hesitation, I found myself reaching for

Courtney's phone. I turned it on, searched for Adam's number, and then quickly sent him a text.

Thanks for always being my constant. Take care—Jackson

Then I turned the phone off and stuffed it away before he had a chance to reply.

Bucket list officially complete.

CHAPTER TWENTY-NINE

Chief Marshall drove the large boat like he'd been doing it all his life. Courtney and I sat in silence as the chilly morning air hit our faces along with the splashes of cool ocean water.

"Why do we need such a big boat?" Courtney asked. "This is made for, like, thirty people."

I stared straight ahead, my stomach in knots, my arms and legs numb with fear. I could have really used a bottle of whiskey or even a couple beers. "Maybe a smaller boat would get sucked down the hole."

Suddenly, just when I thought the blue water could go on forever in the same state, the swirl of a whirlpool came into view. It looked exactly like I'd imagined and even in my scared-shitless state, I couldn't help running over to the edge to get a closer look.

Marshall stopped the boat a little ways away from the phenomenal maelstrom. Even with this distance separating us, the force of the swirling waters rocked the boat back and forth. Courtney was at my side now, her trembling hand resting on top of mine, both of us staring out across the water.

"We'll have to swim out a bit first," Marshall said, coming up behind us.

I closed my eyes, trying to hear my thoughts over the loud hammering of my heart. When I opened my eyes again, there was so much adrenaline running through my veins, it was like I could see more clearly, details were so precise. My fingers buzzed with electricity. I could dodge five bullets at once if I needed to.

But no, I'll be drowning myself instead.

"I guess we're not getting scuba equipment," I whispered to Courtney, loud enough for Marshall to hear.

Courtney glanced warily over her shoulder at Marshall, her face filled with panic. "Can we have a minute? I just need a minute."

"Of course." He walked away, heading toward the opposite side of the boat.

"What are you going to think about?" Courtney whispered. "What's the last thought that will sit in your head forever?"

My limbs and my heart were numb again. "I don't know. I think I'd like to think about nothing. Or maybe everything . . . everything good, at least?"

Tears tumbled down Courtney's cheeks, but she sniffled and nodded her agreement. I stepped closer to hug her and noticed dark clouds rolling over us, a clap of thunder breaking the rhythm of my heart in my ears. I glanced up at the sky, now growing dark, and then over at Marshall.

"Chief?"

Marshall's face was filled with alarm as he raced across the boat. "We've got to go now!"

One look at Courtney and both of us hopped up onto the ledge, trying to balance in place, Marshall moving his tall figure up beside Courtney. I drew in a deep breath, staring at the ocean, focusing on the swirling water and nothing else.

I felt Courtney's hand in mine, and then as I imagined my feet leaving the boat and hitting the cool water, I was falling backwards, my head slamming against the floor of the boat, the weight of a large body on top of me.

With all the force I could muster, I shoved my attacker off me and onto his back, then drew my gun and pressed it to his temple. I didn't recognize him, but he had the familiar features of one of the cloned time travelers. From the corner of my eye, I saw over a dozen more of them popping into view, landing on our boat.

They knew. They knew what we were trying to do.

"Let's go, now!" Chief Marshall shouted.

I pulled myself off the attacker as Courtney reached out a hand to help me up to the ledge.

And then I saw them. Hostages. One for every two time travelers.
"No . . . oh no."

All the faces I had never wanted to see again, especially not here, came into focus—Adam, Mason, Stewart, twelve-year-old Emily, Dad . . . and Holly. Each of them struggled to free themselves from their attackers, but they were halfhearted attempts, as if they'd been knocked out for the time jump.

They didn't just know what we were going to do, they knew what would stop us. There was no point in saving the world if all the people I was dying for would be killed anyway.

"Jackson, now!" Marshall said again, preparing to pull himself onto the ledge.

Before anyone could stop him, one of the dudes grabbed Courtney from the ledge and yanked her back into the boat, holding her upright with an elbow hooked around her neck. I released the guy I was holding at gunpoint as both Marshall and I sprang to Courtney's rescue.

The clouds had turned the sky nearly black, and thunder rolled over us in loud booms. A bolt of yellow-and-pink lightning burst through the sky, illuminating Chief Marshall's stunned expression.

Courtney and I both watched as Chief Marshall fell to the ground, as if in slow motion, blood oozing from his head, his chest . . . everywhere.

I froze on the spot, my eyes following the trail that led to Thomas, holding a gun. Courtney's eyes were wide with panic. Red flashed in front of me. Intense fury coursed through my body and I didn't even bother with my weapon. I used my newfound powers, moved with such speed that I must have been a blur in motion. I extricated Courtney from the cloned time traveler's hold, then knocked him out before he even had time to react.

Without stopping for breath, I headed straight for Thomas. But he showed no fear. His mouth remained a thin line and the second I launched myself at him, one hand reached out, a small metal object clutched in his fingers, barely grazing my skin.

My body hit the deck of the boat hard, my mind clear as anything, unlike whatever he'd done to me at Eyewall headquarters. But everything else was paralyzed.

This is what he did to Blake. He made him watch, unable to move, while Kendrick's family was killed.

Thomas kept the weapon pressed into my gut as he leaned over. Rain fell down in giant sheets, pounding against the deck, hitting me square in the face. I couldn't even blink away the drops. More lightning burst through the sky and thunder clapped. All the time jumps were causing a huge storm to brew. This wasn't the first time I'd seen this happen.

"Look at us," Thomas said to me, knowing that all I had in my line of sight was the dark sky above us. "This is all we have left of the project that took over twenty years to build. Twenty of us. And now you want to go and destroy the timeline that allows my people to use their power. Look at the abilities you've developed, I've never seen any one of us move the way that you just did. Of *course,* I'm going to have to kill you now. You're just too dangerous to live."

I yelled every curse word imaginable at him inside my head. The anger inside me felt so huge, it should have been strong enough to force my frozen body into action. Yet still I remained paralyzed. I had to get free. I had to get Dad and Courtney and Holly and Adam . . . and everyone out of this mess.

"What a waste," Thomas spat, disgust filling his face as the rain soaked both of us.

The sound of a gun's firing broke through the storm and the crashing ocean. Thomas rolled to the side, dodging a bullet before glancing around, panicked. I didn't know if it was the similar DNA or the fact that he and I had met like this a few times already, but it was like I could read his mind, could see him assess the situation and weight pros and cons of staying here with his people and fighting this battle or getting out alive so he could continue to lead this war and take the chance of no longer having a World B to bounce off.

His decision was clearly written on his face and he leaped into action. "Oh no you don't!" I pinned him against the deck and the second I felt him pulling us to another time, I pressed myself, my thoughts, every bit of being into this space in time.

His eyebrows pulled together and he hollered in pain. "You don't know what you're up against, you don't even know what you're destroying!"

I gritted my teeth and pressed all my weight into his shoulders, "This time . . . I'm. Not. Letting. You. Go." Pain shot through my head, but Thomas's yells were louder and more urgent, echoing off the dark sky and emerging even through the rumble of thunder.

"Stop it! Stop it now! You'll kill both of us!" The strain in his voice was all too familiar, taking me back to the minutes following my return to that rooftop after he'd tossed Holly from it.

Holly. Holly is here. I have to win this fight.

He pulled us harder into another time and I fought with every bit of strength I had. Through the pounding rain, I caught sight of the blue beginning to streak up my arms. It's working.

And then someone yanked me up by the collar and the fire of a gunshot right beside my ear deafened me momentarily. Dad was holding me by the shirt collar, his gun in the other hand and his face filled with as much fury as it had been that day in the forest when the memory gas blinded him into thinking that I was Thomas. My gaze snapped back to the man I'd been running from for what felt like an eternity. Blood seeped across Thomas's chest, his eyes wide with surprise, much like Marshall's.

Both Dad and I were breathing heavy, staring down at a lifeless Thomas, but we only had a few seconds to absorb the magnitude of this moment before we became aware of the battle around us again.

"Jean!" one of Thomas's men shouted.

I spun around to see a red-haired young woman just as Blake had described her in his memory files, fall to the deck, facedown, as a bullet from Stewart's aimed pistol hit her square in the back.

In the half second it had taken me to scan the deck and assess the situation, Courtney had reached me, grabbing my arm. "Can we do it now? Without Chief Marshall?"

At that moment, through the storm, all the way across the deck while the others still fought our fight against Thomas's remaining time travelers, my eyes met Emily's and silent words were exchanged.

She knew. She's here to be Marshall's substitute.

As much as it pained me to accept it, as wrong as I thought this was, I could see myself having every one of these arguments with her and the determination to help, to fix the problem showing on her face. She gave me a tiny nod and began making her way through the battle toward us.

"Emily can help us," I shouted to Courtney. "But we can't leave them like this."

I dove into action, moving with my newfound speed and agility, helping Holly take out two really big dudes.

"I knew you were drugging me the other night but I never thought it was to run away to Norway," Holly shouted, throwing an elbow and then a kick into the side of a woman at least a foot taller than her. "I figured you had some mission to do and I trusted you! Why would you come here to fight this battle alone? You have plenty of people more than willing to help."

The storm had turned violent, wind whipping hard, rocking the boat and making it difficult to stand or see. But somehow, only minutes later, the last body had fallen to the deck. Thomas's army had been defeated.

I felt an unexpected surge of elation and satisfaction, but it dissolved the second Adam stumbled across the deck gripping my shoulder for support. "You should go now! Before anything else changes."

Some kind of revelation must have clicked into place in Dad's head because his eyes grew wide and he limped toward me. Blood was seeping through the leg of his jeans.

"Dad!" Courtney said, rushing to him. "You got shot."

Collins whipped out a pocketknife and then sliced a big strip of

T-shirt from the bottom of his shirt. He knelt in front of Dad, tying it around his thigh.

Dad barely took notice of this, his eyes locked on me and Courtney. "What are you doing, Jackson? What are you doing?"

"I'm sorry, Daddy," Courtney said, finally getting close enough to get her arms around him.

I almost yanked her back, afraid Dad might hold her hostage. The storm grew more violent, and I realized that the boat needed to turn back and head for safety before it was too late.

"Let's get out of here," Collins said when he'd finished tying up Dad's leg.

Dad stared at me, over Courtney's shoulder, a pained expression on his face that had nothing to do with the bullet in his leg. "There's no other way?"

I shook my head. "She warned you, Dad, remember?"

He closed his eyes briefly, swallowing hard, and nodded.

"What are you doing?" Holly asked, moving closer, fear dripping from every word.

With great strength, I forced myself to turn around and look at her. Her blond hair clung to the sides of her face, her blue eyes shining and lighting up with every bolt of lightning. I opened my mouth to answer her but no words came out.

"It's the only way to stop the virus," Adam said. "It's the only way."

Everybody held still, forming a horseshoe shape around me, Courtney, and Emily as we stood with our back to the ledge we had already unsuccessfully tried to jump from.

"What's the only way?" Stewart asked. "What the hell is going on? We just killed the last twenty time-jumping cloned bastards and we're about to die out here in this fucking storm if we don't go now."

"If they time-travel from the bottom of the maelstrom, they can destroy the alternate universe and end the virus," Adam said.

I saw the plan click into place in everyone's faces. Shock followed by shouted protests, but the only voice I heard was Holly's.

"No! You can't do this, Jackson! I won't let you. I'll hold you down if I have to." She sprang toward me, like that was exactly what she intended to do, but luckily Adam grabbed her around the waist, dragging her farther away from me and the ledge.

Dad must have known that Adam wouldn't last long against Holly because he hobbled over to me, wrapped his arms around me briefly, and whispered, "I love you."

And then he spun around and moved to block Holly from me. The anger on her face, watching her fight off Adam like that after all we'd been through, the idea of leaving her hating me broke my heart a hundred more times.

Emily took my hand and tugged on it. "Come on, Jackson."

But I couldn't. Not yet. I shook off her grip and turned back to Holly. "This is all you get, Hol. I'm not going to change my mind and you're gonna be okay. But if you don't say good-bye, you'll regret it forever."

As the boat rocked and nearly tipped, I kept my eyes locked on her. She broke free of Adam's grip and knocked Dad over, causing him to tumble right down next to Marshall's body. I braced myself for a fight but instead she jumped into my arms, her legs wrapping around my waist, her mouth colliding with mine, kissing me so hard.

I staggered backwards a few steps before finding my balance and holding her tight. And I just let the moment consume me, standing there in the middle of the storm kissing, both of us crying, our fingers numb from cold and from holding on too tight.

"I love you, Jackson Meyer," Holly said between kisses.

My heart swelled and broke at the same time. *She loves me. This Holly loves me.* "I love you, too, Holly. Forever. It's always been you."

I set her down on the deck and Adam was right behind Holly, pulling her into his arms. This time when Courtney and I climbed up on the ledge, my legs no longer trembled. Emily held my left hand and Courtney my right.

Just as my feet prepared to leave the ledge and head into the cold water, I saw Dad roll over from his position lying on the deck, rip the plastic bag from Marshall's back and crush one of the tiny pills between his teeth. He rolled onto his back again and closed his eyes.

"No!" I shouted. "Dad!"

Courtney's and Emily's jumps had dragged me along with them, and I hit the water with a splash and a sting to every inch of my body. I fought against the waves, trying to turn back, but Courtney grabbed my shirt, struggling to tread water. "It's okay, Jackson. It's okay."

"But he—"

"Did you really think he'd stick around with us gone?" she shouted. "I know I wouldn't."

I felt hot tears rolling down my face, mixing with the cold drops of rain. "I wouldn't either."

The tug of the whirlpool pulled us down and I quickly turned to Emily, looking into her tiny face. "I'm sorry you're here, Emily. It's not fair."

"Everyone will be okay, Jackson," she argued. "I've been hurting so much thinking about everything that's wrong. I need to do this just as much as you."

Under the water, I searched for their hands, reclaiming them in mine, and in no time at all, the current pulled us under. There was no way to fight off that instinct to push toward the surface as my lungs were about to burst.

We sank farther as if a force had grabbed each of our legs and was sucking us toward the ocean floor. Involuntarily, my body started to resist, when suddenly I saw the underwater world in a new light. The buzzing filled my ears and my fingertips. I saw Emily losing consciousness. And then Courtney's face, enlightened as if finally landing on an answer she'd been seeking for a long time. She released my hand as I reached for Emily, whose grip had gone slack.

Already I felt the emptiness of losing my sister again sweep over me. The hole in my heart I could never fill. The part of me that would stay hollow and empty forever.

I love you, Courtney. You're my better half.

My lungs screamed at me, burning and bursting. I reached out through the hazy water and hooked an arm around Emily's waist. Her head jerked and then fell back onto my shoulder, just like it had upon arriving on Misfit Island, and my life played in reverse as Emily pulled us—with her mind—away from here.

Think about the end. Think about nothing but the end of the world. The silence.

That special part of my mind I'd recently learned to access burst to life, making the world underwater come alive, electricity buzzing through my fingers, coursing up my arms, shooting out through every extremity.

Think about the end. Think about nothing but the end of the world. The silence.

As I did this, as I succeeded in pulling myself toward death, I felt the weight of the excess timeline sitting on my chest like a boulder, I felt the floor of the ocean rumble below, the Earth's core cracking beneath it. It was really happening. A whole world was being destroyed in order for another world to survive.

The moment of Holly jumping into my arms, whispering that she loved me, played over and over until I felt her with me, felt the importance of that moment and how it changed both of us. My body sank to the bottom of the ocean, while my heart remained above sea level with a girl I'd loved for so long I couldn't remember what it felt like before.

Mission accomplished.

CHAPTER THIRTY

Some part of my mind registered that I was no longer underwater. I felt Emily's weight pressed against my side. The only thought running through my head was the pills.

I'm still alive and I need those pills taped to my back before the world explodes.

The pressure of my nose being pinched distracted me momentarily. Air was forced into my lungs and then suddenly the world became clear around me, my eyes flying open, taking in the older woman leaning over me. She jolted back, startled by my awakening.

What happened? Did we do it or not?

I rolled onto my side and coughed up what felt like a gallon of ocean water. My teeth chattered. It wasn't cold, but the cool breeze coupled with my soaking-wet clothing had me freezing.

"Courtney," I managed to say. But she wasn't here.

Sirens sounded around me, growing louder and closer. I looked around and took in the crowd of people circled in this outdoor location.

Where am I? When am I?

"Jackson." Emily was stirring beside me, coughing and saying my name.

My muscles were too heavy and full of ocean water to roll over the other way.

"Where did they get wet?" a voice said.

"The pond, I guess," said the woman who until just a moment ago had had her mouth intimately placed over mine.

More water ejected itself from my lungs and finally I had clarity enough to focus on my surroundings.

Central Park. I'm in Central freakin' Park.

I sat up so abruptly, I nearly butted heads with a paramedic. Emily had also pulled herself into a sitting position beside me.

"Son, can you tell us what happened? Have you been in the pond?"

I turned to Emily, whose panicked face seemed to mimic mine. "What happened? Why are we here and not . . . ?"

"I don't know," she said.

"What day is it?" I asked the paramedic.

"Actually, I need you to answer that question from me."

I felt around on my back, smacking the plastic bag Marshall had taped to me. "I need my pills, they're on my back."

Both paramedics looked at me like I was insane but the woman who had been near me when I first woke up lifted my shirt and ripped the bag from it. I let out a yell of pain and then stared in shock at the clear plastic envelope she placed in my lap.

There were no pills. Only a piece of paper with handwriting I recognized immediately. Before I could open it, one person I hadn't expected to see ever again came running toward me.

Dad.

"Oh my God," Emily muttered.

"He's alive," I said, my heart quickening all over again. I didn't know what to feel. What had happened?

Dad froze about twenty feet away, his eyes zooming in on Emily, but then just as quickly he composed himself and tucked his shock away, or maybe he realized it wasn't Courtney. But that meant he didn't know who Emily was.

I pulled myself to my feet, despite the paramedics' protests for me to lie back down. "Dad, I'm okay. It was just one of those fainting spells I'm always having."

He held it together perfectly. "Of course, let's get you home."

"Excuse me, sir," the paramedic said in protest. "He wasn't breathing when they called us, he should be taken to a hospital. The girl, too . . . is she yours as well?"

Emily jumped up beside me, both of us drenched. "Yes, we're

related. I just . . . I tried to go after him when he fainted and then I remembered . . ."

"That she couldn't swim," I finished for her.

I don't know how Dad did it, but he managed to maneuver us away from the paramedics without further questions.

"Are you sure you're okay to walk?" he whispered at me, taking two or three glances at Emily.

"Yeah, I'm okay."

He walked briskly in front of us, his cell phone out and pressed to his ear. "Stewart, we've got a five-seven-two-four situation on the corner of . . ."

His voice faded away as I tuned him out and grabbed Emily's sleeve, halting her. "Where's Courtney? Why isn't she here? What happened? We did it wrong, didn't we?"

Emily's eyes were huge and quickly filled with tears. "I don't know. I felt it happen . . . I thought I did."

"Me, too."

Dad stopped and turned to face us. "Want to tell me who this kid is, Jackson?"

"Emily," I said. "She's sort of my clone."

My own confusion took precedence over Dad's and I snatched the phone from his hand and looked for the information I needed. *March 15, 2009, 5:22 P.M.*

"Holy shit." I showed the phone to Emily. "This isn't happening . . ."

Dad set his hands on my shoulders, lowering his eyes to mine. "Jackson, what happened to you?"

Instead of focusing on his question, my mind turned over a different question—what *wouldn't* happen . . . ?

If I didn't show up in the same place at the same time, something very important might not happen. My heart pounded in my ears, my hands shaking as I broke free from Dad's grip. Maybe it was stupid to even think about this when I had no clue how or why I landed here with only one of the two people I'd jumped into that whirlpool with, but I think my mind and body just wanted to grasp something real and familiar, to ground myself into this time.

March 15, 2009. Again.

I dropped the plastic bag onto the ground and then stripped off my heavy wet coat and sweatshirt, tossing it down beside the bag.

"I'll be right back!" I took off before he could reply, ignoring his shouting my name.

The adrenaline fueled the movement of my legs as I ran toward Ninety-second Street. I had to see her, had to see if she showed up. My life had become this exhausting merry-go-round, constantly bringing me full circle to this exact same spot.

I reached the Ninety-second Street Y in only a few minutes and I leaned against a tree, hunched over catching my breath and clutching my side, trying to rub away the stabbing pain. It probably wasn't the best idea to go for a half-mile sprint just minutes after nearly drowning.

The sun was beginning to set, but I could still see clearly down the block, just like I'd been able to that first time. My breath caught in my throat, my heart nearly stopping as I watched Holly Flynn walk toward the building I stood near, a book open in one hand and a pink smoothie in the other.

What now? Do I bump into her? Introduce myself? Head into the counselor training, leaving Dad with Emily and no explanation for my abrupt departure?

I held my breath, my heart racing as she moved closer.

Go over there! Do something, you idiot.

Just as I placed one foot forward to move toward Holly, her eyes lifted to meet mine and she stopped in the middle of the sidewalk, at least thirty feet still separating us. Her jaw dropped open. The smoothie slipped through her fingers and fell to the ground, splattering all over.

"Oh my God," she muttered.

Okay, this is different.

I tentatively walked a few steps closer as people moved around us. "Do you . . . do you know who I am?" She just continued to stare, the frozen strawberry smoothie forming a puddle at her feet. "Holly?"

She shook her head and seemed to pull herself together, stepping sideways and moving onto the grass beside the sidewalk. "I didn't think I'd see you again."

"Again?"

Where the hell am I? Is this heaven? Have I been reincarnated?

"Oh!" she said, suddenly remembering something. I watched her blond ponytail swing forward as she bent over to retrieve something out of her bag. "I still have your note."

"My note?"

"The one you left me." She stood again, holding a tiny slip of white paper between her fingers. She stepped closer, closing the gap between us.

Slowly, I reached forward and took the note from her hand.

Holly,
Please don't give up on me.
Love, Jackson

I lifted my eyes back to her, staring in disbelief. "You're . . . you're . . ."

She gave me a tiny yet shy smile. "Adam says you call me 007 Holly, but I wasn't sure exactly why . . . ?"

My hands landed on her cheeks before I could think about whether or not this Holly would mind. I had to make sure she was real. "I'm not supposed to be here. This world isn't supposed to exist anymore."

Her eyes dropped down and then slowly moved upward as if taking in my appearance for the first time. "Why are you all wet? Does your dad know you're here?"

"Like here in this world or here with you?"

And that was when my adrenaline rush ran out. My legs wobbled beneath me and I felt Holly struggle to help me sit down in the grass. She leaned close, keeping one hand on my shoulder as she removed her phone and dialed. "He's with me, he's okay."

"Who is that?" I asked warily. "Who are you talking to?"

"Your dad." She glanced around the street before finally sighing with relief as a black car pulled up front.

I mustered the strength to stand and reached for Holly's hand, squeezing it tight. "Please come with me. I don't know what happened and I don't want you to go away."

Her eyes locked with mine, her chest brushing against mine as tears sprang to her eyes. "That's funny because I was thinking the same thing. I don't want you to go away, Jackson. Are you going to leave again?"

Inside my head, it was so much quieter than it had been since my first full jump when I created World B. The silence was beautiful, but replaying my time with this Holly had come a little slower and was finally just hitting me. "Wait . . . you love me. You told me you loved me."

She dropped her eyes to the ground, drawing in a deep breath before nodding. "And then I was gone, right? You haven't seen me since?"

"No."

"So it's been like, what? A year and half?" I asked, and she nodded. I leaned in until my forehead touched hers and I could clearly see the tears trickling down her cheeks. "Holly?"

"What?" she said, sniffling.

"Can I kiss you?"

She surprised me by laughing, her hands shaking as they reached up to touch my face. "Yeah, you can kiss me."

I covered her hands with mine and kissed her quickly while Dad held the door to the car open. "I'm sorry I left you."

I slid into the car beside Emily, who immediately dropped the plastic envelope with the handwritten letter into my lap. I began to read it as Holly and Dad joined us and the car jolted into motion.

Dear Jackson,

I know you're probably very confused and after finding out what's happened, you may be very angry with me. Please know that I had no choice and if presented with the options, you would have never done what needed to be done.

If you're reading this, then you've landed in the place I know you like to call World B. I'm so sorry to tell you this but the destruction to World A was irreversible. This was always the place you'd end up. This was always going to be your home for good but there are things that needed to be done to make that happen. I know how you must feel, leaving that other world behind, but I can assure you, every individual you loved is here with you as they should be and much better off than they'd be under the viral outbreak caused by the convergence.

Of course as you've also probably noticed, Courtney isn't with you and that's because the course of her life has always ended at the same place and there is no way to reverse that. I know it probably seems as though you've been played by Chief Marshall but this was a plan we developed long ago, before you were born. If time travel got so out of hand in the future that it began to affect the past, we had the responsibility of moving life to a world without time travel. Yes, a world without time travel. The future of World B will include the Tempus gene but the evolution of time travelers will never happen here because of the force that you created from the timestorm—a feat that never could have been done if you'd known the truth. The sacrifice and the gravity of what you'd hoped to accomplish is the element that brought your powers to that level. In order for the destruction of World A to be successful, you, Courtney, and Emily needed to believe that you were putting every last drop of your being into that time jump. Unlike the others, both you and Emily use emotions like anger, fear, love, and loyalty to unleash that insurmountable power. The timestorm created a blanket or a sort of force field over World B to prevent human access to the part of the mind used for time travel.

I have one more matter to discuss with you in this letter. I want you to take a moment and close your eyes, count to five and pay attention to what you feel. Don't try to talk Dr. Melvin out of testing you to verify this himself but you can feel it, can't you? Or maybe it's more of an absence of feeling. The electricity you once felt, the expansion of your mind that once allowed you to time-travel has quieted. You have done so much and you've worked long and hard toward these noble goals and the brain can only handle so much. The power is gone. The part of your mind that copies everything is gone, too, and as you've seen what that power has done to Emily, consider this a gift. You're free, Jackson. I imagine the skills that you've learned training under Kevin's watch will all still be around. You're exceptional even without the superpowers. I wouldn't be surprised if you choose to remain an agent for the Tempest Division.

Do not allow yourself to be overcome with guilt because you're alive. You were so brave, Jackson. You're exactly where you deserve to be. Remember to live life for not only yourself but for me and

your sister, too. All we want is for you to be happy,
so that's what you need to do.

I love you always.

Your mother in almost every sense of the word,

Eileen

My hands shook, tears dripping from my eyes down the end of my nose. I turned to Emily and caught her wiping away her own tears. "Marshall tricked us," I said.

"Yes."

"They're gone . . . World A is gone." I took her hand and she leaned against me, her cheek resting on my arm.

I felt a warmer, softer hand wrap around my other wrist. I turned my head to face Holly. "What did Adam tell you? Do you know—"

"That you're a time traveler?" Holly finished, surprising me.

"He's not anymore," Emily said, her head snapping up as the realization hit her. "You're not anymore. Eileen was right. I can't feel you."

"Is your power gone, too?"

She hesitated then nodded. "I think so." Her gaze fell to her lap. "Will I stay here with you, then? In 2009?"

I looked to Dad and then back to Emily. I felt myself smiling. "Yeah, you're staying with me, my fingerprint clone."

"You're not leaving then?" Holly asked. "You don't have to return to some important other place or time?"

I released Emily's hand and turned to face Holly again. "I'm not leaving, Holly. Not ever again. I'm stuck here, just like you."

She closed her eyes briefly, sighing with relief. I leaned in and kissed her forehead. "So, you've really been waiting around for me all this time? Because of my note? I wasn't even sure I'd be back here."

"I guess I wasn't sure either, I just hoped you would." She looked down at our fingers twined together. "I haven't been sitting in my room crying for a year and a half, if that's what you're asking."

I laughed, and the sound of it, the feeling, startled me. "I'd never ever think you'd cry over me for that long. A year, maybe . . ."

The car had stopped in front of the building so we all tumbled out and held our conversations to a minimum until we reached the safety of our apartment. I knew Dad had so many questions for me and I could imagine that Dr. Melvin was probably already on his way, but I had to check Eileen's work and see if her letter was accurate. I led Holly into my bedroom and shut the door behind me. I nudged her toward the end of the bed and pressed on her shoulders until she sat down, then I knelt in front of her, resting my hands on her thighs.

"I need you to answer a few questions for me and not ask for details if it doesn't make sense." I exhaled, looking down at my hands before raising my eyes to hers again. "I'm actually hoping you have no idea what I'm talking about."

Holly smiled a little. "Jackson, just ask me."

"You don't have a . . . boyfriend, do you?"

She burst out laughing. "That's what you wanted to ask me? Are we in middle school?"

I gave her a sad smile in return. "So, no?"

"Besides my mostly imaginary time-traveling boyfriend . . . no," she teased.

A wave of dizziness and exhaustion hit me. I rose to my feet and fell onto the bed beside Holly, before lying all the way back, staring up at the ceiling fan. "Have you ever heard of Eyewall or know anyone named Agent Carter?"

"No and no." She leaned over me, frowning. "Are you okay?"

I shifted my focus from the ceiling to Holly's blue eyes. "I miss my sister," I admitted as pain ripped through me. I'd spent so many days with her and now I'd lost her all over again.

Sympathy filled her expression and she rested a hand on my face. "I know. I'm sorry."

"I'm not supposed to feel guilty for being here when she's . . . not," I said, my voice shaking a bit. "But I'm not sure it's that easy to follow those directions. And I've been nineteen forever and I've missed you forever and I'm so tired—"

Holly shut me up with a kiss, not caring that I was still soaking wet and smelling like salt water and seaweed. I allowed myself to pull her closer, to close my eyes and feel her mouth against mine. And I could feel her love, her understanding, her longing to be with me like I longed to be with her.

And she was okay. No one had hurt her. No one had taken away her free will. She looked beautiful and healthy.

"I've missed you forever, too," Holly whispered against my mouth. "I don't know if that helps you at all . . ."

"It does, Holly. It really does." Before I could kiss her again, the door burst open.

"Break it up, both of you," Adam said. "I can't believe you're back! This is awesome, man! It's been boring as hell without you around."

I sat up slowly, feeling a grin spread across my face. "Boring sounds nice."

Adam pulled me to my feet and I surprised him by hugging my friend. My best friend. "You haven't, like, died recently, have you?"

He released me and stepped back. "Not that I'm aware of. No wonder Dr. Melvin is pacing the living room, waiting to scan your brain."

Eileen had told me to let him do his job even though I already knew the truth. I wasn't a time traveler anymore and that was a hundred percent okay with me.

I sighed heavily. "All right, let's get this updating stuff over with so I can take a nice long nap."

"One more question." Holly and I walked down the hall hand in hand but I stopped her before joining the others. "You're not in the CIA, are you?"

She wrapped her arms around my neck and pulled me closer. "If I told you, then I'd have to—"

I groaned and leaned my forehead against hers. "Why?"

"Oh come on." She laughed. "You know I've had spy ambitions since early childhood. Besides, your dad's just started me on the basics. I'm still going to school now, graduating and all that. NYU in the fall."

"Does your mom know?"

She kissed me quickly on the mouth. "Does she know that I'm interning for a government department that required a full security clearance? Yes, she knows."

"Okay." I sighed and then kissed her again. "I love you so much, Holly."

Her eyes met mine. "I love you, too."

I released her and we continued toward the other room.

"So, seriously," Holly pressed. "Who's the redheaded girl?"

I looked over at her and smiled. "That's a really interesting and complicated story, but for now, just think of her as my family."

"You're related?"

"You could say that."

We had entered the living room and I stopped in the doorway, taking in the roomful of people—Dr. Melvin, Dad, Emily, Adam, Mason, Stewart, Kendrick, Agent Collins, and Holly.

Eileen was right. I had *almost* everybody I loved right here with me. And it was already more than I ever thought I could hope for.

EPILOGUE

Dad smacked my knee, making me aware of the fact that I'd been bouncing it for the entire cab ride from the airport to the East Village. "Three more minutes. Relax, all right?"

I would if I could. The panic had reached a climactic point and there was no going back now.

"What exactly do you think is going to happen?" Dad asked for like the tenth time since abandoning our mission in Hungary nine hours ago.

If my dad wasn't in charge of the division, I'd be getting some serious shit for going AWOL like this. "I don't know," I snapped. "So I'm irrational. Get over it."

"Sleep-deprived and irrational." He laughed and shook his head. "Very bad combination."

The cab was nearing what looked like a wall of traffic and I had zero patience left after enduring a transcontinental flight. "Stop here, please," I said to the driver before turning to Dad. "You'll get Emily from Kendrick's place?"

"Yes, and I told you that five times already."

I flung the door open and took off in a full sprint, running the remaining eight blocks, weaving in and out of morning commuters heading to work and NYU students with 8:00 A.M. classes. As I approached the building, I spotted Holly running toward me.

Well, not toward me, but she was jogging from the opposite direction toward her dorm. Her headphones were plugged in, her cheeks pink from running in the chilly morning air. I slowed down to a walk, waiting for her to notice me.

Finally, about twenty feet away, her gaze met mine, her face lighting up. "Jackson!"

I sighed with relief and scooped her up in my arms, tugging the headphones from her ears. She squeezed me around the neck. "What are you doing here? I just talked to you last night and you were all the way across the ocean."

Talking to Holly on the phone the night before, having not seen her in a month, was what had set this whole panic in motion. That and the date. No matter how much I forced myself to think logically, this date still haunted me in the worst way. I thought I could handle being away today, but I couldn't.

"I missed you." I kissed her cheek and then her mouth. "I missed you so much I couldn't stand it and I had to jump on a plane and come and see you."

"No complaints from me," she said. "Just wanted to make sure everything was okay."

"It is now."

Suspicion filled Holly's expression as she tried to figure out what the hell was going on. Seven months of being together and there were still a lot of things about the future and alternate histories that I'd avoided telling her about. I didn't exactly keep things from Holly, but if she didn't ask and I didn't think she needed to know, I kept it to myself. For now, at least.

Despite my obvious emotion, she seemed to accept that answer for the time being and led me inside her building and up the stairs to her floor. The feeling of déjà vu was so intense, I didn't even realize that I'd just climbed five flights of stairs in less than a minute.

A more intense and not-at-all-pleasant moment of déjà vu hit the second I stepped inside Holly's room. I forced the panic away while she closed the door behind me and headed for her shared bathroom.

"I'm gonna take a quick shower," she said, from the other side of the door. "Lydia's already at class."

Lydia. At least she and I had managed to hit it off much better this time around than we had the first time we met. But I was still glad for her absence right now given my emotional state.

My gaze zoomed in on the brown throw rug not too far from the door. My heart raced, my breath lodged in my throat like a lump. I blinked rapidly, trying to wash away the visions of red blood seeping into the brown carpet.

The last time I'd been in this room, before all the worst events had been set in motion, the last vision I saw before time jumping, was Holly lying in a heap on the floor and red blood on her robe . . . on this carpet.

After five minutes of trying to get my shit together, the bathroom door opened.

"Jackson?" Holly stood in front of me, wearing a robe like she had worn on that day, too. But she was perfect and completely unharmed. "What's wrong?"

I shook my head, unable to speak, and then stepped around her and sat down on her bed. My head dropped into my hands and I focused hard on shedding those memories from my mind.

Holly knelt in front of me, placing her hands over mine and tugging them free. "Are you okay?"

The lump was still lodged in my throat but I managed to nod and whisper, "I'm fine."

She studied my face for several long seconds. "You have to stop trying to protect me from everything."

"I'm not—"

"Yes, you are," she said firmly. "I've let it go most of the time, but I think it's time we accept the fact that neither of us is going anywhere and eventually your secrets will be my secrets, too."

I managed half a smile. "You say that like it's a bad thing."

"It's terrible," she said with mock frustration. "I've always dreamed of having the normal college experience—playing the field, lots of hot drunken one-night stands and excessive trips to the student health center for free contraception. And now I can't do any of that because I'm a little bit too in love with you."

I should have told her to get a different room. Anything but this. I'd thought by not letting it get to me, I was facing my fears.

My gaze flitted back to the brown rug and I felt that rush of panic again. "Do you remember that day I started working at Mike's gym, when he introduced us?"

"Uh-huh." She stood up and crawled over me then tugged my arms until I was lying beside her on the bed. This must be my cue to spill the whole story.

"You already know that wasn't our first meeting for me." I focused on the ceiling and held Holly's hand in mine. "Before that, I'd left 2009. Not just 2009 but October 30, 2009. And it was this room that I jumped from and you were . . . you were—"

"What?" she pressed. "I was what?"

"Shot." I released the word in one big exhale. "Bleeding onto that brown rug. I know it's not logical to think that history will repeat itself but I'm seeing it right now. I can't help it. It's the same room, same everything. And when I talked to you last night, I couldn't shake the feeling that I had to get here. Just in case."

Holly had stiffened the second I said the word "shot," but she drew in a deep breath, composing herself, and then leaned over me. "What time did this happen?"

"I don't know." I dug through memories I'd been avoiding for months. "Around nine in the morning."

She nodded. "That's pretty soon. Okay, all we need to do is find one difference and then maybe you can imagine a new outcome. How did that Holly react to someone with a gun? Or was there time to react?"

"She threw a shoe and used pepper spray." I squeezed my eyes shut, hating how the tiniest of details brought back all the feelings I'd had in that moment. Dr. Melvin said I was experiencing PTSD and I would probably go long bouts without any problems and then one small trigger could bring me right back to the worst times of my life.

"Jackson, look at me," Holly said firmly, and I opened my eyes right away. "I wouldn't need a shoe or pepper spray to disarm and turn a gun on someone and you know that."

True. Even after the loss of my extensive brainpower, I was still a pretty good shot, but Holly was better. Not that this Holly had any experience in the field, but she'd been shooting at the range for months as part of her part-time CIA trainee program.

My body relaxed about ten percent.

"What else is different?" Holly asked, recognizing that her technique might be working.

I reached up, taking her face in my hands. "You and me. We're different. I'd never let that bullet hit you again. I'd never leave without you knowing how I really felt, without professing my undying love."

She laughed and brushed her thumb across my cheek. "See? Your color's back to normal." Her fingers drifted over my jaw, down lower until she rested them at the pulse point in my neck. "Your heart rate is almost normal now."

I slid my hands inside her robe. "It's never normal when you're around."

"What a line." She rolled her eyes and then her face turned serious again. "It sounds like you shut that other Holly out and that didn't turn out well. I know some of what you're going through, but you won't throw that burden all the way on my shoulders. And I think you need to. You can't let me in halfway, Jackson."

"I know. I'm sorry." I rubbed the back of her neck with one hand and pulled her almost all the way on top of me with the other. "But I can't exactly think of each and every possible trigger for memories I've tucked away and spill them all at once."

"But you tried to tell me you were fine a few minutes ago," Holly pointed out. "If I hadn't pressed you for details, you wouldn't have told me what was bothering you. For once, I want you to say exactly what's going through your head. I can handle it."

I looked up at her, studying her expression. Could she handle everything? Yes. But did I want to taint this Holly with all the horrible memories? I wasn't quite ready to decide that but I did have other things on my mind that I could throw her way. "I was just thinking how much I love you and how many times a day I stop myself from telling you because I don't want to drive you crazy. And I want to . . ." I rolled her over onto her back and leaned down, my mouth hovering close to hers, "buy an apartment for us to share, and have a dozen babies with you and send half to public school in Jersey and half to a private school on the Upper East Side and see which half turns out better. Maybe we'll send a couple of them to secret-agent school, too, you know, keep up the family biz. Emily can teach them all eight different languages. And then we'll get old and fat and probably bald, too, and I'll love you even more because you're willing to love the old, fat, and bald version of me."

Holly was laughing so hard, tears were streaking down the side of her face. "You're so full of it, Jackson. A dozen babies in a New York City apartment? And we're not even married?"

I closed the gap and kissed her, then pulled back just enough to see her face. "I'll marry you, Holly. I'm ready right now. I've been ready forever so you just tell me when, all right?"

Her eyes widened, her mouth falling open. "Did you just—?"

"Propose," I finished, giving her another kiss. "I think so. But you said not to hold back."

"Right, I did say that."

I laughed at her shell-shocked expression. "Relax, Hol. Don't freak out on me. I do want to be with you like that, but I also want you to do everything you've ever wanted to do—the second goal trumps the first, so no matter what happens with us, I'm going to feel happy at some level at least knowing you're okay and you're happy."

"I'm happy right now," she said with such certainty. "And I'd be even more happy if you'd admit this whole conversation is just a ploy to take advantage of my roommate being at class all day."

"Yes, it totally is." My lips traveled down her neck and then she was kissing me long and slow, our clothes falling to the floor one article at a time.

A couple hours later, we were exiting Holly's dorm, the sun hitting us in the eyes after having dozed off for an hour or so. I tried to stay calm as we headed toward Holly's first class of the day, but there was no stopping my gaze from roaming the area, looking for a delayed performance of my last attempt at living through October 30, 2009. But there was no threat in sight.

We walked for several minutes hand in hand, chatting about fall-semester class schedules, Emily, my dad, Adam, and also Holly's training. When we reached the building where Holly's calculus class was held, she stopped in the middle of the sidewalk, turning to face me.

"You don't scare me, Jackson Meyer. You, your past, your plans for the future—I'm not afraid of any of it. I'm only afraid of admitting that it doesn't scare me. I hope all these flashbacks and horrible experiences stop haunting you eventually, but even if they don't, I'll be there beside you, helping you through it." She smiled and squeezed my hand. "You're not perfect, but you're perfect for me, and I don't see that changing anytime soon."

I wrapped my arms around her, lifting her off the ground. "Me either."

We stood there in the middle of the sidewalk kissing for longer than would be considered appropriate and then Holly buried her face in my neck, and said, "I'd jump in front of that bullet, too, if it kept it from hitting you. I'm sure that's not something you want to hear, but I'm just as willing to save you as you are to save me."

She lifted her head and I touched my forehead to hers. "You've already saved me, Holly. At least a dozen times."

"Good." She kissed me and then disentangled herself from my arms, reaching for the door of the building. "Then it's settled. We'll keep doing what we've been doing and everything's going to turn out fine. We've got time to figure out all the details."

Time. Yes, finally we had time.

ACKNOWLEDGMENTS

I'd like to thank my husband, Nick, for his continued support and love. My kids, for being proud of these books that they aren't even old enough to read yet. My entire family, who have all gone out on the front lines, preaching the word of Tempest from day one. I have amazing parents, in-laws, aunts, siblings, cousins, uncles, nieces, and one amazing grandmother. I'm the luckiest author alive for all the family support that I have.

Also thanks to my agent, Nicole Resciniti, who may not have had much direct involvement with this series coming into it so late in the game, but she helped me through that emotional turning point all authors must face where we have to answer the question: What now?

Timestorm beta readers, you guys are all so amazing. Some of you went so far above and beyond your beta-reader duties, I should be bequeathing my firstborn to you. I'm sorry in advance if I forgot anyone! You have my permission to harass me via e-mail and I will send you lovely presents—Kari Olson, Mark Perini, Erica Haglund, Malinda Childers, Heather Sheffield, and Chersti Nieveen.

My editor, Brendan Deneen, deserves one of the biggest thanks for the existence of this series. Sometimes I feel like we made a big pot of stone soup, beginning our journey together from basically a one-line premise: A boy witnesses his girlfriend's murder, accidentally jumps back two years in the past, and tries to prevent her death from occurring two years from then. As we got more and more excited about the project, and as it started to become a book, others began to join our party, tossing more ingredients into the pot. And now it's finally finished.

Those contributors to the pot of Tempest-series soup include a blend of author friends, publishing people, and other random non-family members: Nicole Sohl, Jessica Preeg, Rachel Kelleher, Tom Dunne, Joe Goldschein, Breia Brissey, Pete Wolverton, Roni Loren, Anne Marie Tallberg, Brittney Kleinfelter, Eileen Longo, Matthew Shear (who recently passed and I know is greatly missed by the wonderful people at St. Martin's Press), and Beth Revis.

To the Tempest series fans, thanks so much for riding this wild wave with me. I have loved and appreciated all your support, reviews, and feedback. I hope this final installment is everything you wanted it to be. It's heartbreaking for me to leave Holly and Jackson behind, to leave this story and these characters. I've been in this world for nearly four years and I'm attached to it in a way that will probably never be replicated in any future books because it's my first. But knowing that the series can continue to fall into new hands helps me to see this ending as a new beginning.